This Girl for Hire

G.G. Fickling

The Honey West Files
ISBN: 9781936814176
Cover Design:
Erik Enervold/Simian Brothers Creative
Prepress: Lewis Chapman
Editorial assist: Yolanda Cockrell

www.moonstonebooks.com

Chapter One

Wind drove in under the eves, spattering drops of night rain on the dead man's mutilated face.

Lieutenant Mark Storm got to his feet, lit a cigarette and studied the battered corpse. Then he glanced at me.

"You want a cigarette?"

"No, thanks," I said softly. "I haven't got the stomach for one right now. When'll the coroner be here?"

Mark walked to the shade-drawn window and peeked out at the storm. Then he said, "Few minutes, I guess. Honey, gal, you'd better go home. It's late."

"Come on, Lieutenant," I said. "You don't have to play games with me. I've seen blood before."

He whirled around. "I told you to get out of here. Now get out! That's an order."

"Herb Nelson was a client of mine. I've got a right to be here."

Mark took off his hat and nervously dented his knuckles in the crown. "Look, I don't care whether you're a private detective or not. This guy looks as if he's been hit by a freight train. No self-respecting woman would stay in the same room with such a torn-up mess, much less ogle at it."

Music drifted out of the distant night. An odd sound, distorted by the wind in the trees. It was a sad song with a high-pitched trumpet that reminded me of taps being played over a dreary, cold burial ground. It seemed a sorry end for a man who had fought his way to the very top of the entertainment world and then toppled to the very bottom.

"I'll take that cigarette now," I said.

Mark slammed his hat back on his head. He started to form a new argument with his mouth and then gave it up, handing me a cigarette. "You

1

kill me, Honey. A gal with your class, looks, personality..." He shook his head dismally. "What in hell did he hire you for?"

"To find out who was trying to kill him."

Mark Storm, a cynic from the day he was born, lit my cigarette, blew the match out with an expression of disgust and said, "All right, who killed him? A Santa Fe streamliner?"

"I wouldn't be surprised. Know any likely ones with a record?"

"You kill me…" he started.

"You said that."

He turned on his heels and crossed the small, dingy second-story room to a shelf crammed with odds and ends. Under a pile of dirty laundry he extracted an Academy Award Oscar. Also a .38 revolver. He flipped open the cylinder and peered at me through the six empty chambers. "Did he have a permit for this thing?"

"I don't know. Ask him."

"Don't be funny," Mark said, tossing the gun back on the shelf. "When we go out for an evening and you stop off to check on a client who's been hit by an H-bomb, I want straight talk, do you understand?"

The music kept sadly drifting in. In a way this was funny. Not laughable, but the sad kind of funny that makes you say things you don't mean. Mark didn't sound like Lieutenant Mark Storm of the sheriff's office, homicide. He sounded like a little boy who suddenly felt the first pangs of manhood when he told his little sister to go home after they found the dead remains of their dog. And I sounded like the sister, who, fighting back desperate tears, made light of his brave attempts to protect me.

With Mark standing firm-legged and angry in the middle of Herb Nelson's dismal, one-room apartment, I said, "I liked the guy. He was a terrific person. He didn't have any money. He didn't have any close friends. But he had a mountain full of guts. Now stop acting the part of deputy sheriff. I know you liked him, too. Everybody did."

Mark creased his hat again. "This murder!" he said with a little boy's anger.

"How do you know it's murder?" I demanded. "Maybe he *was* hit by a train. Maybe he threw himself in front of it. Maybe someone who knew him picked him up and brought his body back here."

"You know better than that!"

2

I did know better than that, but I didn't want to admit it. You couldn't accept this as murder when you knew what Herb Nelson had been to a generation of children who'd grown up in the thirties and forties. He had been as widely celebrated as F.D.R., Hopalong Cassidy or the Wizard of Oz. I could still remember the songs they had written about him, the jokes that were told, the great performances he'd given on the motion picture screens. I suddenly felt that wave of female nausea Mark had expected me to feel earlier.

"I want to get out of here," I said unhappily.

Mark's legs loosened from their angry stance. He replaced his hat and crossed to me.

"I—I'm sorry, Honey," he said. "Believe me, I'm sorry."

"So am I, Mark. And I'm mad, too, at the very same time. I'm mad because—because—nobody had the right to do this. I don't care what he did after—he wasn't big anymore. Do you know what I mean?"

"Yeah," he said softly, putting an arm around my shoulder. "Yeah, I know what you mean." He swallowed and it was a deep swallow of hate for something seemingly untouchable, but with a hope that it could be touched someday, somehow. "Some dirty bastard!" he said.

The coroner and several men from the sheriff's office arrived a few minutes later. They were all young men in their thirties and they couldn't believe their eyes. It seemed utterly impossible, but there it was. A child's dream all smashed to pieces. The coroner guessed Herb had been dead about four hours.

After they took his body away to the morgue, Mark and I drove south to a little coffee house in Laguna. The rain still pelted down and the surf crashed awesomely in tune with the storm's fury.

I stirred a spoonful of sugar into my coffee and watched the crystals melt away in the black depths. Then I said, "Herb never paid me a cent. I want you to know that. He tried to, but I wouldn't take it."

Mark stared through the open door at the rain drops shimmering in the brilliance of the neon sign. "Who was he afraid of, Honey? Was he really worried somebody was going to kill him?" He squeezed his big knuckles with the weight of his other hand. "Who the hell did he suspect?"

I sipped my coffee, listening to the faint roar of an airliner battling through the stormy sky. "You don't understand, Mark."

Headlights of oncoming traffic on Pacific Coast Highway flickered across the big lieutenant's eyes making them glitter weirdly like cat's eyes caught in the same reflection. "Listen, Miss Private Eye!" he barked. "A man's dead. I've got to explore every possible lead. Now give!"

I shook my head. "All right. About a month ago, Herb landed a bit part in a Bob Swanson TV show. He got into some kind of hassle with the star and cast. There were some pretty bitter words. Herb was apparently hitting the bottle and I guess he went berserk when Swanson ordered him off the set. He started swinging and before it was all over an expensive camera was damaged and a set wrecked at Television Riviera.

Mark scowled. "That doesn't spell murder in my book. Come on, Honey, you're holding out on me. What is it?"

"Well, as I understand it, Swanson threatened Herb at the fracas. Then, a week later, Herb got a letter signed by Swanson, followed by several phone calls."

"Where's the letter?"

"Herb said he was so mad he tore it up and burned the scraps. He said the letter contained insulting remarks about his acting… even suggested Herb would be better off dead."

"That still doesn't add up to murder," Mark said, pushing his cup away. "What about the phone calls?"

"More threats. Herb said it was the same voice each time. It could have been Swanson, but he wasn't absolutely certain. Something was used to muffle the voice… probably a handkerchief."

"Have you checked out Swanson?" Mark demanded. "To a certain extent. He's a baby-faced, muscular schizophrenic actor with a yearly paycheck of at least a million. As far as I could find out, he had no reason in the world to threaten Herb Nelson—aside from his fight on the sound stage at WBS-TV."

"Who else was on the set at the time of the blowup?"

"Cameraman, grips, electricians—the usual TV backstage crew," I said. "The producer on the Swanson show is a guy named Sam Aces. Joe Meeler writes the series and Swanson does his own directing. They were all present when the fireworks started. So were about six actors and actresses."

Mark wiped some of the dampness off his forehead and squinted up at the wall menu. "What do you think of the Swanson theory?"

4

"The whole business sounds too pat. That's why I didn't kick the information over to your office. What do you think?"

"Yeah," he grunted. "Nobody in his right mind sends a letter telling a person he'd 'be better off dead, signs his own John Henry and then drives up with a tank loaded with a twenty-millimeter cannon."

"I went all the way back to the day Herb was born. He never had an enemy in the world. When he worked at Metro, he was the most liked person in the studio—barring none."

Mark, a man who had lived, breathed and formulated his ideals during the era of Herb Nelson, drew an exasperated breath. "Why not? How—how anybody could kill a man of Herb Nelson's stature—and like that..." He drifted off into a niche of chronic hatred all policemen have for a murder which jolts them into the realization that despite the badge and the training, they are still human beings and subject to remorse for the victim and loathing for the wrongdoer.

"He grew up in Pasadena," I said. "An orphan. No record of who his parents were, where he was born, nothing. Not a birth certificate anywhere. Herb started acting when he was in his teens. He was the kind of guy who ended up class president, most likely to succeed, most popular..."
"All right," Mark said angrily. "Where do we stand? Somebody must have hated his guts. Who was it?"

"How do I know?"

"He hired you to protect his life, didn't he?"

I knew what was coming. It was the same old thing. Mark didn't like private eyes. Especially the female variety. He was always trying to prove the superhuman portraits of them in fiction were the most dismal fraud ever perpetrated.

He turned and stared at me with about as much compassion as a little boy would feel staring at the spoon after he'd swallowed the castor oil. "Why didn't he come to me about these threats? We might have prevented this!"

"Sure," I said sarcastically. "You probably get at least a dozen calls a week from people who say their lives are in danger. Do you save everyone?"

"No!" Mark roared. "But we would have saved Herb Nelson!"

"Yeah, I'll bet!" I got to my feet "It's late. I want to go back to my of-

5

fice."

"Sure," he said, tossing some change on the counter. "You might have a customer—with real dough, and an option on a plot at Forest Lawn cemetery."

Anger was forming a big knot in my throat, but I managed to answer, "Why don't you get a new subject, Lieutenant? You've worn this one down to the nub."

We walked out into the rain. It touched my face, recalling days long ago when I waited in the same kind of downpour, blonde curls clinging to my forehead, and hoped my father, a private detective, would come out of the wet darkness, still safe and sound and smiling.

When we reached Long Beach, the rain stopped and the wheels of Mark's car whined dismally on the slick pavement. I listened to the sound for a long time and then said, "Sure, I feel bad about Herb Nelson. I feel partially responsible that he's dead. Wouldn't anybody under the same circumstances?"

Mark kept his eyes on the windshield-wiped panorama of street lights that faintly illuminated Anaheim Street in Long Beach. "Honey, why don't you get out of this business? What are you trying to prove?"

"What do you think?"

"So your father was murdered! That's no reason to keep banging your head against the wall!"

I jerked around in the seat as if I felt the same bullet which had ended Hank West's career in a dirty Los Angeles back alley. "You've got a lot of guts to tell me what I ought to do—where I ought to get off! Sure, I'm a woman! I act like a woman, think like a woman, look like a woman, but I'm mixed up in a rotten dirty business that men think they own by right of conquest! But you've never stopped to consider that half the crimes in the United States today are committed by women—and half of those committed by men are provoked by women. So where does that leave you? In a business operated seventy-five percent by females! All right, so you don't think I'm nice. What are you going to do about it?"

Mark looked at me with the contemptible expression of a man who hates himself because he doesn't understand why he likes something he thinks he should hate. "The only thing nice about you," he said hotly, "are your legs. You should have been a chorus girl."

The left-handed compliment bounced off me like buckshot off a fleeing watermelon thief. It went just far enough in to hurt. "Thanks," I murmured. "If the opportunity ever arises, I'll take advantage of it."

"I'm sure you will," Mark said, spinning the wheels and pulling to the curb outside my office.

I opened the door and stepped out, a jolting angry step that rang on the cement. Mark followed me up the stairway to the third floor. At the end of the hall was a glass door with the words, H. WEST, PRIVATE INVESTIGATOR painted in gold-leaf serif letters.

Mark gestured at the door. "You see, you don't even have the guts to let 'em know you're a woman before they walk in."

"I'm not in this business for my health," I said, inserting my key into the lock.

"What are you in it for?" Mark demanded hotly.

I didn't bother to answer. I was in this business for a lot of reasons, many of which he knew but refused to accept. I was tired of being accused, insulted and pushed around for doing a job men considered wrong for a woman.

The office was cold and damp. A brassiere hung out of an open desk drawer where I'd left it during a quick change earlier in the day.

Mark casually walked over and lifted the article of clothing up. "What kind of business did you say you were running?"

I slammed the door. "You want to know something, Lieutenant?" I said. "I'm going to find the person who murdered Herb Nelson, and when I do I'm going to take that piece of underwear and wrap it around your big thick neck!"

Mark threw down the bra and a grin spread across his face. "That's a deal!" he said.

Chapter Two

Herb Nelson's brutal murder made big headlines the next morning. The Los Angeles press called it, "The worst crime since the Black Dahlia!"

One of the major newspapers handled the story pictorially with two pages of photos, including one gruesome posed shot of Herb Nelson's blood-stained hand clutching his Academy Award Oscar.

Rain continued to pour from the storm sky, filling the gutters. After breakfast I called Fred Sims, an old friend of mine who was a reporter on the *Long Beach Press-Telegram*. Fred walked with a cane, but still managed to cover every inch of mayhem committed in Southern California. He said he was going to have breakfast at a hamburger joint on the Pike and asked me to join him for a cup of coffee.

We sat under a badly worn awning while Fred munched on a sandwich. Finally, he muttered, "Herb Nelson was a client of yours?"

"Yeah."

"You got an exclusive story for me?"

"Nope."

Fred pulled his lean, slightly bent frame around in his seat. He had deep, steel-gray eyes that ate through a person like acid through a piece of tin. "Well, what do you want?"

I created a few half-gestures that were reminiscent of a tired seagull about to set down on the water for a rest. "I hate to admit it, but I need some advice, Fred."

He grinned, lifted up his cane and took a practiced sight, one eye narrowed on the careening, empty rollercoaster cards in the distance.

"How old are you, Honey?" he asked.

"Twenty-eight. Now come on, Fred, let's not kid around..."

"You want my advice?"

"Well sure, but…"

The crippled newspaperman lowered his cane and rapped it on the cement "Look, I don't have time to kid with you or anyone else. Now do you want my advice or not?"

He sounded like a solider I'd read about during the war who refused to quit in the face of tremendous odds and led an infantry assault with his leg practically blown off. The soldier's name had been Fred Sims, and he hadn't changed a bit. He still refused to listen to anyone or wait for an answer. "Go to Hollywood," he said.

"What?"

"Close up your office for a couple of weeks. Go to Hollywood and get a job."

"What for?" I demanded.

Fred chewed on some soggy potato chips, then shoved the plate away. "You want to find Nelson's murderer, don't you?"

"Of course…"

"What do you measure, Honey?"

"What?"

"What do you measure?"

"Where?"

He smiled, got up and with the aid of his cane, circled my chair. "Everywhere," he said pointedly.

"What's that got to do…"

"Answer my question!" he barked stubbornly.

I groaned. "38-22-36. Five feet five. One hundred and twenty pounds. Normal childhood diseases. No dimples. Small birthmark on inside of right thigh. Parents both dead. No known living relatives." I stood up and snapped him a salute. "Anything else, General?"

"Yeah, can you act?"

"Of course not… I've never been on a stage in my life."

"That doesn't matter. With your taffy-colored hair, blue eyes and baby-bottom complexion, you ought to set Hollywood on fire with your looks alone."

"Thanks, pal," I said, "but who would hire me? There must be a thousand real-live dolls living in Hollywood and starving. It's a great idea. Sure, if I could get into the studios through the actor's entrance instead of

9

through the private eye's keyhole, I'd probably land something fast. But without experience I wouldn't get past the casting desk."

Fred wiped his eyes with the back of his hand. "Yeah, 'I guess you're right. Well, it was a good idea while it lasted. Would have made a great story. Terrific headline. Succulent Shamus Shucks Stiletto for Stardom."

"Very funny."

We started back toward town, Fred's metal-tipped cane cracking hollowly on the cement. Thoughts about Herb Nelson's blowup at Television Riviera drummed the same rhythmic cadence in my head. Was the killer affiliated with Bob Swanson's TV show? Was he the director, the producer, the cameraman?"

Sunlight broke through brightening the dull sky as Fred turned off down Ocean Avenue. He grinned, threw me a kiss and vanished in the mid-day crowd.

I continued on to my building, climbed the two flights of stairs and tried the doorknob. It wouldn't budge. The office door was never locked during the day, but apparently I'd been careless this time and snapped the latch on my way out to see Fred.

I rummaged futilely in my bag for the key. Then, recalling that one of my office windows opened onto the fire escape, I went downstairs, around to the alley and climbed up the metal staircase to the third floor.

The window was open just wide enough for me to squeeze through on my stomach.

When I got inside and turned around, the cold ugly snout of a gun was pressed squarely between my eyes.

Looking up the barrel of a loaded revolver is an experience not many people have the opportunity to put into words. For a long instant I was speechless.

Then I managed to say something which didn't make any sense at all, except that it was the truth. "I—haven't paid my insurance premium this month."

"What do you want?" a male voice snapped.

"I might ask you the same question. This is my office."

"Your…" the voice stopped. What are you talking about? This is H. West's office. He's a private detective."

"He was," I said, "until somebody did what you look as if you're plan-

10

ning to do."

"You mean there is no H.West? He's dead?"

"That's right," I said. "I'm his daughter. The name's Honey. I'm running the business now."

The revolver lifted up, and the hand that was holding it tossed the weapon on the desk. I focused in on a short dark mustache, a large hooked nose and a pair of black horn-rimmed glasses. "I—I'm sorry," he said. "I didn't know. I thought you were somebody else."

"Who were you expecting?" I asked, trying to shake off the tingle in my spine.

"Bob Swanson. He's trying to kill me."

"Bob Swanson? The TV actor?"

The man with the mustache had curly black hair and he ran his fingers through it nervously. "Yeah, the very same. My name's Aces—Sam Aces. I produce his show."

"What are you doing here?"

"I—I need help. No kidding. Somebody followed me from L.A. Even came into this building. That's why I locked the door. I figured when H.West came back he'd use a key. Then you appeared at the window and I got all shook up, grabbed the gun and…"

"Why do you think Swanson wants to kill you?"

Aces nervously lit two cigarettes and handed me one of them. "He'd like to get me out and produce the show himself."

"There must be an easier way!" I said suspiciously.

"I own the rights to the show. Besides, I got a long term contract with WBS-TV. He couldn't budge me any other way. He's tried to poison me twice."

I drew a mental picture of the TV star, Bob Swanson. He was the athletic type with a round boyish face and muscular arms. "I've watched him on television," I said. "He doesn't strike me as the poison type. A golf club in a dark alley, maybe. He could always say he was having a couple of practice shots and didn't see you."

Aces blew a few smoke rings. Then he said, "Two weeks ago I was working late in Studio Sixteen. I thought everyone had gone home hours before. Suddenly old B.S. came staggering in out of nowhere with a couple of drinks in his chubby little fists. He said he'd been around the corner

11

at a bar called the Golden Slipper lapping up a few when he thought about poor old Sammy back at the studio. He handed me a drink. It was a screwdriver. That's all I ever drink. Anything with orange juice. So I faked a healthy swallow and sent him on his merry way. The next morning I had the contents of that glass analyzed. It was loaded with four grains of white arsenic."

"Did this report reach the police?" I demanded.

"Yes," Aces said quickly. "Naturally I didn't cooperate when I learned Max Decker, the owner of WBS-TV, had been with Swanson when that drink was ordered."

"You don't think Decker…?"

"I don't know," Aces said, stubbing out his cigarette. "Max has never been fond of me. So you can see what would have happened if I'd spilled my story to the police. They'd have brought Decker in, too. Max wouldn't like that sort of thing. If I couldn't have proved absolutely it was Swanson who loaded that drink—long-time contract or not—Decker and B.S. would have killed me in the TV field."

"You would have been killed, period, if you'd downed that screwdriver," I said.

"Yeah, I know, and that's what brings me here. Last night we did a live Swanson show themed around a bathing-beauty contest. The winner was supposed to be signed to a six-week contract. But we couldn't get together on the choice. Before the show we held the judging in Decker's office. Max liked one, B.S. liked another and me, well, hell, I didn't really care just so we got the show on the road. I got pretty nervous so I went downstairs to a little juice bar on the first floor. I ordered my usual when B.S. suddenly appeared. We got into an argument about the judging and I guess I wasn't watching him too closely. Next thing I knew he'd gone back up to the studio, leaving me with the ultimatum that if I didn't bring a winner up in five minutes he'd personally knock my brains out. So I gulped down the orange juice and rushed upstairs. I folded up right in the middle of Decker's office."

I said, "You figure Swanson slipped something in your drink during the argument?"

"That's what I don't know. Ann Claypool, one of the bathing-beauty contestants, grabbed a glass of milk and forced some down my throat. I was

12

sick as a dog for a few minutes, then I felt fine."

"Did you feel stomach pains after drinking the orange juice?"

"I felt something," Aces said, "but I don't know whether it was really pain or just in my mind."

"But the milk," I said. "It caused a reaction."

"I'm allergic to milk. It makes me deathly ill."

"Did you know Herb Nelson?" I asked.

"Sure," he said, growing solemn. "I was a good friend to Herb Nelson. We worked together years ago when I was producing at Metro. In fact, I was the guy who dug up the script that won him an Academy Award."

"What caused the argument last month when Herb tore up the studio at Television Riviera?"

Aces didn't hesitate. "Swanson, as usual. I hired Herb for a bit part—an old broken-down comedian. He needed work bad and was drinking pretty heavy. Well, old B.S. bitched when he saw what a tremendous actor Herb was. He criticized Herb, changed his part, made a fool out of him. Herb finally blew his top. He told old B.S. off and then started wrecking the set. We had to call the cops."

"How did Swanson feel after they took Nelson away?"

"Mad as a hornet. Herb hit Swanson with a flood lamp and really floored him."

"Who do you think killed Nelson?"

Aces said, "Who do you think I think? Herb was a nice guy. Only a maniac would do something like that."

"Have you ever had any maniacal moments, Mr. Aces?"

"What are you getting at?"

"You were present when the fireworks started. Are you sure Herb Nelson didn't say anything derogatory about you?"

"Of course not!" His deep eyes rolled angrily. "Say, what is this? I came here to hire someone to help me, not to be accused of harming one of my oldest friends."

Sam Aces appeared to be about fifty. He was tall and gangly with an ambling body that seemed plucked out of some animated cartoon about comical dizzy-eyed giraffes. Despite his poor features, he had a look of warmth and sincerity. He was the kind of person you somehow wanted to like.

13

"You're perfect," he said after a moment. "B.S. is crazy about beautiful dames—especially blondes. Will you work for me?"

"That all depends on what kind of work you want done," I said.

"This afternoon I want you to go see Swanson at Television Riviera. We still haven't picked a winner in our beauty contest. Ten to one he'll go for you. All I have to do is second the motion and you'll be in. You've got to be around when we go on location. He's going to get me, I know he is—unless…"

"But, wait a minute, Mr. Aces…"

"Call me Sam, baby."

"Look, Sam," I protested, "this six-week contract—you know I'm not an actress."

"Who cares? With your face and figure…"

"But I can't learn lines…"

"Lines?" Aces said. "Who learns lines in television? This is the modern age, Honey. We've got little men who do nothing all day but type scripts into big letters on machines. Acting's a cinch. Ask Swanson. He spends two days on the golf course, two days drunk and two days in front of a camera, reading from the carding device and looking at women with shapely navels." He shrugged his lanky frame. "What do you say? If I go to the police, the publicity will kill me dead. You're the only one who can really help me now. I don't want to windup like Herb Nelson in an adjoining grave."

I scanned his face for a hint of phony melodramatics, but it revealed nothing but despair. His jaw sagged slightly.

"All right," I said. "I'll see what I can do."

We shook hands. Mentally, I considered the possibility of Sam Aces having killed Herb Nelson then quickly discarded the idea. He seemed honestly afraid. It was the same kind of fear I'd seen in Herb Nelson's eyes the week before his death. As Aces filled out information forms, I kept wanting to tell him I couldn't guarantee his staying out of a six-foot hole. But I never got the words out, because that's exactly where I pictured him. I don't know why, except at that moment Sam Aces' slouched, dejected shoulders and unhappy drawn face gave him the look of a man who was about to die.

Chapter Three

At four o'clock that afternoon I stood in the center of one of Television Riviera's mammoth sound stages wearing a skin-tight bathing suit. Max Decker, a ponderous bear of a man, sat on two wooden chairs, chewing on a black cigar and squinting under thick brows at my torso. Bob Swanson stood a few feet away, flexing his muscles and undressing me with his eyes.

Sam Aces was in a glass-faced monitor booth above the stage floor. His voice suddenly boomed out over a speaker, "Well, what do you think of her?"

Decker grunted, got a new grip on his cigar and continued to peer at me. Bob Swanson glanced at the booth. "You may be a lousy producer, Sam, but you can sure pick the girls. I vote yes. Can she act?"

"Of course," Aces lied.

"Okay," Swanson said. "What do you say, Max?"

Apparently Decker liked looking at females wearing bathing suits, but couldn't cope with the emotional problem that went with it. "Damn you, Sam!" he barked. "You had to go think up this crazy contest idea, then you went and filled up my office with a lot of fat female fannies, now you come up with a dame who's got more dangerous curves than the Indianapolis Speedway, and who makes me feel like an H-Bomb about to be triggered. Get her out of here!"

"But, Max!" Swanson protested. "I want this girl."

"Well, have her!" Decker blared back. "Just get her out of my sight. And keep her out of bathing suits!"

I changed my clothes, signed a six-week contract at four hundred a week, then left with Sam Aces.

"What's wrong with Decker?" I asked.

Aces grinned. "High blood pressure. I don't blame him for getting

15

mad. You must have raised his reading at least twenty degrees."

"What about Swanson? I thought he was going to hang around for the contract-signing business?"

"Honey," Aces said patiently, "there's one thing you'll learn about Swanson. The minute the sun goes down he heads for the nearest bar."

"And where would that be?"

"Just around the corner. You know- the place I told you about. The Golden Slipper."

I said good night to Sam, warned him to stay away from orange juice and then walked to the Golden Slipper. It was a ritzy little place with an ornate front and a bar that was as dark as the bottom of the River Styx. I signaled the bartender and ordered a martini. Two seconds later I was joined by the Golden Boy himself, flexing and snorting.

"Hello, baby," Swanson laughed drunkenly. "I hardly recognized you in clothes."

I smiled half-heartedly. "Thanks for the contract, Mr. Swanson."

"Don't thank me. Thank Sam Aces, the miserable bastard. He brought you in."

"You don't like Mr. Aces?"

"That's exactly right, sweetie. In fact, I hate his guts." He took a big gulp of his drink and leaned against the bar for support.

"I don't see how you could feel like that," I said. "He seems like such a nice guy."

Swanson bit hard on his teeth, scowling angrily. "Why that dirty son-of-a…" He stopped, his eyes narrowing suspiciously. "What's it to you?" He banged for another drink. "You make a lot of observations for a blonde walk-on with no talent but plenty of chest muscle. What's your name?"

"Honey West."

"Where'd you get that handle, in burlesque?"

"It's on my birth certificate, Mr. Swanson. No middle name. I was never in burlesque."

He gave me a knowing look. "Baby, you really missed you're calling."

"Now you're making the observations, Mr. Swanson. Why don't you like Sam Aces?"

"You writing a book?"

"Maybe."

Television star, Bob Swanson, winner of last year's award for best male performer, slugged down his fresh drink, wiped off his mouth with the back of his hand and grinned drunkenly. "Okay, put this in your first chapter, baby. You ever hear of an actor named Herb Nelson?"

"Sure…"

"He's dead," Swanson interrupted. "Murdered. You must have read about it in the papers. You want to know who did it? Sam Aces, that's who, and he's going to kill me next. You understand? That is, if I don't get him first!"

"Those are pretty strong words, Mr. Swanson," I said. "Why would Sam Aces want to kill Herb Nelson?"

"I don't know." He answered quickly as if he knew but didn't want to put it into words."

"Second chapter," I said, staring at my martini. "Why do you think he wants to kill you?"

"Power. I got too much power and Aces doesn't like it. There'd be no show without me. Aces can't stand it. He'd like to blow my brains out."

Bob Swanson talked exactly like the frustrated guy he was supposed to be. Prior to Herb Nelson's death I'd spent several hours digging into the muscle man's notoriously unspectacular past. He had migrated to TV from motion pictures after a sporadic career as a temperamental child star and an even more-impossible-to-work with postwar jungle hero. From that point it had been a series of breaks which had sprung him into the choice situation comedy series about a bachelor-writer who mixed verbs, consonants, and beautiful women.

These criss-cross accusations were puzzling. Sam Aces and Golden Boy suspected each other of murdering Herb Nelson and of plotting the same end for each other. I was more inclined to believe my client's story. A phone call earlier to Daws, Inc., a pharmaceutical lab in Beverly Hills, had verified the presence of arsenic in Aces' drink. L.A. police had backed this up with an official report listing the incident as "closed due to insufficient cooperation."

"Third chapter," I said.

"Third chapter," Swanson said, grinning slyly, "is where beautiful blonde with gorgeous blue eyes throws her book out and agrees to accompany handsome young television star on a tour of the night spots. Come on!"

He whisked me into his Cadillac convertible before I could argue. A quick thought struck me. If Bob Swanson had slipped arsenic into Aces' drink, it was possible he still might have some of the poison lying around. I wanted to have a look at his personal stationary too. Herb Nelson had said the threat note had been typed on bright orange bond with a giant letter "S" embossed in the corner.

"Why waste time in a bunch of dingy bars?" I leaned against his shoulder. "Why not your place? I bet you even have a swimming pool!"

His eyes lit up like a neon sign. "Have I got a swimming pool?" he roared. "This pool was designed especially for you, baby doll. Wait until you see it!"

We zipped out to Beverly Hills in eleven minutes flat. Bob Swanson's home was fantastically modern. It was so low-slung you had to duck to get through the front door. The house was a gigantic flat-roofed square with a swimming pool in the center. There were no inside walls, only a few moveable partitions, and at each corner of the house there were elevated platforms. These were built much like television sound stages with arc lights in the ceiling and steps leading up. There was only one major difference. They were entirely carpeted with thick foam rubber. From each of them, things happening on any of the other stages could obviously have been seen merely by looking over the low-slung, unwalled kitchen, the tremendous indoor swimming pool or the equally unwalled bathrooms. Bob Swanson's home was the most spectacular, and at the same time vulgar looking, place I'd ever seen.

He pointed at the four raised stages. "The bedrooms," he said casually. "This is a four bedroom home."

"But, no beds," I observed. "Where do you sleep?"

"What do you mean, no beds?" Swanson demanded. "Four of the biggest king-size hammocks in captivity. Twelve by twelve. A foot depth of the softest foam rubber you ever snuggled your lily-white rear into, I'll bet!"

"You sleep on the floor?"

Golden Boy grinned. "Natch. Best place to sleep. No falling out of bed. Plenty of room to roam. No pillows. Just pull a blanket over you if it gets a little cold."

I looked at this guy and shook my head. "Did you design the place?"

18

"Every last inch."

"You don't like privacy, I take it?"

"The hell with privacy," Swanson said. "Notice! No permanent walls. A few partitions for those futile numbskulls who have to hide something that nobody gives a damn about seeing in the first place. You ever think about that? Nothing's worth seeing if it's ugly. The partitions are for the ugly ones. I get a few of those now and then."

He led me to the swimming pool. It was immense and shaped like the body of a very large-bosomed woman.

"What are you, a nudist?" I asked.

Golden Boy raised his eyebrows as if he smelled something foul. "Hell, no. Nobody is ever allowed in this pool in the nude. It contaminates the water. We have bathtubs for that sort of thing. Anyone who swims in this pool wears one of my special suits."

"What?"

"Plastic," he said, pulling one of the suits out of a poolside cabinet, "The men wear plastic trunks and the woman have plastic pants and bras."

I examined the two-piecer he handed to me. It was fantastic. And transparent. So transparent not even a mole could go undetected underneath. I wondered what kind of queer psychosis affected this man, but undoubtedly it had no conventional name. It was a perfect blend of nature and sanitation. Bob Swanson was what could have been called a natursanicotic. He was crazy about living in the raw, but wanted to keep the microbes caged while he was doing it.

He asked me to go for a swim.

"Let's have a drink first," I suggested quickly. "I'd like to look around the rest of the house."

"Sure, baby." Then he laughed. He was still pretty drunk. "But don't get lost."

My return laugh didn't feel right in my throat. I wondered who'd get the last laugh. If I couldn't find some of that deadly white powder quick, Golden Boy was certain to have me in one of his peek-a-boo bathing suits. There was only one thing on my mind—arsenic. And only one thing on his mind—my chassis. I had to locate what I was after before his plans began to jell.

Swanson switched on his hi-fi and the throbbing rhythm of *Taboo* filled the house. As casually as possible, I mamboed into the modern kitchen area. The all-electric stove, oven, roaster and charcoal broiler were housed in a long, low-slung orange-colored case. The sink faced a floor-to-ceiling window that looked out into a green landscape. Glancing over at Golden Boy, who was bent over a bar built low enough to serve kids in grammar school, I silently cursed his idea of no walls. You couldn't do a thing around this place unnoticed. I reached quickly down and tried to pull open a cabinet drawer. It wouldn't budge. A try for another drawer yielded the same results. The next instant, he was breathing down my back.

"Wha'cha doing?" he asked curiously.

I turned around slowly. "Oh, nothing. Thought I'd look at your kitchenware. Women go for that sort of thing, you know."

He laughed. I didn't like that laugh. It sounded too much like the last one. "Drawers and cabinets are all electric," he said. "You got to know where to touch them to make 'em work. Cost me a fortune."

"That's a crazy thing. What'd you do that for?"

He led me back to the kindergarten-size bar. "I don't like snoopers," he said. "That's one thing you'll learn about me. I don't trust anyone. I had this setup installed in every moveable object in the joint. It makes me rest easier. This way I know nobody is going through my stuff. Whether I'm here or not."

"But what if somebody learns the spot to touch to open things up?"

He grinned. "Oh, that's easy." He pointed to a tiny metal plate on one of the bar doors. "This is the place to touch, but you got to have this to touch it with. "He held up a piece of metal that was attached to his key chain.

"It's a magnet," he said proudly. "A special magnet. I've got the only one that will spring these locks." He laughed again. "Simple, isn't it?"

I nodded. This was one character who would never be caught with his poison out in the open. In fact, I wouldn't have been surprised if he had a special key and a special vault for such appetizing spices as arsenic.

He handed me an orange-colored drink in a tall glass.

"What's this?" I asked quickly.

"A screwdriver," he said. "If you don't mind my saying so, I make damned good ones."

The drink went crashing to the slate surface that surrounded the swimming pool. Swanson leaped to his feet. I stood, holding an invisible glass, staring blankly at the orange liquid soaking into the stone. It had been a stupid reflex action. Talk about Sam Aces being allergic to milk. At that moment, I was sure I'd never be able to drink anything with even a hint of orange flavor again.

It took a bit of doing, but I managed to cover over the accident without arousing too much suspicion. He did think it was strange when I turned down a second of his "superb" screwdrivers for an "unspectacular" martini.

Then came swim time.

"What size do you wear?" Golden Boy asked.

"I'm a working girl," I said. "It's getting late. I'd better be getting home."

"You just got here," he said, flexing his biceps. "You have to swim in my pool. That's standard procedure for all female visitors."

"It isn't standard procedure for me."

"You can change right here," he persisted. "I won't mind."

"I'll bet!"

"You're almost twice as broad on top as you are in the middle," he said, scanning my figure.

"I didn't think you noticed," I said sarcastically. "Anyway, you're still not going to get me out of my clothes."

"Get into that bathing suit!" he demanded.

I threw the bra and pants in his face. "You put it on! You designed it, you wear it!"

I should never have done that. His eyes, widened into a passionate glare. He obviously liked women when they got rough.

"I love you!" he yelled. "Nobody's ever done that to me! Nobody!"

He uttered a drunken beastly growl which must have been a throwback to the days when he played a poor man's Tarzan. Then he staggered toward me with his arms outstretched. I thought about using some of the judo tactics I'd learned from my father, but decided in favor of some healthier conversation.

"Now look, Mr. Swanson," I argued. "Let's simmer down, brush back your hair and drive me home."

He kept coming with the determined gait of a fullback driving off tackle. The conversation period was over. I sidestepped, brought my foot up and he went straight into the pool. That was exactly what he needed. A good cooling off. I started for the phone to call a taxi, then thought about Mr. Swanson's swan dive. I glanced at the pool. He hadn't come up!

Bubbles gurgled to the surface where Golden Boy had gone down. Maybe he couldn't swim!

I slipped off my shoes, yanked down the zipper on my dress and dove in.

Chapter Four

Swanson was floating face down a foot under water. I slipped the crook of my elbow under his chin and brought him to the surface. A silly thought crossed my mind! Tomorrow's headlines: TV HERO DROWNS IN HIS OWN MICROBES! We reached the edge of the pool and I drifted underneath to get more leverage. I never got it.

His lips suddenly split open sucked in a tremendous gasp of air and he was after me again. With a roar, Swanson rolled over, locked his legs around my bare middle and we went down, straight to the bottom. This guy was one of the greatest actors I'd ever seen. He'd faked the drowning.

His big hands reached for me. I shook him loose for an instant, got a foot up under his chin and kicked. He buckled slightly. Then I caught him again with my heel, a glancing blow that bounced off his left eyebrow. He recoiled, swallowed some water and finally surfaced. I followed him up.

All the fight was drained out of Mr. TV. He sagged on the stone rim of the pool, glowering at me out of the eye that wasn't swelling up. "Get out of my pool!" he bellowed. "Now I'll have to have it drained and sterilized. I ought to sue you."

I climbed up a ladder on the far side and flashed him a smile that was dripping with dislike. "Why don't you sue me, Mr. Swanson? We could bring the jury down here for a swim—in your plastic suits."

He touched his eye and winced. "I'm cancelling your contract, you can be sure of that! You'll never work for the WBS network. In fact, I'll have you so completely blackballed you won't even be able to get a job in Hell!"

"You ought to have a lot of influence down there," I said.

He groaned, the eye closing into a tight black lump of pain. "Get out of my house! Now! This instant! Get out!"

I slipped on my clothes and called a taxi. In the confused rush of leav-

23

ing, I left my bag and had to have the cab driver turn around and go back. It was lying on the front steps where Swanson had obviously thrown it. I looked inside. Everything seemed to be in order, except for one important item. My .32 revolver was gone!

The next morning Bob Swanson marched into Studio Sixteen wearing a patch over his left eye. I was going over a TV script with Sam Aces and his chief writer, Joe Meeler. The muscle man stormed toward Aces when he saw me.

"What's this girl doing here?" Swanson bellowed. "I might ask you the same question," Aces said. "Isn't this one of your golf days?"

"No, it is not!"

Aces grinned. "My mistake. The way you look I thought for sure someone had used your eye for a hole-in-one."

Swanson's face began to twitch with rage. He demanded my immediate removal from the studio.

"Miss West has a contract," Aces reminded him.

"I don't care! She tried to kill me last night!"

"No fooling?" the lanky producer said, grinning, "What'd she hit you with, the side of a house?"

Swanson turned to Sam Aces. "I warn you Mr. Producer!" he hissed. "If you don't get this girl out of here, I'll…"

"You'll what, B.S.?" Aces taunted. "Kill me? Murder me the way you murdered Herb Nelson?"

Swanson stepped back, a jolting wobbly step of a man who takes a jarring right cross and isn't certain he won't collapse from the blow. "What— what are you talking about?"

"You threatened him, didn't you?" Aces answered quickly. "You told him you wished he were dead. You tried to ruin the poor guy, didn't you?"

"That's ridiculous…"

"You hate everybody, Swanson!" Aces continued viciously. "Anybody who gets up near the top, or guys like Nelson who've hit it and gone down— you shove them good, don't you?"

Swanson whirled angrily and left the studio. I glanced at Sam Aces. A small glint flickered in his deep set eyes as he stared after the fleeting figure of Bob Swanson. I tried to analyze the look and the incident. Had Sam

Aces used the element of surprise to stun an innocent man into seeming guilty? Or was Swanson so obviously the murderer, that nothing could help him form a verbal defense against such accusations? Three factors stacked up strongly against Bob Swanson. His name, according to Herb Nelson, had appeared on the threat note. He had accused Aces of murdering Nelson without furnishing any motive for the crime. And it appeared almost certain that he had stolen my .32 revolver.

Privately, I told Aces about the missing gun.

"Great," the producer groaned. "It wasn't bad enough having to filter all my drinks, now I'll have to filter the air for bullets."

"Swanson must have that gun, Sam. We'd better notify the police."

"No!" Aces said sharply. "We can't do that, Honey. The police will think I'm crazy. It was bad enough when I refused to tell them my story about the poisoned drink. What if they picked up Swanson and found nothing? Not even the gun?"

"They'd release him, naturally, but…"

"You two met last night at the Golden Slipper, is that right?" Aces asked.

"Yes."

"Did you open your bag while you were there?"

I thought for an instant "No. He paid for my drink, but…"

"Did you open it after you got to his place?"

"No."

Aces pinched his thin lips together thoughtfully. "Is it possible someone other than Swanson could have removed your revolver while you were at the Golden Slipper bar?"

I nodded. "Sure, I guess it's possible. Why?"

Aces gathered up his lanky frame and ambled nervously across the sound stage. "Honey, I'm in a helluva spot. This gun business really scares me. Rod Caine is an expert with a revolver."

"Rod Caine?"

"He's a TV writer—originated the idea of the Bob Swanson show. I fired him several months ago."

"Why?"

"I didn't like him."

"That's all?"

25

"Not exactly," Aces said grimly. "One night I came home unexpectedly. He was in bed with my wife, Lori."

"That sort of thing does get under one's skin."

"Lori is a very beautiful woman," Aces said, his eyes growing intently dark. "Very beautiful, and very young. She's only twenty. A rare little child. She doesn't know any better. Caine does."

"Where is he now?"

"I don't know. He disappeared. Nobody seems to know where he is. And that's what worries me. I hurt him. Hurt him bad. A cowardly thing. I hit him in the face with a broken glass." He wiped hands over his eyes. "I don't know why exactly. They were lying there, naked and drunk. I grabbed an empty glass from a table beside the bed, shattered it on the metal rim and hit him in the face."

I winced. "How dirty can you get?"

Aces nodded. "I know. There was blood all over the place. I never even saw how bad he was cut. He just put his hands to his face and ran. Nobody's seen him since."

"He must have needed stitches. Did you check the hospitals? His doctor?"

"Sure. He just vanished. Naked, too. The police had no record either."

"Where do you live?"

"Newport. Lido Isle on the bay front."

"Is Caine a good swimmer?"

"I don't know. It was dark as hell. He could have made it to the water. Rain was pouring down and I couldn't follow his trail. But he was bleeding."

"He might be hiding because he's scarred."

"I don't think he's hiding," Aces said tightly. "The incident occurred four months ago. Plenty of time for plastic surgery. I keep wondering if he still has the same features."

"Do you think it was that bad?"

Aces stopped pacing, lit two cigarettes and handed me one. Then he said, "I walk down the street now and look at faces and I ask myself, 'Is that Caine? Where is he? What does he look like? It drives me crazy. I wonder if he was sitting in the Golden Slipper the night my drink was poisoned.

26

I wonder if he was there last night, if he stole your gun, if…"

"Wait a minute," I interjected. "You forget one thing."

"What's that?"

"If he was bleeding as freely as you say, he might have tired and drifted out to sea."

"I thought about that," Aces said quietly.

"He could be dead."

"Yeah, and if he isn't, the tombstone may be on the other grave. If you know what I mean."

While Meeler and Aces made further script changes, I decided to search the dressing room where I'd left my bag during my appearance the day before. An attractive, green-eyed brunette stopped me just inside the doorway.

"Hi!" she said, much too sweetly. "Remember me?"

"Sure. We met yesterday. You're Ann Claypool, one of the contestants."

"That's right." She flashed me a pasted-on smirk that reeked of bourbon. "I'm the contestant who was supposed to win but didn't. Have you ever heard of a fix that was fixed?"

"I don't think I understand."

"Of course, you wouldn't," she said, weaving slightly. Ann Claypool looked like a grown-up doll with a deep dimple in her cheek, long sweeping eyelashes and a small voluptuous figure. She couldn't have weighed more than a hundred pounds soaking wet.

"You want to know something?" she continued. "I was supposed to have signed that contract you got. It was all decided days ago. Then Sam Aces ruined it. He went and killed it just like he killed my husband!"

"What do you mean?"

"He sent my husband to his death deliberately!"

"How'd he do that?"

Ann Claypool said, "Vince was a specialist in underwater photography. Aces sent him on an impossible assignment." She squinted cynically. "Vince never came back."

I glanced out the window at the mountain of white clouds forming over the blue sky. This case was getting almost as obscure as the distant hills. I

27

shook my head. "Now, look, why would Sam Aces want your husband dead?"

"For revenge," she blurted angrily. "Because I told his wife the truth about him. He was always trying to get me alone in his office. He was always trying to take off my clothes and—well—I told her everything. He said he'd kill me for it. But he killed Vince instead!"

She sat down and put her face in her hands. "Now he's even taken the contract away from me! After he promised!" Her large green eyes looked up and there was a glaze of hate over them. "I'd like to kill him, do you know that? And I'm not the only one. Bob Swanson hates Sam enough to strangle him. And Max Decker feels the same way."

"I don't get this," I said, suspiciously. "Why tell me?"

"Because," Ann snapped drunkenly, "I want you to know what you're getting yourself into. You think you're pretty smart, don't you? I don't know how you got that contract, but I'm warning you to watch out. Do you understand? You're sitting on a big keg of dynamite and when it blows you're going to be in trouble. Big trouble."

Ann Claypool flashed those hate-filled eyes at me again and walked all too soberly out of the dressing room. I thought about my missing revolver. Could this girl have taken it?

When I saw Aces later in the day I told him how well-liked he was by Ann Claypool and her associates.

"Brother," I sighed. "You're about as popular around these parts as a Russian-made hydrogen bomb."

"Yeah," Aces said, trying to smile. "I guess I should have told you about Vince's death. I was really sorry it happened, believe me. But I wasn't responsible."

"Was she supposed to get the contract?"

"Yeah," Aces said wincing. "I've been trying to give her every break possible. But it doesn't make any difference. I could star her in a three-hour spectacular and she'd still hate my guts."

"Did you really make a play for her?"

"Yeah."

"Did you threaten her after she talked to your wife?"

"Of course I did!" Aces said. "But I was only trying to throw a scare into her. What would you expect me to do? She nearly wrecked my marriage."

I nodded dismally, then added up the credit side of Sam Aces' ledger. Bob Swanson, Ann Claypool, Rod Caine and possibly Max Decker. Apparently there wasn't a debit anywhere to balance the books.

"What's Max Decker got against you?" I asked, studying the producer as he paced across the sound stage.

"I don't know," Aces said, shaking his head. "I've threatened to take the show to another network several times. Max is a funny guy. To tell the truth, I don't think he likes anyone."

"Sam," I said suddenly, "do you honestly think one of them plans to murder you?"

Aces grinned and put his arm around my shoulder. "I like you, Honey. You have just about everything a woman could want, including brains. Maybe you ought to drop out of this thing before you get hurt."

"If Swanson's our boy," I said, "I'm not worried."

"What about Caine? A butched-up face could go a long way to setting him up for the loony bin. Before I gave him the jagged glass he looked a little like Rock Hudson."

"That's a tough break."

"And if it's Ann Claypool, you're really sitting pretty. You got a contract yesterday she was a cinch to sign. As you said, she's mad as hell about that."

"Swell," I groaned. "Now we're all friends. We ought to throw a big party in Swanson's swimming pool and serve nothing but arsenic-spiked screwdrivers in jagged glasses."

Aces pulled on his coat. "We're leaving for Catalina Island tomorrow aboard my yacht. We'll be filming one of the Swanson shows in and around Avalon and White's Landing. Be gone about four days with the cast and crew. You can make it, of course?"

"Wouldn't miss it for the world. Yachts, Catalina and men are my three favorite sports. This sounds like a Honey West parlay."

"We'll leave around noon. I'm taking my big ship, *Hell's Light*. It's tied up at Wilmington Harbor. Pier Sixty-seven. Just bring a swimsuit and a toothbrush. We'll have plenty of things in wardrobe if you should want to be civilized."

He gave me a copy of the Catalina script. Meeler had already written me in.

"You better start boning up on your lines," Aces grinned, "even if we do have cuing devices. I want to shoot one of your scenes tomorrow."

Great! I didn't have enough on my mind. Now I had to worry about words and speeches and scenes. After Aces left, I stayed in Studio Sixteen wrestling with the script, the puzzle of who hated Aces the most and the question of Herb Nelson's murderer. I could hardly keep them all straight.

I thought about Lori Aces. How did she fit? Was she really in love with her husband? Maybe I could study that situation during the Catalina trip. No doubt, she'd be along. Or would she? Then I got to thinking about Ann Claypool. She had a lot of hate welled up inside her. But she had such a sweet rhythmic voice. It sounded like woodwinds or flutes.

The big clock on the wall of Stage Sixteen pointed to ten-thirty. I could hardly keep my eyes open. I got up, stretched and bent over to pick up my purse.

That's when I heard another sound. It was rhythmic. It was deadly. Bullets have a special sound all their own.

Chapter Five

I straightened up quickly and lunged for cover behind the TV camera as a second shot screamed off the side of the metal case. The character with the gun was somewhere in the metal beams above the sound stage. It was a country mile up there, and dark. I couldn't see a soul. A chill went through me. This reminded me of a horror movie I saw years ago, Lon Chaney in *Phantom of the Opera*. There was no telling who was crawling around in the maze of ventilating tubes, light fixtures, and pitch blackness.

I waited nervously for the third barrage. It didn't come. There was the sudden sound of a door closing high up in the stage loft and then nothing. My sniper friend evidently had decided to call it quits.

About then I became aware of a sharp pain. I felt around. My hand came up red.

Dr. Carter had just completed his examination of my wound when Lieutenant Mark Storm came striding into South Bay Emergency. The big detective was followed closely by Fred Sims.

"What the hell's going on, Honey?" Mark demanded. "Hey Doc, I got a report somebody shot at her from behind. What's the damage?"

"The damage," I said angrily, "is in the report. The word *from* is a lie."

"You're kidding," Fred grunted.

"Think so?" I said, touching the back of my skirt gingerly. "If I weren't a lady I'd show you the Band-Aid."

The white-haired medical man crinkled his face slyly. "Just a flesh wound boys, nothing critical."

Fred and Mark, two guys who had pulled me out of more scrapes and tight spots than Dr. Carter had pills, smothered a pair of grins.

"Same old Honey," Mark said pointedly, glanced at the crippled news-

31

paperman. "Always leading with her chin. Only this time she turned around and stuck something else out."

"Doc!" I yelled. "Get these two nitwits out of her before I commit murder!"

Mark took off his hat, leaned his six-foot-five tower down and stuck his chin out. "All right," he said, "murder me!"

I measured him with my fist, then leaned into his face with my lips. There was something I really liked about this crazy detective. I wasn't certain whether it was his looks, his build, or his personality. He had a rugged face with thick black brows, deep, quiet brown eyes, and solid massive shoulders that tapered down into an Olympic physique. Mark was a boomeranged mixture of wit, tomfoolery, and plain horse-sense.

A piece of finely sanded hickory interrupted us, pushing Mark away from me. "Hey," Fred pleaded, "am I always going to be the other man?"

I grinned, kissed Fred and the three of us walked down to a nearby coffee shop. Immediately they both grew serious. Dead serious. I told them the story of Sam Aces and his "unfriendly" associates.

"Get out of this, Honey!" Mark warned. "There's a real screwball mixed up in it somewhere and he's not going to be satisfied until everybody's got a few extra holes. And I don't mean just from bullets. Arsenic can cut a few capers of its own."

I nodded. "Sure, there're a lot of screwballs mixed up in this case, but I can't tell yet which screwball is the one who murdered Herb Nelson."

At the mention of Herb's name the two men flinched. "Honey," Fred started, "we have something to tell you…"

"Let me tell her," Mark interrupted. He stirred his coffee for an instant and then studied me with the same protective expression on his face that he'd had the night we found Herb's battered body. "Honey, you remember we—we didn't know what sort of instrument had been used on Herb? Well, we've found out. It was the Oscar."

"No," I groaned, "but, we…"

"I know," Mark said. "The killer must have cleaned it in an effort to wipe off fingerprints. The lab says that's definitely what was used."

Fred kept his head lowered. "He was so badly battered identification had to be made from rings and clothing and physical structure."

I sagged in my chair. The thought of the brutal murder of Herb Nelson still made me tighten with shock.

"I'm going to bring Swanson in for questioning," Mark said, sipping at his coffee. "I'm anxious to give him a couple of hours under the sweat lamp." He grinned, an expression that was contrary to what he felt inside. "Of course, we'll install an infra-red bulb for Mr. Muscle Man."

I didn't agree on the idea. Swanson would be a tough man to pump. It'd be better to catch him off guard. Maybe aboard Aces' yacht. Liquor did a lot of fancy things with Mr. Swanson's insides. Even took care of the microbes. I asked Mark to lay off for a few more days.

"We're going to Catalina tomorrow," I said. "The ship will be jammed with partial sets, lights, cast, crew, the works. I don't think he'll pull any tricks."

"I wouldn't bet on it," Mark said.

"What would you bet on?" I asked.

"Murder. Two to one you're going to lose another client, Honey girl. The only way to stop it is hauling in Swanson."

"I'll stop it," I said.

"Yeah," Mark finished, "that's what worries me."

Pier Sixty-seven in Wilmington Harbor looked like D-Day on the beach at Normandy. They were loading half of Television Riviera aboard *Hell's Light*. And at least a hundred cases of liquor. The ship wasn't going to be the only thing afloat during this journey.

Hell's Light was the largest private yacht I'd ever seen. It had two decks, three lifeboats and a fantastic circular bar that could seat fifty people. The bar, stools and built-in-hi-fi equipment were set squarely in the middle of a swimming pool. To get a drink, it was necessary to swim or wade through the comfortably heated water. Now I knew why Aces had said to bring only a toothbrush and a bathing suit. What else did I need?

The swimming-pool bar was already jammed, still an hour until sailing time. I recognized a few familiar faces and bodies: patch-eyed Golden Boy, crocked to the teeth and wearing a blue denim outfit that was soaked to his skin; Ann Claypool sitting on the bar, singing and not wearing much of anything; Joe Meeler, staring at all his drunken associates as if he wished they were all dead; Sam Aces, decked out in a red jacket and captain's hat that was as cockeyed as he was; and a face and figure that I'd never seen before, but recognized instantly as Lori Aces. She was a rare little child all right, just as Aces had said. Sam claimed she was twenty which made her roughly thirty years his junior. Actually she looked closer to sixteen. Lori was the only one without a drink besides Meeler.

Aces saw me immediately, waved and floundered over. Apparently he wasn't much of a swimmer. In fact, he waded the entire distance. He showed me to my cabin, a big comfortable room well enough forward to provide a view off the ship's bow.

"Do you like it?" Aces asked.

"Like it?" I said. "How can you afford a battleship like this?"

"Hell's Light was left to me by my grandfather," he explained. "Provisions of the will make it impossible for me to ever sell. This baby is the granddaddy of all parental nooses.

"Must cost you a small fortune to run and maintain a yacht this size."

"Those expenses are provided for in the will, too. Gramps had only one vice—this boat. He was madly in love with her. When I was a kid I showed a natural interest in the yacht, so when Grandpa kicked off he left it to me, lock, stock and lifeboat."

I smiled mischievously. "Including the swimming-pool bar?"

"Well, no," Aces admitted. "That was my own innovation, paid for out of my own pocket. I put the bar in the pool because I understand ghosts can't swim. I wouldn't want Grandpa to sit next to me while I'm gulping down a barrel of screwdrivers."

"Speaking of screwdrivers," I said, unpacking my toothbrush, "have you been mixing your own?"

"Absolutely. And no bullet holes yet, either."

"I wish I could say the same. "While I slipped on my bathing suit behind a small screen, I told Aces about the twin shots fired at me in Studio 16. He got mad. Real mad.

"I warned you to drop out of this. Is the wound very serious?"

"No," I said smiling. "Practically healed overnight. Maybe it'll teach me to keep my tail feathers tucked in."

"Did you find either of the bullets?"

"One. A .32 caliber. Cinch it was from my gun."

He offered me a cigarette. I reached, but never got it. Lori—child-like, pretty, little Lori Aces—had it between her slim white fingers. And she

34

had something else in that graceful, dainty hand. A .32 revolver.

I knew the gun looked familiar because I was staring straight down the barrel. This was getting to be a nerve wracking habit.

"You crazy little fool!" Sam tore the gun out of Lori's hand. "You want to kill someone?"

Lori seemed stunned. She shook her head. "I didn't know what to do, Sammy. I was taking the gun to Captain Morgan's cabin when I heard your voice."

I came out from behind the screen. "Where'd you get it?" I demanded.

"In our cabin," Lori said. "I wanted some fresh air. It was stuck in one of the windows." She gave me the once-over-lightly treatment. "Are you our new leading lady?"

Aces nodded. He was sober now. I asked Lori too explain exactly how she found the revolver.

"The window is in our bathroom. One of those crank types. I started turning the handle and this thing dropped right into my lap. Scared the life out of me."

"Which direction was the revolver pointing when it fell?" I asked.

Lori shook her head again. "I'm not sure. I was sitting at my vanity table. I think this end hit me first." She pointed at the barrel.

I glanced at Aces. He was slightly green around the gills. "What's at the opposite side of that window?"

"A bathtub," Aces said. "I usually take a bath before dinner."

I took the revolver and opened it. "What were you saying about no bullet holes, Mr. Aces?" I asked casually.

"You don't think someone was planning to pot me in the bathtub?"

"Two bullets missing," I said, showing him the empty chambers. "This is definitely my gun. Don't you think the other four bullets could have done a job on you?"

"But why leave the gun sticking in the window like that?" Aces questioned. "Someone was bound to see it."

"Maybe." I glanced at Lori. She was nervous as a cat. "Did you see the gun when you sat down at the vanity table?"

"No. I told you. I don't think I would have known it was there if I hadn't turned that crank."

35

"What's outside the window?" I asked.

"A passageway," Aces said. "Leads to the swimming-pool bar."

I said I thought somebody was trying the window for size when there was an interruption. In his haste the gunman probably couldn't pry his weapon loose and decided to risk the chance of returning for it later.

"Maybe by that time you'd have been lolling around in the tub," I said to Aces.

I put the revolver away in a safe place and the three of us walked out on deck. *Hell's Light* was pulling away from the pier, heading into the bright blue Wilmington channel that would lead us out to sea. Aces looked sick.

"You can take her back," I said.

"That wouldn't solve anything," he groaned miserably. "We still haven't got a killer."

"No," I said. "But somebody's working on it."

I glanced at Lori Aces. She was such a tiny thing. Really child-like. She was about the same height as Ann Claypool, but smaller in the bosom. She had strong arms and legs that looked as if they were kept in perfect trim with a lot of exercise. I thought about that as we stated off to the swimming-pool bar. It would have taken someone in good shape to swing around on those dark crossbeams in Studio Sixteen. Lori Aces appeared to be in excellent physical shape.

Hell's Light took a little more than three hours crossing through the twenty-mile stretch of placid green Pacific to reach Catalina Island. By that time, nine people had been rescued from the water around the bar. One of them was Ann Claypool. She wore a flimsy two piece swimsuit. Her straps kept coming down and the little TV actress finally abandoned the top in favor of a bright red lei. It would have taken no encouragement at all for her to shed the lei, but for some reason a slight semblance of order was maintained and nobody encouraged her.

Two incidents were unusual during that trip: the sudden appearance of Max Decker, who was supposed to have missed the boat, and a back-slapping relationship that developed between Sam Aces and Bob Swanson.

We anchored about a half-mile off shore at White's Landing, the summer site of a YMCA camp. A camera crew went ashore to set up for the next day's film sequences. I hitched a ride on the small boat. So did Lori Aces, who seemed disgusted with the chaos aboard *Hell's Light.*

"I think my husband likes that cheap Claypool girl," Lori said. "Did you see the way she kept looping the other half of her lei over the men and hugging them?"

The boat angled up beside the pier. We climbed out, then separated from the camera crew and started up the white beach. I asked Lori if she knew what had ever happened to Rod Caine. She denied knowing the writer until I told her I was a private detective hired by her husband. We talked about the night Aces caught Lori and Caine under the covers.

"I was having a drink," Lori said, "I was lonesome. Sammy works so many nights, you know! Rod came by the house and we had a few martinis. He kissed me a couple of times and then—the next thing I knew we were in bed together."

"He must be some man."

"I guess so," Lori said softly. "I'm only eighteen. I haven't had much experience. In fact, with Sammy it was the first time for me."

Now I knew the age score. About thirty-two years difference between Aces and Lori. A wide gap.

"Have you seen or heard from Caine since that evening?"

"You won't tell my husband, will you?"

"This is strictly between us, I promise."

"He called me about three weeks ago. I asked him where he was, but he wouldn't tell me. He said he was so mad at what Sammy had done, he'd like to kill him."

"How badly was his face injured?"

"He wouldn't tell me a thing, but he did ask me the strangest question." Lori looked puzzled.

"What was that?"

Lori's bathing suit had big buttons down the front and she fiddled with them nervously. "He asked me if Sammy's favorite drink was still a screwdriver."

I winced. "You never told your husband about the phone call?"

"No, I was afraid to. He goes mad with jealousy. Like the night he shoved the glass in Rod's face. I was afraid he might think there was more to it than just the phone call."

"Has Sam ever mentioned Herb Nelson to you?"

"Sure."

"When exactly?"

Lori said, "Lot's of times. Sam felt sorry for Herb. He was always trying to get him into bit parts in the Swanson show, but Bob kept saying no. Bob's one hundred percent louse."

We decided to take a swim. Lori was obviously an expert swimmer and her small arms cut the frothy sea with swift, practiced strokes. We sent out about a half mile and then floated on our backs.

The swim did a lot to clear my head. I began piecing things together. Whoever stole my .32 had tried it on me and then brought the revolver aboard the ship planning to use it on Aces. The only suspect who hadn't sailed with us was Rod Caine, unless he was hiding, or was unrecognizable because of a change in his features. I felt like counting Lori Aces out of the race. She was too naïve, too sweet, too much in love with her husband. Or was she any of these?

I considered the phone call to Lori from Rod Caine. The story sounded phony. Knowing Sam Aces, I figured he'd probably been drinking screwdrivers since he was old enough to talk. Who changes an old habit like that overnight? Someone could have faked Caine's voice. Or maybe Lori lied.

Floating on a glittering green wave, Lori smiled at me, "How you doing?"

"Great. What's Rod Caine sound like?"

"His voice?"

"Yes."

Lori treaded water for a moment while she thought about the question. "I don't know. It's sort of deep. A little nasal. Has a nice quality. He should have been an actor instead of a writer—with his looks and a voice like that. Sounds a little like Sammy, in fact."

"Who?"

"Sammy. My husband."

I rolled over in the water and studied this dark haired little porpoise. Who was she trying to kid? That first crack about Caine's questioning of Sam's taste in drink was bad enough, but this took the prize for being obvious. I fried a quick new formula: Lori plus Caine plus revenge plus money equals murder! Sounded plausible. This way Caine didn't have to aboard

Hell's Light. Lori could have faked the whole business about finding the gun in the bathroom window. Maybe she wanted to frighten Aces and make me think he was on the verge of a nervous breakdown. Then powie! The old suicide gag. They slip Aces a pint of poison and make him out a homicidal maniac who hits people with broken glass and who fakes his voice to pin his death on a hated enemy. I was certain now. Lori Aces was in the running. Very much in the running. There was only one disturbing element to my conclusion. Whoever wanted Aces out of the way, apparently wanted to nudge me in the same direction.

"Come on!" Lori suddenly shouted. "I'll race you to that cove."

She struck out, lightning fast, toward a jagged wall that was narrowed in by a couple of white-capped rocks. I hadn't noticed before, but the sea was beginning to push itself up into healthy ridges and the wind blew the top of one into my face. I lost sight of Lori in the swell.

A big wave broke over my shoulders, hurling me under and ripping loose the top of my two-piece suit. I abandoned any thought of heading for the cove and angled toward the beach. Vicious breakers and a strong current drove me into a bed of kelp well beyond the beach and even the cove. I fought wildly, went down once and came up again.

The second time down I felt an arm around my middle.

Chapter Six

He was staring at me when I woke up, a handsome guy with curly black hair that made his head look like a mass of licorice desert. He had a nice nose, straight with wide flaring nostrils. His mouth was wide with plenty of slack and a small smile etched in the corners. I liked this face. But there was something I didn't like. The sound I heard somewhere in the distance. The sound of hard rain and violent wind.

"How are you feeling?" he asked.

"In one piece," I said gingerly. "Am I?"

"Absolutely," he said with a larger smile. "And may I add, one of the nicest I've come across in a long time."

There was a warm blanket over me. I reached underneath and felt around for the top to my suit. It was gone. Apparently he'd pulled me out of the briny deep without a stitch covering the upper part of my body.

"Fill me in," I said, my eyes avoiding his. "Things are rather hazy."

He grinned again. "For my money you're already filled in. And in just the right places."

"Thanks." I felt my cheeks growing hot. "Where am I?"

"In my cabin. On the hill overlooking White's Landing. I was doing a little spear fishing when I found you poking around in my abalone beds."

"Was I alone?"

"Not exactly. There were a couple of wide-eyed fish in the vicinity, but I got there first."

The left side of my jaw felt extremely sore. "You didn't by any chance hit me with a KO punch?"

"Not until you gave me some of the same in the lower intestine. If you want the facts, ma'am, you tossed me one below the belt."

"I'm sorry." Then I suddenly remembered Lori Aces. With her talent

40

for swimming she should easily have maneuvered her ninety-odd pounds to a safe landing place. Maybe even the beach.

He interrupted my train of thought. "How about some coffee?"

"First things first," I said. "How about some clothes?"

"Fresh out of clothes," he teased. "Plenty of coffee."

"How'd you get me here?" I asked, trying to sit up. He pushed me down in a firm, nice manner. "You swallowed a lot of water. I had to carry you up the hill. You weren't about to walk on your own two feet. What were you doing swimming around half naked in the first place?"

"An old custom of mine. It scares the tar out of sharks."

"Great!" he said. "You scared the tar out of me. I thought you were a shark for a few seconds. That is, until I put my arm around your waist."

"And that convinced you?"

"Well, no shark I ever knew had what you've got," he laughed. There was a long silence.

"What's your name?" I asked.

"Ralph—Ralph Smith. What's yours?"

"Honey West."

"The female private eye?"

"You carried me up the hill," I said. "Have you got any doubts about my sex?"

"Not in the least. What are you doing at Catalina?"

"Investigating the buffalo. What's your excuse?"

"I'm writing a novel."

"What's it about?"

Smith walked over to stoke the fire. "That nasty, dirty little business called television."

"You sound as if you know something about the subject."

He was pensive for a moment. "I do. I was around when the first TV show went on the air in Los Angeles."

"Are you still in television?"

"Nope. It got too dirty for me."

"You ever know a writer named Rod Caine?" He bent over the fire and tossed on another log. "Yeah," he said after a pause, "I know him."

"What's he like?"

"Why?"

41

"He may be working his way to the gas chamber. If he's the sensible type maybe I can warn him off before he kills a client of mine."

Smith stood up, turned and looked at me, half grinning, half serious. "You're kidding! Who's your client?"

I told him the story. He listened attentively, especially when I mentioned the poisoned drink mixed at the Golden Slipper and Lori's disappearance earlier in the huge swell. Smith, expressing concern for her safety, pulled on a raincoat and hat.

"You should have told me there were two of you," he said. "Even if she made shore, she might be battered to pieces in this storm."

He ran out of the cabin and the wind lashed the door shut behind him. It was a furious gale leadened with rain. If Lori hadn't found shelter, her chance for survival in this kind of storm was about as good as a hundred-mile-an-hour approach into a hairpin curve with no warning signs. I wondered how Hell's Light was taking the blow. Probably the customers in the swimming-pool bar were so frightened, they were drinking with both hands and getting stiffer than boards. I hoped Sam Aces wasn't too stiff. His kind of stiffness could turn out to be permanent if he didn't keep a weather eye open.

I searched around for some clothes. In the closet was an old pair of white dungarees with the cuffs rolled up. There was quite a space to make up for around the middle, but an old piece of rope helped cinch in the waist. A red-striped cotton shirt, minus any buttons, hung on the same hook. I slipped it on and tucked the tails inside the trousers to keep the shirt together.

Smith returned a few minutes later soaked to the skin and breathing heavily. "I slipped on a rock down near the boat cave and went in up to my shoulders," he explained. "Didn't make much difference. I was drenched by that time anyway."

"See anything."

"Yeah. One of the permanent buildings down on the YMCA site lost part of a roof. Same thing may happen to us if it gets any worse."

I winced. "Nothing of Lori Aces?"

He stripped off his wet shirt. "Maybe she made it to one of the caves at the south end of the beach. She'd be safe there." He knelt before the fire. "How about something to eat? You must be starved!"

42

"What about yourself?" I studied him carefully. His body was deeply bronzed from the sun. Then I said, "You'd better get out of those wet pants."

He grinned and pulled me down next to him in front of the fireplace.

"I don't take orders from nobody," he said quietly. "Especially a female investigator who packs a .32."

"How'd you know I carry a .32?"

"I don't know." He shrugged his shoulders. "A .32 seems about the right caliber for a woman." Then his lips touched mine, and they were warm and soft. He lifted his head finally and whispered, "I told you I was fresh out of clothes. Where'd you get these?"

"In the closet," I said.

He touched the opening at the top of my shirt and kissed me again.

I felt my legs wobble slightly as I forced myself up. "What'll it be? Bacon and eggs, hot cakes, waffles…?" He came after me and his hands pulled me close to him.

"Aren't—aren't you hungry?" I stammered. His mouth kissed the bruise on my chin. "You—must have worked up a big appetite wandering around in the rain…"

"Yeah, I did," he said.

"I'd—better get into the kitchen then…"

His lips moved over my mouth shutting out the words. He picked me up and carried me into the bedroom.

"Look," I said, "I don't even know you…"

Wind suddenly bit furiously into the cabin. The roof trembled and screeched as shingles ripped loose into the stormy sky. One of them hit the bedroom window splintering glass across the room.

He put me on my feet hurriedly, grabbed his slicker and vanished into the night.

I glanced down at the front of my shirt.

The flesh underneath was crimson and I was trembling.

It was still raining when I awakened. The bedroom window had been boarded up, but Ralph Smith was nowhere in view. Wind rustled softly in the distant dark. In the living room I found him curled up like a big dog in front of the fireplace. I shook my head and crossed into the kitchen. The

43

clock said it was a few minutes after midnight.

The old-fashioned wood stove was all set for a fire. I lit a match to it, started some bacon sizzling in a skillet and looked for a fork. The kitchen drawers were filled with everything except silverware.

I walked into the living room, rummaged around in a desk drawer and came up with a couple of knives and forks. Leave it to a man to keep books and papers in the kitchen and sliver in the desk!

Something else in that drawer startled me. A photograph of Lori Aces! Sweet, little, child-like Lori Aces. She got around more than measles. There was a signature on the front of the picture. *I Love You Passionately—Lori.* She obviously was as crazy for Sam Aces as a detonator hooked up to a ton of dynamite. First Rod Caine, now Ralph Smith. No wonder he got excited at the mention of her name.

I shoved the picture back and started toward the kitchen when I saw the bronze statuette of an Emmy, television's equivalent to motion picture's Academy Award Oscar.

The inscription read, *For outstanding achievement in the development and creation of the Bob Swanson Show, WBS Network.*

The winner's name was etched on the face of the plate in fancy letters. *Rod Caine.*

Chapter Seven

I rammed the statuette down hard breaking a glass bowl. The sound brought him to his feet, a startled expression on his face. "What in hell's the matter?" he yelled. "The roof coming off?"

"You can say that again!" I boomed. "The roof, two floors of furniture and the kitchen sink."

He glanced around. "You out of your mind?"

"Yes, I am, *Mr. Caine!*"

The puzzled expression drained out of his handsome face. He took the statuette and placed it back on the shelf. "So, you found out? You've been looking for me, haven't you? Well, here I am!"

"Thanks," I said.

"I suppose I should have told you right away. But I'm not trying to hide anything. Ralph Smith is my *nom de plume.*"

"What?"

"Pen name. Ficitious."

"You mean fake, don't you?" I realized I was shouting. "That's you all over. Just about as fake as they come!"

He shook his head.

"How come no facial scars?" I asked. "Plastic surgery?"

"Some," Caine said. "The wounds weren't as bad as they looked. I was practically healed inside of two weeks."

"Why didn't you go back to Television Riviera?"

"I was fired. Besides, I was glad to be out of there. This new novel's much more important to me. Aces actually did me a favor."

"Now you'd like to return the favor," I said.

"Not the way you think!"

"Did you call Lori three weeks ago and ask if Aces still drink screw-

45

drivers?"

"Don't be idiotic."

"Did you say you'd like to get Aces for what he did to you?"

"No!" Rod insisted. "I haven't seen or talked to Lori Aces for over four months."

"This is important," I said. "Whose idea was it—the martinis, the kisses, bed?"

"Lori's idea. The whole thing. She invited me up with the understanding Sam was out of town for a couple of days. I was floored when he walked in."

"Imbedded is a better word," I said. "Where'd you go after you ran out?"

"Into the bay."

"Then where?"

"To a small yacht that was anchored about a half mile down from Lori's place. There was a doctor on board. I told him I'd been attacked by something in the water. He stitched me up and that was that."

"No questions about why you were naked?"

"No more than I asked you!" He grinned again. Rod Caine had a most infectious smile.

"How long have you been living on the island?"

"About three months. I moved to Catalina after the plastic surgery, bought this cabin and started working on the novel."

"Have you ever been back to the mainland?"

"Sure. A month later for a final examination of my face."

"Any other time?"

"Two weeks ago. I picked up a few supplies and came right back."

"Did you go to Hollywood?"

Rod hesitated, then said, "Yeah. I wanted to see my agent, but it was too late. He'd already left the office."

"Go any place else?"

He shrugged. "Sure, I stopped for a couple of drinks."

"Where?"

He hesitated again. "The Golden Slipper. That was my old hangout before..."

"Did you see anyone you know?"

Rod laughed half-heartedly. "Are you kidding? You couldn't recognize a Siamese twin in that place, even if it belonged to you."

"What time was it?"

"I don't know!" Rod said harshly. He crossed toward the kitchen, then whirled around. "All right, I did see Swanson. He was sitting at the bar. I talked to him for a few minutes. He was so wacked I doubt if he remembered it afterward. He was taking a drink back to Aces at the studio. I wouldn't have thought a thing about it except Bob kidded me about the broken-glass incident. He said it was lucky I wasn't taking the drink to Sam or I might slip in a little poison to even the score." Rod stopped and wiped his hands over his face. "Hell, that's insane!"

"Maybe," I said. "Have you ever been back to the Golden Slipper since that night?"

"No."

"You're certain?"

"Dammit! Of course, I'm certain."

"Have you been in Television Riviera?"

"No!"

"Not even the day after the last Swanson show?"

"No! What would I be doing there?"

I said quietly, "You originated the show. Doesn't it bother you not to be part of it anymore?"

Rod shook his head. "Aces gave me a raw deal, sure. Okay. But I never should have been in bed with his wife, so we're even."

"Are you in love with her?"

"If I were, don't you think I'd be out looking for her right now?"

"Depends on what kind of a man you are."

"Try me sometime."

"I already have. You saved my life. I still haven't thanked you for that."

"You can return the favor by taking me off the hook. I don't want to kill anyone."

I stared at him and in the distance, through one of the windows, lightning touched the dark sea and then disintegrated. I closed my eyes, but the picture clung to my retina like the image of Herb Nelson's body, which was imprinted indelibly upon the mirror of my mind.

"Answer me one thing," I said. "Have you ever worked with Herb Nelson?"

He hesitated for an instant. "Too bad about him, wasn't it? I—I thought he was one tremendous actor. No, I never worked with him on anything. I only wish I had. The last I saw or heard of Herb Nelson, he was working as a bartender's assistant at the Golden Slipper."

"What time is it?"

Rod peered at the kitchen clock. "Twelve-thirty."

"Have you got a boat?"

"Sure," Rod said. "I got a boat. What about it?"

"Could you get us out to *Hell's Light*?"

He did a double-take and then grinned. "Are you kidding? In this storm? We wouldn't stand a chance."

"Sounds as if the wind's eased up."

Rod walked outside to check the weather. I knew I'd better get back to the ship as soon as possible. In all the confusion the wind, rain and whiskey, Sam Aces stood a good chance of getting what someone had been trying to give him for several weeks. A lesson in not breathing!

Rod came in form his weather inspection. "You're right," he said. "The wind's down considerably. So is the water. I think we can make the yacht if you want to try."

"What are we waiting for? Let's go!"

We dressed warmly and started down the face of the hill toward the water. Rain sifted through a sky cross patched with thick black clouds and intermittent stars. His boat, a small cabin cruiser, was stored in a deep ocean cave below the house. Rod lowered her into the water by pulley and cable and we climbed aboard, nearly being thrown into the water, as a big wave smashed into the cave. It took a few minutes to navigate out into the open sea, then we turned toward the faint, distant lights of Aces' floating fun land.

Waves, blown gaily by the wind, crested over our bow, but Rod kept the cruiser straight on course. We approached the yacht from the stern. She was impressive in the storm, her gleaming white sides sloping up into the dark sky. Somebody lowered the landing for us.

It was wild, but between Rod and several of the yacht's crew, they managed to secure the boat and raise her up out of the water. The float was lifted again.

48

The swimming-pool bar was jammed. He didn't even make a dent in the mad conglomeration. Max Decker, flushed, filled and fat, squandered his weighty load on two bar stools, spilling over both. Ann Claypool was providing most of the entertainment with a rock-and-roll version of the bump and grind.

Ann was dancing on top of the bar and her wiggle was a smash hit. All she wore was a blue denim yachting cap. The headdress looked familiar. It had the word CAPTAIN sewn across the front. Sam Aces had been wearing that cap earlier, but there was no sign of the producer. There was no sign of Bob Swanson either.

Joe Meeler seemed to be the only sober one in the place. I asked him about Aces.

"Last thing I know," Joe said, trying to talk above the din, "Swanson and Aces took off for a little stroll around the deck. Lord, you woulda' thought they were a couple of queers, they were so palsy-walsy."

"Have you seen Lori Aces?" I asked.

"Sure," Joe said. "She came back with the camera crew late this afternoon. They had one helluva time in this storm, believe you me."

When I got back to the edge of the pool, even Rod Caine was gone. I started for Aces' cabin. This looked bad. Swanson was out for a promenade with Sam while Rod Caine was rendezvousing with Lori.

I suddenly felt as ridiculous as a jockey seeing his horse break from the starting gate and finding with horror he's still in the chute.

I banged on the producer's cabin door. There were no lights on inside and the door was locked. I ran forward, hammering on doors, trying knobs. One opened and I entered hurriedly. The bed was occupied by two-bit players scrambled together like two crisp pieces of bacon fried into an egg. They didn't even look up. I raced out. The wind was rising again and so was the sea. Whitecaps crackled in the churning water below. I wondered if Sam Aces was down there.

There was a light in my cabin. I opened the door. Aces was sprawled across my bed, legs and arms hanging limply over each side. My heart sank to my knees. I stepped inside and slammed the door.

Aces sat up, stretched, yawned and peered at me. "Where you been, Honey?" he asked. "I have been worried about you."

"Sam, I thought you were dead! Where's Swanson?"

49

"You got me," Aces said, grinding to his feet. "We got to be as thick as thieves in the bar. Then he suggested we take a walk. I didn't like the sound of that, but I went along. When we got out on deck, I don't know whether it was the ship pitching or old B.S. pushing, but I damn near went over the railing. That's when we quit being friends."

"How'd you get in here?"

Aces tried to shake some of the whiskey out of his cranium. "I don't know exactly. I remembered your gun and that's about all I remember until now. What time is it, anyway?"

"About two o'clock."

"How'd you get back to the ship?"

I told him the whole story, including the part about Lori's picture in Rod Caine's drawer.

"You mean that son-of-a-B is aboard my ship?" Aces roared.

"Someplace," I said. "I lost him in the shuffle. But I got a hunch where we might find him."

We headed for the swimming pool. Wind and rain swept the decks wildly, pushing us around like paper dolls. Rod was sitting at the bar with Lori.

Aces waded over with me and grabbed Rob by the arm.

"Get out of here, Caine! Get off this ship before I throw you off!"

Rod didn't ruffle a feather. He gently lifted Sam's hand away and said, "Now, that isn't being very hospitable, is it, Mr. Aces? Is that all the thanks I get for bringing your blonde bombshell back to her base?"

"Don't do my any favors, Caine. I don't need your kind of help. Now get out of here!"

Lori tried to intercede. "Sammy, please! Rod saved Miss West's life. Let's let bygones be bygones."

"No!" Aces roared.

His voice barely caused a ripple in the noise and confusion. Ann Claypool, still dancing and singing on the bar, was shouting her lungs out. And beyond, in the wet darkness, the storm was creating its own impossible clamor.

Rod grinned, his usual grin, and quietly mixed Aces a drink. Then Swanson appeared out of nowhere, breasting the water in his inimitable muscular style. He looked at Caine, then at Aces and exploded wildly.

"Let me at him!" he roared. "Let me at Caine! I'll kill the bastard!"

He flailed and stumbled around drunkenly but never even got close to Rod Caine. Sam Aces intervened with a smashing blow to Swanson's mouth that caught the muscle man completely off guard. He stood for an instant, eyes widened, blood spilling from the wound, then slowly submerged in the water of the swimming pool. Rod helped me drag him to the side of the pool.

"What is this?" I said to Caine. "You and Swanson were supposed to be pals. What happened the night in the Golden Slipper that you haven't told me about?"

Rod shook his head. "Nothing. I told you everything. Now forget it!"

I shook my head angrily. Rod Caine wasn't telling me half of what he knew. Had he seen Swanson put something in Aces' drink? Or was it the other way around? Or was it that everyone had a hankering to hang one on the capricious Mr. Caines' jaw? But the biggest riddle was why Sam Aces suddenly stepped in between the two and lowered the boom on Golden Boy.

Swanson was all out of the fighting mood when he came to his senses. He growled a few times and skulked off to his cabin. Rod was about to head back to the beach when things really went haywire.

Aces stopped him. "I'm sorry I flew off the handle, Caine. Why not stay the night? You'll have a tough time making shore the way the storm's going now."

Rod accepted gratefully. We joined Lori at the bar again and immediately Decker floated over. There was one thing about Max Decker. Drunk or sober, he didn't have to shout to be heard.

"Good to see you again, Rodney," he bellowed, pumping Caine's hand. "I thought maybe you were dead."

This time it was Rod's turn to get nasty. He didn't hit Decker, but he might as well have. He gave the big man one of the roughest five minutes on record. When it was over, everyone seemed willing to call it a night, but we got naked little Annie instead. She obviously knew Rod Caine well.

She flopped into his lap. "Hi, honey man! I been missing you, where you been?"

"In a clothing store," Rod quipped. *"Why don't you try one for size?"*

"Now, sweetie," Ann said drunkenly, "when the public clamors, you

51

got to give them what they want. Isn't that right, Sam boy?"

Before Sam Aces had a chance to answer, Lori cried, "Can it, Clay-pool! Can it and sell it on Main Street where you can make yourself a buck."

The two gals were about the same size and weight. I thought for a second they'd square off in another fight but they never had a chance to get up out of their corners.

Sam Aces suddenly turned green grabbed his throat and screamed as if he'd just swallowed a pint of broken glass.

The bar patrons stopped dead in their drunken tracks. Aces lurched through the water toward me with a tall orange drink in his hand and as I tried to catch him, he went down. I got the drink instead.

While I juggled the glass, Aces sank and came up again, still screaming, still of balance. Several people tried to stop him, but failed in their efforts. He crawled up the side of the pool, staggered, fell and got up again, finally disappearing onto the storm-drenched upper deck.

"He's poisoned!" someone yelled.

Rod Caine ditched Ann in the pool and came after me. Apparently he wanted Sam's glass, but I wasn't about to give it up.

Clutching the glass firmly, I waded to the edge of the pool and started after Aces. Caine was hot on my heels. So were a few others, including Decker, Meeler, Ann Claypool, and Lori Aces.

If there was poison in the glass, I had to get the contents to a safe place. More important, I had to find Aces and dig up an antidote in a hurry.

A light burned in a cabin up ahead. I recognized it as Aces' and turned in. The bit players were gone. I went into the bathroom, opened the cabinet and took down a small ceramic figurine used for storing old razor blades. The container was almost empty.

I shook out the blades and poured the contents of Aces' glass into the narrow slot. Replacing the piece of pottery, I noticed a bottle of orange-colored medicine bearing the label, *Suspension Co-Pyronil Antihistamine*. It looked like concentrated orange juice. A bright thought struck me. I poured a small quantity of the thick liquid into Aces' glass and added water. What a break! It looked enough like the original contents of the glass to fool anyone.

Suddenly the cabin was swarming with people. Caine extracted the glass from my hand and grinned.

"I'll take care of this," he said. "I can analyze it at my place tomorrow. I've got lab equipment there." Lori stood behind Rod.

"Remind me to analyze you sometime, Mr. Caine," I said. "Especially if we find Sam Aces dead."

We split up and searched *Hell's Light*. The wind, rain and darkness made it difficult. I finally tried my own cabin. The door was banging loudly in the wind and it was pitch dark inside.

The hair on the back of my neck began to twitch. And with good reason. Something was hanging from the ceiling. A rope with a body attached to it. Caine appeared behind me in the open doorway, a flashlight in his hand.

"What's the matter?" he shouted over the roar of the storm.

I didn't have to answer. The flashlight beam caught the round white face under the rope. It was Bob Swanson.

Chapter Eight

I switched on the cabin light. Golden Boy was hanging from a rope looped through a metal ring in the ceiling. The cord was hooked under his arms. We lifted him down.

"What the hell do you make of this?" Rod peered at me through narrowed eyes.

I examined Swanson's head. "Big lump, here, over his right temple. He must have been struck by a pretty solid object."

Swanson began to make sounds. He opened his eyes and looked at us. "What hit me?"

I grinned. "From the looks of the lump, I'd say the Twentieth Century Limited. Where'd this happen?"

He looked about the room dazedly. "Right here. I was going through some of your drawers."

"What for?" I demanded.

"Your gun," Golden Boy grunted. "I knew you had one. Lori told me you did. I wanted to find it so I could blow his brains out."

"Whose brains?" Rod asked.

"Aces'! That dirty bastard!" Swanson tried to get up. "I'll kill him, so help me, I'll kill him!"

"You wanted to do the same thing to Rod Caine twenty minutes ago," I said. "What is it with you, anyway?"

Swanson felt the lump over his right ear. "Caine knows why I said that to him. That's not important now. Aces is. He's hit me for the first and last time. When I see him I'm going to put a hole right through his middle."

"Who do you think jumped you in here?" I asked. "Did you see or hear anything?"

Golden Boy grimaced. "No, I was bent over. There was a lot of noise

54

outside from the storm. I didn't even hear the door open."

"Serves you right for going through a lady's drawers," I said. "Did you find the gun?"

"Do you think I'd still be here if I had?" Swanson tried to stand up, but his legs were like rubber.

I gazed about the room. A chair was over turned a few feet from where the rope dangled from the ceiling. Then I spotted a piece of pipe lying under the edge of the bed. I picked it up in a small towel and showed the weapon to Caine.

"Half-inch," Rod said quickly. "Looks like a fitting for a gas or steam line."

Swanson grabbed the pipe before I could stop him. "So that's what hit me! Wonder it didn't crush my skull."

"I'll go along with that," I said angrily. "With as few brains as you've got I'm surprised you weren't flattened right down to your oxfords."

"What do you mean by that crack?" he howled.

"If you hadn't smeared your fingerprints all over the weapon, we might have found your friend."

Golden Boy groaned, touched the patch on his eye and said, "This is all your fault! Everything's gone wrong since we hired you!" He staggered through the door into the drenching rain.

Rod helped me search the yacht but we found no trace of Sam Aces. About four o'clock we checked the bar again. Everybody had gone to bed.

Exhausted, I slumped down on the edge of the pool and glanced at the weary-eyed writer. "Well, what do you think?"

"Maybe it's all a joke," Rod said, stretching his arms. "We're not absolutely certain there's poison in that glass. Maybe he took one of his own small boats."

"None of the boats are missing."

"Okay," Rod continued. "Maybe he swam to shore."

"Very funny!"

"He was drunk. Maybe he carried his joke too far."

"Listen," I said. "I don't care how drunk he was, nobody would go into the water during a storm like this."

"A good swimmer might. I've seen a lot of fools attempt it."

"Not Sam Aces," I insisted. "He can't swim a stroke."

"How do you know that?"

"I watched him earlier. There's only one way he'd have gone into that ocean peacefully—and that's dead!"

Rod scanned the swimming-pool area. "All right," he said, "let's assume he's dead. That he was poisoned and thrown overboard. Who slipped him the arsenic?"

"Any number of people could have, not excluding present company."

He smiled. "Thanks for the compliment. Maybe you figure I was the one who slugged Swanson and hung him from the ceiling, too?"

"It's possible."

"Now wait a minute," he argued. "I was in the bar with you and the others when Aces staggered out. I couldn't have been in your cabin at the same time."

"You forgot," I reminded tightly. "We searched for Sam about twenty minutes before discovering Swanson in my cabin. That was plenty of time for you or anyone to string him to the ceiling."

Rod threw his hands up in a mock pretense of surrender. "You got me, pal."

"I didn't say you did it."

"Then who do you think did it?"

"Could be Bob Swanson."

"What?" Rod stared at me for a moment. "Are you kidding? I suppose Bob knocked himself out, then strung up the rope, took a running jump, leaped into the noose and at the same time pushed the poisoned body of Sam Aces overboard."

"Nope," I said. "Maybe Swanson poisoned Aces' drink in the wild melee at the bar, then waited outside on deck and hurled Sam over the railing when he came outside…"

"Now wait a minute…"

"Afterward he could have gone to my cabin and fixed a noose, stood up on a chair, slipped his arms through the loop and pushed the chair way as he hit himself with the pipe."

"May I say something?"

"Sure, go ahead."

"Nobody in his right mind would take the chance of fracturing his own skull."

"It's quite possible Bob Swanson is not in his right mind."

"It's a cinch somebody isn't," Rod agreed. "I'm beginning to wonder about you. Why would a beautiful gal get involved in this kind of business anyway?"

I brushed a few wet strands of hair away from my forehead and looked at him. "I was brought up in this business. My dad was a private detective."

"What do you mean was?"

"Six years ago he was murdered in an alley behind the Paramount Theater in L.A. I hired myself to find the killer."

"So you found him, brought him to justice and decided to keep on going in the private-eye game!"

I shook my head. "No. I've never found him—but I will someday."

"I believe that," Rod said quietly. He handed me a cigarette. "You asked me about Herb Nelson earlier. Was he by any chance a client of yours?"

"Yes." I glanced at Rod out of the corner of my eye. "I know what you're thinking. I haven't been doing too well lately, especially if Sam is…"

Rod grunted. "Honey, have you ever considered the idea that Aces might have been poisoned earlier?"

"Sure. Depending upon the amount, you can never tell how long arsenic will take to do its dirty work."

"Have you thought also of the possibility—if Aces is dead—that you'll never find his body?"

"No," I said. "I never thought of that."

"Well, baby, if he went overboard in this storm and was already dead, it may take years to find his body. Maybe it never will turn up."

I didn't like the way he said that. It sounded too positive.

"Why did you take Aces' glass?" I demanded.

Rod glanced at me and smiled. "I knew it would be safe in my possession. If you'd kept that drink I have a feeling someone would have been after you with blood in his eyes."

"You're taking the same chance."

"I'll risk it." He got up, said good night, and left for his cabin aboard the yacht.

After a few minutes I went out on deck. The storm still slashed at the darkness, ripping it intermittently with crooked orange daggers. *Hell's Light* rolled and pitched with a new vigor. It was difficult making my way to the bow and I fell several times, once nearly going over the side, and almost losing the oversize dungarees Rod had loaned me.

I came to a large wooden chest anchored to the bow deck. It was big enough to store a body, if anyone had such inclinations. Gripping the heavy lid with both hands, I swung the chest open. Darkness shrouded its contents.

Suddenly the chest became illuminated by a faint circle of light.

Rod Caine stood over me. "What gives?" he said. "I thought you were going to bed?"

"Give me that flashlight," I probed inside the trunk with the beam. "Would you recognize blood stains if you saw them?"

He nodded slowly.

The faint light, dimmed considerably by the night mist, touched two dark pools which were drying on the bottom of the chest.

Rod swore. I couldn't tell whether it was in anger or from surprise.

"How in the devil did that get there?" he demanded.

"I'm sure they weren't left by the Easter Bunny."

'But Aces wasn't bleeding!" Rod protested.

"How do we know," I said. "We haven't seen him for over two hours."

Rod's face was grim. "I thought for sure this thing was a joke. You know, like in a comedy. You open a closet and out jumps Aces laughing like mad."

I looked at the blood spots again. "Losing this much of this stuff leaves a body any way but laughing."

We went to my cabin. The noose still hung from the ceiling. Rod took it down. I watched him carefully. Here was a guy who'd helped me out of a hazardous situation, yet I didn't trust him. I checked to see whether my .32 was still in its hiding place.

The revolver was there, but it was wet. I flipped open the cylinder: Another bullet was gone.

"Tell me something, Rod," I said, holding up my gun. "Are you in cahoots with Lori Aces?"

"Don't be silly."

"There's another bullet missing from my revolver. Lori and Sam Aces were the only ones who saw where I hid the gun. Now what were you doing up on the bow of this ship a few minutes ago? You'd already said good-night."

"Looking for Aces. What do you think?"

"I don't know," I slammed angrily. "As dark as it was, and with all the trouble I had getting up there, it would have been possible for you to take the starboard passageway, reach the bow before I did, lift Aces' body out of that trunk and dispose of it somewhere else."

"You're out of your mind!"

"You knew I had a .32 revolver," I argued.

"That's crazy!"

"You also knew who I was before I ever told you."

"You're way out, baby, way out."

"Why don't you like Max Decker?"

"Because he's a big slob and I wouldn't trust him as far as I could throw him. Which is about nothing minus nowhere."

"Why don't you trust him?" I demanded.

"Because," Rod countered, "He's a four-carat, no-good bastard. He hates everything and everybody. If he can't get what he wants, he'll kill it so nobody else can have it. He's tried to crush me several times in my career."

"Did Decker like Aces?"

"It was a screwy relationship. Sometimes Max was so kissing sweet to Sam he would drip with good fellowship. Times like that made me wonder if Aces had something bit on the old man."

"Blackmail?"

"Yeah!"

I thought about that. Aces had hired me to track down a poisoner. Two days ago I had agreed with his choice of Swanson and suggested bringing in the police, but Aces had declined fearfully. Had, he been afraid of the police? Blackmailers usually are.

After Rod left, I sat up until daybreak thinking about the cast of characters aboard the good ship H.L. One of them was lying and I had a pretty good idea who it was.

Around noon, a few hours after the sun sliced through the dull sky, Lieutenant Mark Storm arrived aboard Hell's Light. He looked tired and his shoulders drooped slightly as he walked up the steps from the float.

"I got your message, Honey," he said wearily. "What gives? Has Aces checked out or not?"

I showed him the two blood stains in the bottom of the chest and then filled him in on the details of Aces' disappearance.

"I took the remains of his drink into Avalon this morning and had it analyzed," I said. "It was loaded with arsenic."

"You're positive?"

"Of course I'm positive. I wouldn't have called you if the test had shown plain vodka and orange juice."

Mark scratched his head. "All right, let's talk to a few people. Especially... this guy Swanson."

"He's on the beach right now at White's Landing." I said, pointing toward shore. "So are most of the others. They're going ahead on their shooting schedule for the next show."

"Without Aces?" Mark demanded.

I explained, "He's the producer. Swanson does most of the directing. In fact, he claims he can get along very nicely without Aces."

"I'll bet," Mark said. "Where's Mrs. Producer?"

"She went with Rod Caine to his place to analyze the phony contents of Aces' glass—an orange-colored antihistamine solution. They still don't know I switched drinks."

"This should be interesting. What if they return with the report that the supposed vodka and orange juice was unadulterated?"

"In that case, I think you can make an arrest." Mark shook his head decisively. "We've got to have a body, Honey. You know that. We don't stand a Chinaman's chance without a body."

"Okay," I suggested. "Let's find one."

We scoured the ship. Down in the engine room we talked with an old beetle-browed sailor named Carruthers. He told us someone had been below deck during the night going through some tool boxes.

"Was his name Swanson?" I asked. "What did he look like?"

"Couldn't tell you his name," Carruthers said, "Husky critter, though, with a baby face—I remember that."

"Don't you ever watch television?" Mark inquired.

"Nope—never," the old man answered.

We went back up to my cabin. Mark looked at the piece of pipe used on Swanson. He thought the business with the rope sounded pretty ridiculous, but not incriminating."

"You can't hang a man for that," Mark said.

"Don't be funny!"

"What about this Claypool dame?"

"Cute. Maybe too cute. She hates Aces' guts."

"You say she was prancing around in her birthday suit most of the evening?"

"Except for Aces' yachting cap."

"What happened to the cap?"

"I wouldn't know. I imagine it wound up in her cabin."

"Let's take a look," Mark said, going to the door. "We just might find something in the lining."

"What?" I asked.

"Traces of arsenic, baby. That stuff's got to be hidden somewhere."

Ann Claypool's cabin was near the swimming-pool bar, next to Aces' stateroom. We had been there before, but hadn't noticed the yachting cap. It was no place in sight and even after a thorough search we couldn't find it.

A few minutes later, back at the swimming pool, Mark spotted the cap submerged in a few feet of water.

"That's that," he said. "There's nothing left in this lining, not even the label."

Mark had brought a few changes of clothing from my apartment. I was happy to get into a snug comfortable swimsuit after wearing Rod's battered shirt and sloppy dungarees for the past twelve hours. About this time, Rod and Lori returned to the yacht, grim-faced and tense. Rod studied me angrily.

"No arsenic," he said. "Not one-fiftieth of a milligram."

"Just plain screwdriver?" I asked.

"Not so plain," Rod answered. "I think it was some kind of medicine. A pretty unusual drink for Sam Aces, wouldn't you say?"

"I switched glasses on you," I admitted.

61

"That was a dirty trick! You should have told me. I went to a lot of trouble!" Rod snapped.

I glanced at Lori. "That's too bad. Aces' drink contained more than four grains of white arsenic. Enough to kill two guys the size of Max Decker."

Lori swallowed enough air to last her a week.

Rod shook his head in amazement.

Decker came out of his cabin, a big smile creasing his jowls. It was a dirty sort of smile that I felt like wiping with the flat of my hand to see if it might come clean.

"Good morning," he roared cheerily. "Lori, I want to thank you for your hospitality, but now I must take my leave. My own yacht is anchored in Avalon Harbor. I'm joining some of the New York network people who are on board. Thank Sam for me when you see him."

"He may be too dead to thank," I said.

"Oh, Miss West," Decker continued, as if he hadn't heard me. "I had a chat with Mr. Swanson this morning and we have decided to dispense with your acting services on the Bob Swanson show. You have been re-placed by Miss Claypool."

"What about my six-week contract?" I said angrily. "You can't fire me. I signed a legitimate agreement with Sam Aces."

Decker laughed awkwardly. "Your contract will be honored, naturally. Four hundred a week for six weeks, wasn't that the arrangement?"

I nodded. "I have a copy of the contract in my cabin." Decker contin-ued to carry on like the cat who ate an entire aviary. "You stop by my of-fice next week. A check for twenty-four hundred will be waiting for you. Good day."

Mark brought the fat man to a halt. "Mr. Decker, my name is Storm. L.A. Sheriff's office, homicide bureau."

"What are you doing here?" Decker demanded.

"A large quantity of arsenic was found in Sam Aces' drink. We have a strong suspicion your producer is dead."

"Impossible! Sam'd never pull a trick like that!"

"I didn't say it was suicide," Mark snarled.

"You mean someone murdered him?"

"You're on the right track," I said. "Maybe two someones."

Mark studied the big television magnate. "Yours was the only state-room we were unable to search this morning."

"Well, I was still sleeping when you knocked," Decker said, losing most of his gaiety. "You can check it now if you like; I'm all packed and moved out. In fact, my bags are being loaded aboard a water taxi now."

Mark bolted for the landing float. He took the steps three at a time. In the side pocket of the first suitcase he opened Mark found what he was looking for—a small package of white powder.

Chapter Nine

Mark showed the contents of the package to Decker. "New brand of tooth powder?" he asked.

"Never saw that before," Decker said. "Was it in my luggage?"

"That's right," Mark said. "Can you explain how this quantity of arsenic happens to be in your possession?"

Decker appeared baffled. "Why, no, I can't."

"You're sure?"

"Absolutely. I wouldn't lie!"

I studied the big-bellied emperor of television. He was in a tight spot, and he knew it. If Sam Aces turned up with a stomach full of that powder, not all the TV in Chinatown could save the lord of WBS. But, for a moment, there was no corpse. That made a big difference.

Mark signaled for one of the crew of *Hell's Light* to bring Decker's luggage back aboard ship. "You're going to have to stick around awhile," Mark said.

"You can't hold me!" Decker said hoarsely. "I could have your badge in five minutes."

"I didn't say I was holding you, Mr. Decker. It's just that in the absence of your host, Sam Aces, I'm holding a little party, and I would become very unhappy if any of my guests should refuse to attend."

Decker stomped angrily back to his stateroom. Mark took my hand and we started down to the float.

"Where're we going?" I demanded.

"Out looking for a body," he said. "Dead or alive, we've got to find Sam Aces."

A blue sky stretched cloudlessly over the water as Mark and I climbed aboard a small cabin cruiser he'd borrowed from the chief of the Avalon Police Department. We spent the afternoon searching in deep water and along a sharply irregular shoreline. We found no trace of Sam Aces.

About an hour before sundown we doubled back to White's Landing. Mark noticed the ocean cave below Rod Caine's cabin.

"Let's take a look in there," he said. "Never can tell where a body will wind up."

We steered the boat inside. Rod's cruiser was gone.

"He's probably still out aboard *Hell's Light*," I guessed. "Let's check the cabin."

Mark tied the cruiser, *Clementine*, to the dock and we trudged up the winding path. The door was unlocked, so we helped ourselves to the invitation and entered. Nothing much had changed since I'd been there. A few more dishes in the sink. A few more ashes in the trays. The bed cover wildly thrown back.

We searched for the lab equipment but found nothing except Aces' glass. It still contained a small amount of the antihistamine. And something new had been added. A lipstick stain on the rim.

Mark examined the lip print. "Was this on the glass last night when you gave it to Caine?"

I shook my head decisively.

Mark held the glass up to the light. The remaining liquid had turned a vivid orange. "It's possible Caine caught on to the switch without putting the contents through a lab test."

"What does that mean?"

"He could have tasted some of it," Mark said.

"You think he figured the drink never contained poison?"

"Either that or he knew it was loaded with arsenic, invited Mrs. Aces back here to examine it with him, gave it a clean bill of health and suggested that she try some."

"Intending to murder her?"

"That's right," Mark said. "Then, when Mrs. Aces laughed, instead of pitching over on her face, and said it tasted like medicine, Caine grabbed the glass and gulped some himself. That's when he guessed what you pulled in the bathroom."

"Rod Caine wouldn't do a thing like that!"

"Are you kidding, Honey? If those two are in a murder plot together,

Caine would do anything to prevent her from implicating him."

We searched Rod's closet and found a typed note in the pocket of his suit coat.

> CAINE: MEET ME ABOARD MY YACHT WEDNESDAY
> NIGHT. WE'LL ANCHOR OFF WHITE'S LANDING. I
> MAY
> ACT ANGRY IF ANYONE IS AROUND BUT DON'T LET
> THATUPSET YOU. I HAVE AN
> IMPORTANT PROPOSITION I'M
> SURE WILL INTEREST YOU. SAM ACES.

There was also a faint penciled notation at the bottom which read: Little Harbor.

"Wednesday was last night," I said. "The night Aces disappeared. Caine never said he had an appointment with Aces!"

"Where's Little Harbor?" Mark demanded.

"On the other side of the island," I explained. "It's desolate. Nothing but rocks and beach. I hiked over Mt. Orizaba once to get there."

"Nice place to bury a body?"

"Lovely. Nobody would find it in a million years without a detailed map and an oversize crane. Even then I wouldn't bank on it."

Mark studied the piece of paper. "What time did Caine and Mrs. Aces leave Hell's Light this morning?"

"About eight o'clock. They were gone almost four hours."

"Did you check Caine's boat after finding those blood stains in the chest?"

"No," I said. "I'd searched it twice earlier. I didn't think there was any reason—You don't believe Rod Caine moved Aces body from the chest to his boat while I was on my way to the bow?"

"It's possible."

"That's ridiculous," I said. "Then you figure Aces' body was aboard Rod's boat this morning when he left with Lori?"

"Right." Mark slapped the note. "I also wonder if Mr. Sam Aces isn't buried at Little Harbor."

I threw my hands in the air. "Do you mind if I present my theory?"

"Why not?"

"I think we've barking up the wrong tree."

Mark said, "What do you mean by that?"

"I mean someone is leading us around like we've got reigns in our noses. I don't even think Sam Aces is dead."

Mark brought his hands to his face in a quick, resigned gesture of here we go again! He said, "Four grains of arsenic in a man's drink, another bullet missing from your gun, blood stains in a deck trunk and you come up with the straight-faced opinion you don't think Sam Aces is dead."

"I thought he was until you found that arsenic in Decker's suitcase— then I changed my mind."

"A woman's prerogative," Mark said resignedly. "What wrought this great change?"

"Max Decker's expression when you showed him that poison. He was telling the truth. He didn't have any more idea of how that stuff got there than the man in the moon."

"You're sure of this?" Mark said with a tinge of sarcasm in his voice.

"As sure as I am that I caught Sam Aces in my office looking for the threatening letter which had been sent to Herb Nelson."

"What?"

"He told me he was hiding in my office because someone had followed him from L.A. I believed his story at the time, especially after I checked with a Beverly Hills lab and they verified a previous poison dose brought in by Aces. But I don't know. Something's phony about this guy. Mark. He doesn't ring true—the way he was so afraid and yet he wouldn't go to the police, the way I caught him in my office, the way he hired me to help him and then suggested I quit because I might get hurt. Even the poisoned drink—the way he handed it to me in the bar—the way he ran out before anyone could get to him. To me, these things only add up to an amateur try-ing to act like a pro and getting away with it because of good breaks."

Mark studied my face. "Are you trying to say Sam Aces killed Herb Nelson, that he was in your office looking for a letter which might have im-plicated him in the crime, and that now he's trying to confuse everyone into thinking he's dead?"

"Something like that," I said faintly. "I know it sounds weird..."

"Weird?" Mark roared. "It sounds positively absurd. You expect me to believe Sam Aces left some of his own blood in a trunk aboard Hell's Light, planted arsenic in Decker's luggage, and also in his own glass, slipped this note into Rod Caine's pocket, stole your gun, took two shots at you, hung Swanson from the rafters…"

"All right," I interrupted.

"This would be the greatest one-man act in history…"

"I still don't think he's dead."

"Want to bet?" Mark extended his hand.

I hesitated, then accepted the challenge. Sam Aces had to be alive. He was not the kind of man to die without a struggle.

Stars blazed over Little Harbor as Mark headed the cruiser toward shore. The sea was calm, unusually calm for the windward side of the island, and a bright full moon illuminated the water.

We had used the cruiser's searchlight intermittently in our trip around the northern tip of Catalina. Once to identify a dark object which turned out to be a floating log, and again to intrigue a few flying fish out of their depths. But no Aces!

For two hours we toured the smooth sea outside Little Harbor, carefully avoiding treacherous reefs that sometimes lurked a few inches under water.

I shook my head. "If we keep fooling around in this place, there'll be two bodies floating around for sure. Us."

"Let's anchor and swim to shore," Mark suggested. "It's light enough. Maybe we'll come up with some kind of lead."

He stripped to his swim trunks, fastened a flashlight to his waist and we plunged in.

The reefs were impossible. A jagged coral edge tore a gaping hole in my suit. Mark was raked by a row of greenish needles, which ripped off the flashlight and gashed his leg. Then we got mixed up in thunderous breakers that were ten feet high and weighted a ton. They bounced us both on the beach like a pair of dice on a crap table. When Mark crawled over, I breathlessly lauded him for the most sensational bit of inventive thinking since dynamite.

"How did I know it'd be that rough?" He examined the slash in his leg.

"The water was like mush out there around the boat. But it's high tide. The breakers will simmer down in a couple of hours."

"I hope so," I said as I looked toward the shoreline. A dark shape was stretched out about a dozen yards away on the sand.

"Look!" I pointed.

Mark got to his feet slowly. "You stay here!"

"Why?"

"If it's Aces, he won't look his Sunday best."

"Well, I wouldn't exactly pass as a princess," I said. "Besides, it's probably seaweed."

We crossed the beach and discovered it was seaweed. But a few feet away, illuminated by the moon, was a wet crumpled piece of clothing under a rock ledge. A red jacket... the initials S.A. were stitched boldly under the left breast pocket and below the initials we found something else—a bullet hole and an ugly dark blood stain!

Chapter Ten

"Now what do you think?" Mark demanded. "You recognize this jacket?"

I nodded slowly. "Sam was wearing it the last time I saw him in the bar, but…"

"You still don't think he's dead?"

"I didn't say that."

"That's what I thought." The lieutenant, clutching the jacket in his hand, limped up the beach a few yards. When he returned, he said, "This will do until a body comes along. We will check these blood stains with the ones in the bottom of that chest. I think they will match."

"And where do you imagine Sam Aces is now?"

Mark looked out at the thrashing breakers and the needle-sharp reef beyond. "There," he said. "Probably caught below the surface in one of the caverns. The jacket must have floated to the top and was washed in by the heavy surf."

"Maybe," I said. "But until we find a body all bets are off."

"We'll find him."

"How?"

"After daybreak when the tide's down, I'll…"

Suddenly, the sound of the cruiser's engines starting up hoarsely in the tiny bay attracted our attention. Clouds of vapor boiled up from the twin exhausts and quickly the cabin cruiser-whirled around shooting up a curtain of spray. Before we could let out a protest, it vanished in the inky darkness of the open sea.

It seemed an eternity before we could find words to replace our surprise. Half joking, half bewildered by the sudden turn of events, I whispered, "Don't—don't tell me your corpse came up out of the reef?"

"We had a stowaway,' Mark said in a dazed voice. "He must have been

70

hiding down in the cabin."

"But where'd he come from?"

Mark scratched his jaw thoughtfully. "Darned if I know. He must have climbed aboard while the boat was tied up in that cave."

"But, Mark—who?"

"If we knew that, baby, this case would probably be closed as of here and now. Thing to do is get back to *Hell's Light* and count noses. Find out who's been missing for the past few hours."

"How do we manage that trick?" I asked.

"What do you mean?"

"There's nothing on this side of Catalina. To reach White's Landing, we'd have to hike over Mt. Orizaba or search for Two Harbors' Road and try for Avalon. Either way we could never make it in our bare feet."

"How far to White's Landing?"

"About seven miles," I said, "Mt. Orizaba is over a thousand feet high. And she's rugged!"

Mark flinched. "That's out. I'm a lousy mountain climber. Besides, I've got flat feet."

"That figures. So what do we do? Build a seaweed hut, catch fish, and start our own civilization?"

Mark put his arm around my shoulder and squeezed in a tender, intimate way that meant more than any words. The gesture said, I like you, Honey. When do we start with this wonderful new world?

I broke the emotional connection. "Come on, Mark. What are we going to do?"

"That's a good question," he admitted, grinning wolfishly. "Said with just the right amount of feminine naivety." His eyes drifted to my torn bathing suit. "You might never guess it, but I'm an excellent tailor."

I smiled, "I'll be all right."

"Just happened to bring a needle and thread with me. I'd be very happy to make a stitch here and there."

"Mark," I said, "we're in a serious predicament. Now will you stop making jokes?"

"Honey, you're no joke, believe me." His eyes fell upon the blood-stained jacket and his grip tightened. "Why don't you quit this damned business and get married?"

"But, Mark," I teased, "Fred hasn't asked me yet. And besides…"

"Fred?" the lieutenant boomed. "Why that dirty, no good…"

The blinding glare of a searchlight cut Mark's retort into word less mouthings that literally fell apart in midair.

"You all right, Lieutenant Storm?" a voice boomed from behind the glare.

Mark cupped his hands around his mouth and shouted. "Who is it?"

"Chief Clements of the Avalon Police Department. What's going on?"

"We're marooned," Mark returned loudly. "Have you got an auxiliary boat you can put ashore?"

"Sure," came the reply. "I'll bring it in myself."

Mark glanced at my torn bathing suit. "Oh, and bring a blanket with you, Chief. I've got a body to wrap up."

When we were aboard the Avalon patrol boat, Mark introduced me to Chief Clements. The old, white-haired police officer had a devilish twinkle in his eyes as his mind seemed to recall the moment we met on the beach before Mark got the blanket around me.

Clements examined the blood-stained jacket after Mark told the story of our mishaps at Little Harbor.

Mark explained, "This article of clothing belonged to a man named Aces. Sam Aces. A television producer."

"From the looks of things, he'd been producing all right," the chief said, poking his finger though the bullet hole.

Mark nodded. "How'd you happen to find us?"

"Important message came through from L.A. for you. I decided to run it out to *Hell's Light* myself. They told me you'd been gone since noon, so I thought I'd scout around a bit."

"We're certainly glad you did," I said.

Clements continued. "About three miles out from Little Harbor we sighted a small boat's lights. She didn't respond to my blinker, so we let her go by."

"That was the cruiser, Chief," Mark said grimly.

"I realize that now," Clements said. "How'd the bandit get possession?"

"I figure he was stowed away somewhere during our trip around the island. As soon as we'd anchored and gone ashore, he took off."

"We'll find him," Clements assured us.

"I hope so," Mark answered. "He got away with my clothes, my revolver and a very important piece of evidence. A typewritten message Aces sent to a former associate named Caine."

Clements wiped some spray out of his eyes. "Did you say Caine? That's the man I talked to aboard *Hell's Light*. This man, Caine, said the TV people were worried about their big television star—what's his name—Swans-down!"

"Swanson," I corrected. "Bob Swanson."

"Yeah, that's the one," Clements agreed. "Caine said this Swanson disappeared about four o'clock while they were shooting a picture at White's Landing. Nobody's seen hide nor hair of him since."

Mark looked at me, gripping the edge of his upper lip in his teeth. I knew what he was thinking. I was thinking the same thing. We had arrived at Rod's cabin about six o'clock. Bob Swanson had vanished on the beach around four. During that time he could have gone to Rod's cabin and planted the note, then waited around for our arrival and stowed away aboard Chief Clements' boat.

Mark asked the Avalon police chief about the urgent message from his Los Angeles office.

"They want you back tonight," Clements said. "A new lead has turned up in the Nelson case."

"That's what I thought," Mark said, glancing at me. "We've been tracking down some of Herb's old pals. One of them, Ed Walker, was seen going into Nelson's place an hour before the murder."

The stern lights of Aces' yacht shone in the dark night. It was after midnight and I was tired and suddenly angry because Mark hadn't taken me into his confidence about this new twist in the Nelson case. I started to complain when something stopped me. Chief Clements's racy cabin cruiser was tied up at *Hell's Light* boat landing.

"Well, what do you know?" Mark said. "This is going to be easier than I thought. Maybe we can wind this case up tonight before I go back to L.A."

Everything aboard the *Clementine* was intact, except the handwritten note we had found in Rod's coat pocket.

73

Mark dressed quickly and we went aboard the yacht. Max Decker met us in the passageway outside the swimming-pool bar.

"Now see here, Lieutenant," the TV magnate roared, "I've had just about enough of your stalling tactics…"

"Where's Swanson?" Mark interrupted.

"I haven't seen him all day," Decker said. "He went to White's Landing to shoot an important scene and he hasn't returned."

Mark pushed the fat man out of the way. "I know he's somewhere on this ship. Now where is he?"

"I told you, he didn't come back…"

Rod Caine walked out on deck. Mark pounced on him. "Where's Swanson?" the lieutenant asked.

"You got me," Rod said. "Haven't seen him. Nobody has. There's a scouting party over at White's Landing now."

Mark pointed to the cruiser. "That cabin job pulled in here sometime in the last hour. Now who was at the helm?"

"I don't know," Rod said flatly. "I was in the bar. I didn't even hear the boat arrive."

People poured out of the bar. One of them was Lori Aces. Mark repeated his questions, but no one would admit having seen the cruiser tie up at the boat landing.

While Mark, Chief Clements and two Avalon policemen searched for Swanson, I changed from my torn suit and blanket into something more practical. Lori Aces followed me to my cabin. She broke down when I told her about Sam's jacket.

"I've got to tell the truth," she said. "I've really never loved Sammy. But he's such a nice guy, you got to like him. Do the police really think Sam's been murdered?"

I nodded and went back to the bar. The music, laughter and whiskey were still flowing. It made me sick. Sam Aces might be dead but nobody seemed to care.

I glanced at Joe Meeler, the writer who had replaced Rod Caine on the Swanson show. He was slumped forward on the bar, apparently sleeping off his good time. That seemed funny. I didn't think little Joe drank.

I waded over to rouse him. He couldn't be roused.

Joe was dead, a butcher knife stuck between his ribs.

After examining the weapon, Mark questioned the drunken patrons at the swimming-pool bar. "How long's he been sitting here, anyone know?"

"Not long," one of the cameramen answered. "I'd guess a half hour. Maybe less."

"Did he come in alone?"

No answer.

"Was Swanson in the bar during the past half hour?"

Still no answer.

"What the hell do you people do?" Mark burst. "Pour this stuff on your eyeballs?"

A few inarticulate grunts.

"Did Swanson dislike Meeler?" the lieutenant continued.

"He was always shouting at him," another cameraman said.

A little red-haired starlet added, "So what? Bob Swanson shouts at everyone on the set."

"Did they ever argue?" Mark demanded.

Ann Claypool said, "They did today. It was pretty violent. I thought Bob was going to chop Joe into little pieces."

"What was the argument about?" Mark asked.

"A sailboat scene," Ann continued. "According to the script Bob was supposed to follow me down the ladder into the sailboat. But he wanted to reverse the procedure. I was wearing a full circle skirt…"

"I get the idea," Mark said. "What happened?"

"Joe called Swanson a twisted lecherous bastard and the sparks flew."

"Did Swanson fire Meeler?"

"No," Ann said. "Bob just went haywire, shouting and raving. That's when he disappeared. We couldn't find him after that."

Mark looked at me and his mouth tightened. I knew what he was thinking. How could Golden Boy have entered and left the swimming-pool area without being seen by one of his television compatriots—much less silently commit a murder which involved something as unwieldy as a butcher knife. Meeler must have been completely unaware that he was about to die. If he'd had any kind of warning, the TV writer surely would have alerted others in the bar.

After Meeler's body was loaded aboard the Avalon patrol boat, I walked down to the float with Mark and Chief Clements.

"The Coast Guard will probably send out an investigating party," Mark explained. "I got a blood-sample scraping from the chest and will try to match it with the strains on the jacket. I'll be back tomorrow, after I check out this character, Walker, who turned up in the Nelson case. Meanwhile, stay out of mischief, understand?"

"That's a pretty tall order, Lieutenant, but I'll try. Incidentally, why did you fail to tell me about this guy Walker?"

Mark ignored the question, climbed into the patrol boat, then turned and took my hand. "I understand Decker skipped out on a water taxi while we were searching for Swanson. He isn't out of this by any means. I want him back on this ship by tomorrow. If the Avalon police can't find him, it's up to you, Honey. There are some places a dame can get into that even a cop can't."

I nodded, kissed his cheek and thanked him for our exciting sojourn to Little Harbor.

"We'll have to do it again sometime," Mark smiled. "Under different circumstances."

The patrol boat rocked, kicked up a dark crest that washed over the float and moved away into the night.

"Don't forget the prints on that knife!" I yelled.

"I won't!" Mark called back. "And don't you forget to keep yourself out of trouble!"

I walked up to the main deck, meeting Rod Caine at the top of the steps. He was strangely apologetic about Meeler's death.

"I can't understand how it could have happened," he said dejectedly. "Joe was a damned good writer. He was doing a better job on the show than I ever did. I'm really sorry about this, believe me."

"Did Lori tell you about Aces' jacket?"

"Yeah."

"Were you surprised?"

"Hell, yes, I was surprised," Rod said. "I still can't believe he's dead, though."

We walked to the bow of the ship. Rod lit two cigarettes and handed me one. I thought of Aces' habit of doing the same thing.

"Did Aces ever send you a note inviting you aboard this ship?" I asked.

76

"Many times," Rod said quietly. "I've spent some wonderful days aboard *Hell's Light*."

"I mean recently."

"Of course not. I told you I didn't see or hear from Sam from the time I ran out of Lori's bedroom until last night."

"You're absolutely certain?"

Rod cocked his head suspiciously. "Now what does that mean?"

I flipped my cigarette overboard. "We found a note in your coat pocket."

"When?"

"Early this evening in your cabin. One thing we didn't find was your lab equipment."

Rod shook his head dazedly. "You were in my cabin early this evening?"

"That's right."

"And you didn't find my equipment? Did you look in the metal case on the kitchen table?"

"We didn't find a thing. Not even the metal case."

"But I left it on the table in the kitchen. Lori will tell you. She watched me make the tests.

"We found Sam's glass and that's all."

Rod appeared genuinely dumbfounded. If this was an act, it was a good one. But then, I was surrounded by a ship full of actors, so his performance didn't convince me entirely.

"Believe me," Rod said, "that equipment was on the table when Lori and I left. Someone must have taken it while we were gone."

"Who steals that sort of thing?"

"I don't know."

"What about the note?"

"I can't explain that," Rod said. "If there was a note in my pocket, someone planted it there."

"Let's lay a few things on the line," I said. "What was Swanson talking about last night when he said you'd know why he got mad in the bar?"

Rod didn't answer for a long time. He pinched out his cigarette and tossed it into the water. "You want it straight?"

"Straight as you can make it."

77

"All right. I guess there's nothing to lose now. Swanson found out I was living on Catalina. I don't know how he found out, but he did. He came to see me about three weeks ago. Said his visit had to be strictly confidential. He told me if it didn't remain secret, if his personal dealings with me ever came out in the open, he'd kill me dead in the writing field."

"What was he after?"

Rod wiped his hands across his forehead. "A personal contract for my services on the Swanson show."

"I don't understand."

"I didn't understand at first myself. Then he explained that he and Decker were planning to force Aces out as producer. They had some kind of gimmick. I don't know what it was, but he wanted me back as writer. I told him I didn't want the deal, that I was happy with what I was doing. Then he really got tough. Promised me nothing but trouble if I didn't sign the contract. So I signed. What else could I do?"

"Now we're getting somewhere," I said. "You met him that night in the Golden Slipper, not accidentally, but on purpose."

"That's right. He told me to be there after the show because he wanted to iron out a few last details."

"And what were these details?"

"I don't know," Rod said vaguely. "He was crocked when I got there. Loaded to the gills. I told you how he kidded me about the drink he was taking to Aces."

I nodded.

"Decker was there, too. I tried to get something concrete out of him, but he was flying three ways to the moon himself and I got nothing—except an ultimatum from Swanson to show up in his office on the twenty-fifth."

"You mean last Monday? The day I signed my contract?"

"Yeah. I know I told you I hadn't been back to town since that time in the Golden Slipper, but I had to lie. Don't you understand? Swanson had me. I figured if I told you everything, it would get back to him. My writing career would have been out the window. I couldn't take the chance."

"Okay. I understand. What happened last Monday?"

"Swanson told me Aces would be out inside of two weeks. That meant Meeler, too. I argued. Told him Joe Meeler was doing a damn good job and ought to be retained. I said the same thing about Aces, and Swanson nearly hit the ceiling. He said if he could, he'd send Sam Aces right to the scrap heap."

"Then Swanson thought you were pulling a fast one when he saw you last night with Aces."

"Sure," Rod said. "He probably thought I was breaking his confidence and making a separate deal with Sam. Certainly he never expected to walk in that bar and see the two of us talking together."

I searched for holes in his story. There was only one opening I could find. "How come none of your old cronies recognized you in the Golden Slipper, or last Monday at Television Riviera?"

"It took a while for the plastic surgery to heal. During that time I couldn't shave so I grew a pretty heavy beard. Swanson didn't even recognize me the day he came over from the mainland. I shaved for the first time the afternoon I found you wading around in my abalone beds."

He flashed that infectious smile. I liked this guy. I couldn't help it.

"Mister," I whispered, "I'm very glad we met."

"So am I. I saw you Monday at the studio and you know what I said to myself? There's the most beautiful woman alive. Why don't you ask her to marry you, buy a hunk of your crazy island and never come back to civilization again?"

"Why didn't you?" I teased.

"Because," he said, "I knew there'd be ten thousand guys ahead of me in line."

"What if I told you there weren't ten thousand guys?"

"I'd say you're the biggest liar in the world." He took my face in his hands and kissed me.

He looked at me tenderly, "You know, I started something the night we met that I never got a chance to finish."

A crazy hot feeling boiled up in my stomach. Before I could make a move, Rod picked me up, carried me to my cabin and locked the door.

The horn of a big ship passing outside tore the darkness with its sound. He unbuttoned my sweater and slipped it gently off my shoulders.

Suddenly there was another sound. Loud footsteps running hurriedly on the deck. It was a sound filled with urgency—with deadlines.

Rod whirled toward the doorway, snapped open the lock and stepped outside. He disappeared as the night wind pushed the door closed. I waited tensely as Rod's footsteps faded in the distance. New rain pattered on the windows. When I peeked through one of the curtains, a yellowish face rose up, stared at me and disappeared.

Then there was a knock at the door. For an instant I was frightened. Really frightened. A killer was loose aboard Hell's Light. I forced back my female instincts, assumed my role of private detective, and answered.

"Who is it?" I asked.

"Carruthers, ma'am."

"Who?"

"Carruthers. One of the ship's crew, ma'am. I found something I think you and your police friend ought to see."

"Just a minute." I switched on the table lamp and crossed to my closet for a negligee.

Carruthers, his weather-beaten face damp with rain, stood outside the door. He was wearing a yellow hat and slicker and looked like something hauled straight out of the Sargasso Sea. But what really shook me was the instrument he held.

It was a knife. A butcher knife. Exactly like the one Mark had pulled from the dead body of Joe Meeler.

Chapter Eleven

Carruthers shoved the knife toward me. "Found it down on B Deck near one of the lifeboats," he said. "Looks like a trick gadget of some kind."

"What do you mean?" I asked.

"Here, I'll show you, ma'am." He took the butcher knife in his right hand, swung it back and rammed it squarely in his chest.

He shouldn't have been ready for a pine box or leaking so much plasma the blood bank could have closed down for a week. But he wasn't even scratched.

The old man smiled. "Amazing, ain't it?"

"Let me see that again. "I examined the knife. It was apparently spring-loaded, allowing the blade to collapse on contact into a narrow slit in the handle.

Carruthers chuckled, remarked about weird inventions and vanished into the night. A short time later Rod appeared, breathless and wet from the rain.

"I don't get it," he said. "There was somebody out there, but he vanished before I could catch up with him."

I showed Rod the trick knife and gave Carruthers' account of the discovery on B Deck. "What do you make of the gadget?" I asked.

"It's what they call a breakaway. Must be a Swanson TV prop." Rod examined the instrument. "Wonder how it got down there. I understood from Lud Norman that all props are kept on main deck in back of the swimming pool."

"Looks exactly like the one we found in Meeler," I said.

"Yeah, but that was no breakaway."

I pointed to the handle. "Did you notice this brown stain?"

"Makeup," Rod nodded. "TV people just don't know when to stop with the stuff. Ann Claypool's one of the worst. She spreads it on every part of her that shows."

'Speaking of Ann Claypool, what gives between you two?"

"What do you mean?" Rod demanded. "I—I'm an old friend. Vince Claypool and I went to college together."

"Vince was her husband?"

"Yeah. A nice guy. We opened up a sporting-goods shop together after graduation. That's when Vince met Ann. I never liked her—must have told him a thousand times she was no good. But he married her anyway."

"Was Ann really crazy about him?"

"Are you kidding? She's crazy about only two things—Ann Claypool and sex. She's one of those physical combinations that spells dynamite. Little woman, big bust. She's always out to prove something. Little people usually are. I imagine you can guess what she's trying to prove."

"You don't think she was sorry to see her husband die?"

"Hell, no! Vince had a ten-thousand dollar G.I. term policy. She's been having a ball on that poor bastard. If he only knew."

"But Ann gave me the impression she hated Aces' guts for sending Vince Claypool out on that underwater assignment."

"Sounds like Ann all right. Always with the sad story when she's in the chips and living high. The time to be careful of Annie is when she acts deliriously, sexapatingly happy like she did last night."

"Do you think she and Swanson could be in this together?"

"Who knows?" Rod shrugged his shoulders. "What would Ann get out of it?"

"The female lead in the Swanson show."

A stunned look sprang onto Rod's face. "Hell! I'd forgotten about Decker replacing you with Claypool!"

"It was apparently a joint decision introduced by Swanson and approved by Decker," I added.

"And meted out the morning after Aces disappeared." Rod rubbed his hands together vigorously. "I think you've got something, Honey. Something big."

"Think back," I suggested. "It would have been pretty tough for Swanson to poison Aces' drink. He was around only a few seconds. But with

82

Annie it was different. A lot different."

"You can say that again," Rod agreed. "She was all over the bar. It wouldn't have been easy, but nothing's too tough for little Annie if there's money in the deal."

I picked up the breakaway knife again. "But why murder Joe Meeler? Do you suppose he saw Ann or Golden Boy slip something in Aces' drink?"

"Could be!"

"Maybe Meeler was mixed up in the plot himself."

Rod shook his head. "Not Joe Meeler. He wouldn't hurt a gnat if he could help it."

"Joe never drank, did he?"

"Used to," Rod said. "Plenty. He cut off the alcohol after his operation."

"What was his trouble?"

"Peptic ulcers. Bad. Damn near killed him."

"If that's the case, why was he always hanging around the bar?"

Rod said, "Habit, I guess. In the old days he always did his best writing in bars. Liked the atmosphere."

"Seems almost prophetic he had to die in one."

"Yeah."

"What time is it?" I asked.

"Little after three. Why are you always so interested in the time?"

I stepped into the bathroom, slipped out of my negligee and into a swimsuit. "If the swimming-pool area is cleared out, I'd like to try to reenact Meeler's murder. Are you game?"

Rod's forehead ridged slightly. "I don't know. What do you want me to do?"

"Play the murderer."

"Will you cut it out?" he said angrily.

"All right, I'll play the murderer if it makes you any happier."

Just as long as you don't substitute that breakaway knife for the real thing."

I whirled around and grabbed Rod. "That's it!" I exclaimed. "That's how it was done!"

"What do you mean?"

"Somebody who knew Meeler could have substituted a real knife for the phony while they were discussing a scene."

I tossed a sweater over my shoulders and took his arm. "Come on, I'll show you."

The bar and swimming pool were dark. I switched on some lights and led Rod through the water to the exact stool where Meeler was found.

"You sit here," I said.

He followed my instructions resignedly. "Okay, now what?"

I waded back to the edge of the pool. "Now, I'm Swanson. You're Meeler. The bar is filled with people having a wild time."

"Yeah," Rod said. "Only if you're Swanson and these characters have been looking for you all day, don't you think you'd better come in with a tent over your head? Nothing would be more obvious than Golden Boy's chubby jowls and thick arms."

That made sense. Swanson couldn't have walked in unnoticed. He'd have attracted as much attention as a man wearing kilts and playing a bagpipe in the ladies' lounge of the Statler Hotel.

"Check," I said, circling around the edge of the pool. At the deep end, I stopped to survey the bar. "How about an approach from this direction? He could dive in and swim underwater. Swanson's a crackerjack at that sort of thing."

Rod pointed out a very important factor. There was no way into the pool area from the deep end. Swanson still would have had to pass through the game zone on the shallow side in order to reach the nine-foot depth.

I took off my sweater and plunged into the water. In the middle of the deep end wall I noticed a small porthole. Through the thick glass I could see a narrow passageway on B Deck. Then I saw something else. There was a lifeboat suspended along the side of the corridor. I surfaced.

"Rod!"

He almost fell off his stool. "What's the matter? You find another body?"

"No!" I yelled, swimming quickly to the bar. "I think I've got the answer to how the murderer entered and left unnoticed."

"Don't tell me he was in the pool all the time using a snorkel and pretending to be the Creature from the Black Lagoon!"

"Don't be smart!" I climbed over the top of the circular bar to the inside where the glasses and liquor were stored. The floor, about two-feet-wide and made of steel plating, was dry and raised well above the level of the pool bottom. Obviously a circular area the size of the bar was built underneath. I searched for a trap door.

About three feet from Rod's stool I found one. The door rose easily. I climbed down a ladder into a storeroom that was dark and foreboding with its stacked cases of whiskey. Rod's face appeared in the trap door opening.

"What's down there?" he asked.

"Enough giggle juice to float a battleship. Take a look for yourself."

Rod accepted my invitation. He was overwhelmed by the quantity of liquor in the storeroom.

"Courtesy of Grandpa Aces," I said. "No doubt Sam got around certain provisions of the will by listing this as necessary ship's stores."

"Holy smokes," Rod exclaimed, "I didn't know this room was down here. Sam always carried enough stock on the shelves around the bar to last any trip we ever made to Catalina and back. This looks like enough for a three-year cruise around the world."

"That's for sure," I agreed. "Let's see how they got this stuff in here. They couldn't have brought all these cases through the swimming pool."

I was right. A watertight door led us out onto B Deck only a few yards from the lifeboat, I'd seen through the underwater porthole in the pool. Carruthers said he'd found the trick knife on B Deck near a lifeboat. I was willing to bet this was where he'd made his discovery.

"Okay," Rod said, "how'd Swanson do it? And, more important, why?"

"Meeler saw the Clementine arrive," I explained. "He recognized the man at the wheel. He probably exchanged friendly greetings with the killer not realizing he was signing his own death certificate. They retired to the bar where Meeler was shown the breakaway knife. Then, in the confusion of my arrival with Chief Clements, while everyone poured out on deck, the killer plunged the real blade into Meeler and escaped through the opening in the bar floor."

"Sounds reasonable up to a point," Rod said. "But you still haven't explained Bob Swanson's presence in the bar and why no one besides Meeler recognized him."

I answered quickly, "He must have put on some sort of disguise before joining Meeler. This would explain the makeup smudges on the breakaway handle."

"Fantastic, Honey. Then you really believe Swanson's the killer?"

"I don't know."

"But, you just said…"

"Forget what I said, Rod. I don't know what's wrong here, but something's haywire."

"I don't get you."

"Herb Nelson was bludgeoned to death. Sam Aces was apparently poisoned and then shot at close range. Joe Meeler—stabbed. All three murders about as brutal as possible. I'm convinced they were committed by one and the same person. But who? Swanson's almost too obvious. Decker had arsenic in his possession. You said you were going to test for arsenic and yet we couldn't find any of your equipment. We did find a highly suspicious note which led to Aces' bloodstained jacket."

Rod Caine reddened. "Now, listen, once and for all, I'm not the killer!"

"If you're not," I said, "the real villain in this piece is trying mighty hard to make you look guilty. Believe me, Rod, you'd be behind bars right now if Chief Clements hadn't verified your presence aboard *Hell's Light* while Mark and I were searching for Aces. The murderer probably hoped you'd leave the yacht and go home so that you'd be the logical stowaway suspect."

Rod glanced away for an instant. Then he said, "I was on the float ready to go back to my place when Chief Clements pulled up in the police boat."

"Now you're talking the killer's language."

"But that's the strange part," Rod said uneasily. "I didn't plan to go home at all until Ann Claypool told me Swanson faked his disappearance in order to meet me at my cabin."

I recoiled, "You're joking!"

"No. She said he wanted to talk more about the show. I asked her how long he'd been waiting and she guessed about two hours. I really blew my top when I heard that."

"Did you go to your cabin then?"

"Of course. But Swanson wasn't there, so I waited around thinking he'd come back."

"How long did you wait?" I demanded.

"All evening. I got back to *Hell's Light* a short time before you did."

"And you mean to tell me you never noticed your lab equipment was gone from the kitchen table?"

"No—no, I didn't," Rod stammered. "I don't think I even went into the kitchen. That's why I was so surprised when you said the portable case was gone."

I felt like tearing my hair out by the roots. Why hadn't I thought to ask someone if Rod had been missing during the evening? Clements had talked to him aboard the yacht, but neither Mark nor I had bothered to ask what time that discussion occurred. Could it have been early enough for Rod Caine to swim unseen to the boat cave and stow aboard the *Clementine?*"

"I know it sounds suspicious, Honey, but…"

"Why didn't you tell me this before?" I demanded, suddenly on the defensive again.

"Because I figured Ann Claypool and Swanson decoyed me to the cabin to try and hook Aces' murder onto me. But it didn't add up somehow. I wanted to talk to Ann before I spilled the story to you."

I climbed over the bar into the pool. "All right. Let's visit Miss Claypool and get her version of the story."

"You don't expect her to admit anything if she's mixed up in this, do you?"

"I don't know what to expect," I said angrily. "Do you want to come along while I ask her?"

Rod vaulted over the rail into the water. "You're damn right! I'm getting tired of being the fall guy around here!"

We went to Ann's cabin. There were no lights. I knocked gently. No answer. Rod banged. Still no answer. He tried the knob and it turned. We entered and switched on the light. The bed was turned back, but Ann wasn't in it.

"She's gone," Rod said. "Skipped. Does that answer your questions?"

"No!" I opened the closet. Her clothes were still there. Then I heard Rod's voice from the bathroom. It sounded twisted, as if someone had gripped him about the throat.

"She's in here," he said.

I entered the bathroom where Rod was bent awkwardly over a pink tub. In the water, Ann Claypool floated face up, stark naked, long black hair curled around her face like thick strands of seaweed. Her bright green eyes were wide and watery and she stared up at us for a long moment before Rod straightened up.

"She—she's dead," he managed. "What in the hell could have happened?"

I leaned over the tub. Two livid thumb prints were on her white neck. There was no point in answering Rod's question. It was too obvious.

Chapter Twelve

Strangulation is a brutal way to die, but in death Ann Claypool seemed quietly and beautifully resigned to her fate.

Her bathroom was a dismal wreck. The medicine cabinet was half torn from its hinges. A cocktail glass was shattered on the floor. Broken fragments lay glittering in tiny pools of water that had spilled over the side of the tub as she apparently had struggled with the killer. An ashtray and several lipstick-stained cigarette butts floated around the lifeless nude body.

Rod Cain stood beside the tub; arms limp at his sides, eyes riveted on Ann. "I don't understand," he murmured. "This isn't possible."

"Why not?" I asked quickly.

"Well—I don't know," Rod stammered. "This just doesn't make sense. Who—who'd want to kill Ann?"

"Maybe somebody had to."

"What do you mean?"

We walked out onto the deck. The black sea was growing amber with the coming dawn. I looked at his unshaven face. "Maybe she was about to reveal the killer's identity."

"Honey, quit looking at me like that! I didn't do it. How could I? I've been with you all night."

"I'm not blaming you Rod," I said, shaking my head. "I'm blaming myself for being so dumb. For not sticking to my guns."

"About what?"

"About a certain theory I had concerning Sam Aces." I glanced toward Ann's stateroom. "Listen, Rod, after the police arrive I'm going into Avalon. For the next twenty-four hours you must not leave this yacht for any reason. Do you understand?"

"No, I don't. Why can't I go with you?"

"Because I've got a hunch," I said. "A real big hunch that somebody else is going to die and the killer will want you in the vicinity when it happens."

"You mean Avalon?"

"That's right. You've got to be able to prove you were aboard this yacht. I don't care whether you get a death warning, a secret message or a vision—don't leave this ship!"

Rod grinned. "Honey, what's going on? What'd you find in there? A death image in Ann's eyes? An important clue? What?"

"I'll let you know when I get back from Avalon. Maybe I'm crazy. But, believe I'm going to find out."

Glittering spray danced in the brilliant morning light as the patrol boat sliced through the waters outside Avalon Bay. Chief Clements sat beside me, his wrinkled mouth closed in stony silence. He'd been that way ever since the bathroom, when he looked into Ann Claypool's wet staring eyes. Three murders in one night had been too much for the old police officer.

I chipped through his marbleized exterior with a question about Decker.

"We haven't been able to find him," Clements admitted wearily. "After dropping Lieutenant Storm at the airport last night, we searched Decker's yacht. We found absolutely nothing."

"How's Avalon as a hideout?"

The chief scowled. "Best this side of the French Riviera. You know the setup. Hundreds of cabins in the Villa, homes on the hill, homes in the canyon, all sorts of ocean caves, two piers, the casino—it's endless. If Decker's on the island, it might take us a month to blast him out."

"And if he's aboard another yacht?"

"Then it's hardly possible unless we get a strong lead. Yesterday there were almost three hundred boats anchored in Avalon Bay."

The red-tiled roof of the huge casino building appeared out of the swirling spray. Over the roar of the police-boat engines could be heard the hillside chimes, pealing from the white tower above the bay.

I asked the chief if any efforts were being made to retrieve Sam Aces' body.

"Two divers have been down exploring the reefs at Little Harbor since dawn," Clements said. "Frankly, I doubt if we'll ever find the body."

Our boat swept past a fabulous triple-mastered schooner. The police officer pointed at the words, Decker's Dilemma, painted on the side of the huge sailing vessel. Obviously, the ship belonged to Man Mountain Max. That gave the two of us something in common. A dilemma. It was my job to find a dead man before he committed another murder.

I phoned Mark from the Avalon police station. He hadn't slept all night and admitted he was up to his ears with the Nelson case. "We still haven't located this suspect, Walker," the lieutenant said. "He seems to have vanished into thin air."

Mark was jolted when I told him about Ann Claypool. "Holy smokes!" he roared. "We're dealing with a maniac!"

"A clever maniac," I said.

"We've got an APB out on Swanson," Mark told me. "The same goes for Decker. But it sounds to me like they're still in your vicinity. Has Clements found Aces' body yet?"

"No. And he's not going to."

"What do you mean?"

"I don't believe Sam Aces is dead."

"Here we go again!" Mark cried. "Where do you get these ideas?"

"It all fits a pattern, Lieutenant," I said angrily. "Do you want to hear it?"

"Go ahead."

"Ace murdered Herb Nelson."

"Why?" Mark demanded.

"I don't know yet," I said hesitantly, "but when I find him I'll know the answer to that question."

Mark Storm groaned wearily. "Before you waste anymore of the taxpayers' money on this telephone call, let me tell you something."

"What?"

"Remember the blood-sample scrapings I took from the trunk?"

"Of course I remember. They don't match with the stains on the jacket, do they?"

Mark swiftly squashed my theory. "They match perfectly. In fact, from corresponding medical samples we've proved conclusively the blood stains in both cases belonged to Sam Aces. You want to know something else?"

"Go ahead."

"You won't believe this, Honey, but Herb Nelson wasn't the little white god we all thought he was. For the past few years he's been pushing heroin."

"You're lying!"

"I wish I were," Mark said. "This morning we picked up a couple of jokers in the vicinity of Nelson's apartment. They had needle marks clear up to their armpits. They admitted Herb's been selling junk to them and dozens of other punks for years."

"Can they prove it?" I demanded.

"They don't have to. We went up to the apartment, ripped open a few suspicious wall boards and discovered a hiding place. There were a number of needles, old spoons and H caps. So we made another autopsy on his body about a half hour ago. He'd been using the stuff himself."

"Oh, no!" I felt for a chair and slumped down.

"Then a few minutes ago," Mark continued, "I got a call from the San Diego police. They've just made a big roundup of Southern California heroin suppliers at the border. One of them had a junk list."

"What's that?"

"Names of pushers in various areas and who kept them supplied. Herb Nelson's name was on that list."

"Who was his supplier?"

"A man named Sam Aces."

For a long moment I couldn't get my breath, then I said, "It—it couldn't be the same one."

"We don't know for sure," Mark said. "There may be another Sam Aces, but I doubt it. Too many strong links; the old friend routine; Sam trying to get Herb a spot on the Swanson show. It all adds up. Honey, I'm afraid your two clients were a couple of bad boys.

"Mark," I protested, "I can believe it of Sam Aces, he was no angel— but, Herb Nelson…"

"Yeah, I know what you mean. I felt sick when they brought in that stuff from his apartment. I didn't believe it until I got that phone call from San Diego."

"So where does that leave us?" I asked after a moment. "Well, this suspect, Walker, is a known user. It's my guess he went to Herb's apartment, demanded some junk, didn't have the money and was forced to kill him to get what he wanted. Where we go from there, I don't know. My theory is that Bob Swanson murdered Aces and then killed Meeler to conceal the crime. He added Ann Claypool to the list when she threatened to reveal her part in the plan."

I glanced up as Chief Clements came into his office. "Listen, Mark, the Avalon lab is making a set of prints from the thumb impression found on Ann Claypool's neck. The chief says he'll have them flown to the mainland as soon as they're ready. I imagine they'll do a lot toward straightening us out, once and for all."

Mark said, "I hope so."

"When will you be able to get here?"

"Tonight," Mark said, "at the earliest. But I'll call Clements just as soon as we've matched those prints."

"Okay. Hey, I almost forgot! How about fingerprints on that butcher knife?"

"Plenty of them," the lieutenant answered. "All belonging to Mr. Joseph Meeler."

"Great," I said. "Now all we have to do is find out if the thumb marks on Ann Claypool's throat are her own and that Sam Aces shot himself."

Mark growled, "Rotten business, isn't it? Well, are you about ready to settle down and get married?"

"Who thinks about marriage when they're having a ball at Catalina?"

Mark missed the humor, swore loudly and said, "Have it your own way, you voluptuous blonde bird-dog. But one of these days you're going to get yourself into a hole six-feet deep and then nobody's going to be able to dig you out except a guy with a shovel."

"Remind me to call for Perry Mason."

He finally softened, warned me to keep on the alert for both Decker and Swanson and ended the conversation.

I walked to the island villas and rented one of the small cabins. The day was hot and the air acrid as if someone had shipped in a slice of Los Angeles smog.

I freshened my lipstick, slipped into a cool dress and walked outside along the front cabins. That was a mistake! One of the doors suddenly flew open and a large hand pulled me inside the room.

Before I could get my bearings I was flat on my back and a big kid with thick reddish hair was trying to get my dress up. I put my heel in the middle of his stomach and he reeled across the room, landing on a small table.

The piece of furniture collapsed, pitching the startled young man to the floor. He got up slowly. I thought about reaching for my .32 but vetoed the idea in favor of some juvenile rehabilitation. The kid couldn't have been more than nineteen.

"What's your problem?" I asked, dusting myself off. "You the island doctor, or was the physical examination just for kicks?"

"I thought you were somebody else," he said, shaking his head. "I been expecting a girl named Toni. You look just like her."

"Toni must be quite a gal," I said.

He had a bad complexion and thick eyebrows. He said, "Don't get me wrong. I didn't want to hurt you. It was all a mistake."

"Look," I said carefully. "Let's level a little, what do you say? You saw me through the window, liked what you saw and decided to have some. Isn't that about it?"

He ran his fingers nervously through his hair. "Well—I—I wasn't going to hurt you."

As I turned for the door, a rusted tin box caught my eye. It was surrounded by a collection of bright shells.

"Where'd you get that?" I demanded.

"What?"

"That metal case."

He looked frightened. "I dunno. I picked it up somewhere. Why?"

"Where'd you pick it up?"

"In the water. It—was at the bottom in a nest of sea anemone."

"Where?" I asked. "White's Landing? Little Harbor? You don't pick up articles like this every day. Where'd you find it?"

He made half gestures. "In the bay. Late yesterday afternoon. I'm an undersea diver. I work with the glass bottom boats. Is something wrong?"

The initials RC were engraved in the top of the case. I opened the lid. No mistake. Rod had told the truth about owning lab equipment, but how in Hades had this case wound up at the bottom of Avalon Bay?

"Look," I said to the kid, "a friend of mind lost this, and it's important that I find out where."

The kid seemed confused.

94

"Could you locate the spot again if you had to?"

"I—I guess so," he said.

"Will you take me there?"

"Well—sure," he stammered. "When do you want to go?"

"As soon as I change into a swimsuit. Is that okay with you?"

I returned a few minutes later. He glanced at the V-slashed neckline of my tiger-striped suit, swallowed hard and introduced himself. "Name's Marble. Danny Marble. I bunk with a couple of guys from my hometown. They went over to the mainland yesterday. I guess I've been lonesome. That's why I wanted to talk to you…"

"No explanation needed," I said. "Come on, Danny. Let's go for a boat ride."

We walked to the Pleasure Pier where Danny borrowed a small five-horse putter from a friend, and we headed out into the bay. The sun was blistering hot.

Danny cut the engine about a hundred yards off from the red-roofed Casino. "This is the spot," he said decisively. "I did a special dive here yesterday because there's a lot of Iodine Kelp for the people to see."

"What's that?"

"Iodine Kelp is the ocean's tallest plant." Danny handed me a face mask with an extra-large window. "Here! Stick you head over the side and take a look for yourself."

I fastened the mask over my eyes and followed his instructions. The bottom was about twenty feet below the surface and very sandy. Giant ribbons of green kelp twisted up from the ocean floor and, like weird ballet dancers, seemed to sway in a soundless, fantastic rhythm. It was beautiful, but I was more interested in the treasure that Dan had brought up from the deep.

I flipped off the mask and studied the surrounding area. Twenty yards away lay the three-masted schooner, *Decker's Dilemma*.

"Danny, do you know that ship?" I pointed at the large sea craft.

"Sure. She's been around for several days. A big television man owns her."

"Has she moved at all to your knowledge?"

"I don't think so," Danny said. "She's secured bow and stern."

I held up the metal case. "How much would you guess this thing

95

weighs?"

"About ten pounds, maybe less."

"How far could you throw it if you wanted to?"

"I dunno," Danny said, scratching his head. He examined the case. "You can grip it pretty easy by this metal handle." He surveyed the waters around the putter. "I guess I could heave it about as far as that schooner."

I nodded. "That was about my guess, too. Let's go over there."

"Where?"

"The schooner. I want to go aboard."

Danny groaned. "Are you crazy? You can't go aboard a ship just because you've got an urge to do it. Especially that one."

"Why?"

"Rough crew," Danny said. "Real rough. I think this television guy keeps 'em around for protection."

"How do you know they're rough?"

The youth shook his head. "Couple of the boys and I got—drunk the other night during the storm. We went for a boat ride and swamped near the schooner. We barely managed to climb aboard when these three big goons jumped us. And I really mean jumped! We put up a whale of a battle, but they had us on size, weight, experience, everything."

"What finally happened?"

"What do you think? We got tossed in the drink. It was just lucky none of us drowned."

I scanned the quiet decks of the schooner. "Nice guys! I'd like to meet them."

"You're kidding!"

"Cross my heart. Want me to drop you somewhere first?"

The big kid swallowed hard. "I'll stick. I might get killed doing it, but I'll play along."

I patted his cheek. "That's my boy! Let's go!"

Danny fired up the engine and we cleaved the short distance to Decker's schooner. Nobody appeared. He tied the boat to the landing ladder and we started up the steps.

"I hope you know what you're doing," he said. "I've got to work this afternoon and I don't want to do it in splints."

I didn't answer. My thoughts were concentrating on Decker's disappearance and the discovery of Rod's metal case near the TV king's yacht. Someone had stolen the lab equipment and apparently brought it back to Decker's schooner. But why? Bob Swanson and Max Decker were around somewhere and I had a feeling I was getting closer by the second.

The three bodyguards suddenly popped up out of a hatch. They had more muscle than a herd of bulls. I was hoping, in contrast, they had less brains than a pack of fleas.

"Hey, you two!" the ugliest yelled. "Get off this ship before we throw you off."

"I'll bet you three gentlemen combined couldn't throw an oyster into a pot of stew," I answered.

They rose up out of the hatch with Herculean precision. They must have weighed two hundred pounds each.

"Lady," the second ugliest boomed, "I could personally toss you over the Casino with my little finger!"

I laughed. "I'll bet your little finger is so muscle bound you can't raise it high enough to scratch your own elbow."

Danny was shaking all the way down to his toes. "What are you trying to do?" he whispered.

I smiled at him. "Don't worry!" Then I said to the three bodyguards, "If you're so tough why don't you take us on one at a time?"

They grunted. The ugliest came on, wrapped his hairy arms around my waist and squeezed. I got a leg up under him and ripped hard with my knee. He grabbed his stomach, bent over and I drop-kicked him neatly over the side. He made a tremendous splash and disappeared.

Chapter Thirteen

The second muscle man advanced angrily and reached for me. I caught him by the wrist, snapped his arm over my shoulder and leaned into the wind. When he hit high C, I flipped him in a circular arc. He hit the water head first.

The third pug, refusing to believe his eyes, got off to a bad start even before he moved out of the starting gate. He made some King Kong noises, flexing and snorting as if he were working up to an appearance before the crowds. Then he was off and running. But he hit a newly waxed section of deck. The next time I looked, he was stretched completely out, pawing at the sky as he catapulted into the water, pancaking with a sickening swoosh.

By the time the three of them had surfaced, a thin, white-haired man in an expensive-looking robe came out on deck, swearing and waving violently at them.

"You bums," he yelled. "You patsy-faced, weak kneed rascals! You couldn't lick an old lady with her hands tied behind her back. You're fired!"

He aimed a shotgun at the bobbing figures. "Swim for shore before I put a pound of buckshot in your yellow-bellied drawers!"

They headed for the beach, ripping the water open with their powerful arms. Danny Marble heaved a big sigh of relief. I approached the skinny little man with the shotgun.

"Thanks," I said.

"Don't thank me," he said angrily. "When I see more than six hundred pounds of beef being tossed around by a woman, I know it's time Max Decker got some new hands aboard this yacht."

He introduced himself as Philip Hickman, president of the Radio-Television Corporation. "We own a sizable interest in Decker's WES network."

"I'm looking for Decker," I said.

"Everyone is," Hickman returned. "You a female cop?"

"Private investigator. Sam Aces was my client until he disappeared. I suppose you've heard about the blood stained jacket?"

Hickman winced. "Yes, the police told me last night. I liked Aces. He had a lot of executive ability. Too bad this had to happen right now."

"What do you mean?"

"During our meeting," Hickman explained. "Four of us flew all the way from New York for this get-together. Unfortunately, Aces never learned of our decision."

"I don't follow you."

"Well," Hickman continued. "Decker owns the largest block of stock in World Broadcasting System, but a board of directors actually runs the network. None of the board, including myself, have been too happy with Max's operation of the Western net at Television Riviera. This has been going on for more than a year. He's incompetent when it comes to mixing with people and personalities. So the board voted to move Decker back to WBS headquarters in New York and replace him in Hollywood with Sam Aces."

I caught my breath.

Hickman continued. "We had only one obstacle, that was Decker. He'd always been jealous of Aces for some reason. But Max finally gave in last Monday morning and agreed to turn his desk over to Sam."

"Why didn't someone tell Aces?" I demanded. "That was one of Decker's stipulations. Aces wasn't to be notified until after the Catalina trip." Hickman shook his head. "I don't know exactly why. Max is a strange man."

"You can say that again. Did you know Decker had been secretly planning to oust Aces?"

"No, I knew nothing about such a thing."

"Did you know Bob Swanson was hoping to take over producer of his own show after Aces was fired?"

"I can't believe that," Hickman said.

"Why not?"

"Swanson's a lousy producer. I've even hitched about his job as director. This was another example of poor executive power on the part of Max Decker."

"Do you think Swanson could be blackmailing Decker?"

Hickman put away his shotgun. "I doubt it. Max is a powerful man. If he wanted to, he could break Swanson down to a latrine keeper."

"Maybe," I said. "That all depends on whether Swanson saw a certain party dump a quantity of arsenic in a glass two weeks ago. And whether that certain party was Max Decker."

"I—I don't follow you," Hickman stammered.

I smiled. "You should sometime. I'm told it's like watching a cobra about to shed its skin."

Hickman tried to catch my humor but it didn't penetrate. Danny Marble and I climbed down the ladder into the boat.

"Where to?" he asked, "I don't know of any wars that need to be won. How the devil did you manage those three guys anyway?"

"Judo and a little deck wax," I said. "Don't worry. If they'd had an ounce more brains between them we'd have been in trouble, you can bet on that."

The wind was rising cool off the water. "Looks like we might have another storm," Danny said, scanning the sky.

"That's all we need. What time do you go to work on the glass-bottom boat?"

"Soon as the steamer arrives. About twelve-fifteen."

"Could I go down with you?" I asked.

"Sure," Dan said enthusiastically. "So you're a private detective, huh? This ought to be fun."

We landed again at the Pleasure Pier and walked down Crescent venue to the Jolly Inn. I wanted to talk to the bartender, Joe King, an old friend of mine from Lake Arrowhead. Joe had been the power behind the bar at The Chalet for many years. He was a dark complected, nervous type with more ulcers than a sultan has wives.

"What'll you have, Honey gal?" Joe asked.

"A fat man," I said.

"Never heard of one," Joe teased. "What's it made of, vinegar and brandy?"

"Blubber and belly," I corrected. "This one's bald, weighs about three fifty, needs two stools to sit. Seen him around?"

Joe grinned. "Sounds like Max Decker."

I nodded. "When's the last time you saw him?"

"Yesterday afternoon."

"Was he with anyone?"

"Yeah," Joe said. "Cute little doll. He called her Lori, as I remember."

"Smart remembering," I said. "Do you ever watch the Bob Swanson show on TV?"

"Never miss it. Swanson was in here this morning."

"What?"

"About an hour ago. He looked bushed, like he hadn't slept for days."

I practically crawled over the bar. "Did he say anything to you, Joe? About where he's been staying or what he's been doing?"

"He didn't say a word. Just tossed down a double and walked out. He was pretty dusty. I'd say he'd been on a camping trip or something."

"Thanks, pal. What would private eyes like me do without open-eyed guys like you?"

"Live a little longer," Joe said. "Get out of here! I'd rather associate with alcoholics. At least they're having fun while they're trying to kill themselves."

Outside the Jolly Inn, warm mist dampened the sidewalks as Dan and I headed up the street toward the steamer terminal. The massive white hulk of the channel liner, *Catalina*, was sliding into view around the Casino, its decks jammed with waving, wet tourists.

"Time for us to go to work," Danny said. "What are you going to be looking for?"

"You'll know if I find it!" I said. "Come on, let's not miss the boat."

We climbed aboard the glass-bottomed *Phoenix* and Danny took me to a small dressing room. He brought out two sets of long underwear and two orange rubber diving suits.

He smiled embarrassedly. "We usually dive off a tub called Davey Jones. She's got separate dressing quarters. Aboard the *Phoenix* this is it, and we don't have time to take turns."

"That's convenient," I said, "for you."

He swallowed a large lump. "I won't look."

"Danny," I said. "I'm a big girl, remember?"

"Yeah," he said uneasily. "That's what I'm trying to forget. I am

101

human, you know!"

"So I noticed back at your cabin."

With his jaw set tight, Danny turned his back and we tugged on our long underwear. After we got into the rubber suits, he looked at me. He was blushing enough color to paint the Empire State Building.

"The captain wants me to talk to the passengers on the public address system before we go down," Danny said. "I'll introduce you as—Dolores West, a very experienced female skin diver. Do you think you can live up to the fanfare?"

"I'll try."

The Phoenix paddle wheel was churning us out into the bay by the time Dan and I came up topside in our orange suits. Despite a steady mist, the boat was crammed with eager passengers. We breezed over to a spot near Decker's schooner while Danny did his microphone bit. Then we plunged into the water.

Immediately I became tangled in Iodine Kelp but managed to extract myself with a few healthy kicks of the rubber flippers attached to my feet. Dan pointed out the bright colored fish to a watchful audience while I pretended to search for abalone. But my mind was not on any citizens of the briny deep. I was looking for something man-made; an article a killer might discard as he tossed over Rod's metal case. All that turned up were two soda bottles and a rusted beer can.

It was late afternoon before Dan and I got back to the villa. The sky had opened up into a heavy downpour and we ran all the way from the pier. The poor tourists were in for a foul trip home on the steamer.

I was in for a shock myself. Dan's pals were back from the mainland, apparently three-sheets-to-the-wind, glassy-eyed and very belligerent. They took one look at me in the tiger-striped swimsuit and growled.

"Danny boy," one bellowed, "you've been holding out on us. Let's spread the wealth."

"This is off-limits," I returned abruptly. "So stop undressing me with your eyes."

"Wow!" howled another. "She's tough. How tough are you, baby?"

Quickly Danny moved in between us. "I'll answer that one," he said. "She's tough enough to send you back to kindergarten, Hank, so take my advice and button your lip."

"Fancy that," Hank retorted. "Even our pal and soul-mate, Danny boy, is getting muscular around the larynx. Perhaps it will be necessary to perform a tonsillectomy, right Arch?"

Arch, a runt with a gutsy-looking face, arched his back. I could see we were going to have trouble. Real trouble. Danny's three friends were feeling no pain, but aching to create a little. It suddenly struck me that there were neither glasses, liquor bottles, nor the smell of alcohol in the small room. These kids were *high*, but from what? They all wore long sleeve shirts. If there was any possibility they were on heroin, I had to bare their arms to check for needle marks.

"How about a game of strip poker?" I suggested quickly.

Arch unarched and grinned out of the side of his mouth. "Now you're beginning to talk like a lady," he said.

The third member of the clan, a mop-headed brute with buck-teeth, giggled girlishly. "You can say that again. I've got a deck of cards."

Dan flashed me a suspicious look and started to argue with buck-teeth.

"That's fine," I interrupted. "We'll play five-handed, one card a piece. Low man sheds, okay?"

Hank flipped open a card table as the trio grunted favorably. The odds were roughly thirty-to-one against me. One low card and I would lose my tiger stripes. But I wasn't going to leave my fate in the hands of luck.

"I'll deal," Arch said, shuffling the deck.
"Wait a minute!" I lifted the cards from his chubby fists. "Low man deals each hand. When I say low, I mean the person with the least amount of clothes. You all have me about seven to one at the moment. It's my deal."

"Okay," buck-teeth agreed. He was shaking so hard he would have agreed to anything. The rest followed suit. Only Danny tried to call off the game, but he was out-voted.

I shuffled, cut and flipped out five cards, face down. "All right," Arch said. "You first Danny boy. Then me, then Hank, then Buck. The lady is last. Go ahead, turn it over."

Dan had a queen. The trio grinned. Arch had a ten. They banged the table happily. Hank had a jack. They clapped each other on the back. Buck had a king. The place nearly flew apart.

"Now it's your turn, Blondie," Arch said, licking his chops. "Remember, this was your idea. No sore losers!"

103

I turned over my card. The trio flattened out.

Ace of spades.

Grumbling bitterly, Arch took off his shoes.

I reshuffled and dealt a new hand. All four had jacks. Arch lined them up in a formidable row.

"Beat that!" he bragged.

I took all four jacks and stacked them one on top of the other. Then I flipped over my card and covered the pile with it. The trio flipped.

Queen of hearts.

All four of them removed a piece of clothing. But no shirts.

I dealt out five more cards. Arch was getting hot around the collar. "This time around," he said, "the lady shows first. We'll reverse the table. I'll show last." I nodded and turned up my card. The trio cackled like a bunch of hens. Three of diamonds.

Hank had a king. Buck had an eight. Danny had an ace. Arch chuckled and flipped over his card.

Deuce!

Arch was down to his shorts and shirt.

After ten more hands the whole trio was in the same state of undress and I still had my tiger stripes. Danny had lost only his jacket. It was getting so dark, Hank had to turn on the lights.

"Hey, Arch," buck-teeth moaned all of a sudden. "How come we keep losing?"

"I dunno," Arch said. But I'm beginning to get a pretty good idea. I think the little lady is dealing off the bottom."

Arch demanded the next deal. He shuffled and issued out five cards. I had a bad feeling. Especially since this was the first hand I hadn't dealt— and, as Arch had guessed, off the bottom of the deck.

The trio flipped over their cards. They groaned. Three treys. Dan had a ten of hearts.

My card was a black one. Very black. Deuce! The plan was wrecked. I'd wanted to see a few bare arms. Now they were clamoring to see a few parts of my anatomy.

"Well?" Arch roared, jumping up, "are you going to do it, or should I?"

"I've managed to undress myself since I was five," I said, stalling. "I don't need any lessons now."

104

"Okay," Hank said impatiently. "Commence!"

The tiger-striped suit was held up by two shoulder straps. I shrugged and unfastened one, edging slowly toward the door. A big storm had turned the early evening pitch black and rain smashed heavily on the roof. The second strap finally gave. Holding up the front of my suit, I eased down the zipper, simultaneously stepping back and grasping the doorknob. Their glazed eyes saw nothing except the fabric easing away from my body as they waited for the unveiling.

As I was about to turn the knob, the lights went out. The cursing and screaming was riotous.

"Who did it?" roared the runt's voice out of pitch blackness. "Who did it? I'll kill 'em! I'll kill 'em!"

"Nobody done it, Arch," boomed back the nasal voice of buck teeth. "It musta been the storm. The electricity is off."

"Well, get it on again!" Arch screamed wildly.

I whirled around, flung open the door and dashed out into the night. Rain drilled in my eyes. I stumbled, snagged my swimsuit on something sharp and tried to break loose. The fabric ripped apart below the zipper as I lunged free. Then a biting chill swept over me. My suit was gone!

I searched frantically for my cabin, but the rain and darkness obliterated everything. A hundred and fifty cabins and they all looked alike. I wound up on a side street, lost, angry and naked. The street was apparently deserted, but I couldn't be sure. Lights were out all over Avalon.

I stopped and listened. Drenching rain pelted against the pavement. There was one other sound, distant and weird. The chimes. They were pealing wildly up on the hillside.

I ran for the police station. It would be embarrassing, but I had no choice.

Chief Clements almost knocked me down in the doorway of the police building. He wore a black slicker and apparently was in a big hurry. He gave me a quick rundown with the flashlight and bellowed, "Miss West, for God's sake, don't you ever wear clothes?"

He swept me into his office and a warm blanket as I explained the circumstances. His face had an expression of exasperation and worry.

"We've been looking for you," Clements said. "Decker's been found."

"Where?" I demanded.

"Up in the chimes tower," the police chief said.

"What was he doing up there?"

Clement wiped a wet hand across his old face. "He was hanging by a thick rope. Decker's dead!"

Chapter Fourteen

I nearly dropped my blanket. "How'd you happen to find him up there?"

"The chimes started ringing at five o'clock," Clements said, "and they never stopped. One of the Island Company repair men went to check the trouble. Decker was strung up on a rod that controls the timing device."

"But the electricity," I said. "I thought there was a power failure."

"There is," the police chief explained. "Decker was hung up on a timing rod. His weight created a jam-up in the bell mechanism."

"Where's the body now?"

"In the island morgue. He's had a .38 caliber bullet lodged in his heart. That's what really killed him."

"It must be Swanson," I said, shaking my head. "But it just doesn't add up."

"How big is this TV actor, Swanson?" Clements asked.

"About average. He's in terrific shape, though. Strong as a bull physically."

"That's what I thought."

"I don't get you."

Clements produced a crumpled piece of paper and handed it to me. The typewritten note read, MEET ME IN THE CHIMES TOWER AT FOUR-THRITY THIS AFTERNOON. VITALLY IMPORTANT. B.S.

I examined the note. "Where'd you get this?"

The old police chief struck the table with a match and applied the flame to his cigarette. "We found it in Decker's coat pocket. Swanson's first name is Bob, isn't it?"

I nodded. This note looked exactly like the one Mark and I had found in Rod Caine's pocket. All capital letters and an unusual typeface. Both messages were probably from the same typewriter. Swanson had a portable in his stateroom aboard *Hell's Light*.

"Any trace of Swanson?" I asked.

"No. The storm's loused us up completely," Clements said. "It's been pretty dusty around the tower. We might have followed his trail if the rain hadn't obliterated everything. I've got men covering the airport and both piers."

Dusty! That coincided with Joe King's description of Swanson. Golden Boy could have investigated the chimes area before sending his message to Decker.

I studied the old police chief's face, then said, "How would you guess it was done? It's no easy matter to hang a man who weighs three hundred and fifty pounds."

"There's a ledge next to the timing rod," Clements said. "I figure Swanson got Decker up on that ledge at gunpoint, then ordered him to slip on the noose. The bullet did the rest."

Clements loaned me some trousers and a shirt. "I'm going back to *Hell's Light*," I said.

"You want a lift out to the yacht?"

"No thanks, I'll find a way. Do you have a flashlight you can spare?"

The grizzled police officer bought one out of a drawer. "Incidentally," he said, "we still haven't been able to get to the mainland with those thumb impressions from Ann Claypool. All the airstrips are closed over there."

I rolled my eyes dismally. "Listen, Chief, do me a favor. Check Decker's arms for needle marks. He might have been a narcotics addict."

The chimes had stopped and raindrops slackened into a mist by the time I reached the Villa. My footsteps rang loudly on the wooden walkways as I searched for my own cabin. When I found number thirty-six the door was ajar.

Hadn't I locked it? My mind, conflicted with thoughts about Decker's murder, couldn't come up with a positive answer. I stepped inside and closed the door, automatically flicking the wall switch. Nothing happened. The power was still off.

Then a metal instrument flashed in the darkness. I ducked, but not far enough. The weapon caught me on the side of the head just as one of my fingernails tore into something. I crumpled to the floor, rolled over and

108

crawled for the door. A dark figure was stumbling clumsily down the walkway. Struggling to my feet, I started in pursuit, collapsing after a few steps. My head felt like a full-scale assault at Iwo Jima.

When I finally reached the street, it was deserted. My first impulse carried me to the Jolly Inn. Candles flickered on the tables and behind the bar. The place was alive with music, laughter and the jangled chorus of glasses, bottles and people bumping around on the dance floor.

Fighting a blackout, I grabbed the edge of the bar and shot a flare up in the general direction of Joe King. He got my signal and breezed over.

"For God's sake, Honey," Joe said angrily. "You look like Hell-warmed-over for the Fourth-of-July. What's happened?"

"Have you seen Swanson in the last few minutes? I demanded.

"No. Haven't seen him since this morning."

"You're sure?"

"Of course I'm sure," Joe said. "What are you doing in men's clothes? I hardly recognized you."

"My dressmaker's on vacation!" I said, holding my head. There was a lump on the left side that would have frightened an ostrich. I studied the crowd. The character who leveled me with the blunt instrument had to be around somewhere. And I felt certain that character was Swanson.

I dashed across the street to the Hi-Ho bar. The same sort of candlelit fandango was going on. One difference. Danny Marble was sitting at a table with a blonde about my size. One difference here, too. This gal didn't have a lump on her topside. I joined them.

"Gee, Honey," Danny said warmly, "where you been? I looked for you." He glanced at his partner. "Oh, I'd like you to meet Toni."

Toni was about twenty and stacked to the rooftops in a flashy orange dress.

"I owe you an apology, Danny," I said. "I was sure your story about another gal was a phony."

The big youth grinned. "Well, I didn't tell you the absolute truth. I knew you weren't Toni in the first place."

I scanned the surrounding populace. No Swanson. "Listen, Danny," I said quickly. "Did you go to my cabin after the card game?"

"Yeah, I was worried. It was raining bad, and I knew you weren't exactly dressed for the weather."

"How'd you know that?"

Danny said, "I found your bathing suit. It was caught in a fence outside our cabin. So I took it to your place."

"Did you try the door?"

"Sure. But I knocked first."

"Was it unlocked?"

"Yeah, it was," Danny said. "That surprised me, because you weren't there and I saw you lock it when we left for the *Phoenix*."

"You did see me lock it?"

"Of course. I even tried it after you turned the key. Don't you remember?"

I nodded dazedly. Blackness was drawing in again and I needed air. Without an explanation, I headed for the street. The night mist felt cool to my face. I walked up one street and down another. More than anything I wanted to come face to face with Robert Swanson, television's gift to humanity. I wanted to take that gift and give it back to the Indians, piece by piece.

I wound up at the police station and quickly phoned the Los Angeles Sheriff's office, homicide.

"We're socked in solid, Honey," Mark explained, after he got on the phone. "I've been trying to charter a plane for the past three hours, but everything's grounded. You might have mist, but we've got the works. Lightning, thunder, hail. It's like pea soup outside."

"You should crawl inside my head," I groaned. "Pea soup doesn't begin to describe the weather conditions. Somebody slugged me."

Mark swore. "I told you to stay out of trouble. What happened?"

I gave him the details and then said, "I suppose you know about Decker?"

"Know about him? Clements had me on the phone for forty-five minutes. Why do you think I've been trying to break every law of aerial navigation to get over there?"

"I thought you wanted to see me," I said miserably, trying to make light of the situation. "Now I know the truth. All you want is to gaze at Decker's body and take notes."

"Whose body do you want me to gaze at? If it's yours, I won't bring a note pad; I'll bring a deck of cards."

"Where'd you hear about that?"

"What difference does it make?" he said. "Next time I find out you've been playing strip poker, I'm going to slap you in the pokey so fast you'll think you came up with seven aces!"

"That does it!" I retaliated. "I'm going out and start the biggest strip-poker game in history. By the time you get here, you'll think Catalina is a nudist camp."

"Is that so?" Mark said, suddenly serious. "You're a sassy blonde with plenty of guts and body, but when it comes to the think department, you've got another thing coming."

'What do you mean?"

"You think Swanson hit you, right?"

"Right!"

There was a slight crackling pause. "Okay. If your Villa door was open after you locked it earlier, someone must have opened it with a key, right?"

"I—guess so," I stammered. "I never thought about it."

"Of course you never thought about it," Mark said. "Hot heads die young. You've got a brain that's saturated with gasoline."

"Who says so?"

"I do. Someone throws a match and you blow, every time."

I thought about that with my muddled tank of gasoline. Mark was so right. I had been hurt and gone haywire. Ignited was a better word. I'd blown when the chips were down.

"Okay," I said, "I've just installed some asbestos. Fire away!"

"Check with the manager of the Villa," Mark advised. "If your cabin wasn't broken into, then someone used a key. Maybe Swanson gave a song and dance about being your husband and the manager opened the door."

"Think you're smart, don't you?"

Mark said, "It's easy when you're born that way."

"Very funny," I said. "Well, make a joke out of this. I think I've found a connection between the Nelson case and the four murders over here."

"What's the connection?" the lieutenant barked.

"The metal case containing Rod Caine's lab equipment. I believe it was used to transfer heroin."

"Do you know for sure?"

"No. But I'm going to find out. You'd better break up the atmosphere as soon as you can and get over here before I win that bet of ours by default."

Mark told me to stay out of dark cabins, promised to tear holes in the sky and then hung up. I walked to the manager's office after reaching the Villa and rang the bell. A squat little man clutching a candle came to the door.

"Did you open up cabin thirty-six for someone this afternoon?" I asked.

He stared blankly at the candle, then shook his head. "What about the woman who rented the cabin to me this morning? Maybe she opened it."

"That's my wife," he said. "I'll ask her." He disappeared.

He returned shortly. "Yes, she opened up thirty-six. It was early this evening. About six-thirty or seven. The man said his name was West. Said he was your husband—that you misplaced your key."

"I haven't got a husband. What'd he look like?" The manager's face dropped a foot. "This is terrible. Was something taken? It was raining so hard and my wife probably thought…"

"What'd he look like?" I repeated.

He hurriedly disappeared inside again and returned with his wife, a dumpy blonde in a faded negligee.

"What are you trying to start anyway?" she bellowed. "You were with the man when I gave him the key."

I tried to unscramble that one.

She continued, "I don't give out no keys unless the renter is there, and you were there. Now what do you say to that?"

"What was I wearing?"

The dumpy one chewed for an instant on a fingernail. "A raincoat and hat, and—and an orange dress. I seen it under the coat."

"What'd the man look like?"

"Hard to say. He was wearing a trench coat and hat. I never got a good look at his face. He had a lot of pimples, that's all I saw."

"That's enough," I said. "Thanks."

I bent into the wind as I walked down the main street again. Rain drove in under my jacket, drenching my skin.

They were still sitting at the table in the Hi-Ho bar. I crossed over to them and plopped down beside blonde, busty Toni. She did resemble me in many respects. I studied Danny's pockmarked cheeks.

112

"Did you open my cabin door tonight?" I asked him carefully.

"Yeah, I told you," Danny said. "The door was already unlocked."

"Who unlocked it?"

"I dunno."

"The manager's wife down at the Villa says you unlocked it, Danny."

"She's crazy!"

"She said I was with you at the time."

"Well, now you know she's crazy for sure," Danny said.

I glanced at the other blonde. "Except it wasn't me she saw, was it, Danny? It was Toni."

"Does that make sense?"

"No, it doesn't," I said. "That's why I want to know why you did it."

Danny looked at Toni and swallowed hard. "The manager's wife is wrong." He got to his feet. "We better go, Toni."

I shoved the kid into his chair. "Now, listen, mister," I said, "Someone was waiting for me inside my cabin tonight when I got back. He didn't care about playing strip poker or diving for abalone, he just wanted to split my skull in half. And he would have done it if I hadn't dodged. Now, why'd you open that door, Danny?"

"I didn't!"

"You wanted that metal case back. You wanted to be absolutely certain you hadn't left any heroin caps inside, didn't you?"

Danny got to his feet. "You're crazy!"

I pushed him down again and reached for his right shirt sleeve. "Show me your arms, Danny!"

"No!" He pulled away.

I grasped Toni's left arm and straightened it out. In the slender white hollow was a blue vein, punctured with tiny, dark needle marks.

"Now what do you say, Danny?"

"That doesn't prove anything. Now leave us alone!"

"You were in my cabin, weren't you?"

"No!"

"You're a liar. Who's supplying you with junk? Swanson?"

"Na!"

"Who?"

"Nobody! I didn't open your door. I wasn't in your chain."

113

I kicked his chair and Danny went head-over-heels into another table. Chairs, people, food, glasses and candles went hurtling every which way. The Hi-Ho bar seemed to rise up in one stupendous wave and break for the front door. In the wild excitement two people vanished into the night rain—Danny Marble and blonde Toni.

I could have kicked myself I was so mad. Nothing was damaged in the Hi-Ho except my hopes for a quick solution to the cabin attack. Mark was absolutely right. My temper always got the better of me at the wrong time.

Outside, the street lights went on and the rain stopped. I returned to my cabin, made certain the metal case was gone, then climbed the long flight of steps to the chime tower.

The hillside area, above the dark, dimly lit city, seemed deserted until the crunch of footsteps rose behind me. I whirled. A big shape loomed up in the darkness. I caught the man in the glare of my flashlight. It was Rod Caine.

He wore a sleeveless shirt and on the lower part of his right arm was a long, deep scratch.

Chapter Fifteen

"Rod! What are you doing on this island?"

"Honey, am I glad to see you alive," he said, trying to put his arms around me.

I stepped back. "I told you stay aboard the *Hell's Light.* Why didn't you?"

He frowned at my cool reception. "I got a message."

"You were supposed to ignore any messages." I stared at the slash on his forearm.

Rood shook his head. "This one I couldn't ignore. It was from Bob Swanson, a note saying he was going to kill you."

"Where is it?"

He shrugged his big shoulders. "I don't know. I guess I lost it. It shook me up so much I just hopped a water taxi and came on into Avalon. Thank God you're all right."

"Who delivered the message?"

"It came by the same water taxi," he said, irritated by my questions. "What's the matter?"

"What time did you arrive in Avalon?"

"I don't know. Four-thirty. Five. What difference does it make?"

"It makes a big difference," I said. "Max Decker was murdered around that time."

"Yeah," Rod winced, "I heard about Max. Too bad."

"Who'd you hear it from?"

"Chief Clements. He told me you were staying in number thirty-six at the Villa. I went there. The door was open, but nobody was around, so I finally came up here."

"What time did you see Chief Clements?"

"About two hours ago," Rod said. "What is this, anyway? Am I a suspect again?"

"Where'd you get that scratch on your arm?" Rod looked at the long deep wound. "I got mixed up with a woman. Does that answer your question, Miss District Attorney?"

I took a firm hold on the butt of the flashlight. "I never thought you'd do anything like this."

"Like what?" Rod's nostrils flared angrily. "If you must know the truth, Lori scratched me with her fingernails. We got into an argument about you. She got mad and drew blood. Is that what you're talking about?"

"When did this happen?"

"About an hour before I received the message from Swanson. Lori wound up with a black eye, but I had to do it. She would have cut me to ribbons. What's this all about?"

"Is Lori still aboard *Hell's Light*?"

"As far as I know she is," Rod said. "I don't think she'd travel far with an eye like that."

"All right," I said, "let's go see her."

I started down the path toward town. Rod stopped me abruptly. "What difference does it make if Lori has a shiner? I didn't mean to hurt her. What's the matter with you?"

I studied him in the glare of the flashlight. "If Lori Aces doesn't have a black eye, or if she's gone, Rod, you're in trouble. Big trouble. Understand?"

"No, I don't. What the hell is this? I came into Avalon to help you; is this the thanks I get?"

"I don't know what kind of thanks you're looking for," I said, "but whatever it is, you'll get it. It'll see to that personally."

We walked down the long flight of steps. I checked with the water-taxi service. There was no record of a message being delivered to *Hell's Light*, but the log did show a boat had gone out to Aces' yacht around four o'clock. Chief Clements, several policemen and a half dozen Coast Guardsmen were on the pier. I asked the police officer whether Rod Caine had reported to the police station and the chief confirmed the incident.

"It was about an hour before you came back and phoned Lieutenant Storm in Los Angeles," Clements said.

116

I gave the police chief a description of Danny marble, his girlfriend Toni, and the three strip-poker players.

"If you find them, hold all five on suspicion of narcotics possession." I glanced at Rod and added, "They might lead us to the murderer."

On the water taxi out to Hell's Light, Rod was ominously quiet. I wanted to check one phase of his story—Lori Aces' black eye.

My mind kept searching for a connection between the murderer and Danny Marble. Had the metal case actually been found in the bay by the kid? This was a vital question. So was the whereabouts of the boys from the strip-poker game. The manager had said they'd checked out "in a hurry" around the time I'd left the card game. Their cabin, stripped to the bare furniture, revealed no evidence of narcotics.

Rod interrupted my thoughts. "I overheard your conversation with Chief Clements. What's Danny Marble got to do with all this?"

"You know him?" I asked.

"Sure. He's played a lot of tough-kid parts in TV films. I've seen him around Television Riviera. He pals around with a hype named Toni Scott."

"A voluptuous blonde with blue eyes?"

"Yeah, that's the one," Rod said. "They were great pals with Sam Aces. Sam gave Marble a couple of bits in the Swanson series. Toni likes to act to, when she isn't on the needle."

"How friendly are they with you?" I asked.

"We say 'hello', that's all. I dated Toni once, about a year ago. I headed for the nearest exit when she brought out her little kit and a handful of caps."

"Is Marble a user?" I demanded.

"I don't know. I don't think so. He's always been a heavy drinker. The two don't usually go together."

"Rod, did you have any hypodermic needle in your lab case?"

"Sure. Why? You don't think I take junk, do you? Here, look." He held out his arms. They were unmarked except for the scratch on his right forearm.

The gleaming white hull of *Hell's Light* became visible through the mist and spray. Carruthers was on the float to help steady the taxi as Rod and I climbed out. We thanked the old man and proceeded to the main deck.

Lori Aces was not in the swimming pool. We checked her cabin. We searched up forward, the stern, the lower deck, the engine room."

"She's somewhere," Rod said. "She's got to be, unless she left the ship."

"That's possible." I glanced over the railing. "How many feet to the bottom?"

He caught my arm. "Don't be funny. I don't like that kind of joke."

"I don't like the kind of joke someone played on me back in Avalon. It was a lead-pipe cinch to fold me into all kinds of laughter, but I dodged the punch line."

Rod gritted his teeth. "Honey, you burn me right to the ground. Make sense or quit beating your gums."

I twisted his forearm to reveal the long scratch. "Who gave you that?"

"Lori! How many times do I have to tell you?"

"You're lying!"

"I'm not lying!"

I held up my left hand and pointed to the index finger. The nail was torn off to the quick. "It's my hunch," I said, "this nail did the trick."

"You're crazy!"

"You were in cabin thirty-six in the Villa, weren't you?"

Rod swallowed. "Yes, but..."

"Somebody swung at me in the dark and I clawed him with my finger-nail. How do you explain the coincidence?"

"I—I don't know. But Lori can explain..."

"Did anyone see you and Lori tangle?" I demanded.

"No. We were in her cabin."

"Did you make any noise?"

"She screamed when I hit her." He opened the front of his shirt revealing deep scratches across his chest. "Do you want to credit yourself with these, too?"

I winced. It looked like the work of a wildcat. "I'm sorry, Rod. I wanted to believe you, but the coincidence was just too much for me."

He said, "Would you call this the luck of Swanson? Even when he doesn't try, the evidence still comes up with my name on it."

"What do you think has happened to Lori Aces," I asked. He started aft. "That's what I'd like to know. Maybe she went to my place. I'm sure she didn't see me leave on the water taxi."

We checked with the people in the bar. Nobody remembered seeing Lori since lunch. Rod got a pair of binoculars and peered through the mist at the shore.

"I think there's a light," he said, lowering the glasses. "But I can't be sure. It's pretty hazy out there."

"Let's go look," I said. "I'd still like to hear Lori's side of the story."

Rod shook his head. "I think you were born skeptical. Come on!"

We started for the float, then he stopped abruptly. "Have you got your .32 along for protection," he asked.

"Naturally," I said. "You don't think I'd trust you entirely, do you?"

"Or course not," Rod grumbled. "I just wanted to make sure."

Rod's cabin cruiser wasn't tied up at the float. I asked if Lori might have taken it.

"Nope. I ran the cruiser over to the cave when the blow started up this afternoon. I was afraid if the storm got as bad as it did a couple of days ago, she'd be knocked galley west."

"How'd you get back?"

"Carruthers followed me over in one of the putters." We climbed into a small boat and started toward shore.

I tried to unlock this case as we cut though the dark waters. Lori Aces had one of several keys. She could definitely eliminate Rod Caine form the cabin attack. But, more than that, she could explain the significance of her meeting with Max Decker in the Jolly Inn bar the same day Aces' blood-stained jacket was found at Little Harbor. I had a hunch Lori held the major key to the whole case. But whether she'd turn it for me was another matter.

Then there was Danny Marble. A clever kid. A very clever kid. He'd probably known all along who I was. He held a big key. Maybe the most important one. He was getting paid off to pull a few stunts and, obviously, the payoff man was the killer. Was it Swanson? There were only three logical suspects left. Golden Boy, Rod Caine and Lori Aces.

I glanced at Rod out of the corner of my eye. I know this was the work of a very clever dangerous maniac. This fact bothered me plenty. The finger of suspicion pointed all too clearly at Bob Swanson.

Rod veered the boat into the cave and we stepped out. His own cruiser was raised out of the water on its pulleys. As we walked up the path to the cabin, I had a raw feeling in the pit of my stomach. A kerosene lamp burned in the living room.

Rod opened the front door. "Lori? Lori, where are you?"

No answer. We looked through the house. In the bedroom we found a pile of feminine garments. A sweater, dark slacks, a small bra, panties and high heels. They belonged to Lori Aces.

Rod picked up the shoes. "I don't get it," he said, shaking his head. "She was wearing this stuff the last time I saw her."

I walked outside and checked the grounds. When I returned Rod was still studying the shoes. I lighted a cigarette and sat down.

"Let's conjure up a vision, pal," I said. "Where is she, taking a midnight swim in the nude?"

"I—I don't know," Rod stammered.

"I suppose you noticed there weren't any other boats down below. What do you make of that?"

Rod tossed the shoes on the bed and threw up his hands. "I tell you I don't know. Honey, believe me, I'm as much in the dark about this thing as you are."

"If you saw there were no other boats, why'd you call her name when you walked in?"

"There was a light," Rod said. "I did it instinctively."

"You do a lot of things instinctively, don't you?"

"No," he said angrily. "I don't kill instinctively, if that's what you mean!"

"How do you kill, Rod?"

"I don't!"

He stormed into the living room, poured a shot of whiskey and slugged it down non-stop.

"You want one?" he asked, holding up the bottle.

I shook my head.

Nervously, he poured again, spilling some on the floor. "What gives you the idea Lori's dead?" he asked.

"I didn't say I thought she was."

Rod gulped down another shot and wiped off his mouth with the back of his hand. "Cut the doubletalk," he said. "Maybe she is out for a swim.

Lori's always been cracked on swimming in the raw."

"So I understand. But where's the boat that brought her here?"

"Maybe she swam from *Hell's Light*?"

"She swam nearly a mile in high heels?"

Rod set the bottle down hard. "I told you, I don't know!"

"Well, I do. She couldn't have done it unless she carried the shoe in her teeth."

He threw himself in a chair and groaned. "All right. If the merry-go-round ring fits, I'll wear it. I guess we've been working up to this, haven't we?"

"I don't know," I said. "That's a question you'll have to answer."

"Okay," Rod said. "I'll answer it. Maybe I am a pigeon for Aces and Meeler and Decker. But what about Anny Claypool? I couldn't have done that one. We were together the whole time."

I pulled out the .32 and leveled it at him. "Were we, Rod? I thought about that while I was in Avalon. Remember, you heard someone running outside my cabin. You disappeared for a few minutes. Long enough to stop off for a short visit with little Ann. Long enough to…"

"No! Rod got to his feet. "For God's sake, Honey, what would I want to kill Ann Claypool for? Or Aces or Meeler or Decker? I didn't like Sam, true, but Meeler was my friend. And as for Max Decker or Ann Claypool, I had nothing against either of them. Maybe I disliked Sam Aces enough to want to kill him, but I didn't kill him! And the other three—sure, they had their bad points—but so do I."

"I'd like to believe you, Rod," I said softly. "But there are only two people now who can possibly clear you in this mess—Lori Aces and Bob Swanson."

Rod paced around the room nervously. Finally, he stopped and stared at me. "Look, Honey! Lori Aces may be mired up with Swanson in this business. If she is, I'm in trouble! Don't you understand? They could vanish. Head for South America and hole up for ten years if they wanted to. And where would that leave me?"

"In a gas chamber," I said.

"Yeah, that's right!" Rod retorted. "And don't think these clothes of Lori's and anything else Swanson wants to plant around the island, won't contribute to sending me there."

He picked up the whiskey bottle, juggled it an instant and then swung it hard in my direction. Glass and whiskey sprayed in all directions. So did the gun. Before I had a chance to pick up the right piece of merchandise, Rod had the revolver in his hand and was pointing it straight at my middle.

"I'm sorry to have to do this, Honey," he said, "but you leave me no choice."

I stood my ground, tight as a drum. "If you didn't kill anyone, you have nothing to worry about. Give me the gun."

"Not this trip, baby,' Rod said. "I'm the guy with the merry-go-round ring, remember? That entitles me to a free ride to the gas chamber. Only I'm not accepting the prize."

"You'd never die for something you didn't do!"

Rod smiled unhappily. "Sing that lullaby in church, Honey. You'll get a better collection."

"What do you plan to do?"

"Get out of here," Rod answered. "I can take a piece of that South America bit myself. I'm not proud. Maybe I'll run across two old friends of mine. If I do, I'll send you back their skulls—after I shrink them down to size." He started for the door.

"Running away won't help, Rod. That's what Swanson wants, don't you see? You'll never clear yourself this way. He could turn up in a week with lily white hands and an iron-clad alibi. And when the police caught you, you'd hang for sure. You can bet on that."

Rod said grimly, "Either way, I've had it." He reached the doorway. "Now take my advice. Don't come down that path for at least fifteen minutes. I like life and I don't plan to give it up for anyone, understand?"

I nodded half-heartedly, and he was gone. I considered several plans to stop him, but discarded them all. If Rod Caine were the murderer, he wouldn't hesitate to add me to the score.

If he weren't it didn't really matter if he escaped. I was certain he'd turn up sooner or later.

I examined Rod's portable typewriter, a brand new Royal with a blue chassis. I fed a piece of paper into it. The type was distinctive. I recognized it immediately. It had exactly the same characteristics as the type of the notes found in Rod Caine's and Max Decker's coat pockets.

I entered his bedroom again and checked the closets and bureau drawers. Then I looked under the bed.

A battered nude body stared sightlessly at me.

Chapter Sixteen

Sweet childlike Lori was a nightmare. She'd been viciously beaten to death and there were bruises all over her body.

I pulled her out from under the bed. There were several needle marks in the crook of her arm. I shook my head dismally. Apparently she had been a narcotic addict. Now there'd be no more fixes. No more caps or spoons or needles. Lori Aces had met with the same violent end that had taken five others, including Herb Nelson.

It made me sick inside just to look at her.

I walked down the hill to the cave. Rod had taken the small boat. I lowered his cabin cruiser into the swell, climbed into the pilot's seat, fired up the engines and steered her into the open sea.

After tying up the cruiser at the yacht's float, I went aboard *Hell's Light* and down to B Deck. The watertight door leading into the liquor-supply room was open. I walked inside and turned on the light. Above, in the swimming-pool bar, noise, clinking glasses and confusion reigned as usual.

Several cases of liquor were dumped on their sides and heel marks indicated that they had been split open from repeated blows of a heavy shoe or boot. Bottles of scotch rolled loosely on the floor of the storeroom.

I searched through the cardboard debris. Then I found what I was looking for. A small heroin cap. In a still unopened case there were a dozen more caps and two hypodermic kits. Nearby, a handkerchief was caught under one of the broken cases. The piece of silk bore the initials L.A.

Mark Storm arrived aboard Hell's Light about an hour after I discovered the heroin cache. He was accompanied by Chief Clement, two Avalon policemen, a Coast Guard commander and three other officers. They escorted a very tired, dusty, ominously silent prisoner in handcuffs. Rod Caine.

I took Mark aside, showed him the heroin caps and told him about Lori Aces. The big lieutenant rolled with the punch, grimly wiped a hand across his eyes and swore.

"Honey," Mark said, "this guy's a maniac. It's a wonder he didn't get you in the bargain."

"Where'd you find him?" I asked.

"A couple of Clements' men caught him on the hillside near the old Wrigley home."

"What was he doing there, Mark?"

"Burying a metal case full of lab equipment."

They took Rod into the yacht's dining room for questioning. Two other men form the L.A. Sheriff's office joined the group as Mark began the interrogation. Rod said he had gone into Avalon to search for Swanson.

"Why?" Mark asked.

"Swanson's been trying to swing me for these murders. I had to find him to clear myself."

"Did you find him?" Clements demanded.

"No."

"What were you doing up near the Wrigley home?" Rod glowered angrily. "Looking for my stolen gear." Clements said, "When you were apprehended by two of my officers, they claim you were trying to bury a metal case containing some instruments."

"That's crazy!" Rod said. "I got a tip from one of Danny Marble's pals that a case with my initials was buried up on the hillside. He drew a map for me and I went to get it."

"Where's the map?" Mark demanded.

Rod shook his head. "I don't know. I guess in the excitement of the arrest, I lost it."

Mark bent toward the handcuffed man. "You have a great faculty for losing important evidence, haven't you, Mr. Caine?"

"No! Anyway, what's so important about a map? I told you the truth. I was digging up the case, not burying it."

"Why?"

"It substantiated part of my original story," Rod said. "I used the equipment to analyze the liquid in Sam Aces' glass. The case and contents were stolen. I wanted to get them back to prove I wasn't lying."

"How did you get to Avalon?" Clements asked. "In a putter. I went as far as the old seaplane airport and then swam ashore. I suppose you found the boat?"

"Yeah, we did," Mark said carefully. "When's the last time you saw Bob Swanson?"

Rod wiped a nervous hand across his face. "Let's see. Thursday morning. The day he disappeared. Two days ago."

"You're sure of this?"

"Absolutely. I wouldn't have been looking for him last night if I'd seen him since then."

Mark lit a cigarette and regarded Rod carefully. "When's the last time you saw Lori Aces?"

Rod pursed his lips. "Yesterday afternoon. We had a fight. I walked out and haven't seen her since."

"You're certain?"

"Of course I am. Did you ever find her?"

"Yes, we did," Mark said quietly. "Or rather Miss West found her."

"Where?"

"Where you left her," Mark continued casually.

"You mean in her stateroom," Rod said.

"No. Under the bed in your island cabin."

Rod shot to his feet, "Are you crazy? She's not—dead?"

"I think you can answer that one."

"No!" Rod exclaimed, shaking his head. "No, no, no! Lori can't be dead! She shouldn't be dead."

Mark said, "You're right this time. You just kicked a little too hard."

Rod slumped back in his chair. "You—you got this all wrong. I hit her, yes, but I never kicked her. I never struck her more than once, believe me.

"Where was the argument?"

"Lori's stateroom."

"What time?"

"Around two o'clock."

"Want me to tell you exactly how it happened?" Mark said quickly.

126

"You and she were in this together. You were afraid Lori would crack pretty soon, weren't you, Caine? You knew she had a monkey on her back and couldn't be trusted, so you took her to your cabin on the island and beat her up."

"No!"

"You knocked her down and kicked her to death."

Rod lashed, "You're crazy!"

"Then you stuffed her under the bed until you decided how to dispose of the body."

"No! For God's sake!"

"We found blood stains on a shirt and a pair of pants that belong to you."

"That was from me," Rod said. "She ripped me to pieces. But Lori didn't bleed. Don't you understand? Swanson did this. He's trying to frame me.

"That alibi won't work anymore," Mark said tightly.

"What do you mean?"

"We've found him."

Rod's eyes blazed. "Where is he? That dirty, rotten bastard. I'll kill him!"

Mark looked at Chief Clements and shook his head unhappily. Then he grabbed Caine angrily by the shoulders, lifting him out of his chair. "You're a card, aren't you, Caine? Why don't you spit it out? We found Bob Swanson about a half-hour before you were apprehended. He was lying on the rocks below the chimes tower. He has a bullet smack between his eyes and he's dead! He's about as dead as you are, brother, believe me!"

Rod Caine folded up like a collapsible toy.

I nearly fainted. Mark hadn't said one word to me about finding Swanson's body.

"I've had it," Rod groaned miserably. "Really had it!"

"You should have pushed harder," Mark said. "If he'd hit the water, it's possible he'd never of been found. Your story always was pretty thin, but with Swanson missing indefinitely it might have held up."

Rod glanced at me, his mouth twisted horribly. "Why'd you do it, Caine?" Mark asked. "Mass murder is serious business."

The handcuffed writer was silent for a long moment, his breathing punctuating the air like a rapid-fire shotgun. Then he broke, "I didn't do it!"

Mark cocked his hat back on his head. "You said you were being framed. That Swanson was framing you. Swanson was shot hours before Lori Aces was murdered. Now, how did he frame that one?"

"I don't know! I don't know how anything could have happened!"

"You don't expect us to believe that!"

"I don't know what I expect you to believe, but I didn't do it!"

Mark demanded, "You did have reason to kill Sam Aces, didn't you?"

"Not exactly, no!"

"He disfigured your face, didn't he?"

Rod leaned forward in his chair, cupping his face in his hands. "A little," he whispered. "But I didn't want to kill him for it."

"Joe Meeler took your job on the Swanson show," Mark continued to hammer, "isn't that right?"

"Yes, but I was glad Joe got the job," Rod said. "He was my friend."

Mark paced around the room for a moment, then he said, "You hated Ann Claypool, didn't you?"

"No!"

Vince Claypool was your friend in college, wasn't he? You told him to stay away from Ann, but he refused. He married her while you two were in business together. She destroyed that business, didn't she?"

Rod was on the ropes and reeling. He swayed back in his chair. "Yes—yes, in a way she did, but she wasn't the only reason we folded. Vince drank a lot. He kept digging into the till…"

"He drank because of Ann, didn't he?" Mark argued hotly.

"I guess so…"

"You hated her for that!"

"Yes—No! I didn't really hate her—I…"

Mark continued, "You knew what kind of man Max Decker was, didn't you?"

"What do you mean?"

"Ruthless, hard, scheming," Mark drilled. "You said right here, aboard this ship, that Decker would go to almost any lengths to crush someone, didn't you?"

"I've said that a lot of times."

"Did he ever try to crush you?"

Rod twisted miserably in his chair. "He's tried to ruin a dozen people."

"Did he ever try to ruin you?"

"Yes!" Rod exclaimed. "But that's all part of this rotten game. That's why I got out of it. It's cut-throat! They'll shrink your head down to a walnut and crack it if they get half the chance!"

Mark surveyed the group. Clements shook his head as if to say, this guy's as loco as they come! The chief asked Rod, "Where's the .38 you used on Decker and Swanson?"

"Did you throw that in the ocean along with Swanson?"

"No!"

Clements produced a .32 and handed it to me. "This is your revolver, isn't it, Miss West?"

I nodded.

"Caine was carrying it when my men tagged him on the hillside," Clements continued. He studied Rod's haggard face. "Did you use this weapon on Sam Aces?"

Rod tried to rise out of his chair. "I never fired that weapon in my life!" He slumped back and looked at me. "Believe me, Honey, I only took the gun because I knew you'd use it to bring me in."

Mark got to his feet again. "You faked that message to Decker from Swanson, didn't you?"

"I don't know what message you're talking about," Rod said.

"The one where Swanson said he'd meet Decker in the chimes tower yesterday at four-thirty."

"I didn't send any such message," Rod argued. "I got one myself signed by Swanson. That's why I went into Avalon. Swanson said he was going to kill Honey."

Mark leaned over Rod. "Where is this message?"

"I—I don't know."

Mark studied the group for an instant, then turned his eyes on Rod again. "Miss West says you met her up at the chimes tower last night, is that correct?"

"Yes," Rod said. "I was worried about her. I heard about Decker, went

129

to her cabin… and when I found she was gone I went up to the tower."

"Or was it this way?" Mark hurled. "After murdering Decker and Swanson, you went to Honey's cabin to look for your case which, before it was stolen, had contained heroin caps for your confederate, Lori Aces. Honey walked in. You hit her with the butt of your gun and ran. But she managed to scrape your arm with her fingernail; isn't that nearer to the truth?"

"No! I told you Lori did this to my arm. If you want further proof, look at this!"

Rod opened his shirt to reveal the long, hideous marks on his chest.

"You know what I think?" Mark said. "I think you did that yourself."

"Are you crazy? Why would I?"

"Because you knew Honey would remember inflicting the wound on your arm. You remembered your argument with Lori, so you hauled off with your own fingernails and raked yourself."

"Run a test on Lori's fingernails then!" Rod said hotly. "You'll find bits of me under every one of them."

Mark grinned. "Maybe we will, Caine, but hat won't prove a thing. Naturally, if you beat the hell out of her she was bound to get you a couple of times."

Rod slumped over in his seat and ran the cool hardness of the handcuffs over his forehead. "Like I said," he moaned dismally, "I've had it! You've really got me."

"You can say that again!" Mark taunted. "You shot and killed Swanson because you hated his guts for not reinstating you with the show."

"He signed me to a contract," Rod argued. "He wanted me back on the show. The contract must be filed somewhere in his office at Television Riviera."

Mark shook his head. "No such luck, boy. We went over his office with a fine-tooth comb. There's no contract with your signature on it anywhere."

"I—I don't get this," Rod stammered. "It all falls into place, I know, but I didn't do it. Someone's clever…"

"You, Caine," Mark interrupted. "You were the clever one. Up to a point. You made it look like Swanson. You were framing him and saying all along that he was framing you. But you made two major mistakes. Pushing Swanson's dead body off the cliff at low tide was one of them. And the other—you fought too hard with Ann Claypool when you drowned her in the bathtub."

"I didn't drown her!"

Mark glanced at me. "The coroner's official verdict was death by drowning, not strangulation." Then he crossed to Clements. "Chief, could I have those blowups now, please."

Clements removed two photographs from a briefcase and handed them to Mark. The lieutenant showed them around the room, finally ending with Rod Caine.

"These are enlargements of the thumbprints taken from the neck of Ann Claypool," Mark said. "They match the prints we took from you exactly. Now what do you say, Mr. Caine?"

"Okay," Rod murmured, head hung low, unable to look up at the undeniable evidence of the enlarged thumbprints. "I'll tell you the truth."

"It's about time," Mark said, surveying the group. He smiled triumphantly at my stunned expression.

"You're right," Rod continued. "Those are my prints, but I didn't murder Ann Claypool. I—I was in Honey's cabin. We were talking about Joe Meeler when we heard a sound outside."

"What kind of sound?" Mark growled.

"Somebody running on deck," Rod explained. "It came like a volley of shots. Honey will back me up on this. I went out to see who it was. The sounds lead me to Ann's cabin. The door was open a little, so I went in. It had been Ann all right. She was wet and out of breath. I asked her what was going on. She was drunk. She shouted at me to mind my own business. I told her it was my business. She'd tricked me earlier into going to my island cabin on the ruse that Bob Swanson was there waiting to talk to me. I demanded the truth, but she ordered me out. I guess I got excited. She tried to push me out the door and I grabbed her by the throat. Believe me, I didn't strangle her. She tried to scream and I threw her over the bed and walked out. The next time I saw her she was in the bathtub—dead."

Mark said, "I'm surprised, Caine. Being a writer I thought you'd come up with a better story than that."

"It's the truth, believe me," Rod pleaded.

"I don't buy it," Mark said. "And I don't think anyone else here does either." He stared into Rod's sullen eyes. "You're the last man standing, Caine. You eliminated every possible suspect except yourself. Maybe you even got Herb Nelson. If you did, that makes seven. And if you could have nailed Honey it would have been eight. A nice round number in any man's luggage. Especially in the tongue of a psychopathic killer."

The lieutenant gestured at one of the men from the sheriff's office. Together they lifted Rob Caine out of his chair and started him toward the door.

I went after them, whispering, "Mark, you got the wrong man. I'm sure you have."

"Are you kidding?" he said, "Don't you believe in evidence?"

"Sure, but…"

"You're just sore because you lost your bet."

We reached the end of the dining room. Mark opened the door.

Outside on the deck, his face illuminated by starboard rail lights, stood Sam Aces.

Chapter Seventeen

Sam held his left hand behind his back. There was blood on his white shirt and he weaved as he stumbled toward the door, a pained expression around his mouth.

I rushed to him, slipping his arm around my shoulders.

"I'm hurt, Honey," he whispered. "I didn't think I'd make it."

While I helped Sam into the dining room, Mark had one of the deputies remove Rod Caine to another part of the ship.

For an instant, Rod and Sam surveyed each other in the doorway, then Chief Clements helped me ease Sam Aces into a chair. He cried out from the pain, staggered to his feet, pushed several helping hands away and crumpled to the floor. In the middle of his back was a bullet hole.

"Get a doctor, quick!" I yelled at Chief Clements.

Mark rolled Sam over and said, "Who did it, Aces?"

"I—it must have been Caine," the lanky producer whispered. "I didn't see him. He got me through the window from behind. I fell and didn't move for a long time. I guess he thought I was dead."

I wiped a trickle of blood out of the corner of his mouth with my handkerchief. "Where did it happen, Sam?"

"In a little house we rented near the chimes tower."

"What do you mean we, Sam?"

"Swanson and I. We—we were trying to outsmart Caine. But I guess he was much smarter than we figured." Aces choked, gasped desperately for breath.

Mark leaned over the wounded man. "Aces, we've sent for a doctor..."

"It—it's too late for that," Sam whispered. "I got to tell you something. I—I came all this way because—because you got to know the—truth."

"All right, Aces, tell us as much as you can." Sam closed his eyes for an

133

instant and said, "I—I've been handling narcotics. The yacht's loaded with heroin. Caps are packed in liquor cases down in the storeroom."

"Why, Sam?" I asked. "You didn't need the money. You don't take the stuff. Why'd you fool with it?"

The producer shook his head and groaned. "It was Lori. She was an addict when I married her. I didn't know. When I caught her taking junk she threatened to leave me if I didn't help her get the stuff. I—I couldn't let her go. I love Lori. I love her more than anything else in the world."

I glanced at Mark. It was obvious Sam Aces didn't know his wife was dead.

"To save my marriage," he continued, "I got involved. It wasn't much at first. Then the big operators backed me against the wall. They—they threatened to ruin me if I didn't cooperate. They turned *Hell's Light* into a floating warehouse and forced me to supply the pushers."

"Herb Nelson was one of your clients, wasn't he?" Mark said.

"Yes."

"Do you know who murdered him?"

"No."

"Why did you hire me, Sam?" I asked.

Aces peered up at me, his eyes glazed with pain. "Because—because I couldn't go to the police. They might have traced down my narcotics connections. But I had to know who was trying to poison me."

"You were searching for something that day in my office, weren't you, Sam?"

"Yes."

"Was it Herb Nelson's file?"

"Yes. I was afraid you had some information about his being a pusher that might lead to me."

"Do you know who stole my gun?" I asked.

Aces tried to smile. "I took it, Honey."

"Why?"

"I—I got scared. I wanted you to quit the case. You were much too smart. But—I knew you'd only be more suspicious if I fired you. So, I took your gun out of your bag."

"And you took two shots at me."

Aces winced. "Yes. I only meant to frighten you, but you moved at the wrong moment. I—I was very sorry about that."

Mark said, "Did you really believe Swanson was trying to poison you?"

"Yes."

"You said you and Swanson rented a cabin together in Avalon. When did you change your mind about him?"

"The night I disappeared."

"What happened that night?"

"I—I faked the poisoning," Aces said, struggling for his words. "I wanted to confuse Swanson, bring him into the open. Let him trap himself. But, I was wrong. B.S. wasn't the guy who was after me. I realized that after somebody cracked him on the skull and hung him from the ceiling in Honey's cabin."

I wiped another trickle of blood for Aces' mouth. "You hid in that trunk up on the bow, didn't you, Sam?"

"Yes," Aces whispered. "Then later I moved down below to a place you never would have found. There's a false bulkhead on the stern end of the engine room."

"You were bleeding," Mark said. "We found blood stains in the bow trunk. What happened?"

Aces tried to smile again. "I saw red when B.S. came into the bar and started swinging at Rod Caine. You remember, Honey. I hit him pretty hard with my fist." He held up his right hand. His knuckles were lacerated. "Lucky it was raining," he added, staring at me, "or you could have followed my trail straight to that trunk."

"Then what?"

The wounded producer lifted up slightly, groaning from new pain. Finally, he said, "We—decided Rod Caine was our man."

"Who's we? You and Swanson?"

"No."

"Who?"

"I—I can't tell you," Aces said slowly. "I met with B.S. during the night—down in the secret room. I told him Caine was out to get us both. He was skeptical, but agreed to help me find out. The next morning we went to Caine's island cabin. We planted a note in his coat pocket and then took my jacket to Little Harbor."

"You smeared it with blood, put a bullet hole through the front and dumped the jacket on the beach," I said.

"Yes. We wanted to cast suspicion on Caine so the police would take him into custody after finding the note and the jacket."

I added, "Then Bob Swanson actually did order Ann Claypool to send Caine to his island cabin for a meeting?"

Aces nodded.

"This is supposed to attract us into following Caine and searching for his cabin."

"Yes."

"And Swanson's disappearance on the beach at White's Landing was another ruse.

"Yes. He met me at a secret cove and we went into Avalon to the house near the chimes tower."

"Who made the arrangements for the rental?" Mark asked.

"Danny Marble."

"Does he work for you?"

Aces said, "He's a pusher. He handles the young island crowd during the summer. I supply him—that's all."

"Sam," I said quietly, "did you ask Danny Marble to do you a favor?"

"Yes."

"What was it?"

"I—I gave him some heroin caps to plant in Caine's lab case. Something went wrong. I never found out what."

I glanced at Mark Storm, then said, "I'll tell you what I think went wrong, Sam. We almost caught Danny in Caine's cabin. He must have grabbed the case and ran to Rod's boat cave. He was going to escape in our boat, but we came down the hill too soon. Then he tossed the case into the water and hid."

"So, Danny Marble was our stowaway," Mark said, shaking his head.

"That's my guess," I continued. "He took the *Clementine* back to *Hell's Light*, tied her up and then swam to shore where he retrieved the metal case containing the heroin caps."

"Why did you want H planted in Caine's lab case?" Mark asked.

"To make him break when the police questioned him." I asked, "Who planted my gun in your bathroom window?"

"I—I don't know," Aces whispered. "Caine, I guess. I thought it was

Swanson until we got together. Caine must have had an ally on board the yacht."

"Sam, did you plant the arsenic in Decker's luggage?"

"I—don't know what you're talking about?"

"Did you and Swanson send Decker a note asking him to meet Swanson yesterday at four-thirty at the chimes tower?"

"No. You can ask Decker if you don't believe me."

"Decker's dead, Sam."

Sam Aces tried to get up, choked several times and then fell back, gasping for air, blood streaming from his mouth again. "It—it—isn't-possible," he whispered.

"He was shot and hanged in the chimes tower."

"Where's Swanson?" Aces looked around weakly.

"Dead."

"Ann Claypool?"

"Dead."

"And Joe Meeler?"

"Stabbed."

"Lori? No, not Lori, too!"

"Sam, she's…"

Tears welled up in Sam Aces' eyes and ran down the side of his face. He trembled violently. "I—I should have known," he said, trying to catch his breath. "I—should have known all the time, but I was too stupid to realize…"

The producer rolled over on his stomach, his hand searching for the wound that was draining life out of him.

Mark got up, gestured to Chief Clements. "Have Caine brought in here immediately."

Clements went into the swimming-pool bar and brought Rod Caine back into the dining room. He was assisted by a deputy sheriff and the seaman, Carruthers.

Sam Aces was so near death that he couldn't move. His head lay twisted sideways on the floor and a stream of red ran across the planking. He stared at me as I kneeled down and lifted his head into my lap. He seemed awesomely pathetic, like a dog crumpled on the highway, trying to make me understand what he felt, but unable to say it except with his eyes.

Mark bent over the dying producer, "Aces," he said softly, "will you point out the man who shot you in the back?"

For a long moment, Sam didn't move. His eyes remained riveted on mine as if he were trying to convey some vitally important message. Then, very slowly, he looked across the room.

Rod Caine took a step toward Aces, but was held back by the three men around him. "Tell them the truth, Sam," the writer pleaded. "Tell them I didn't do it! Tell them!"

Then, with the last ounce of strength in his body, Sam Aces lifted his arm and pointed across the room to where Rod Caine stood with his three guards.

"You were my friend," he whispered. "I—I should have known." His arm dropped to the floor and he was dead.

I watched them carry Sam Aces' body down to a Coast Guard launch. The blood-stained boat Sam had used to travel from Avalon was also tied to the float.

Mark patted me on the shoulder as he prepared to board the launch with Rod Caine. "I'll see you on the mainland tomorrow," he said. "Come on, smile. You look like you've just lost your last friend."

I glanced at Rod. "Maybe I have. Mark, what did Aces' mean when he said, 'I should have known? Known what?"

"That Caine was the murderer."

"But," I argued, "he'd already said he thought Rod had been the one who shot him through the window."

"That's right," Mark agreed. "But he was stunned when we told him about the others—especially his wife."

The other police officials and Coast Guard officers climbed aboard the launch. Dawn was beginning to light the morning sea and a breeze scattered salt spray across my cheeks.

"Look, Mark," I insisted, 'Aces said, 'you were my friend.' Rod Caine wasn't his friend. He hadn't been his friend for a long time."

Mark pulled his hat firmly on his head. "Honey, you're just sniping in the dark. The thumbprints check. Aces pointed out the man he thought was the murderer. So there it is. Sure, a few loose ends here and there, but we'll leave those to the prosecution to nail down. See you tomorrow."

The Coast Guard launch slid away from the float, gained momentum and disintegrated in the shadow of the island. I walked back up the steps. Music still drifted from the swimming-pool bar where a few diehards were still drinking Sam Aces' whiskey. On deck, at the head of the stairs, was Carruthers. He smiled in a drunken, half-lidded manner, and moved toward the bow. I called to him.

"Yes, ma'am?" He tipped his hat and grinned broadly.

"Who has charge of all the small boats attached to Hell's Light?"

"I do, ma'am."

"Have you noticed any of them missing during the past few days?"

"No ma'am."

"You're sure?"

Carruthers nodded. His grin seemed like an idiot's grin, fixed and cemented on his old face. "Is that all, ma'am?"

"No," I said. "How long have you worked on this yacht?"

"Long time. Years, ma'am. Why, I was just thinking, there ain't been so much excitement aboard *Hell's Light* since old man Aces fell off the bridge and broke his neck." He laughed raucously. It seemed like a poor thing to laugh about. His eyes rolled weirdly, seeming to whirl like pinwheels on the Fourth-of-July.

Suddenly, I stepped back, for the first time really listening to his voice, really hearing his laughter. They didn't seem to belong to the body.

He took a .38 revolver out of his pocket and leveled it at my heart. His hand trembled, but he still laughed. He seemed like some awful mirth machine at the Pike in Long Beach that got stuck and wouldn't stop until somebody smashed the mechanism.

"You're too smart, Honey," the laughing voice said over and over. "I always knew you were."

I shook my head, trying to shut out the sight, the sound, the laughter. "It—it couldn't be possible," I said.

"Ever hear of the wrong man," the voice laughed inside of Carruthers. "Well, I'm the wrong man and you're the wrong woman and this is the wrong world! Funny, Honey? You kill me! Really fracture me! Your expression."

"Then you're the one Aces really was pointing at."

"Yes, yes, yes," the laughing voice continued. "I thought he was dead.

139

I was down taking a fix and when I came up they were having a little trouble with Caine so I volunteered my services. Then, when we got inside and I saw Sad Sam..." The laughter choked him, choked him double, choked him until he couldn't stand, choked him until he was lying face-down on the deck.

I kicked the revolver out of his hand, grasped him by the shoulders and rolled him over. He wasn't breathing. The idiot's smile was still cemented on his face. I reached inside my skirt pocket and produced a handkerchief. The cloth lifted a coat of makeup form the man's face. Underneath was a deep scratch on his right cheek. Underneath another layer was Herb Nelson.

Chapter Eighteen

It was daylight before the coroner, Mark Storm and Chief Clements came out of the stateroom where the man who had died laughing lay, the idiot's smile still frozen on his lips.

Mark seemed brutally dazed as if he couldn't believe what his eyes had found under Carruther's makeup. He stared at me for a long time and then shook his head.

"It's Herb Nelson, all right," Mark said. "Narcotics killed him. Stopped his heart like a clock." He tried to steady himself against the yacht's railing. "Honey, I just don't get it. Call me stupid. Call me anything. But—we were so certain that the corpse we found at Herb Nelson's place was…"

"Were we, Mark?" I felt sick at the pit of my stomach. "We weren't so much certain as we were stunned. We found a man Herb's size, weight and age, with his head and face bashed in, carrying Herb's wallet and wearing Herb's rings, and we were shocked to think it was guy we'd idolized when we were kids. A guy who'd been a prince, a champion…" I covered my face with my hands. My God, I can still hear him laughing!"

Mark put his arm around my shoulders. "I'm sorry, Honey."

I wiped my eyes and glanced up at the big lieutenant. "You said a skid-row bum named Ed Walker was seen entering Herb's place about an hour before the murder. You said he'd vanished. How do we know he's not our mangled body in the morgue?"

"Yeah," Mark said. "I thought of that, too. From what I can remember, his build and characteristics were similar to Nelson's"

"You said he was a user. He could have been on the prowl for H, found Herb gone and torn the place apart looking for junk. Instead, he came across Herb's identification, his wallet and two of his rings. He even discovered an old coat of Herb's with initials embroidered on the pocket and he put it on. As he was leaving with the loot, Nelson appeared. Herb had probably been down the hall in the bathroom getting ready for bed and in a narcotic frenzy he grabbed his Oscar and started swinging. End of story."

"Oh, no," the lieutenant groaned. "Beginning of story."

"That's not the beginning, Mark. The beginning was…" I shrugged my shoulders. "Who knows—probably when Herb Nelson took his first pop. A big star trying out a new thrill and it sank him right to the bottom. And when he got to the very last rung, one guy tried to give him a hand—Sam Aces.

"Are you kidding?" Mark said, arching his thick brows. "Aces was the good Samaritan who supplied Nelson with junk."

"Sure," I defended. "Sam even supplied his own wife, but he didn't want to. He admitted he was trapped—caught—probably even worse than one of his hypes."

"How did he help Nelson?"

"The only way he knew how. He tried to get him bit parts in TV shows. Then came that disastrous day when Swanson threw Herb off the set at Television Riviera. Herb's pride was deeply hurt. His drug-twisted mind craved revenge."

"So, what'd he do?"

"Rod told me that last he'd heard about Nelson was that he was working as a bartender's assistant at the Golden Slipper. I have a hunch Sam got him that job. I have another hunch that one night Swanson and Decker were sitting together at the bar drinking heavily when Golden Boy ordered a screwdriver. The bartender mixed the drink and while it was waiting to be served, Herb slipped in some arsenic. I'm sure he didn't know that drink had been ordered for his friend, Sam Aces."

"Nelson poisoned Aces' drink intending it for Swanson?"

"That's how I figure it," I said. "He never admitted the truth to Sam because the mistake provided a brand new idea. Since Aces thought Swanson was out to get him, Herb decided to make it appear as if Golden Boy were threatening his life, too. Then he picked me out of the phone book, planted a few seeds of suspicion about Swanson and—you know the rest."

"But I don't know the rest," Mark said. "All I knew is Nelson must have killed Walker like you said. Sure it was a mistake on our part. The body was so badly battered we couldn't go on facial features. He had no living relatives, no birth certificate. He'd never driven a car, never registered his fingerprints with the Department of Motor Vehicles. He'd never been in the service or belonged to any special clubs or secret orders. I don't think he'd ever been fingerprinted in his life."

"Sure," I agreed, "we thought the corpse was Herb Nelson. But he didn't know we thought this until the next morning when he saw the headlines. So, after the murder, he went to his friend, Sam Aces, and pleaded for help and Sam hid Herb aboard *Hell's Light*."

"And then Seaman Carruthers was created when they realized a mistake had been made."

"Right. Being an old-time actor, Herb knew plenty about make-up and he developed a most convincing character. When the Catalina voyage began, he probably told Sam he'd keep a watchful eye on Swanson. From there he embarked on a warped, neurotic plan—to murder Sam Aces and have Swanson swing for the crime."

"But, Honey, that doesn't make sense. Sam was his friend."

"Mark, we're talking about a man who'd hit the very bottom—narcotics, murder. The needle was his only friend."

"All right, where'd he go from there?"

"He stole my gun out of Sam's stateroom and was planning to shoot Aces through the bathroom window, but somebody caught him off-guard."

"Who?"

"My guess is Ann Claypool. Herb was probably in the corridor checking the angle of the shot when she came along. He left the gun in the window and ran thinking she'd seen everything. But it's my hunch Ann wasn't in the least suspicious."

"You think he killed her because he was afraid she'd seen him with the gun?"

"Yes."

"But, Honey, how do you explain Caine's thumbprints on her neck?"

"Sam Aces verified the fact that Ann Claypool told Rod to meet Swanson at his island cabin. I believe Rod's story. But it was probably Nelson we heard running outside on deck that night. Rod went to Ann's cabin. Meanwhile, Herb came back to my window. I caught him, so he pretended to be bringing me the breakaway knife he'd used earlier on Meeler."

"But, why the devil did he murder Joe Meeler?"

143

"Because Meeler must have been on deck when Danny Marble arrived with the *Clementine*. Nelson saw what Meeler saw—Danny tying up the cruiser and swimming away. He knew, also, that if the police tracked down Marble they'd find Aces. And he couldn't trust that the trail wouldn't lead to him. Somehow he got Meeler into the bar. He'd probably planned to show Joe that breakaway and then, when nobody was looking, give him the real thing he'd taken from the kitchen. But we made it easy for him."

"What do you mean?" Mark demanded.

"Remember, we arrived back here with Chief Clements and everyone came out on deck? That's when Herb plunged the real knife into Meeler. Then he wiped off his own prints, put Joe's hands on the weapon and escaped through a trapdoor behind the bar."

Mark wiped his big hands across his eyes. "Okay, I'll buy it. What about Claypool?"

"After he left my cabin he went back to Ann's door. He probably heard the windup of the fight between her and Rod and sensed the opportunity. He waited until she'd undressed and climbed into her bath. Then, he slipped in, struggled with her and finally pushed her under the water."

"That explains the coroner's verdict," Mark said. "Where do we go from there?"

"It's pretty obvious Nelson planted the arsenic in Decker's suitcase. Why he did it we'll probably never know. Evidently he was the one who picked up Decker's luggage that morning and carried it down to the float. When you discovered the poison he must have been afraid Max, under severe questioning, might recall who had the best opportunity to make the plant. So, after Max's disappearance, Herb found out where he was and sent that phony note about Swanson wanting to see him at the chimes tower at four."

"So, he maneuvered Swanson to the tower using the same excuse and left Aces alone at the house."

"Right. He also sent a note to Rod Caine claiming my life was in danger, hoping to lure him into Avalon."

"Smart," Mark said, rapping his knuckles on the rail. "But, look, this is four o'clock in the afternoon. How could he hope to pull this thing off in broad daylight?"

"The storm, Lieutenant, remember? It was raining so hard you could hardly see your hand in front of your face."

"Okay," Mark said. "He hung Decker, then took Swanson to the edge of the cliff and shot him. Then what?"

"He returned to the house where he'd left Aces and put a bullet in Sam's back."

"Then it's true," Mark murmured. "Aces never really knew who shot him."

I said, "He didn't know what had happened until we told him Decker and Swanson were dead and he saw Herb come into the room. Then he realized the truth, but it was too late."

"What do you figure he did after he left Aces in the house in Avalon?"

"He must have been badly in need of a fix. He went to the Villa looking for Danny Marble, saw Danny and his girlfriend coming out of my cabin and figured he'd find some caps inside.

"And while he was rummaging around," Mark continued, "you came back and he clipped you with the butt of his gun."

"That's the way I see it. From there he headed for Hell's Light where he guessed Sam had a big supply of heroin stashed away. He finally tried the storeroom, tore into several cases and found some caps."

"I'm with you now," Mark said. "Then Lori, also needing a pop, came wandering on the scene."

"Right. I don't know how he managed it, but he got her into a boat and over to Caine's island cabin where they apparently had a small blasting party which wound up with Lori dead."

Mark took out a pack of cigarettes and offered me one. "It all adds up, Honey," he said, staring blankly at the distant island."

"Does it, Mark? Does it add up?" I leaned over the railing and watched the sea push up against the polished white hull of the yacht. "Eight people are dead and for what?"

"Don't ask me," Mark said faintly. "I told you this was a rotten business. It squeezes your guts right down to nothing."

"Yeah," I said, taking a deep breath.

I walked toward the bow. The wind was cool. It whistled strangely in my ears. It sounded like laughter. Wild, unreasoning laughter that wouldn't stop.

I began to run.

Suddenly I remembered that laughter. It was the laughter of a little girl with blonde curls sitting in a dark motion-picture theater. The laughter of a little girl for a great comedian, for a man who'd always made people happy, a man everyone had loved. A man who'd been such a genuine humorist that at the peak of his career he'd predicted that, come what may, he'd have the last laugh.

I ran to the bow of the yacht and I threw my hands over my ears, but I could still hear it. Only now it wasn't my laughter anymore, it was Herb Nelson's. His wild, maniacal laughter. And I suddenly knew his prediction had come true.

Herb Nelson had had the last laugh. Even if it killed him.

The End

A Gun for Honey

G.G. Fickling

The Honey West Files
ISBN: 9781936814176
Cover Design:
Erik Enervold/Simian Brothers Creative
Prepress: Lewis Chapman
Editorial assist: Yolanda Cockrell

www.moonstonebooks.com

The Honey West Files published 2012 by Moonstone Entertainment, Inc.,
1128 S. State Street, IL 60441. All rights reserved. Produced under
license. With the exception of review purposes, this book may not be
reprinted in part or in whole without the express written consent of
Moonstone and Gloria Fickling.   Printed in the USA.

Chapter One

Lightning flashed down over the dark sea, illuminating the figure of a man standing at the rocky edge of the cliff. Thunder creased the night and then subsided in the inky sky over Shark Beach.

I climbed from my car, tugged at the low neckline of my gown and listened for a moment to the sound of the breakers.

"Are you all right?" I called over the surf's din. "Hey, where are you? What's the matter?"

I took the .32 revolver from my purse and moved toward the edge of the cliff, strands of hair clinging to my forehead as the rain began.

"Are you in trouble?" I called, wishing I'd thought to swing my car's headlights onto the cliff edge.

As I crept nearer to the precipice, one of my heels snagged in a rut and threw me off balance. Suddenly two strong arms caught me from behind, locked tight around my breasts and sent my gun sprawling.

Lightning bit into the sky again, explosively plunging its crooked blade into the sea. A man bent down for my revolver. In the brief flash of light he looked like a silhouette cut from luminous paper. He had curved horns and a red cape swirled up from around his shoulders in the wet wind.

I fought to break loose, but the arms held me like steel rods.

A voice said, "This one's a wildcat, Hel. What'll I do with her? She's liable to kick something loose in a second!"

The red man moved nearer in the darkness. "Tear off her clothes," he roared, "and throw her into the sea!"

"Look," the man behind me protested, "fun's fun, but—"

"Wait a minute!" Satan interrupted. "This feels like a real gun. Reed,

151

hand me your flashlight."

A third figure moved toward the red-caped Satan, casting a yellow glow onto the barrel of my revolver. One of the men whistled as he clicked open the cylinder.

"Holy Geronimo, this doll plays for keeps. Gimme that flashlight!"

The beam was raised to my face and slowly lowered over my bare shoulders and down the clinging gown I'd worn for the New Year's Eve party. The whistle was repeated. This time it was long and low with a bend in the middle.

"Man alive, if it isn't the Dragon Lady with peach parfait piled on top of her head. Are you a blonde all over, baby?"

"What do you think?"

"I don't know," Satan chuckled. "It might be interesting to find out. What's with the artillery?"

"What's with the judo lessons?" I asked. "Don't you keep office hours around these parts?"

"Baby, with parts like yours we don't keep any kind of special hours. What are you doing here on the Collier's road?"

"Attending a party," I said. "I didn't expect to be greeted by the devil and two of his henchmen."

The arms around my chest relaxed. One of the men laughed. "Who were you expecting, baby? The kissing killer?"

I hesitated. "Perhaps."

The New Year's Eve's electrical storm, a rarity along California shores, lit up Shark Beach's rocky cliffs once more and revealed a smile on Satan's thick mouth. He tossed the revolver into my hands.

"Smart girl," he muttered. "So that's why you carry the rod! Afraid you might be his third victim?"

"Maybe."

"Maybe, nothing." He laughed. "I've never seen you around Shark Beach. Where you from anyway?"

"L.A. I know Rote Collier from the days he directed horror movies," I said, stretching the truth a little. "I'm sure you three are not with the police."

"Nope," Satan said. "I'm a magazine photographer. Name's Helmet

Gandy. Better known to my friends as just plain Hel." The flashlight beam flickered over to a tall, lean-faced man wearing a Buck Rogers outfit. "This is Reed Walker. Captain, United States Marine Corps. Jet pilot extraordinaire. And the muscleman behind you is Wolf Larson famed for his exploits at thirty fathoms and fathomless bedrooms. He won't admit it, naturally, but we're all convinced he's the kissing killer."

The man with steel-band arms stepped in front of the light. "That isn't funny, Hel. I ought to bust you one for that."

"Speaking of bust," Hel said, "don't you gentlemen agree that our fair captive has a generous amount of same? What do you do in your spare time, baby? If it's what I think, you can count me in any time."

"You're counted in, Mr. Grandy," I said, touching the neckline of my gown. "I'm a model. A photographer's model. Name's Honey West. Ever hear of me?"

I was hoping he hadn't. A private detective, especially a female of the species, did hit the front pages once in a while. In my business, sometimes once was too many.

"Don't recall the name," Hel said. "But, I'm sure I've seen you in some magazine. Maybe one of the nudie books, huh?"

"Perhaps," I said, with a hint more *yes* than *no*. "Why don't we adjourn to the party and talk more about it there?"

The jet pilot winked. "Good idea. I'm tired of standing out here trying to scare all the single dames that come along. This was a rotten idea from the start, Hel."

I crossed the road to my convertible. "Why don't you three ride with me? There's plenty of room. How far is Rote's house from here?"

Hel laughed in his devilish sort of way. "You mean you can't hear the screams and music? It's just up the road. You've never been to one of Rote Collier's fabulous New Year's Eve parties before?"

"No, I've never had the pleasure."

Hel Gandy and the jet pilot climbed in beside me. Wolf Larson vaulted into the back. He was as strong as an ox and dressed in nothing but a loin cloth.

"You're going to love this party, baby," Hel said, squeezing in tightly. "Of course, a lot of my pictures have to be censored before they hit the magazines. You know what artists' balls are like!"

"I can imagine."

"Just keep that gun handy, baby. You may have to shoot your way out."
He laughed raucously. "Are you in for some surprises! Watch out for the
vaults!"

"The what?"

"Shut up, Hel," Wolf said. "You're always spoiling the fun. Maybe
she'll like the vaults. Do you swim, Honey?"

Loud and sensual rhythm swelled up from a massive, spiral-topped castle at the end of the road.

I drew the car to a stop. "Sure, I swim, but I didn't bring a bathing
suit."

Reed Walker brushed my bare shoulder accidentally with his hand. It
felt warm, almost too warm. "We'll dig you up a suit," he said.

"That's what I'm worried about," I said, getting out of the car. "You
mean one with cement sleeves? Come on, now, let's have the truth. Which
one of you is the kissing killer?"

"That's for you to figure out, baby," Hel answered, following out my
side. "Just be careful who you pucker up with. Right, Wolf?"

Wolf didn't answer. He took my arm and walked me down a steep dark
staircase to the front door of the Collier mansion.

"This place looks at least a hundred years old," I said, glancing at Wolf's
face. He was ruggedly handsome, the Marlon Brando type with sensitive
deep-set eyes and a broad nose that was slightly flattened at the tip where
he'd apparently taken one too many punches. His mouth was thin and hard
with a trace of bitterness chiseled in the corners. He suddenly smiled and
the change was quietly disturbing. On each side of his mouth Wolf had two
fangs that seemed almost fake in their needle-sharp perfection. Now I
knew what had inspired his name.

Hel stepped around us and banged on the oak door. "Open up! The
Devil's here, you filthy sinners!"

In an instant, the old bronze handle turned and we were staring into a
strangely half-lit madhouse. The living room could have passed for a small
amphitheatre with its domed ceiling and ornate balustrades. Colored
streamers fluttered weirdly in the semi-darkness, like hungry tentacles of an

octopus, touching the costumed figures and making them thrash with abandon. In the center of the huge room, bathed in a purple spotlight, was an elevated platform with two pillars rising almost to the ceiling. It was difficult to see through the smoke and colored ribbons, but the grimly spectacular structure seemed reminiscent of the sacrificial altar used in the old movie, King Kong.

Wolf pushed me into the room. The music stopped. It was almost as if everything suddenly and brutally froze as the figures stared at us, their bodies stiffly caught in the rhythm of their fantastic dance. Even the thick smoke seemed to pall at the interruption. The ribbons hung limp and lifeless in the soundless vacuum. Hel stepped forward and raised his arms high in a garish salute.

"She has come!" Hel's voice was a thundering roar in the huge room. "Out of the dark night! Out of the empty deathless regions of time, a blonde princess has come to light the sacrificial fire of the New Year. All hail!"

The masked figures, seemingly supported by a myriad of hidden strings, fell forward on their knees and arms raised, they echoed, "All hail!"

"Bring the torch!" Hel bellowed. "Bring the torch!" The crowd picked up the chant.

A bent and horribly disfigured man got to his feet. His huge misshapen head was formed in the image of the famed Quasimodo from Victor Hugo's, *Hunchback of Notre Dame*. Slowly, he dragged his legs across the room to a lighted torch flickering in an earthenware urn in the corner.

"What is this?" I whispered to Wolf. "Maybe I'm at the wrong party!"

The hunchback brought the torch to me. I shook my head, but Hel shoved the flaming stick into my hands. Wolf pushed me toward the sacrificial alter. The weird figures moved back, prostrate on their knees, creating a path across the deathly silent room.

"Courage, baby," Hel whispered as we reached the bottom step leading up to the pillars. "She won't feel a thing."

"Who won't?" I asked, peering through the semi-darkness at the red-suited Satan, wondering when the joke was going to end and how. I trembled from the grisly realism they were injecting into this rite.

Hel pointed up to the sacrificial altar. My eyes followed his gesture.

Chained to the pillars was a nude woman, her head hunched forward, dark hair dangling limply over her eyes, body slumped into unconsciousness. Splintered pieces of wood were piled under her body.

I dropped the torch and screamed. I screamed so loud the rafters caught the sound and hurled it back in a wild, unreasoning echo. Wolf caught me as I started up the steps toward the altar. The prostrate figures leaped to their feet. The music began to roar. The screams and laughter of a hundred throats joined in mine. The ribbons rose into the air as the crescendo of sound reached a defying pitch. Then it stopped as quickly as it had begun. Quasimodo limped to me and tore off his grisly headpiece. It was Rote Collier!

"Happy New Year, Honey!" Rote said, wrapping his warped arms around my shoulders. "I'm so glad you could make it!"

I gestured futilely at the nude figure chained to the altar.

"A dummy, baby," Hel said, grinning. "Rote pulls this gag on all his first-time New Year's Eve guests. What do you think we were doing out on the road? This was planned, baby, planned. We were your reception committee."

I shook my head dismally. "Leave it to the master of horror. I should have known, but it was all so—"

"—realistic," Rote finished. "Listen, Honey, maybe my directing days are over but I can still create a pretty convincing scene."

Rote Collier was a femininely handsome man in his early fifties. His costume was a strange contrast to his well-groomed features: finely-trimmed mustache, pink cheeks, delicate blue eyes. He ran his rubber-covered fingers through his thinning gray hair and laughed. "I always did have a yearning to play the Hunchback. Silly quirk, I guess. Gee, it's good to see you, Honey." He squeezed me again, then leaped onto the steps. "Everybody!" he roared. "I want you to meet Honey West. The prettiest gal to come along the pike in a long, long while—except my wife, Helena, naturally." Rote's exception came out too flat and he knew it. "Have fun, everybody," he added with more enthusiasm. "The night is yours!"

Wolf Larson reached around my waist and squeezed tightly. "How about that swim? Rote's got a pool down on the water. You'll love it."

"I bet she'll love it," Rote interrupted. "But later, Wolf. Honey and I have something to talk about. Privately."

"Okay," Wolf said, his fangs bared slightly, "I can take the hint. I'll see what I can do about digging up a bathing suit. Don't be too long—and don't get caught in a vault, get me?"

"I got you," I said. "Just be sure to come back with a bathing suit."

Wolf shook his head and disappeared in the myriad of dancing, costumed shapes. Rote steered me into his study. It was another tremendous room tinged with the weird flavor of his old movies. He offered me a chair and a cigarette.

"What's your problem, Rote?" I said. "You didn't really say much over the telephone."

"I think you know, Honey." Rote walked to the window. "Two women have been murdered in Shark Beach during the past six months. Two beautiful women. They were smothered. Or, as the police and newspapers call it—kissed to death."

"Fantastic," I said, using his favorite word.

"Yeah, fantastic is right," Rote turned and looked at me. "I couldn't have thought up a better idea for a picture of mine. That's what bothers me. The whole business has been too close to home. The police have called me in for questioning several times. Luckily I've managed to keep it out of the papers. They claim the bizarre method of murder is too reminiscent of a movie script.

"Is that really what bothers you, the fact that you've been suspected?"

Rote slumped into a chair and wiped twisted fingers across his pink forehead. "No, of course not, Honey. That's only added a little flavor to a dull winter down here. What I'm worried about is my wife—and Fawn."

"Fawn?"

"Yes—a child—from my first marriage. I don't think you've ever met Fawn." Rote got up, grinning sheepishly. "But of course you've never met Helena either. They're the same age."

"What?"

"Fawn's the same age as my wife Helena," Rote continued in an embarrassed tone. "In fact, Fawn's a few months older. As you can imagine that's somewhat of a conversation piece in this small town."

"How old are they, Rote?"

157

"Twenty-three."

"I thought you had a son, too, about the same age."

"I—I did have. But, unfortunately, he was killed, in Korea."

"I—I'm sorry."

"Me, too. But, now I have Fawn—and Helena. And a fear. A cold sort of fear, Honey, like in the old days when I started in pictures. This kissing killer is going to strike again soon. Perhaps even tonight here at this party."

"Sounds like a story conference for one of your movies, Rote. Are the police worried at all?"

"Sure they are. But, in a small town they're not equipped for this sort of thing. They asked me to call off the party. What could I do? It's been an annual event here in Shark Beach for the last five years. Fawn and Helena wouldn't hear of a cancellation. So, here we are. A couple of policemen in costume have been mingling with the crowd." He shook his head. "I doubt if they can prevent anything from happening, if it's going to happen. The killer's after a woman. Knowing we're on guard he's going to take particular caution—and that'll be that."

I stood up and crossed to an old Egyptian mummy case that lay flat on a table in the middle of the room. "In other words, Rote, you want me to prevent our osculating friend from using his talents on Fawn or Helena."

"Right. They're both beautiful. Exceptionally beautiful. And, I might add, very gullible."

The mummy case lid raised easily. It was empty and smelled of mothballs. "Gullible to what extent, Rote?"

"Well," Rote said hesitantly, "Helena's extremely naïve, easily taken in by people, if you know what I mean."

"Are you trying to say your wife's been straying a little?"

He grimaced. "I—I don't know. It's possible. She's young, impulsive, beautiful. Men go crazy for her." Rote frowned and he stopped to stare at new flashes of lightning out over the sea. "It's possible she might be lured into a compromising situation. But, I'd say that was true of almost any young woman at a New Year's Eve party, wouldn't you?"

I moved to a gun case and peered through the glass at a collection of old-fashioned revolvers. "Considering I'm a female, and over twenty-one myself, I don't think I should answer that question." I smiled. "What about

Fawn?"

Rote shook his head. "Dangerously familiar with people. Just too damned friendly for her own good. Fawn's the sort of person who gets mixed up in something and then doesn't know how to get out. Weak, impulsive, unconventional. That's Fawn. Worries the hell out of me."

I lifted a long-barrelled .45 our of the cabinet. "I take it, then, you want me to lure the killer over to my side of the parlor."

"Right. As I said over the phone, you're my old friend Hank West's daughter, down for a brief holiday in Shark Beach as my house guest. You're a model, an actress—anything but a private detective. You're beautiful—"

"Thank you."

"Well you are, Honey. You saw how Wolf Larson was acting out there—and Hel Gandy and Reed Walker and all the rest. I don't blame them. You've got 'em drooling." Rote put his rubbery hands on my bare shoulders. "Look at you. Blue eyes, taffy colored hair, a real baby bottom complexion. You're gorgeous." He moved in closer, touching the tip of my nose with his own."

"Rote," I said carefully, "this isn't getting my spiderweb spun."

"That's what you think. I'm stuck already."

His pink mouth lowered toward my lips, but before he made contact a low, husky voice bounced Rote Collier back on his heels harder than I was planning to myself.

"Dad!"

Inside the study door stood a figure in black mesh stockings, an old-fashioned corset and a mask with long, sweeping, false eyelashes.

"Fawn!" Rote stammered. "I—I thought you were down at the pool with Doctor Erik." He glanced at me still holding the .45 and laughed nervously. "Fawn, this is our house guest, Honey West. She's a model and an actress. In fact, when you came in we were just going through a scene from one of my old pictures—for fun."

"It did look like fun," Fawn said knowingly, moving toward Rote. "I'll bet Helena would have loved seeing it."

Fawn Collier had slim, well-rounded legs that swung in long, sexy strides when she walked. She kept the lower part of her body forward and held her shoulders back in an effort to emphasize to the fullest extent, her small breasts. That part of her face which showed from under the mask was astonishingly like Rote's—full-tapered mouth and pink rounded chin with a slight dimple.

Rote glanced at the clock on his desk. "It'll be midnight soon. What do you say we all get back to the party?"

"What party?" Fawn laughed huskily. "Everybody's either passed out drunk or down in the vaults doing what comes naturally."

"That isn't possible," Rote said, moving to the door. "They were dancing a few minutes ago. You two get acquainted. I'll be right back."

After Rote was gone, Fawn looked at me for an instant through curved eyeslits, then smiled and removed her mask. She had green eyes almost the color of jade and short black hair tumbled carelessly about her head like tiny whirlpools. She took a lipstick from her purse and touched the red tip to her mouth.

"Stuff wears off in no time at a party like this," Fawn said, smiling slyly, "Don't you find it so?"

"Sometimes," I answered, replacing the .45 in the cabinet. "Depends upon the party. Have you seen Helena around?"

Fawn's eyes hardened. "Are you kidding? She's probably exhibiting herself before one of her boyfriends. She's an expert at that, don't you know? Or maybe you do know since you're a friend of hers and a model."

"I have no idea what you're talking about."

"You don't have to play games with me, sister," Fawn said angrily. "I know your type. Helena's exactly the same. Cheap and aggressive. You get what you want one way or another, don't you? Like with Father a moment ago."

"Look, that was nothing more than a brief New Year's Eve flourish. If your father hadn't been drinking and having fun he'd never have tried it. I'm sure. Now, if you'll excuse me, I'm supposed to join someone down at the pool."

"Of course," Fawn said, surveying my evening gown. "But, I'm warning you, darling, you'd better hang onto your pantie girdle because it's mighty rough down there. Mighty rough. Especially if you run into Doctor Erik Ford."

160

I told Fawn I would watch my step and walked out of the study. The high-domed living room was now ominously dark. Even the purple light was turned out over the sacrificial altar. Someone brushed against me.

"Honey?"

"Yes."

"Wolf Larson. I have that bathing suit for you."

"Really? What happened to the rest of the party?"

"Coffee break. Come on, let's go."

I resisted his big hands. "No, I'm serious, Wolf. There could be a murderer loose in this house. These lights shouldn't be out."

"Have you still got your gun?"

"Well, yes, but—"

"You're safe. Come on!"

He pulled me toward a faint glow at the far end of the living room. Ribbons fluttered in the darkness, touching my face and twisting around my body.

"Where are we going?" I asked, breaking free from one entrapment only to be caught in another.

We reached a long spiral staircase that seemed to go down into the very depths of Hell. Wolf backed me up under a pale light that illuminated the top of the stairwell.

"I'm going to kiss you," he said, baring his fangs. "I'm going to kiss you like you've never been kissed before."

My heart leaped up into my throat. I reached for my revolver, but he wrapped his sinewy arms around me and pushed my face toward his mouth. In an instant, his lips were crushing against mine.

Chapter Two

A NOT-SO-OLD adage with the punch line "relax and enjoy it" raced through my mind, but I couldn't make myself believe this particular moment was going to end up in any sort of enjoyable state. Wolf Larson was crushing the very life out of me. Footsteps suddenly clanged on the metal treads below the platform.

"Hey, you two up there!" a voice blared. "We need some more drinking material down at the pool. How about helping us out?"

Wolf pulled back angrily. "Get it yourself! Who was your barmaid last year?"

"You were, Larson. What the devil are you doing anyway?"

The footsteps moved nearer. Wolf released his hold and bent over the railing while I caught my breath.

"Oh, it's you, Erik," Wolf said in a more pleasant tone. "Sure, I'll bring it down in a second. Just breaking in the new girl."

The man below laughed and started back down into the stairwell. "Take your time. We're not going to die."

Wolf whirled around and looked at me, a triumphant grin on his lipstick-smeared mouth. "Not bad, huh?"

"Not good," I said, disgust heavy in my voice. My face hurt where he had ground his against it. "Don't try that again, Wolf."

"What are you talking about?" he demanded, drawing strong arms across his bare chest. He chuckled. "I suppose you think I was trying to kill you. Well, maybe I was. Can you think of a better way to die?"

I touched my mouth with the back of my hand and it stung. "I'm not laughing, Wolf. You're drunk and having a hilarious time, okay. Let's leave it at that."

162

"Ah, come on. I was only trying to scare you a little, Honey. Can't you take a joke?"

I started down the staircase. "No, I'm sorry, Wolf.."

"But, the boys and I just cooked this up because we knew you were from out-of-town," Wolf argued, following on my heels. "There's nothing to this kissing killer business, believe me. The newspapers only coined the word because it sounded sensational. We know who the murderer is."

I stopped and stared up at his huge bulk. "Now, what are *you* talking about?"

Wolf hunched his shoulders complacently. "The police don't believe it, but we do. There was an old character living here in town named Butler. He was as ugly as sin and a little nuts to boot. He was a gardener. Used to work at all the big homes along the cliffs. And when he got drunk down at the Booby Hatch he'd talk about these beautiful dames he'd like to smother with kisses. Well, two of those dames he worked for were smothered. So, you take it from there."

"Where is this old character now, Wolf?"

"He's dead. Got drunk one night, walked out on the Pleasure Pier and fell in. We found his body the next morning. There hasn't been another murder since."

"No, just a near miss," I said, feeling my lips again. "have you seen Helena Collier in the last hour?"

"Sure. She was lying where I left her...in a pool of kisses."

"Very funny."

"Naturally, I'm a very funny guy." He blew me a kiss. "Now, if you don't mind, I'll go murder somebody else. Good night." He disappeared into the dark living room.

Before I walked down to the pool, I thought for a moment about his story of the old man. If my mouth hadn't been hurt so badly I might have believed it, but there was that one big difference.

Rote Collier's swimming pool was carved out of rock against the edge of the sea. Mountainous waves maintained it with salt water at high tide, which happened to be the height of the sea on this New Year's Eve. A full moon winked hazily through scattered clouds in the still, lightning-lit sky.

At the edge of the pool, a masked, dark-haired woman in a black cat

163

costume bumped into me. She was drunk and her outfit was open at the top exposing the raw edge of one starkly flushed bosom. "What's the password?" she asked.

"You got me," I said. "Are you Helena?"

She shook her head. "Are you kidding? I wish I was. That Helena's really something. The men go gaga over her. She was around here a little while ago. Swimming in the nude! Dancing! Doing just about everything. And, boy, does that gal know how to do it." The catwoman staggered past me into the stairwell.

I scanned the swimming pool area. Costumed figures were huddled and strewn in various and sundry clumps. Glasses and bottles were spaced in between like way stations on a local bus line. Two shapes—sans anything—were in the pool, deathly white in the semi-darkness. I started toward them when a familiar voice stopped me.

"Going somewhere?"

A man with coppery red hair stood up and touched my arm. He was wearing the tattered remains of a fantastic half-man, half-woman costume.

"You're Erik," I said.

"That's right. How'd you know?"

"We sort of met indirectly on the staircase a few minutes ago."

"Oh, yes with old Fang Larson. Did he bite you?"

"Almost," I said. "Is he poisonous?"

Erik nodded. "Deadly. If I were a woman I wouldn't go near him with asbestos underwear."

I smiled, enjoying his unsubtle humor. Erik Ford seemed pleasant, fairly young and easy-going.

"You're a doctor."

"Right again. You've got me pegged. Now how about a rundown on yourself?"

"Weren't you upstairs when I came in?"

"No," he said frowning. "I didn't have the pleasure, I was what you might say—out on a call."

"Was her name Helena?"

Erik exhaled. "Wrong again. But, I'll have to admit you're close."

"Fawn?"

"Uncanny," he said. "You must be a psychic. I bow to your powers. Care for a drink?"

"No, thanks."

"We mix some fancy cocktails around these parts."

"So I've noticed," I said, glancing at one of the more intimate huddles. "You haven't seen Helena, then, in awhile"

"My dear, I have not only seen Helena Collier in a while, I have seen her after a while. Which is just about the state of her physical condition at the present time. That's *she* in the pool. Would you care to converse with her?"

I studied the two white beings in the water. "No, thanks. I can wait until another time."

"Why wait?" Erik said. He crossed to the pool and bent over the edge. "Hey, you two, break it up! This is Dr. Erik Ford. I want to examine the female of the species."

One of the swimmers laughed in a high-pitched feminine way, rolled over on her stomach and moved to the metal ladder. She was thin-faced and bosomy with stringy blonde hair clinging to her back. She raised her dripping face up to Erik, lips puckered, eyes half-closed. The doctor got to his feet, leaving the woman unkissed and slightly bewildered.

"Wrong female," he said to me. "That isn't Helena. Funny, I'm sure she was in the pool not too long ago."

"Have you seen Rote?"

"That, my dear, is a good question. I hope I haven't. At least, not while Helena's prancing around in the nude. He doesn't go that rout a bit. He'd tear the hell out of everybody if he ever caught her, I'll tell you that."

I scanned the shoreline south of the pool. Steep rocky cliffs rose up out of the sea forebodingly.

"What's down in that direction?" I asked.

"A few caves. One is sort of a lover's nest, if you know what I mean?"

"Could Helena have gone that way?"

"Sure. Want to take a look?"

"Would we be intruding?"

Erik grinned. "Probably. But, that's the fun of it. Helena wouldn't mind."

"Why do you say that?"

The doctor winked and slipped his arm around my waist. "That's one thing you'll learn about Helena Collier. She's ambidextrous as hell."

As we crawled over jagged rocks on the way to one of the caves, I tried to create a composite picture of Helena out of four amazingly varied descriptions. Rote had said she was beautiful and naïve. Fawn branded her stepmother as cheap and aggressive. The catwoman was envious of her romantic abilities with the male sex, while Erik claimed she worked the same kind of racket on the other side of the fence. All in all Helena Collier was some strange conglomeration of womanhood.

Erik helped me down a slippery bed of moss into the opening of a cave. Behind us the ocean struck against the rocks, shooting up a cold biting spray.

"That was close," I yelled to Erik over the roar of the breakers. "The tide seems to be building. Sure this is safe?"

The doctor nodded. His face wasn't exactly handsome, but it had a certain pleasing appeal that radiated from his warm brown eyes. He took my hand and led me into the cave. Drops slithered down from the ceiling. It was cold and impossibly dark. This didn't seem a likely spot for lovers.

"Are you certain we're in the right place?" I said, my voice reverberating hollowly.

"Of course. I've been here many times. They call this Collier's Cave. Rote used to shoot a lot of his horror scenes here."

"I can believe that."

A misstep almost sent me sprawling until his arms caught me from behind. I regained my footing and lifted his hands away from where they had rooted on the top of my gown.

"You're a very large girl," he said quietly, backing me against the side of the cave.

"And you're a very large faker," I added. "There's nobody down here. Why'd you do this?"

"Because I like you, Honey, and because I was bored with the company back there."

"How'd you know my name?"

"I didn't. Is your name Honey? How convenient."

What he was saying didn't sound convincing anymore. The natural-
ness in his voice had tightened. I was sure that business about my name was
a lie.

"Let's go back," I said.

"Not on your life."

"Okay, I'll find my own way."

His hands stiffened on my bare shoulders. "Not before you answer, a
few questions."

"All right, Erik."

"Why are you so desperately anxious to find Helena Collier?"

I winced. "Because she's an old friend of mine and I wanted to see her
before going back to L.A."

"That's a lie," Erik said. "You just met recently."

"How do you know this?"

"Because she told me. Helena's a patient of mine. She happened to
let your name slip yesterday during a visit to my office. Now tell me the
truth."

"I don't have to tell you anything."

His hands squeezed even tighter, this time nearer to my throat.

"You won't get away with it, do you understand? You and Helena think
you're pretty smart, but you're not. You can only go so far with your little
scheme. And I've had it, do you understand! I've had it up to here!"

His fingers clamped on my windpipe. I tried to kick him loose, but my
gown was too tight and we fell over into a pool of water. His hands broke
free.

"I'll get you! I'll get you both if it's the last thing I do!" Erik said, half
screaming.

He leaped for me and missed in the darkness. I got to my feet and
staggered toward a faint strip of sky when a wave crested over the rock
ledge into the cave. It struck chest-high and flung me over into whirling
foam, choking my nostrils and dragging me down into jagged rocks. By the
time I reached the surface, the sea rose again stabbing brutally through the
black cavity with another mountainous breaker.

Over the rush of the sea, Erik called, "This way, Honey, this way!
You'll never make it to the ledge!"

Thinking this might be another trick. I fought even harder to reach the mouth of the cave. Then the third breaker convinced me it was impossible, as it hurled me against a wall. Erik came through the dark foam. He caught my arm and dragged me up onto a rock.

"Quick!" he yelled. "The next one may hit the ceiling!"

We climbed hurriedly to a cement retaining wall. The fourth wave was stupendous. It struck with awesome fury forcing us to crawl to another ledge and up a flight of block steps into the warm night. The spray hissed its anger below.

We found ourselves in a small garden only a few yards from Rote Collier's spiral-topped castle. Erik fell to his knees, coughing violently, his costume ripped down both sides. My evening gown was in far worse shape. There was just enough left to cover the important parts. We both looked as if we'd been through an atomic war.

Erik rolled over and groaned. "You know we almost had it down there. Another minute…"

"You mean another second—for me," I interrupted, touching my throat. "You tried to kill me down there. Why?"

The doctor wiped the spray from his face clumsily. "That's not true! You—you misunderstood."

I bent over Erik and examined several cuts on his chest where he had scraped on the rocks. "Listen, mister, you did your best to put me out of commission. Now either you give and give fast or I'm yelling for a cop. There are several on the premises, you know."

"No, I didn't know. What are they doing here?"

"Don't be naïve."

"No, I'm serious. You've got to believe me. I didn't mean you any harm."

"Save it for a police court."

I got up and walked to a lower side door leading into the Collier mansion. He ran after me.

"You're not serious, Honey?"

"What do you think?"

He followed me up a stairway into the still darkened living room. "It was a joke, Honey. I was only trying to scare you."

"That's what Wolf Larsen said. One of they days you people will joke your way right into the gas chamber."

Rote Collier appeared out of the gloom, sweat beading on his pink forehead, breathing loud. "Honey, I've been looking for you everywhere. I can't find Helena. Have you seen her, Erik? What——what in the world's happened to you two?"

"We ran into a tidal wave," I said tightly. "Rote, where do you turn on the lights in this room?"

"Over there," he directed.

I crossed to a switch and flicked it on. The huge room sprang to life. The sacrificial altar was almost obliterated by the jungle of colored ribbons, its pillar chained nude figure barely visible.

"Who thought up the altar bit, Rote?" I asked.

"I did. It was my idea. Just another gimmick to add some color. Why?" Rote stammered.

I traced my nails thoughtfully around my ears, trying to untangle some matted curls. "Have you checked the dummy lately?"

"What?" Rote Collier's eyes widened. "What are you talking about? What is this?"

"Is Helena's hair long and black?" I asked.

"Yes, but…"

"As far as I can tell, Rote, nobody's seen Helena in quite a while. You take it from there."

Slowly the ex-movie director turned and stared up at the sacrificial altar. The white, nude figure hung from the chains, weirdly lifelike with its face concealed by long black hair.

"You—you don't think…" Rote began.

"Around this place I've stopped thinking," I said, glancing at Erik's expressionless face. "Why don't you go look?"

Rote Collier, still garbed in his warped Quasimodo costume, seemed like a man on his last walk to the guillotine as he moved up the long flight of steps to the altar. Finally, he reached the white figure, hesitated a brief instant and then lifted her hair. The glassy, bulging eyes that peered down at us were horribly real. Rote dropped the black strands, grasped his heart and staggered back on the altar.

"Honey," he stammered. "Don't ever do that to me again. Of course, it's a manikin. What did you expect?" He walked down the steps, slowly and unsteadily.

I glanced at Erik. He was deathly pale.

Rote joined us again. "Come on, let's all have a drink," he said, clapping his costumed hands together. "Hell, it's well after midnight. We've got some celebrating to do. Helena will show up pretty soon. She probably drove downtown for more liquor."

Erik shook his head. "I'm sorry, Rote, but I'd better bow out. I've really had it." He glanced at me. "I'm going home to get some sleep, if you don't mind?"

"Of course we mind, Erik," Rote said. "And Helena would be very disappointed. Come on, one for the road, at least."

He pushed Erik and me into the study where Captain Reed Walker lay sprawled asleep on a couch in the corner.

Rote laughed. "Well, even old Buck Rogers ran out of space juice. The party's falling apart at the seams. This calls for a shot of my hundred-year-old Scotch."

He went to a cabinet and lifted out a bottle of liquor. Erik stood inside the door, his face growing whiter by the second.

I took three glasses from another cabinet and placed them on top of the mummy case. They didn't set very level. I peered down and noticed the lid was not fully closed.

Rote raised the bottle and shouted, "Happy New Year everybody!"

I raised the mummy case lid a little. The wind of fear whistled through me like a lance. A nude woman with long black hair was lifelessly crumpled inside.

Chapter Three

The glasses crashed to the floor as I swung the lid open far enough for Rote and Erik to see the contents.

For a long moment, neither man moved. Then Rote set his bottle of hundred-year-old Scotch on the desk, and moved trance-like to the mummy case.

"Helena," he said, staring at the dead woman. "Helena, my God, I knew it couldn't last. I knew it." Tears began to squeeze out of his eyes, rolling down his pink cheeks in pathetic ribbons.

I closed the lid and went to the telephone. "I'm sorry, Rote. Believe me, I'm sorry. Erik, would you ask the people down at the pool to come up to the house, please?"

There was no answer. I glanced toward the door. Doctor Erik Ford was gone.

Shark Beach police and several men form the sheriff's office arrived thirty minutes later. Rote' mansion was considered to be on the city line and came under joint jurisdiction of both law enforcement agencies. One member of the group was a massive, broad-shouldered deputy in a battered felt hat and a blue suit too small for his large frame. His squarish, handsome face wore a scowl three inches thick and this expression deepened even more after he cornered me alone in a room just off the study.

"I'm Detective Lieutenant Mark Storm, sheriff's office, homicide," he said, squinting at the tattered remains of my gown. "I'm confused. Are you the old or new year?"

"You're the third funny man I've met tonight. One more and we'll have

171

a quartet of jokers for the burial."

Mark cocked his hat, opened the button on his coat and groaned. "I should've known you'd be here Honey. Nowadays in this county we spell murder H-O-N-E-Y. Who did it?"

I slumped into a chair in the corner. "The mummy, naturally, who else? Any other questions?"

"Yeah. How did you get counted in on this deal?"

"I was invited."

"Why?"

"Because I've got a birthmark inside my right thigh. You want to see?"

"I've already had the pleasure," Mark said, pacing around the room. "Now will you, please get down to facts."

"How factual can you get, *ma'am*," I kidded. "Oh, come on, Mark, the gal's dead. You know as much as I do. She was smothered to death, right?"

"I'm not the coroner."

"What are you, Lieutenant?"

Mark groaned again. "I'm a tired old man called out of a warm bed on a hot New Year's Eve. Now, make something out of that."

"Well, speaking of tired old men, did you ever know one named Butler here in Shark Beach?"

"Sure. Hospital report was DOA. There weeks ago. Drowning. Why?"

"No reason."

"I'll bet." Mark opened the top button of his shirt and loosened his tie. "Don't kid me! You're not down here for your health."

"That's for sure," I said, fingering the remains of my expensive gown. "A couple of characters named Wolf Larson and Erik Ford have seen to that."

"I met Larson in the study. Who's Ford?"

"A doctor of sorts," I said. "He disappeared after I found the body. Helena was a patient of his."

Mark grunted. "Fine time to run out on a client. What do you make of the Marine officer, Reed Walker?"

"Very young, very nice and very drunk. I don't think he killed her."

"What makes you say that?"

172

"Just a hunch."

"You're slipping, Honey." He took a pair of tin wings from his pocket and held them up. "Interplanetary Space Pilot, Commander."

"Where'd you get those?"

"In the mummy case. *Under* Helena Collier's body."

"So what?"

Mark hunched his shoulders. "So, your very young, very nice jet jockey probably dropped them when he tossed her body into the case. Several people have already identified them as belonging to Captain Walker's costume.

"I can corroborate that testimony. He was wearing them when I met him earlier."

"That's all I wanted to hear." Mark walked to the door.

"What are you going to do?"

"Arrest Walker on suspicion of murder."

"I wouldn't do that, Lieutenant."

"Why not?"

"Yours truly dropped those wings in the mummy case," I said, trying to cover the lie with a smile. "He pinned them on me during the evening for meritorious service under fire."

Mark's eyes hardened. "You're either drunk or lying, which is it?"

I crossed my legs and lighted a cigarette. "Ask the captain if you don't believe me."

Mark took his hat off and scowled. "You must be drunk. This doesn't sound like you, Honey. Do you realize what you're saying? Not only could this implicate you in the murder, but…"

"—make me into a bad girl."

"I didn't say that."

"You don't have to," I said. "A girl can't be good all the time. It gets monotonous. Especially on New Year's Eve."

He grabbed me by the wrists and jerked me to my feet. "You dizzy dame, I ought to…"

I turned my face defiantly toward his. "What's holding you back, Lieutenant? You don't like female private eyes anyway. Now's your chance. Start the New Year out right."

He hurled me back into the chair. "Why you ever got into this business, I'll never know. Just because your father was a damned smart detective doesn't put you at the head of the class by any means. You'll never be able to fill his shoes! And don't think your body will ever open any doors—unless they're bedroom doors! You're just one flight up from the street as far as I'm concerned. Even a prostitute's got more pride in her profession that you have in yours!" Mark hammered his fist on the desk. "Oh, you give me a big, fat, bellyache!"

"Okay Lieutenant, why don't you arrest me and get rid of the pain?" I demanded, knowing he was so mad he hardly knew what he was saying.

"How did those wings get into that case, Honey?"

"They flew in."

Mark crushed his hat angrily. "Now who's being funny? I want a straight answer, do you understand?"

"All right," I said. "At one point in the evening I was in the study with Rote Collier. A mummy case, as you will admit, isn't a usual fixture in most American homes, so I took a peek inside for curiosity's sake. Is that straight enough?"

"Where was the mummy?"

"Out at the bar getting stiff." I grinned. "Mark, you're making much too much out of nothing."

"Yeah, I don't know who was making much too much out of who around here this evening, but I do know there was plenty of it going on. We ought to arrest the whole bunch of you."

"You have no holiday spirit, Lieutenant," I said, hating myself for acting this way. I was stooping pretty low to deceive a guy who'd plucked me out of a dozen tight spots during my detecting career. But it had to be done.

"Tell me just one thing," Mark said, grinding his hat back over rumpled black hair. "Who's the bigger liar, you or Fawn Collier?"

"I don't get you."

"Fawn claims she spent most of the evening with Reed Walker—until he passed out."

I nibbled on my bottom lip. "That, my friend, is for you to find out."

Mark tossed the tin wings into my lap. "Okay, you earned 'em Commander. They're yours. But I'm warning you to keep your eyes open because I'm just liable to shoot Buck Roger's space ship right out from under him."

New Year's morning I awakened in one of Rote's funeral-like guest rooms wondering why I'd stopped Mark from arresting Reed Walker. My reasons had seemed important the night before. But now, examined under daylight, they appeared as empty and shallow as the massive swimming pool beneath my windows, drained almost dry by low tide. I still felt the tin wings were an obvious plant. Or were they? What possible motive would a handsome Marine Captain have for murdering Helena Collier? I shook my head dismally. Maybe Mark was right about getting out of the detective business. My female spotting system had gone completely haywire at Reed Walker's first blip on my sensitive radar screen.

After a quick shower, I slipped into a sweater and skirt, painted my mouth and hurried downstairs. The dummy was still chained to her sacrificial pillars, reeking of the same sickening mothball odor that permeated the mummy case. At the altar's base, partially covered by scattered pieces of paper-mache' was a shiny black slide from a four by five camera.

I showed this to Rote at breakfast.

"Must belong to Hel Gandy," he said. "he was taking pictures last night and probably left it behind after we found..."

"I—I'm sorry I couldn't have been more help, Rote." He touched my arm, a warm expression in his moist blue eyes. "You did help, Honey. At least, you saved Fawn."

"What do you mean?"

"You said something to Fawn which really upset her last night while you two were alone in the study." Rote sipped nervously at his coffee. "She left the party afterwards and didn't come back until just about the time we discovered Helena. I think the killer was really out for Fawn."

"Why, Rote?"

"Just—just a feeling I have. That's why I want you to stay on here for awhile, Honey. I *don't* want to loose Fawn."

His emphasis was poorly placed. It sounded too much as if he hadn't minded losing Helena.

"Rote," I said, "Fawn told the sheriff's detectives she spent the evening with Reed Walker, but never mentioned leaving the party. Did she take the

Marine Captain with her?"

"I—I haven't the slightest idea."

Fawn, her short black hair combed into frothy bangs, whirled onto the breakfast porch in a filmy, expensive negligee. Her full lips were red around the edges where they apparently had been bruised by too many hard kisses. I wondered when she had had time to run up against Wolf Larson.

Fawn pecked her father on his pink forehead and glanced at me. "How nice you look this morning, Miss West. Like a bright picture *torn* out of a magazine."

Rote winced. "Fawn, you'll catch your death of cold in that ridiculous outfit. Go put some clothes on."

"Father, I feel very light and gay this morning." Fawn laughed. "This is the beginning of a new year. Let's bare our souls to the sunlight."

Rote got up from the table, anger searing his red-rimmed eyes. "Need I remind you, Fawn, that Helena is dead. This is no time for frivolities."

"On the contrary, Father," Fawn said lightly, slipping into a chair. "This is the happiest day of my life. I'm glad she's dead. Aren't you?"

"Fawn! Fawn, we have a guest!"

The dark-haired woman flashed green eyes in my direction. "Guest—pest! Why don't you go home, Miss West? You rhyme so delightfully."

"Fawn!" Rote emitted an anguished roar, stepped around the table and slapped his daughter hard on the cheek. "Either you'll learn some better manners or else I'll…"

"Or you'll what, dear Father?" Fawn rose slowly, a hand covering her flushed, dimpled cheek. "Kill me? Why don't you say it. You've always wanted to."

Rote Collier began to tremble, tears springing into his wide, hurt eyes. "Get out!" he whispered. "Get out, you…"

"—darling," Fawn finished, glancing at me. "If I didn't know better I'd say Father killed Helena. And with good reason. With very good reason." She crossed the porch, hips swinging loosely under her negligee, and vanished into the house.

Rote slumped into his chair, head in his hands. "I must apologize for Fawn, Honey. She's terribly upset. We all are."

I examined my fork absently. "Rote, if you want me to work for you,

you've got to work for me."

"Of course, Honey, of course. But, don't pay any attention to Fawn. She's exactly what I said last night. Irresponsible, irrepressible, irrational. I—I love Fawn and I've never had any reason to want to kill Helena." It sounded forced and tinged with insincerity. "Now does that answer your questions?"

"Almost," I said. "Was there ever a real mummy in that case, Rote?"

"Not to my knowledge. The case and the manikin came together. I borrowed them from a friend of mine at the studio."

"Okay, that'll do for now. I'll see you later." I patted him on the cheek and went into the house.

During a search of the living room, I discovered a narrow staircase leading to a lower level where several doors opened into dark dingy rooms with bunk beds built along the walls. Undoubtedly, these were the vaults I'd been warned about. Below this floor was a large, high-ceiling chamber with fixed theatre seats and a side movie screen. Numerous film cases were racked and labeled on a special shelf. I recognized some of the titles; horror pictures made by Rote Collier in his heyday. One case, stuck obscurely at the bottom, was labeled: HELENA. I removed the metal disc and lifted the cover. It was empty.

The room was suddenly plunged into darkness and the rush of a projection machine whirled over my head. From a square slot near the ceiling a stream of yellowish light fanned down. I went for the door, but it was now bolted from the other side. Music filled the room—light, airy music with woodwinds and flutes—and color splashed across the white beaded surface of the movie screen revealing a forest with green trees and low hanging branches. In the background, a dark-haired woman astride a sleek gray horse rode into view, her well-developed body starkly naked, a sensuous smile creasing her painted mouth. Sunlight cascaded down through the trees casting twisted shadows on her pink-tipped breasts. I was startled to discover it was Helena. She climbed from the animal and moved languidly nearer, slim legs taking long sexy steps, hands cupped under marble-white breasts, moistened lips curled back over straight, gleaming teeth. She came into such a tight close-up that the skin texture of her rounded stomach revealed a tiny mole near her navel. The image blacked out, only to lighten again as Helena moved on, her dimpled bottom jutting out below a curvaceous sloping back. She fell into an exotic dance which carried her from tree to tree, fingers stretching hungrily for branches high on gnarled trunks. The music pounded and Helena's body throbbed fantastically to the rhythm. When it was over, she lay exhausted in the forest, her body covered with beads of perspiration, gasping for breath, tongue pushed through her lips.

The scene changed abruptly, darkening into a close-up of a partially opened door that gradually focused onto a weird bedroom through the narrow opening. Black mesh curtains hung from the ceiling of the room, halfway encircling an elevated slab of slate, creating an eerie frame for two naked bodies that were sprawled passionately on a bare black mattress suspended on the rock. I couldn't immediately identify either of the thrashing figures until the woman sat up seizing her long black hair and piling it on top of her head. It was Helena again, but the man's face was turned away from the obviously-hidden camera. His back was broad and sinewy and sweat streamed down his sun-tanned flanks.

A startled voice from the projection booth drew my attention away from the screen. "My God, what's going on here?"

The clicking hum of the projector died, eating up the yellowish beam and erasing its lurid image. New light sprang from a fluorescent tube in the ceiling as Rote Collier's pink face glowered down at me in angry judgment.

"Honey, are you responsible for this?" he demanded.

"For what, Rote?"

He gestured over his head. "For this machine being turned on. It's a very expensive piece of equipment and shouldn't be tampered with by an amateur."

I smiled thinly. "The entire performance was at someone else's insistence. I'm locked in from the other side."

Rote's face paled. "How much did you see?"

"Enough to reveal you didn't give me the straight dope on Helena. She was hardly naïve, Rote."

"I ought to kill Fawn for this. No one was ever supposed to see that film. I should have burned it long ago."

"But you didn't," I said. "Who was the man with Helena?"

"I—I don't know. I mean—I can't tell you. It has nothing to do with her murder," Rote stammered.

"Let me be the judge of that."

"I can't Honey! This is just one of those things you'll have to take my word for. That footage was shot a long time before I even met Helena. It has nothing to do with what happened last night."

"You'd better be telling the truth, Rote, because this film provides you with a sizable motive for Helena's murder."

"Yes, yes, I know. That's what's so awful. Believe me, Honey, I'm innocent."

"You intimated last night Helena was straying a little, but you didn't say with whom."

"That was New Year's Eve talk. I even made a play for you, didn't I?"

"Rote, you're hiding something or somebody. Now which is it?"

"All right, if you must know, I—I'm hiding Helena. Her past. She was a bad girl until I met her. She modeled in the nude, acted in pornographic movies, even participated at closed stag parties where the women did absolutely everything. I'm ashamed to admit it, but I met her at one of those parties."

"Then why'd you give me all that business about naïvete'?"

"Because she was naïve. That's why I married her, despite what I knew about her background. She had a very sensitive nature, was easily swayed, men were always taking advantage of her." Rote stopped and ran his tongue over dry lips. "I knew she was swimming in the nude last night. But, she was drunk. She never would have done that otherwise."

"Tell me something truthfully, Rote. Did Helena like other women?"

"Of course. She had a very friendly nature."

"No," I said, hesitating. "I mean—physically."

Rote's face hardened in the dull yellowish light. "Who said that about Helena?"

"Doctor Erik Ford. He didn't come right out and actually accuse her, but he hinted at it strongly."

"That dirty bastard. She did a lot of things in her life, but Helena was-

179

n't *that* kind. There wasn't an abnormal bone in her beautiful body. Thank God!"

"It's a known fact that a large queer element does exist in Shark Beach."

"Of course. That's why I worry about Fawn. Just drop by the Gay Blade here in town sometime. It's very modern, exquisite, with gorgeous men parading around like a bunch of bronzed fairies. They're deadly, Honey!" Rote drummed his fist on the ledge above. "Every one of them psychologically twisted into a knot, touching each other, rubbing baby oil on each other. They seem to quiet and demure. But they're not! They're capable of anything—even murder!" He paused. "Whatever drove them into this abnormal niche can just as easily push them farther. They're frightened, Honey. And when a man's frightened—no matter what kind of man he is—he can kill so easily it isn't even funny."

"Rote," I said quietly, "you must suspect someone. Who?"

"I—I don't really know. Everyone. No one, I can't fathom why Helena was murdered in the first place. Obviously someone's crazy. You've got to help me find out who that is before he gets to Fawn."

"You said a moment ago that you thought Fawn locked me in here and turned on the film. Why?"

Rote shook his head. "Because Fawn hated Helena. I told you they were the same age. It was hard for Fawn to accept Helena. There was always a great deal of animosity on Fawn's part. Attempts to discredit Helena were always being made. I'm sure this was one of those attempts. I think you can understand why. Fawn did see us together last night."

"Yes, I know. But, one thing I don't understand, Rote, is why you've kept this film, why you never burned it."

"That I can't answer," Rote said sadly. "Not truthfully anyway. Just remember I'm in my fifties and Helena was not even twenty-five. I guess there's a bit of abnormality in us all. Does that answer your question?"

I nodded. "Now would you be so kind as to come down and unlock this door?"

He hesitated just long enough to make me wonder if he'd ever planned to let me out. I would have been a sitting duck from his vantage point.

180

Who could say for certain Rote Collier hadn't been the one who bolted the door? Or that he wasn't in the projection booth the entire time? The film had stopped at a strangely crucial moment. In another second the faces of Helena's lover most certainly would have been revealed.

Chapter Four

Mark Storm was propped up at a desk watching the Rose Bowl game on television when I walked into his temporary office in Shark Beach.

"Is this how you solve murders?" I asked.

"This is New Year's Day," he said gruffly. "People don't solve murders. They watch football games. Go away."

I took a pack of cigarettes from his coat pocket and lighted one. "What's the score?"

"Fourteen to fourteen. We're down on State's three yard line with twenty seconds to play."

"I mean the score on Helena Collier. What'd the coroner say?"

"Oh," the big lieutenant groaned. "Time of death about one hour before discovery. Cause—suffocation. Bruises around her mouth. No violation of the lower regions except her fanny was red as if she'd been spanked. Final score—nothing-nothing. Now scram."

"Is that any way to talk to a lady," I said, blowing smoke in his face.

"You were no lady last night. Our engagement's off."

"Who ever said we were engaged?"

"I did. But, I've made a New Year's resolution."

"Oh, drop dead," I said, kissing him on the cheek. "Can't," Mark said, "even if I'd like to oblige. Got to see the end of this game."

Grim-faced helmeted men lined up against each other across the TV screen, then rammed together brutally. I picked up the coroner's report from Mark's desk and scanned the neatly typed page. One line really threw me for a loss, almost as abruptly as the West team was hurled back by the dark-uniformed players from the Big Ten Conference.

"Hey," I said. "It says here Helena was pregnant."

182

"That's right."

"I thought you said the score was nothing-nothing?"

"Oh, yeah," Mark muttered, his eyes glued to the television screen. "There was a field goal made before the game even started." The coroner guesses it was scored about two months ago. "Maybe a little more. I called Dr. Ford but he claims he didn't know a thing about her pregnancy."

"Do you believe him?"

"Of course," Mark said. "It's possible Helena Collier didn't even know herself."

"Oh, come off it," I roared. "You know better than that."

"I beg your pardon," Mark said. "I've never been pregnant."

"Well, if you get any closer to that television set you'll have a pretty good idea. You're liable to swallow the football."

"That," Mark bellowed, "would be a refreshing idea. At least, I could carry that damned ball over for a touchdown, even if those pip-squeaks can't. Come on, team!"

"What time is it?" I asked, reaching for the telephone.

"Eight seconds. They'll never make it."

I shrugged my shoulders and dialed Erik Ford's home phone number. He answered instantly.

"I can't talk now, you idiot! They've only got five seconds to play!"

"You've got even less than that, Doc," I said. "This is Honey West. Meet me at the Gay Blade in twenty minutes."

The crowd went berserk in the Rose Bowl, blotting out the doctor's faint argument. A big fullback bolted around right end, evaded three tacklers, became trapped along the sidelines, reversed his field and with the mammoth stadium erupting into pandemonium, raced into the end zone standing up.

"I'll be there," Erik said finally. "The game's over."

"You can say that again," I said and hung up.

Mark had his arms around the TV set and was hugging it for dear life. I walked out into the faint warmth of a late Shark Beach afternoon. The sea crashed awesomely in the distance. So awesomely that it made me wince as I crossed Forest Avenue on my way toward Pacific Coast highway.

The Gay Blade was known as a "queer" joint to the outside world. It squatted on the sand, wedged in by two rocky cliffs, the highway and a turbulent sea that smashed at its thick plate windows. The fancy restaurant-bar itself was about as queer as the word could indicate. Magnifying glass across the front created an unusually frightening sensation. When a wave began to gather along the rim of the water it was optically enlarged into a tidal wave sweeping vengefully toward the café. The bar curved around in front of these windows and each stool tapered up into two electrically-controlled steel pods. These were called "love-seats" and could be lowered or raised according to the two patrons' desires by a flick of a switch."

Doctor Erik and I shared one of these stools. He ordered two dry martinis and then grinned at me nervously.

"We won twenty to fourteen," he said. "I suppose you know Helena was pregnant."

"The police told me this morning. I didn't know until then."

"You told me you examined her last week."

Erik sipped at his martini. "My examination was—not for pregnancy. Helena had a kidney ailment. She drank too much."

"Is that so? Why'd you disappear last night after I discovered the body?"

"It—it shook me up—badly. I couldn't stand to see her that way."

"You're a doctor. I presume you've been around corpses before. Why did seeing Helena bother you?"

Erik downed his drink and ordered another round. "I'd never seen Helena that way. Never visualized her in that condition. I—I couldn't take the shock."

"You don't sound convincing."

"Well, dammit, I'm telling the truth. I wouldn't expect a lady lawyer to believe anything I say, naturally. Especially one hired by Helena."

His statement rocked me back. Since when was I a lady lawyer? I tried to conceal my surprise with a quick sip of my drink. Now I was beginning to understand a little more why he went berserk down in the ocean cave.

"What did you expect?" I asked. "For me to dump my whole case into your lap?"

"Why not?" Erik said, grimacing. "There's no overtime in a football game. You're dead! Helena's dead and you're dead and that's that. Period."

"Not exactly. I can still take my case to court."

Erik laughed grimly. "Not in a million years. It's a hung jury. You'll never bring in a verdict now."

I took a wild stab in the dark. "You did make her pregnant, didn't you, Erik?"

"Are you crazy?" he demanded. "I knew nothing about Helena having a baby. I'm not an obstetrician."

"No," I said, "but you're a man—or are you?"

"Very funny." He downed most of his new drink in one gulp. "And very aptly said in the Gay Blade. Do you see those fine-feathered gentlemen over there?"

I nodded.

"They're about as odd as a couple of ducks in a flock of ostriches. See those two doors marked *ladies*? Well, one of them, as you might notice, is spelled with a capital L. Don't ever go in there unless you want to be as embarrassed as hell."

"Which one do you use?" I asked, angry because I'd lost my hold on the conversation.

"That's for you to answer, counselor" Erik said, finishing the dregs of his second drink. "But if you're really interested in your former client, why don't you ask Hel Gandy a few questions. He's the one who killed her."

"Why do you say that?"

"Because he's a lousy skunk, that's why. He'd choke his own mother for a spare buck. He sits up there on top of that hill in a fancy studio shooting pictures of naked women. He ought to be shot himself!"

"You sound jealous, Doctor. Would you like to trade professions?"

"Are you joking?" Erik said, gripping his glass. "Sure, he makes a lot of money selling smut. But do you want to know how he does it? He takes these young rosy-chested girls just off the farm. Some of them arent' even eighteen when he gets his hands on them. They're cute girls out here alone, looking for a break in the movies or television. They've probably never had a drink or smoked a cigarette or taken their clothes off in front of man before. Then they meet Hel Gandy. Before long Miss Country Bumpkin is

185

posing in bra and panties, and not long after that, after one drink too many, she winds up with everything hanging out and Hel shooting pictures of her in every perverted pose known—and a few that aren't. The gal is stunned. Hel shows her some of the prints, offers her another drink, and from then on she never stops taking—or giving—for the rest of her life. End of story."

"Not very pretty," I said.

"That's right. So, now you know what kind of a man Helmet Gandy really is. He started Helena Collier out the same way five years ago. She was Helena Warren then. A real sweet dark-eyed Susan right off the pickle boat from Lincoln, Nebraska. Last night you saw the last stop on Hel Gandy's twisted trolley car ride to ruin. He killed her all right. He kills them all, eventually, some way or another." Erik got up from his half of the stool. "Now if you don't mind, the defense would like to rest its case. I'll see you around."

I stopped him near the door on his way out. "Erik, I—I want to apologize for the way I acted last night. I really thought you were going to..."

The doctor smiled. "Strangle you? No, I was only trying to describe how high up the anger was inside of me for what you and Helena were doing." His hands encircled his own throat. "You know the old expression, 'I've had it up to here.'"

"Of course." I drew close to him and fingered the lapel of his coat. "You wanted to kiss me last night, didn't you?"

"Sure I did, but..."

"No one can see us now," I whispered. "Do it now, Erik. I want you to kiss me."

His arms went around my shoulders quickly squeezing me tight against his chest. His lips were tender and restless on my mouth. My hands were a little restless, too, but not so tender. One of them slipped inside his coat pocket lifting out a ring of keys. I tucked them, unnoticed, into my purse and then pulled away.

"Thank you, Erik," I whispered.

"Honey, you're wonderful, let's go someplace..."

"I've got another appointment, but I'd like to take a raincheck," I hedged.

"It's a deal. You know my phone number. I'll be home all evening."

He glanced at my sweater and skirt and the way my hair was mussed. "I thought Helena had it. You've really got it."

"You're sweet," I said, visualizing his rage if he knew I'd lifted his keys. "Now, go home."

"Okay." He started for the door.

"Erik!"

"Yes?"

I tried to say it as casually as possible. "Did you know Hel Gandy took flash pictures last night at the party?"

"No," he said, and then after an instant, "Yes, I guess I did. Why?"

"Nothing. I just wondered if he took one of you in that crazy half and half costume. I'd love to have a print if he got anything of you."

He grinned, tossed me a kiss and vanished onto the sidewalk. I waited about fifteen minutes in the Gay Blade, dawdling over a martini, to be certain he hadn't guessed I'd tricked him when he missed his keys. He didn't return.

The telephone directory listed his office as opposite the Pleasure Pier in the Muldrup Building. As I strolled along the boardwalk, my mind pincered in on two distinct possibilities concerning Erik Ford's mistaking me for a lawyer. Either Helena had threatened him with a court action concerning her unborn child or else she'd gained information implicating Erik in the two earlier Shark Beach murders. The first thought seemed the most practical. If she'd had any real evidence of his guilt as a killer, she'd have gone to the police. Or would she? There was always the possibility of blackmail. Helena Collier didn't seem above such measures.

A short-sleeved, cotton dress crowd, clutching impish kids and ice cream cones, streamed monotonously along the boardwalk. At the foot of the Pleasure Pier, a rickety, wooden roller coaster trellis sprawled aimlessly on the sand, climbing at one point to a perilous height of almost a hundred feet. Screams and terrified laughter rode with the steel cars as they zoomed around the banked tracks screaming back their own fear of the slender rails that seemed hardly able to control the hurtling hunks of flesh and metal. A huge sign on the pier announced: The most chilling Experience of a Lifetime! Don't Miss It! WOLF LARSON'S BATHYSPHERE. I smiled. They had forgotten to mention one other chilling experience. WOLF

187

LARSON'S KISS.

A hand suddenly caught my arm. "Well, fancy meeting you here."

I glanced around at a neatly-pressed Marine officer's uniform. The handsome, sun-tanned face above belonged to Captain Reed Walker.

"Hi," I said, feeling a warm glow rush through me. "Happy New Year."

"The same to you," he said, squeezing my arm, "and that goes double." He had big brown puppy-dog eyes that sort of devoured you with their affection. "Say," he continued awkwardly, "how about an ice cream cone or something, huh?"

"Sure," then remembering, "but I'm in a hurry to get somewhere..."

"And this is the somewhere," he finished. "I've been lonesome wandering around this darned pier by myself. Come on."

He led me to an ice cream stand and ordered two vanilla cones without asking my preference. It didn't really matter. I felt too warm inside to care about anything, including the search I'd planned of Dr. Ford's office. We walked onto the pier in the gathering, fogtinged dusk.

"You ever been to Shark Beach before?" he asked.

"Once or twice. I—I don't remember exactly."

"You a California girl?"

"Uh-huh."

"Me, too. I mean, I'm a native son myself. Where you from?"

"Long Beach."

"Great town. Real great town. I'm from Frisco."

His small talk didn't seem insincere or boring, in the least. I bit down on the ice cream cone and shook my head. Get a hold of yourself, Honey, I thought. You're a big girl. This sort of thing is for the tourist trade. Besides, those Buck Rogers wings weren't in the case courtesy of the mummy.

We passed Wolf Larson's Bathysphere, but the diving bell was submerged in a frothy pool of green. Apparently, the muscleman was down inside describing his wonders of the deep.

"You're a model," Reed said, repeating what I'd told him last night. "Does it ever get sort of rough in your business?"

"Sure," I kidded, "almost as rough as it gets for a jet pilot when his after-burner blows."

He laughed and I was suddenly glad I'd lied to Mark Storm about the wings. This guy, as far as I was concerned, was definitely not a murderer. I was willing to stake my life on it.

We reached the end of the pier and Reed peered silently at the waves breaking over the pilings, arms braced on the wooden railing. Finally, he said, "Why'd you tell the police I pinned my wings on you?"

"Because you didn't kill Helena Collier."

"What makes you think so?"

I rubbed my bare arms from the chill of the fog rolling up off the water. He slipped his hand around my waist.

"I just have a feeling, that's all," I said, after a moment.

His grip tightened warmly, "You're crazy, you know that? Just plumb crazy."

"Reed, how did those wings get into the mummy case? Do you have any idea?"

"No, the evening got too drunk for me."

"So I noticed. Don't you remember anything?"

His face drew so near that I could count the tiny wrinkles around his eyes. "I remember you, Honey. I remember you out on that cliff with the lightning.

I felt his lips and they were even warmer than his and..." eyes. They moved up from my mouth, across my cheek and down again. I suddenly realized my arms were around his waist and my legs felt like a couple of those ribbons after the New Year's Eve party was over. I pulled back slightly to catch my breath.

"Reed, believe me, I—I've got to go someplace."

"Sure." He kissed me again. "My place."

"No—no, you don't understand."

His lips felt like molten lava pouring down the side of my face. "I—I have a real nice house. On the side of the hill. Big stone fireplace. We could build a fire. You're cold."

"Are you kidding?" I whispered, the heat in my limbs practically choking off my words. "I—I can't, Reed. I just can't."

His arms closed me against his body. "I never heard of that word," he said faintly.

"You want to know something?" I said, still trying to get

my breath. "Neither have I."

The huge gold wings over Reed's fireplace were hewn out of wood in an exact replica of those he wore over his heart. He poured two very *very* dry martinis and led me to a persimmon-colored couch that lay almost on the floor beneath fifty feet of windows framing Shark Beach's sea of neon light below.

Reed placed his warm hands on my cheeks and smiled. "I hope you don't think I'm just another Marine out for a good time."

I shook my head. "And I hope you don't think I'm just another girl out for a good Marine. Call me old-fashioned if you want to, Reed, but I like things to develop slowly."

"Honey," he protested, "I'm a jet pilot!"

"I know," I said. "But we're not at thirty thousand feet. Not yet. I—I want to ask you a question."

"Fire away."

"Were you with Fawn Collier last night?"

"If I say 'yes' will you be jealous?"

"I don't know. Were you?"

Reed took his hands away and wiped them over his broad forehead. "Yes. For a while. Until I passed out."

"Did you give her your wings?"

"No! Hell, no. I wouldn't touch her with a ten foot pole. She may look good, but she's funny. You can't get close to her. I've tried."

"How do you mean?"

"Oh, you know how people get sometimes when they're drunk," Reed said.

"How do you get?"

He smiled and his fingers touched the top of my sweater where several open buttons revealed a deep white cleft. "How old are you, Honey?"

"Twenty-eight."

"I'm thirty-two. Have you ever been married?"

"No."

"Neither have I. Funny, isn't it? Two people as old as we are having never fallen in love."

190

"We're not that old, Reed."

His face hardened in the faint light. "I guess not. My mother got married when she was fifteen. She was a beautiful woman—but she married a lush."

"Your father?"

"Yeah, he drank them both into a grave by the time they were thirty. First with lousy prohibition gin. Dad made it in a bathtub. Then he bought the cheapest junk he could find."

"What happened to you, Reed?"

"I—I was fourteen when my mother died. I knocked around for a few years and then went into the Marines. Been in ever since. Crazy, isn't it?"

"Not so crazy," I said softly. "My mother died when I was born. I lived most of my life with my father."

"Where's he now?"

"He was shot and killed in a back alley behind the Paramount Theatre in L.A. four years ago. He was a private detective."

Reed stiffened. "Who did it?"

"Nobody knows. It was raining. All they ever found was a diamond-studded tie clip lying in the gutter."

He shook his head, poured a new round of martinis and joined me again on the couch. Then he said, "A couple of damned orphans, huh?"

"Yeah."

"Honey," Reed paused for an instant before confessing, "I—I know you're not a model."

"What?"

"You're a private detective like your father. I know because I checked."

"How did you..."

"The Marine Corps has its ways. I went in to the base this morning. It didn't take long."

"But why, Reed?"

"You lied to protect me. I had to find out the reason. Now I know."

"That's what you think."

"You believe in me, don't you, Honey?" A private detective wouldn't lie otherwise.

"I don't know what you're talking about," I said, touching his mouth

191

with my hand. "You're still under suspicion and don't you forget that."

"Yeah," he said. "From the police, maybe, but not from you. I can feel it."

"All right, Reed, you've convinced me. So what?"

"But that's where you're wrong, Honey," he said simply. "I did kill her. I killed Helena."

Chapter Five

"Now who's talking crazy?" I asked.

"No, its true, Honey." Reed got to his feet. "I didn't actually commit the crime, but I might as well have. Helena was in love with me."

"What does that mean?"

"She didn't love Rote. She told me that at least a hundred times." He whirled around angrily. "She was always after me! What was I supposed to do? I'm only human!"

I set my martini on the floor and got up. "You're trying to tell me something Reed. You don't have to pull any punches."

He crossed to the windows, glowering down at neon lights and dark sea. "All right," he said, "I went to bed with her. What could I do? She'd come up here and take off her clothes and dance. My God, she was a woman. A beautiful woman."

"You knew she was pregnant, didn't you, Reed?"

"Yes."

"She accused you of being the father."

"Yes." It was hardly audible.

"Were you?"

"I—I don't know. I guess so."

"Are you certain?"

"No. I was drunk. I don't remember a thing that happened. The next morning I woke up and she was curled around me like a kitten. How certain can you get?"

I nodded.

"That was the only time," Reed said, not looking at me. "I had enough chances, but she was married and Rote Collier was a friend of mine. You want to know something real crazy?"

"What?"

"She used to actually beg me. I couldn't figure it out. There are a dozen guys in this town who would have jumped at the opportunity. Helena didn't want them."

"How do you know?"

"She told me."

"And you believed her, Reed?"

"Why shouldn't I. She never lied to me. At least, I don't think she did."

I patted his arm. "Reed Walker, you are either the most naïve Marine I've ever met in my life or the most egotistical. I don't know which. Where's your bedroom?"

"What?" His mouth fell open.

"I'm not going to beg you," I said, fluttering my eyelashes.

"Honey, you said you were an old-fashioned girl."

"See what I mean." I took his hand. "You even believed *me*."

The bedroom was down a narrow hall. It had a conventional double bed, plain striped wallpaper and a shelf crammed with model airplanes. There were no signs of black mesh curtains, slate rock or an uncovered mattress.

"Okay," I said, "Have you got a car?"

"Honey, you confuse the devil out of me. Of course, I've got a car."

"Good. I'd like to borrow it for about an hour. I want to confuse the devil out of somebody else."

"Who?"

"Helmet Gandy. His satanic costume last night couldn't have been more appropriate. In fact, he ought to wear it all the time."

"Honey, you can't leave now," Reed protested. "We were just beginning to…"

I kissed his cheek. "I'll be back in an hour. Then we'll have some real fun."

His eyes widened again.

"We'll break into an office building," I finished. "That should be a ball."

The path leading down to Hel Gandy's photography studio-home created the illusion of immense grandeur. The small, sparkling stones embedded in the cement walk appeared to be diamonds and the grandiose structure at the top of the road a solid gold miniature of the Eiffel Tower. The building itself, which was set perilously close to the edge of the hill, was extremely modern and constructed of aluminum and glass. It seemed the perfect setting for a bedroom with black mesh curtains draped around a slab of slate rock.

Hel was a long time coming to the door. He was dripping with perspiration and his eyes were red-rimmed.

"Hello," he said, a disturbed note in his voice. "And to what do I attribute this unexpected visit?"

"I told you I was a model, Mr. Gandy. I thought perhaps..."

He didn't move, not one hair. The half-opened door was blocked by his large bulk. "You want to pose, huh? His eyes were locked on the front of my sweater.

"That's right, I'd..."

"Come back tomorrow at three." He tried to swing the door closed in my face.

I stopped it with my shoulder. "I'm going home tomorrow. I won't have another chance—with you."

A knowing smile gathered in the corners of his mouth. "I've got a girl posing at the moment. Can you wait a half hour?"

"Sure. Why not?"

The door pressed against my shoulder as he tried to close me out once again.

I wet my lips with the tip of my tongue. "Why don't I wait inside? I won't get in the way. I promise."

He hesitated just long enough for me to push against his shirt provocatively with my chest. The door slipped from his fingers and I stepped around him into a garish hallway lined with numerous photographs of naked women, none retouched.

He whirled around, brow wrinkled in anger and gestured toward the living room. "Wait in there. You'll find liquor in a cabinet next to the fireplace. Pour yourself a drink."

When he was gone, I singled out a door leading off the hallway and tried the knob. It wasn't a bedroom, as I'd hoped, but it had a desk, six filing cabinets and a rack of books on *How To Take Pictures* in every language except Greek. I went after the cabinets. The first three didn't furnish a thing except thousands of routine pictures of nude women. Then I hit the pornographic drawer. It was bitter! The positions and angles were brutal and numberless. In almost every case the girls involved seemed pathetically young, half-closed eyes peering from white, horrified faces. They looked like a bunch of lipstick-smeared zombies unable to comprehend the acts being perpetrated upon them. Hel Gandy was noticeably present in several of the poses.

I gritted my teeth and went on until I found a thick file on Helena Collier. Her earliest poses hardly resembled the woman I'd discovered in the mummy case. This Helena was lithe and vital with long jet-black hair swept back in a pony tail. Her partially clad body reclined in youthful abandon on a leopard skin. The remaining photos told a different story. They degenerated into a stock lewdness which was stamped indelibly into the fiber of each licentious figure. Helena had stopped at nothing, including a wickedly harsh scene involving two other women. I slammed the file closed and tried another door. This one led me, all too unexpectedly, into Hel's studio.

The girl before the camera ranked in Hel's "breaking in" class. She was one of those rosy-chested types Erik had described; all bosom and hips with apple cheeks and electric blue eyes that were still unmarked by Hel's rigorous processing. She colored with embarrassment, trying to cover herself, when she discovered my presence.

Hel, on the other hand, nearly hit the ceiling. "Miss West, I thought I told you to wait in the living room! Dammit, get out of here!"

I slammed the door closed fast and was almost out of his office before he caught me. His grip on my arm was vicious as he backed me against the wall.

"You had no right to do that!" he roared. "You've embarrassed that girl to death!"

"I—I'm sorry," I stammered, trying to drum up a good explanation. "The—ah—liquor cabinet was jammed. I couldn't open it."

196

"You're lying," he spat. "It doesn't have any doors."

"Oh," I countered. "I must have been trying the wrong cabinet. You see, I'm just dying for a good belt. I guess I got excited. I—I get that way when I need a drink. I shake something terrible."

He steeped back and hunched his big shoulders. "You must have been trying the one on the other side of the fireplace. It's locked."

"Yeah, I guess that's what happened. Please, couldn't I have a drink?" My hands began to tremble.

He wiped sweat from his forehead and nodded, seemingly convinced that my mistake was one of a frenzied alcoholic in search of a bottle. This pleased him immensely and he smiled. "Drink all you want, baby. I'm going to send Lois home. We'll have a little New Year's party. Just the two of us, okay?"

I wet my lips and winked. "Sure, sweetie."

While Lois dressed behind closed studio doors, Hel followed me into the living room, watching eagerly as I filled a water glass to the one-third mark with bourbon. My hands continued to tremble the way I knew hands were expected to shake under such circumstances. He scrutinized each movement closely. My throat seemed to catch fire as I swallowed half the drink in one paralyzing gulp. I stifled a choking sensation with the back of my hand, laughing as the last drops ran sickeningly down my chin.

"Now I can live for a few minutes," I said. I'd never felt more like dying in my life.

Hel raised the bottle. "Have another, baby. Really get you on your feet."

"Oh, no!" I pressed my fingers on his lips. "I've got a big head start. I'll fix you."

And I did. I fixed him with a shot that would have choked a small horse and thirteen ponies. His eyes widened as many notches and his Adam's apple quivered. Lois slipped out the front door and vanished in the night.

Hel picked up the glass and winced. "This would kill me. You drink it."

I didn't have to pretend very hard at intoxication. My words lost their crispness like a bowl of corn flakes soaking in milk. I pressed the glass against his sweaty chest. "I thought you were a man. I guess maybe I was wrong."

His eyes showed his anger. He didn't hesitate a second, draining the glass before I could take a deep breath. He choked, blinked several times and quickly poured another drink. He should have been flat on his back, but his eyes weren't even glazed. His guts must have been made out of steel.

"Your turn," he said, handing me the glass.

I threw up my hands as a signal of surrender. "No—no," I stammered. "I quit! I'm sick, where's your bathroom?"

He led me through his studio to another door. Once alone, I tried a knob on the other side of a brightly-tiled sunken bathtub. It led me into a large, high-ceilinged room with charcoal colored walls. In the center hung black mesh curtains partially concealing an elevated slab of blue slate rock.

Hel came through a door on the other side of the room.

"Take off your clothes," he said. "You're not sick."

"That's what you think," I answered. "And I don't want to pose, thank you."

"You haven't any choice," he threatened. "Take off your clothes!"

"How long ago did you pose in that movie with Helena Collier?"

"What movie?"

"Must bring in a lot of change from pornographic minded home movie owners!"

"You must be an alcoholic," he said, advancing toward me. "You talk like one."

"Was she blackmailing you, too, Hel? Did she accuse you of being the father of her unborn child?"

He stopped dead in his tracks. "Just who are you anyway?"

"A friend," I said tightly. "A friend to just about anybody but you. I don't think you've go any friends. You're rotten. Rotten clean through. Why'd you kill her, Hel? Because she was going to expose you? Because she couldn't stand your sickening filthy racket any longer?"   ·

"Get out of here!"

"Sure," I said drunkenly, "I'll be glad to oblige—*after* I see your dark-room."

His lips pulled back over crooked yellow teeth and a hollow laugh escaped through the ugly opening. "I thought so. You're just a cheap drunk like all the rest of them. Helena was like you. Bitchy and fiery and mean. But she still wanted it. She wanted it in the worst way. Sure, I'll be glad to show you my darkroom. I got a bed in there just big enough for the two of us."

He came after me fast, but I got the door partially closed before his hand clamped over my arm. He groaned as I sank my teeth into him, still he wouldn't let loose. His other fist came out of nowhere against the side of my head, spinning me across the bathroom. He got the door open and leaped for me. That was his one mistake. I drew my leg back and the heel of my shoe caught him squarely in the stomach evoking a screaming howl that didn't stop until his head struck the edge of the sunken tub. For a long moment, he didn't move or utter a sound. Then he rolled over, without using either his arms or legs, as if he were tied up in a burlap bag. He tried to get to his knees, lost all sense of balance and toppled over in a crumpled heap at the bottom of the sunken tub.

Half-stunned from Hel's savage blow to my head, I staggered through the studio, stumbling around furniture, falling once and barely managing to make the darkroom. Several metal hangers of negatives hung inside a rubber tank and were bring washed in the sink. I grasped one of the wet four by five sheets and held it up to the green safe light. The image of a naked woman on a diving board glinted into view. Another negative revealed a group of costumed figures chaining a dummy to two awesomely tall pillars. I reached for a third, but never got it. Hel Gandy stood in the doorway, a stream of blood slanting down his forehead.

"What are you doing?" he growled. "I ought to kill you."

This time there was no way out. He pinned me against the sink and tore my sweater all the way down to my waist. His beady red eyes gaped down at me.

"You—you don't wear a brassiere," he said. "My God, you're beautiful."

I caught his stomach flush with my fist; a driving low blow that doubled him over.

I was halfway across his studio when he yelled. And the bullet squashed into the steel catwalk over my head.

Chapter Six

Hel Gandy aimed a German Luger at the gaping hole in my sweater. His gun hand trembled and blood still streamed down from a cut one his forehead.

"You don't scare me," he whispered. "You don't scare me on bit. What were you looking for in my darkroom?"

"A self portrait of a murderer," I said, staring at the muzzle of the gun. "You like to take pictures of yourself, don't you, Hel? Is that how you really get your kicks? Admiring yourself after a conquest? Where's your file on murder?"

"You—you think I killed Helena?"

"You're getting the idea."

His finger tightened on the trigger. "Why, I ought to…"

"—add me to the list," I finished. "Not this trip. Too many people know where I am. Put down the gun."

He wavered for an instant, then raised the barrel to my eyes. "Get out of here! Get out of here while you still got a chance! I never killed nobody, but I'm liable to right now!"

Another bullet bounced off the metal platform where Hel's overhead lights were rigged. I backed toward the door. He began to tremble again as sweat ran down his cheeks.

"Sure," he whispered, "I knew Helena was pregnant. But, I didn't get her that way, even if she said I did." He lurched toward me slowly. "You're right on another count. She was blackmailing me. Not for the reason you think. She was bleeding me for every rotten cent she could get and I'm glad she's dead."

He wiped some blood from his forehead and sneered. "Find me the

201

murderer and I'll pin a medal on him, do you understand? Now get out of here before I tear the rest of your clothes off and…"

"Why was she blackmailing you, Hel? What'd you ever do wrong—besides running this crummy racket—that you wanted to keep a secret?"

His eyes deepened into two fiery bits of black glitter. "Look!" He spat. "I ain't no queer, understand? I don't care what anybody ever says about me, but that's one thing I'm not and never will be. And nobody's ever going to accuse me of that! Nobody!"

"Why did she call you a queer?" I demanded. "What'd she have on you, Hel?"

"Nothing! Get out of here! I'm warning you for the last time!"

I could see his finger tighten on the trigger. I backed out the door into the hall, grabbed my purse and ran up the path to Reed's car. The night air felt bitterly cold through the hole in my sweater. Pinkish-blue goose pimples began popping out all over and, under the dashboard light, I noticed a deep scratch across one bosom. Now, how was I going to explain all this to Reed Walker?

I wrapped a car blanket around my shoulders and drove straight to Reed's place. He met me on the front steps.

"What happened to your promise of an hour?" he said. "You've been gone nearly three."

"I'm sorry, but I was held up. And that's no joke."

We went into the living room where flames licked over a eucalyptus log in the fireplace. I bent down to warm myself.

"What's with the blanket?" he asked.

"Hel Gandy got a little rough in the clinches. My sweater's torn."

"That dirty so and so." Reed touched a corner of the blanket. "Maybe we can mend the tear. Let's see the damage."

I caught his hand. "There's nothing to see! I—I mean,"

"Well, *what* do you mean?"

"Just take my word for it. I'm going to have to go back to the Collier place and get some other clothes. The tear is pretty severe."

He hunched down beside me and grinned. "I've got something in the closet that might fit you. My sister left a sweater behind the last time she visited me."

"I didn't know you had a sister."

"You don't know a lot of things about me." He went into the bedroom. "She's about your size. Real big bosom." His voice continued above the sound of drawers being yanked open. "She's a bachelor girl. Like you. Nice kid. She tells me all her secrets and I tell her most of mine."

Bits of glitter, reflected by a lamp, suddenly caught my eye. I crawled over and discovered lots of gold sequins scattered on the carpet near the coffee table. I shrugged my shoulders and returned to the fireplace before the realization hit me. Incredulous, I looked toward the bedroom.

"Reed?"

"Yes, Honey." His voice still carried over the sound of his movements.

"Didn't someone tell me Helena wore a bathing suit as her costume for the party?"

"That's right. Not a very novel idea, but the suit did emphasize Helena's best features. She was well stacked in the upper story."

"I wonder what happened to that suit. The police couldn't find it anywhere."

"Probably got washed away by the tide while she was swimming in the nude."

I examined some of the sequins. "What did the bathing suit look like, Reed?"

"A real hot number," Reed shouted back. "Must have been specially designed for her. Slashed all the way down to the waist. I'll never be able to figure out how she stayed in the damned thing. Of course, when you come right down to it, she didn't stay in the suit, did she?"

"No," I murmured, then louder, "what color was it?"

"White." Then he added, "With little gold sequins running all over. A sensational outfit with her long black hair. Hurray! I found the sweater."

Before he reached the living room, I scooped up a few of the shiny gold discs and crouched by the fire again. He tossed me a fluffy gray cashmere sweater and grinned. "Go ahead, try it on."

"I turned my back toward him, lowered the blanket and slipped into the cardigan sweater. Before I had a chance to close the first button, his arms moved around me from behind.

"Honey," he said, in a half-whisper. "You're not wearing a bra! Am I seeing things?"

I whirled around, my palm open revealing the gold sequins. "I don't know, Reed. Am I?"

He stared at the bits of glitter for a long moment, then slowly his arms came loose from around my waist. "Where'd you find those?"

"On the floor near that table."

Reed made a gesture of futility and sat down. "I should have known you'd find out somehow. Okay, if you must know the truth, I've got the bathing suit."

"And just how did you get possession of such an interesting item?"

"After the police left last night, I circled around the house and went down into one of the vaults through a side entrance. I found her suit shoved under one of the mattresses. The material was torn over the left breast."

"Why?"

"Those tin wings. I pinned them on Helena not long after your arrival at the party. The murderer apparently ripped them off her suit."

"And it's your contention that he planted them in the mummy case with the body, right?"

Reed nodded. "Your lie actually put both of us in a helluva spot. If the police'd found her suit first we would have wound up behind bars before you could have batted an eyelash."

"If I hadn't lied you would have been there anyway. Alone. Why didn't you tell me all of this before?"

He got to his feet and moved toward me. His body was lean and quick, almost cat-like. Reed was the human version of one of his jet planes; sleek, well balanced and extremely powerful. He grasped me in his arms. "Honey, you're beautiful."

"You're the second person to say that to me today. Be careful, I'm liable to get a complex."

"You? Hardly." He kissed the tip of my nose. "Why did you lie for me, Honey?"

I took a deep breath and suddenly realized I'd forgotten all about the buttons. "I—I like you, Reed. You know that's the reason. Now, let's get out of here."

Our lips touched lightly. Rain began to caress the windows in the same manner. His hand reached down to my sweater.

"Reed, I told you…"

"I'm going to button the sweater. You'll catch cold."

"Reed, I'm a big girl. I can take care of myself."

His hand didn't keep its promise. I tried to pull back, but couldn't. Suddenly he knew I was a big girl in more ways than one and his fingers trembled from the realization.

The telephone rang. Then again.

"You'd better answer, Reed."

"Tomorrow."

The bell rang again, grating insistently.

"Reed, it might be important."

"No." His fingers slipped under the top of my skirt and touched my stomach.

I broke loose and picked up the receiver. "Hello." "Who's this? Honey? Is that you? What the hell are you doing there?"

"Mark, I…"

"Don't tell me you're investigating the Collier case," he said angrily, "because you don't know which end is up. But I'm sure your boyfriend does."

I glanced at Reed. "What are you talking about?"

"Fawn Collier that's who I'm talking about—and your handsome Marine? They were seen together about two hours ago at the Booby Hatch—a local bar down here on the beach. They had an argument. A big one. And then walked out. Rote Collier just called me. Fawn was supposed to have been home more than an hour ago, but she hasn't shown. Now what gives? If she turns up dead, Honey, you're going to be dead, too, believe me."

My hand tightened on the receiver. I stared down at the glittering gold sequins scattered on the carpet. Reed followed my line of sight and his face tightened.

"I'll call you back."

"No you won't!" Mark said. "I got a feeling something's going to happen, if it hasn't already. I don't want you involved, do you understand?"

"You're a nice guy."

"You're damned right I am," he said in that gruff tone that never really hid his warm interior. "And besides that I'm charming. Now get out of there and leave Buck Rogers to me. It's just possible he's polished off Fawn Collier. You might be next."

"All right," I said faintly, trying to close the conversation without making Reed suspicious. "I'll take care of the situation."

I hung up and buttoned the sweater. Reed studied each movement carefully.

"What was that?" he asked finally.

"I've got an appointment, Reed. I told you that long ago."

"I know, but you didn't leave. What's changed your mind?"

"Nothing."

"You're lying to me, Honey, and I don't like people who lie when it isn't necessary."

I started for the front door. He blocked my path.

"Please, get out of my way, Reed."

"No! I told you not to answer that phone. We were doing fine until that thing rang."

"Were we?"

"I thought so. You were so warm and receptive. A telephone call can't make that much difference. Please don't go!"

"Is that what you said to Fawn Collier two hours ago?"

"I guessed as much!" His fists tightened. "Why do women always do this to me? Why do they always have to make me mad?"

Chapter Seven

"So women make you mad, do they, Reed?"

"You're damned right!" He tossed a new log on the fire and pinched the bridge of his nose. "Fawn Collier called me after you left for Hel's studio. She asked me to meet her at the Booby Hatch. I said no, but she said it concerned you and was very important, so I went. What she told me really made me blow my stack." .

"Go on."

He hesitated, then continued, "Fawn accused you of making time with her father. She said you were planning to take up where Helena left off. She even claimed she caught you two in an intimate situation last night."

"How intimate?"

"You know what I mean?"

"That isn't true, Reed. He tried to kiss me, that's all."

"I guessed as much." His face reddened. "Well, I damned near knocked her out of her chair. Accused her of having a filthy imagination, a father complex, a split personality, sex problems, men problems, money problems…"

"What then?"

Reed smacked a fist into his palm. "She threatened to expose your lie about the wings to the police. She said you were nothing but a high-class pro working every single angle you could manage. She threatened to stop you from moving in on her father, even if it meant sending you to jail."

I shook my head. "How'd she know about the wings?"

"She saw me pin them on Helena." Reed walked to the fireplace and stared into the flames. "I told her she'd never be able to prove Helena had those wings and, furthermore, she was all wrong about you. She said the pictures Hel took at the party would verify her point about the wings. So, I dropped my bomb and blew her higher than a kite!"

"What bomb was that?"

"I told her you were a private detective."

"Reed, you shouldn't have done that!"

"Yes—I know. I was so mad the whole business just slipped out before I realized what I'd said. I wanted to tear her apart I was so burned up."

"That was Lieutenant Storm on the phone. Fawn's disappeared."

"Well, don't look at me," Reed said. "I don't know where she is. She got into her car and drove away—alone."

I studied Reed's tense face and saw more than a little apprehension. Reed Walker just didn't add up. His story about Helena's bathing suit sounded phoney. The bit about the tin wings didn't jibe and, to top it all off, he had obviously lied to avoid any further questions about the scattered sequins. He was definitely hiding something, but what? I hoped it wasn't murder.

I thanked him for the loan of his car and the sweater and walked downtown. Light rain fell softly and felt cool on my flushed cheeks.

Things had quieted considerably on the Pleasure Pier. A few neon lights still burned, but they were faint and hardly recognizable in the dark mist. Wolf Larson's concession was locked tighter than a drum. So was the Muldrup Building. One of Dr. Erik Ford's keys solved that problem. His office was on the second floor toward the rear. It was spacious, modern and had a strong antiseptic odor.

I went after the file cabinet in the outer office. The folders were monotonously dull, stuffed with lengthy descriptions and prescribed treatment for every kind of ailment down to the South African wrist itch. In a bottom drawer I found a medical history on Helena Collier which covered two years. Besides numerous penicillin shots for viral infections, she had been treated for a broken arm, severe sunburn, an earache and had received minor surgery for a growth of her left breast. Nothing was mentioned about a kidney ailment. Her recent visits, dating back three months prior to her death, were listed as "minor checkups." These increased in frequency from once a week to every other day during the week preceding New Year's Eve. It was possible she'd developed kidney trouble during this period and her

208

visits for this ailment had been listed in such a manner, but I seriously doubted it.

Erik Ford's private office was handsomely furnished, indicating prestige, wealth and honor. His polished mahogany walls were lined with plaques naming him such things as Doctor of the Year, Great Humanitarian and Distinguished Medical Scholar.

His desk drawers provided no further data on Helena Collier. They did yield further proof of his feats in the field of medicine, including a citation from a New York Hospital lauding him for a brain operation performed successfully in the face of impossible odds. The patient had been the five-year-old son of poor immigrants. Erik had refused to accept a penny for his twelve long grueling hours at the operating table. Instead, he had provided the youth with an annuity for his future college education.

After reading that citation, I didn't feel like going any farther in my search. This man was obviously a great healer. Why should I investigate him for murder? The bottom drawer of Erik's desk was locked. I fingered the ring of keys indecisively. Five men had figured prominently in Helena's last years of life: Rote Collier, Helmet Gandy, Wolf Larson, Reed Walker and Erik Ford. Which one of them had hated her enough to commit murder? I knew I had to find the answer to that question no matter how low I stooped.

I inserted the correct key into the lock and opened the drawer. My relief at discovering a stack of medical books was short-lived. Underneath was a brown folder stained with finger marks. I flipped open the cover. Inside were at least a dozen newspaper clippings concerning the murder of two prominent Shark Beach women. At the bottom of the pile was a slip of paper with the scrawled words: Dr. J. Smith, Webster-9-34855, Helena.

The operator got the number for me immediately. It rang five times before a small, hesitant man's voice answered. "Hello?"

"Dr. Smith?"

"No, I'm sorry, I'm afraid you have the wrong..."

I pressed dire intensity into my voice. "Please, wait! I know your real name isn't Smith, but that doesn't matter, does it? I'm in trouble—terrible trouble—and you've got to help me, please!"

There was a long empty silence through which his deep nervous breathing penetrated like bursts of machine-gun fire. Finally he asked vaguely, "Smith? Where did you get that name?"

"I'm going to have a baby," I whispered tightly. "Don't you understand? I can't have another child. I'll die if I do."

"You may die if you don't," he said. "Do you realize what you're asking?"

"Yes, yes! But I'm two and a half months pregnant. I know it's dangerous, but I'll take my chances. If my husband ever found out…"

"I'm sorry," he said. "I don't perform such operations. It's against the law."

"I know that. I've got money!" I pleaded. "I'll pay you a thousand dollars, only, please, please, help me!"

"I…"

"I'll sign papers! I'll do anything! Oh, please say you'll perform the operation on me!"

The silence was longer this time. The breathing deeper and more constricted. Finally, "Who's calling, please?"

"Mrs.—Mrs. Arnold Kenilworth."

The name sounded like it might belong to a prominent society woman. I counted on his thinking he'd read it somewhere in the newspapers.

"What's your telephone number, Mrs. Kenilworth? I'll call you back in a few minutes."

I hadn't counted on that.

"No! No, wait I can't!" My voice lowered into a frightened whisper. "My husband's downstairs. He'll answer the phone. I—I can't take the chance."

"Did—did you say a thousand dollars?"

"Yes, yes. I'll pay before the operation. Oh, please!"

The silence became unbearable this time. I even wondered if he was having my number checked.

Then, "I can't guarantee anything, Mrs. Kenilworth."

"I know that. Will your perform the operation?"

"I'll call you tomorrow when your husband is not at home. What is your number?"

"Dr. Smith, I must have an answer now! *Will you perform the opera-*

tion?"

His answer was still evasive, not legally incriminating, but satisfactory as far as I was concerned.

"I believe you can count on me, Mrs. Kenilworth."

"Thanks you," I sighed relievedly. "I'll call you tomorrow and make an appointment."

"But, I thought…"

"Good-bye, Dr. Smith."

I hung up and stared at the file of newspaper clippings spread out on Erik's desk. My eyes moved to the citation. One of the neatly typed lines sprang up boldly:

No man has ever done more for the cause of good in the history of the world. For what more can any man do, but to save a life.

I read it over again slowly. Then I looked again at the newspaper clippings and at the tiny sheet of paper which contained the fictitious name and telephone number of an abortionist. But the thing I really saw was ten times more frightening. A huge shadow twisted across the desk. The shadow of a man standing in the doorway.

Chapter Eight

Doctor Erik Ford was dripping wet from the rain, his coopery red hair glittered in the light reflected from the outer office.

"You sneaking little thief! You stole my keys. I'm going to call the police." He started for the phone.

"Good idea," I said. "And while they're here you can show them your newspaper file. What happened? Haven't you had a chance to add Helena's clips to the group yet?"

He stopped abruptly and stared at the material spread out on his desk. Apparently he hadn't noticed the clippings before.

"You—you've been in my bottom drawer," he stammered. "You had no right to do that."

"And I had no right to call Dr. J. Smith either, Erik, but I did."

His face turned bone white. He staggered for an instant and then caught the edge of his desk. "You—you couldn't have…"

"I made an appointment for an abortion, Erik. He said he thought he could fit me in."

"But, why? Helena's dead. You can't——You had nothing to gain…"

"Except a murder, Erik. I'm not a lawyer, I'm a private detective hired by Rote Collier."

He fell back into a chair in the corner and his shoulders trembled. A plaque hung over his head. Great Humanitarian. Now I remembered two other folders filed under his list of clients in the office cabinet. They had belonged to the two other prominent women recently murdered in Shark Beach. Lorraine Reynolds and Joan Lacey.

"I've been reading your citation, Erik, for that brain operation you performed on a five-year-old boy. I almost cried."

"What are you, Erik, the modern Dr. Jekyll and Mr. Hyde?"

He shook violently, hands crushed over his eyes. They still couldn't hold back the wetness that trickled down his cheeks. "You—you don't understand."

"What don't I understand, Erik? That you knew Helena was pregnant and was arranging for an abortion? That you were the father? That she wouldn't consent to the operation? That she was blackmailing you and threatening to ruin your magnificent career? That the two other murdered women were also former clients of yours?"

"It's all true," he broke. "It's all true. I—I admit it. But I didn't kill them. I didn't kill Helena."

I glanced at the newspaper clippings and got to my feet. "Erik, you don't sound very convincing."

"I don't care," he groaned. "I tried to arrange an illegal operation for Helena. I admit my guilt on that charge."

"And what about these newspaper clippings? A man just doesn't save and hide this sort of thing for fun."

"They were clients of mine," he admitted, still unable to look at me. "If—if you must know the truth they were more than clients. I was in love with—with both Lorraine Reynolds and Joan Lacey. I was in love with Helena—once. You think I'm crazy, don't you?"

"Yes—in a way," I said quietly. "Tell me something, Erik. Have you ever been married?"

"Don't! Don't, please!"

"You want me to call the police, Erik? Believe me, they won't be so easy with their questions."

"No, Honey, listen…" He stopped and glanced at me. His face was twisted almost beyond belief. "I—I'll answer anything, but don't…"

I surveyed the wall plaques again. "All right, Erik."

"I've been married. Once. A long time ago. She was a student nurse."

"What happened to her?"

He couldn't answer. His lips moved, but nothing came out. Then, he managed, "She died."

"What was the cause?"

It was hardly audible. "Negligence. I—I was the doctor. I killed her.

213

I didn't mean to, but I didn't know…"

"What didn't you know, Erik?"

Tears streamed down from his nostrils and he tried to wipe them away with the back of his hand. "I didn't know enough about childbirth. I was only nineteen. She was going to have a baby. She—she had a placenta previa. We lived out in the middle of the desert. A hundred miles away from the nearest doctor. I tried to save her, but I couldn't. They both died."

I opened a humidor on the desk and place a cigarette in his mouth. "What has that got to do with Helena—or these two other women?"

"You asked the question," he murmured, drawing hard on the flame I held up. "Now I'm forty-one. I spent seven years in medical schools trying to learn why she had to die. And I still don't know. I still don't why anyone has to die. Or why anyone has to kill. It—it doesn't make sense to me."

"Are you trying to say that's why you've kept these newspaper clippings?"

"Yes." The word was an interminable whisper.

I shook my head, pushing back a few wet curls from my forehead. "How much was Helena blackmailing you for?"

"Twenty thousand dollars."

"How do you know you were the father?"

His face sagged again. "I—I don't, but it didn't make any difference. I'd been to bed with her. She even had a movie to prove the fact."

I froze in my tracks. "What kind of a movie?"

He almost choked on the words they were so bitter. "Oh, you know the type. She must have had a camera rigged in the closet."

"Erik, did this episode take place in Hel Gandy's bedroom?"

"No, no, of course not," he managed. "At her house. Rote was gone for the week. He still has big holdings in several motion picture companies. I—I never should have done it, I know, but…"

"You actually saw the film?"

"A print," he said angrily. "The original she kept safely tucked away where nobody could find it."

"Did you ever try to get the original or that print?"

"Yes, once." He gripped the arms of his chair. "I couldn't stand it any

214

longer. I knew I had to do something—had to find that film. Rote was in L.A. overnight. I went to her house. I reasoned with her, pleaded, but she laughed. She laughed in my face. So I started looking. I tore that house apart from one end to the other." He shook his head. "But, it wasn't there. Or, at least, I couldn't find it."

"What did you do then?"

"She—she was standing at the top of those steps. You know the ones that lead down to the swimming pool. She laughed at me again. Something snapped inside my head and I hit her. She fell almost all the way to the bottom. I—I thought she was dead when I reached her, but she'd only broken her arm."

"Erik, you had every motive in the world to kill Helena."

"I know. Perhaps, subconsciously, I was trying to murder her that night when… Believe me, Honey, I didn't try again last night."

"Last night was more than a try, Erik."

"I—I know. I had a feeling she was going to die. That's why I wanted to get out of there. I've never done a wrong thing in my life, Honey. Except, possibly to love. I've always loved too much. I can't seem to stop myself."

"You really were in love with Helena?"

"Once—yes. But, I swear to you I didn't kill her. Killing—just isn't my business."

My eyes fell on the note on Erik's desk. "You tried to arrange an abortion for her. Why?"

"To save Rote. To save me. To save anyone who might have been caught in Helena's deadly web."

"Why did you say you thought Hel Gandy killed her?"

"If it hadn't been for Hel Gandy she never would have died—not that way. Did you know Hel way secretly photographing Lorraine and Joan in the nude before they were murdered?"

"No, I didn't."

"Well, he was. Their husbands—a couple of immature Marine officers like Reed Walker—were in the dark, I'm sure. If they'd known they probably would have strung him up on the nearest tree."

"They didn't know about you?"

"No."

"You think your association with them was any different?"

"I wasn't trying to expose them on film for a bunch of pornographic magazines."

"What were you trying to do, Erik?"

"I—I told you I was in love with them!" he nearly shouted. "I couldn't help myself. Every attractive woman I meet looks like Marie—talks like Marie—even you, Honey. It's some kind of horrible fixation that I just can't seem to escape."

"And I can't seem to escape the fact, Erik, that you fit the murderer's shoes exactly. You were in love with three women. And now they're all dead. It almost couldn't be a coincidence."

He got to his feet shakily. "I'm glad you said, 'almost'. Please, give me a chance to prove I'm innocent."

"How?"

"I—I don't know. When I was a little boy and my mother was about to whip me for something I didn't do, I used to say, "The executioner always hangs himself first.""

"You must have been a pretty grown up boy to spout that sort of philosophy."

"I was. Uncomfortably so. I lived with my mother—alone. My father left us when I was ten. She was always afraid I would emerge in his image."

"And have you?"

Erik seemed lost in a grave reflection. "Funny, isn't it? You think you're grown up. You get a few more lines and lose a little hair, but things never really change, do they? You still wake up facing the same realities, asking the same questions, hearing the same answers."

I flipped the file closed on his desk and rubbed my forehead. "Okay, what's the answer to this one? Why didn't you pay her the blackmail? You seem to have enough money."

"I may appear wealthy," he said. "That's the mistake Helena made. Do you want to see something?"

"Yeah," I said softly, "anything but a gun."

"I don't own a gun," he said, crossing to his desk. "You've been through my drawers. You didn't find one, did you?"

"No."

"See this?"

He handed me a letter which; I'd overlooked. It read:

My dear Erik:

It is beyond human bounds to thank you enough for your interest in our research foundation. Your check for $20,000 (twenty thousand dollars), which has just been received, will help save hundreds and thousands of lives. This is a fantastic amount of money considering your previous gifts. There are tears of gratitude in my eyes. Of course, there have been tears in my eyes for many, many years.

Best Always,

F.

"Who's 'F', Erik?"

"My father," the doctor said. "He's been the head of cancer research foundation for the past twenty years. We never see each other. I always receive a letter after I've sent in a contribution. That's been the extent of our association. Funny, isn't it."

"No!" I said, circling his desk angrily. "There's something wrong with you, Erik. You know it and I know it. Now what goes?"

"He left us, Honey," Erik continued, not hearing my words. "Thirty-two years ago. He left my mother and me—flat. Now he's trying to make up for his mistake. Okay, so I contribute. Every time I get a few spare dollars I contribute. Why? Not because of all the poor suffering people, but because I feel sorry for him and because I hate his guts!"

"I suppose that's how you felt about that five-year-old boy when you operated on him?"

Erik Ford's eyes deepened into two infinitesimal pools of despair. "No—no, I loved that boy. He was almost like a son. He didn't ask for anything and I didn't give him anything more than he deserved."

"Do you ever correspond with him?"

His face furrowed perceptibly. "No. He writes to me—often. I don't know why he does. I didn't really help him at all. He would have been all right."

217

"That isn't how this citation reads."

"Well, he would have been!" Erik growled. "People don't need doctors. They can take care of themselves! Ninety-five percent of my patients are a bunch of hypochondriacs. They don't have a thing wrong with them!"

"Like Helena?"

"Yes. I told you she had a kidney infection. She didn't. All she had was an ache—a basic elementary ache that bothers about thirty million American women daily. I treated Helena. What a mistake that was."

"Erik, you're sounding more like a murderer every second."

"All right," he said, sliding into a chair. "What are you going to do?"

"I've got a basic ache, too," I said, "But, at the moment, it's not the kind you've described. Mine's curiosity. Come on, let's go!"

"Where?"

"Helmet Gandy's studio. I want to take another look at some of his negatives."

Rain and darkness obliterated the reproduction of the Eiffel Tower as we stumbled down the polished path to Hel's front door. Erik held my arm and his heels clattered on the wet cement.

I knocked several times and then tried the knob. The door swung open revealing a picture frame twisted and broken on the entryway floor. Bits of glass were ground into the carpet where someone had crushed them through the photograph in an effort to blot out a nude figure.

Erik picked up the remains of the picture and glanced at the blank space on the wall where it had once hung.

"Helena," he said. "Hel took the photo about four years ago. The wind must have broken the wire on the back of the frame and sent the whole works crashing."

I examined the remain of Helena's picture. A piece of glass had gashed a hole in her stomach. "And I suppose the wind jumped on this afterwards with two big muddy feet just to confuse us into thinking Kilroy was here." The entry was tracked with crusty red clay impressions left from a pair of flat-soled shoes.

"Hel must have stepped on the picture accidentally…" Erik started.

"Hel my foot," I said. "Look at this place!"

The office door stood ajar. File drawers and photographs were strewn from one end of the floor to the overturned flood lamps and scenery that created a ulately-arranged studio. The faint green bulb still burned over the darkroom sink. I searched for the negatives, but found only an empty rubber developing tank and a few wire hangers mashed into the wooden-slatted floor.

Erik stood framed in the door. "What a mess. I wonder if Hel knows about this?"

"Why don't you ask him?"

"He isn't here."

"How do you know?" I demanded. "Did you call for him?"

"Well, no, but…"

"How do you know he isn't in the bedroom or outside someplace?"

"I don't. I just imagined…"

"You imagined what, Erik? He wasn't here when you came after the negatives, so it's fairly easy to imagine he wouldn't be here when you came back. Is that it?"

"You—you think I did this?"

"What do you think, Erik?"

"How could I, Honey?" he argued. "Even if I'd wanted to—and God knows for what reason—how would I have gotten here? You had all my keys."

"You have a second set, Erik. Your car was parked out in front of the Muldrup Building when we came out of your office. It wasn't there when I went in."

The doctor shook his head. "You're crazy. You just didn't notice. I parked there this afternoon before I met you at the Gay Blade."

"I'm afraid not, Erik. Let me tell you how I think it was. You discovered your original set of keys were missing when you got home. Fortunately, for me, you'd walked downtown. The possibility that I'd lifted the keys from your pocket didn't cross your mind. You were too concerned with what I'd told you about Hel Gandy taking pictures at the party. You wondered if it was possible he'd taken a shot of you and Helena in—shall we say—an unflattering pose. One that might have given the police the *wrong* idea. Finally, you couldn't stand it any longer. You dialed Hel's num-

219

ber, but there was no answer. So you drove up here. It was raining and dark. A perfect opportunity. You tore the place apart, found the negatives and left—destroying Helena's picture on your way out. Then, it suddenly struck you what happened to your keys."

"No, Honey, you're way off, believe me."

"I don't think so, Erik. Let me look at the soles of your shoes."

Erik's face flushed as bright as his coppery hair and he swallowed hard. "No, I told you I didn't do this. Now let's get out of here."

"You have metal clips on your heels," I said. "I heard them clatter outside on the walk. You should be more careful, Erik, when you break into someone's house. You left some magnificent footprints in that entryway, indicating a metal clip in each impression. Now, what do you say?"

Erik's pale eyes pinched down. "All right" he said. "All right, I was here. You guessed right to a certain point. I did worry about Hel's pictures after you mentioned them. Helena was unusually nice to me last night. I thought maybe she had changed her mind about a law suit. We—we wound up down in one of the vaults—early—while Hel was wandering around shooting some of his filthy pictures. She was being so nice—until I realized she hadn't changed. Not one bit! And I—I got mad. Almost as mad as the night I pushed her down the staircase. Then something popped like a flashbulb. I don't know if it really was a flashbulb or just my own brain bursting from anger. I remembered that incident when I got home today after talking to you. I realized any such picture in the hands of the police would make me a prime suspect for Helena's murder. So, I called Hel Gandy. You're wrong on that count. Somebody did answer."

"Who?"

"I don't know. Hel probably. There was a dead silence on the other end and then he hung up. Probably had one of his pictorial prostitutes all lined up for a shot. I was only going to ask him if I could see the negatives."

"Go on."

"I was furious when he hung up on me like that. Certainly I'd planned to destroy any damaging pictures if there were any, but the darkroom was cleaned out just as it is now. Same state of upheaval all over the house. I must have stepped into a mud puddle and tracked that red clay into the hall without realizing."

I leaned an elbow on the sink and examined his face as a mother might investigate her tiny son's dirt-smudged features after he'd promised to stay clean for church. "You're an amateur, Erik. That's obvious. Some amateurs can be awfully smart. I don't know what to think about you."

"What do you mean, Honey?"

"I didn't see any identifying marks in those footprints out in the entryway. I said that just to trick you into an admission."

"You're very clever."

"Yeah," I groaned miserably. "So clever I can't even begin to explain how you might have placed Helena's body in the mummy case and still mingled with guests at the swimming pool all at the same time. That case was empty ten minutes before you called up to Wolf Larson and me on Rote's spiral staircase. To have achieved that feat you would have needed Mandrake the Magician or a—a jet plane."

He tried to smile. "And there were neither in the vicinity. Honey, I'm glad you've finally added two and two together."

"Have I, Erik? I was never much good at arithmetic." I walked past hhim into the studio. "Who would have had more reason to tear this place apart, than you?"

"Ask Hel Gandy," he said, still standing in the faintly-lighted doorway, his coppery hair all abristle, his hands, so deft and gentle over an operating table, now clenched into big hard knots. "I told you Hel Gandy was the one who murdered Helena. He framed this whole business just to throw suspicion on someone else. You ask Hel Gandy."

Something splattered against my cheek. I wiped it away and my fingers felt sticky from the thick substance. I looked up at the dark metal platform which support Hel's overhead floods.

"Turn on the lights, Erik."

"I—I don't know where the switch is, Honey."
I lifted one of the fallen light standards, pointed it toward the platform and flicked the button. A bright yellow beam lunged up toward the ceiling.

There was no sense asking Hel Gandy anything. He was slumped over the platform railing and beads of crimson ran down into his wide, sightless eyes from a hole in the center of his forehead.

Chapter Nine

Doctor Erik Ford peered up at Hel's dead body like a man peering at a ten-ton piano plummeting at him from the top story of the Empire State building. He tried to put his warning into words and the warped fragments of his fear barely escaped his trembling lips.

Hel Gandy's lantern jaw twisted around on its thick neck and his eyes seemed to roll with the motion of his body. He tipped forward on the platform railing, hung there for a long instant, arms pinioned back like a puppet with his strings all tangled. When he fell, arms flailing limply, he missed Erik by inches, plunging head-first into a mass of jumbled scenery.

I don't know who screamed the loudest. Erik's throaty cry was like a big bird's bewildered squall as a hunter's bullet pierces its chest. He staggered back, gaping at the tangled remains of Hel Gandy and at my blood-smeared cheek and hand. He whirled and ran for the door, but never quite made it. Mark Storm, grasping Hel's Luger in a handkerchief, blocked Erik's way.

"I wondered how long he was going to hang there like that, didn't you?" Mark snapped handcuffs on Erik's trembling wrists. Then he held up a folder filled with newspaper clippings. "You left your morgue file behind, Doc. That's all right, though, when you take up residence on San Quentin's death row you can subscribe to a clipping service." Mark jerked the ashen-faced surgeon toward the door. "Come on, Doc, we don't want to keep the gas chamber waiting."

I argued with Mark until almost midnight about Erik Ford's arrest, but the deputy wouldn't budge an inch toward turning the key on the doctor's cell. He just kept drumming a pencil on his desk and staring at the distant lights of the new hospital where Hel Gandy lay quietly dead in an air-conditioned morgue.

"It's physically impossible, Mark," I repeated for about the fifteenth time.

He grinned suddenly. "You mean sex between two porcupines? That I agree."

"You know exactly what I mean!" I blurted angrily. "Erik couldn't have murdered Helena. He didn't have enough time to put her body in that mummy case!"

Mark nodded. "Okay. Okay. He did have time to put a bullet in Hel Gandy and his lips on the mouths of those two other dames. Now, why don't you go home?"

"Why would he shoot Hel Gandy if he hadn't murdered Helena? There's no logical reason."

The detective lunged to his feet, seizing me by the shoulders. "There's no logical reason for you hanging around this town either, but you do, don't you? All right, you lied your Marine friend out of being arrested last night, but you're not going to pull the same gag twice in a row."

"Why, Mark Storm, I actually think you're jealous."

"Well, what if I am?" he said, swinging his gaze back to the hospital lights. "Now get out of here. And put on a brassiere! You can see right through that damned sweater!"

"I—I'm sorry," I stammered. "I forgot to bring any bras a long on the trip and all the stores were closed today. What can a girl do under those circumstances?"

"Wear a raccoon coat!"

Fawn Collier entered Mark's office, winked at me and tossed a paper on his desk. "Is that what you wanted, Lieutenant?"

"Yes," he said, examining the paper. "In complaints of this sort we need a fairly comprehensive statement from the missing person. Your father's had this department in quite an uproar."

"I'll bet," Fawn said, tucking back some of her dark curls. "I've told Father over and over again not to worry about me, but he doesn't seem to understand that I've grown up. Silly sending half the sheriff's office after me when you've got so many other important things to do." She wet her lips with her tongue and smiled. "Gee, can't a girl take a moonlight walk on the beach alone without creating a national emergency?"

Mark scanned her slim figure which was partially hidden in an expensive-looking orange silk sack dress. "There was no moon, Miss Collier. It was dark and it was raining. We're after a vicious killer and you're not helping one damned bit by pulling a barren-beach-Garbo like you did tonight."

"I'm sorry. It won't happen again."

"Okay." Mark got to his feet. "Would you mind giving Miss West a lift since you're both heading for the same destination?"

"Not at all," Fawn purred graciously. "I'd be glad to."

I flashed Mark a perturbed look and started for the door.

"Oh, and Miss Collier," Mark added, "would you do me another big favor?"

"Why, of course, Lieutenant."

"Loan Miss West one of your brassieres, will you?"

"What?"

"Oh, never mind," he grunted, forcing back a snicker. "Wouldn't fit anyway. Just go home and get some sleep. Both of you. And don't stop anywhere on the way. Fog's starting to roll in."

We got as far as the Booby Hatch when a billowing white wall forced us off the highway and isolated Fawn's convertible in its misty wet grip.

Fawn switched off the ignition and shook her head. "Now what do we do? Father will probably have federal troops with bayonets looking for me. I know. Let's have a drink. Maybe the fog will lift in a few minutes."

We climbed from Fawn's car, stumbling over a shrouded curb. Even the bright neon tubes spelling out BOOBY HATCH could barely be seen as we groped along shop fronts. On one side of the big sign was the word BAR and on the other side the last two letters were transposed to spell out BRA.

"What's the gag," I asked, pointing up at the transposition. "If I didn't know better I'd suspect Lieutenant Mark Storm worked with the local sign company."

"No gag," Fawn said. "That's just Jules Cadillac's way of promoting a 24-hour-a-day gold mine. From eight until five this place is the most fabulous bra shop you ever dreamed existed. By five-thirty the display cases are neatly converted into tables and a sixty-foot bar. White manikins are stripped of their lacy under things and glisten under faint lights like gorgeous pieces of nude statuary just shipping in from the Louvre Museum. It's absolutely fabulous."

Fawn was so right. The interior of Jules Cadillac's Booby Hatch was a quaint blend of ultra-modern and bizarre. In the corner of the massive, smoky room were the remains of an old schooner's bow with a naked, fish-tailed sea nymph fastened to the hull. She was noticeably a shade lighter around her bosom where a brassiere had kept out the sun and dust during her daytime shift.

We found a table and ordered two martinis. Fawn sipped her drink for a moment and then said, "I owe you an apology, Honey. I've been a real bitch and I'm sorry."

"Reed Walker told you why I'm here in Shark Beach, didn't he?"

"Yes." She placed her hand on mine. "I had you pegged for a gold digger. Another Helena. How stupid can one person get?"

"You know about Hel Gandy?"

"Yes, that, too. Word got around pretty fast at the sheriff's office. I can't believe that Erik would…"

"I don't think he did. At least, not to Helena. Tell me something honestly, Fawn. Were you in the projection booth this morning?"

"No—no, of course not." She wet her lips nervously. "What would I have been going there?"

"How do you know what projection booth I'm talking about?" I asked suspiciously.

"Well, I don't, but I assume you're referring to the one at home. Father was a motion picture director, you know. I've been exposed to a home projection booth all my life."

"I thought Rote said you lived with your mother up until five years ago."

"That's right. But I used to visit him a lot during the summers. What's this all about anyway?"

"Do you know your father has a lewd movie film with Helena as the principle subject?"

"Yes."

"Have you ever seen it?"

Fawn took a quick sip of her drink and said, "No, I haven't. Father usually keeps the film under lock and key."

"Do you happen to know where it came from? Who shot the reel?"

"I believe Hel Gandy made the film several years ago. About the time I came to live with father. What difference does it make?"

"As far as I'm concerned this case will never be closed until I see that film in its entirety."

Fawn leaned forward intently. "Have you seen part of the real?"

"Up to a point," I said. "A very crucial point. Do you think—if your father hasn't burned the film—you could help me find where it's hidden?"

"Of course. We'd have to break into the wall safe. I don't really believe that's possible." Her green eyes flashed suddenly. "Father would be furious if we were successful."

"So what? You two certainly weren't on the best of terms this morning."

Fawn regarded me for a moment. "You sound as if you might suspect my father. I don't understand. Aren't you working for him?"

"Of course," I said. "He hired me to keep you alive and that's exactly what I'm trying to do. One way or another."

A faint smiled sliced into her overly-painted mouth. "I didn't know. Now isn't that crazy? He never told me. Is that really why you're here?"

I nodded. "Why did you call Reed Walker early this evening?"

She drew an imaginary R on the table with her fingernail. "I wanted to see him. I was worried about him and wanted to be sure he was all right."

"What made you think he wasn't?"

"The police last night. They were going to arrest him until you lied about those wings. Why did you do that?"

"Just a hunch," I said. "Now I'm not so sure about our handsomely-naïve Marine Captain."

Fawn lighted a cigarette and pushed the pack toward me. "He's a prince, Honey, believe me. Even if we did have a terrible argument this evening."

"Is that why you took your stroll on the beach?"

226

"Yes. Reed doesn't go for me. I don't know why. He was almost like a maniac this evening while I was accusing you of—I'm sorry. He had every right to get angry. You're in love with him, aren't you, Honey?"

"No."

"You're lying. You ought to see your face when his name is mentioned. Have you gone all the way with him yet?"

I sipped my drink, ignoring the question.

"You must have!" Fawn exclaimed delightedly. "Reed likes women with big breasts. Like Helena. He was crazy about her. I saw them together one time."

"When?" I demanded.

"Not too long ago," she said, eyes glazing in retrospect. "Father had gone to Los Angeles. They thought I went with him. Helena took Reed into her room and made love to him! It was sickening!

"How long ago was this?"

"Two months. Maybe longer. Helena was vicious. She'd resort to almost anything in the book for a thrill."

I tried to make my next question as casual as possible. "Did she ever approach you, Fawn?"

"What do you mean?" It sounded disturbed and contorted.

I probed the wound quickly. "Did she like you? Did she ever make a play for you?"

Fawn's heavily made-up eyes narrowed. "Are you kidding? She hated my guts. And the feeling was mutual. She played my father for a sucker for years. I tried to tell him over and over again. He wouldn't believe me. I am glad she's dead, Honey. She was the most wicked woman I've ever known."

"And Hel Gandy?"

"The cruelest man. They both deserved to die. SO did those two other women. All four of them were living miserable, treacherous lives. I only hope they bring up that fact at Erik's trial."

"I don't think he'll ever go to trial, Fawn."

"I hope not."

"Has Erik ever treated you for anything?"

"No. I guess this balmy Shark Beach climate really agrees with me.

I've been unbelievably healthy for the past five years. He's an excellent doctor, though. Won numerous awards."

"So I noticed at his office. I also discovered Helena was pregnant. Did you know that?"

"No!" Fawn said eagerly. "Was she really? I should have guessed as much."

"Who do you imagine was the father? Rote?"

"Hardly. He's been sterile for ten years. The result of an accident. That's one of the reason's why Helena liked my father—besides his money."

"Who do you think was the father?"

"Reed perhaps. He was the only one I ever saw with her. I know there were others. Erik for instance. Helena had a horrible case of nymphomania."

"What about Wolf Larson and Helena?"

"I don't know. He has a bed in his Bathysphere. He took me down alone one time."

"What happened?"

"Let's not talk about the dirty—All I can say is he's crude. Terribly crude. Let's leave him at that."

"Okay," I said. "We'd better be getting home. Your father's going to have the National Guard after us for sure."

Fawn grinned. She had a nice smile. "If the fog hasn't lifted, what do you say we curl up in the car and the hell with everybody? No sense endangering our necks just to satisfy a whim of my father's."

We walked outside. The mist had cleared enough to see the other side of the street, but it still lay heavy over the lamp posts and the hills behind Shark Beach. The seats were wet when we climbed into Fawn's white convertible. She shook her head and put up the top.

"I should have known better," she said, starting up the engine. "This weather's murder on the upholstery."

"Making a U-turn on the coast highway in this kind of soup is murderous, too," I said. "We might have been hit broadside."

She nodded. "I don't know what's the matter with me. I just didn't think."

Fog began to pile up on the windshield, erasing everything but the faint double line down the center of the road. Fawn didn't slow her speed a bit.

"What time is it?" she asked suddenly.

I glanced at my watch under the glow of the speedometer. "One thirty-five a.m. Much later than you think, Fawn," I said, kiddingly. "Hadn't you better let up on that accelerator?"

"Sure," she murmured, relaxing her grip on the wheel. "I guess I should admit the truth, Honey. Something you said has been bothering me."

"What's that?"

"You said Father hired you to protect my life. Do you really believe anyone would want to murder me?"

"That's your father's feeling."

"What's yours?"

"Anything's possible. Three women have been murdered in a town with a population of six thousand. Those are pretty good odds. Why do you ask?"

"Because I felt like I was being followed tonight on the beach. I didn't tell the police or Lieutenant Storm. There was no positive proof. Just a feeling I had. A little while ago, before we went into the Booby Hatch, I got the same feeling!"

"How about right now?"

Fawn peered into the rear view mirror. "I don't know. This fog's so pea thick I can't see through the window. I do have a strange sick sensation in my stomach. Like maybe something is going to happen. That's why I was going so fast. Honey, you don't believe..."

"Steady," I said, lifting the .32 from my purse. "Let's not take any chances. I still don't see Erik Ford as a murderer. Let's pull over to the side, Fawn!"

She glanced down at my gun and her eyes widened with terror. "No—no, I'm afraid! Really afraid, Honey! I've never felt like this before. It's horrible!"

Fawn jammed down the accelerator. The needle leaped toward seventy.

"You're going to pass the turn-in," I said. "Slow down!"

"I—I can't! You're right, he is after me. He does want to kill me!"

"Who, Fawn, who?"

"Reed! He would have finished me this afternoon, but there were too many people. And this evening on the beach—I ran! I ran, Honey. I ran until I thought I'd drop! Until I reached the police car!"

Angry tires, whirling under the convertible's frame, clawed at wet pavement as we skidded around a slight curve.

"Listen to me, Fawn! Get a hold of yourself! Slow down or we'll both be killed."

"All right! All right, Honey! But, please protect me! Please, save me from him!"

She braked suddenly and jerked the wheel into a sharp left turn. We screeched across the highway, striking a dark embankment at a severely sharp angle and slid off in a searing, metal-bending roar that carried us up a small rise before Fawn could brake us to a full stop. She was thrown over the steering wheel, while I landed in a crumpled, skirt-over-my-head heap on the floor.

I located my revolver and got up fast. Fog was piled thicker than ever on the windows and the car's engine throbbed achingly.

"Are you all right" I asked, bending over Fawn's slumped shoulders as I drew her back form the steering wheel. She had a crimson slash in the corner of her mouth where she'd apparently struck the pushbutton controls in the center of the driving shaft.

"Yes—yes, I think so." She lifted her head and groaned. "What in the world happened?"

"I don't know exactly," I said, still clutching my revolver. "We hit something. I'd better check the damage."

She stopped me before I could climb from the car. "No, wait a minute! Don't leave me! I know he's outside somewhere! Please, don't leave me!"

"Fawn," I said, trying to quiet her hysteria, "you just made one of the sharpest turns in automotive history. Nobody could have followed us. Not even Henry Ford."

"Don't make jokes, please!"

"I wasn't trying to." A roar pierced the foggy night. "What's that?"

"I—I don't know—" Fawn whispered. She flipped open the door on her side and lunged into the night.

"Wait you crazy fool!" I yelled.

The roar increased in fury, ripping the night in three shrill wailing shrieks. I clamped down on my door handle and stepped out into the fog. Then I heard another sound.

Ding ding ding

A crossing bell!

The train's brilliantly-ominous eye pierced out of the fog and caught me flush in the face.

I was too terrified to move.

Chapter Ten

The train curved out of the mist, its steel plates gnashing ruthlessly into the narrow space between me and death. My nervous system erupted like an H-bomb as I tried to move from the tracks. The glistening monster bellowed at the top of its metallic lungs, looming off my shoulder, veering toward my body with such a violent roar that it splintered my eardrums and scattered the embers into a hideous, boiling cauldron of sound.

Mark's resonant voice, as if squeezed through a narrow tube, reached me first and forced me to open my eyes to his face, which was circled by a bright field of lights beyond.

"Honey, can you hear me?" he said, his voice a distant echo from an impossibly deep well. "She must be able to hear me. Her eyes are open. Honey, say something, please!"

What do you want me to say? I thought dazedly.

"I'm sorry, Lieutenant," another voice said in that same aggravating whisper. "She doesn't respond. Her nervous system seems paralyzed from the severe shock of the accident."

"But she wasn't hit by the train," Mark argued. "you said you were absolutely certain of that when we found her in this gully an hour ago."

"Yes, I know. But do you have any idea, Lieutenant, what you'd do if you looked up to find a train coming at you at thirty or forty miles per hour?"

"I'd probably jump clean out of my skin," Mark said.

"And that's apparently what Miss West tried to do. She jumped. The train missed her, but she was still standing on those tracks. At least, that's what her brain thought. The impact of that image, hinged with the terrible

232

sound of the train striking the automobile, probably stopped her nervous system like a clock."

You're kidding, I thought. You must be kidding! I can hear you! I can see you! My nervous system is all right. Here, I'll show you!

I tried to move my lips, but nothing happened. The words, formed on the blackboard of my mind, just hung there.

"Somebody bring another blanket!" Mark yelled angrily at a rim of faces that glittered weirdly in the fog-dimmed lights.

Now I could hear other sounds. The wet slap of tires as they rolled along the distant highway, the shudder of a diesel engine warming up, the creak of chains and wheels and the noisy voices of the men who ran them.

Another figure moved into the gully. He was short and his pinkish forehead was beaded with moisture. I realized it was Rote. He handed a blanket to Mark.

"Is she any better?" Rote asked.

"Can't tell yet."

"Don't you think she ought to be moved?"

"No!"

Mark! I yelled soundlessly. Look at me! I'll wink at you! I know I can do that. That should be easy. You watch!

The big detective stared at me. I pushed every ounce of available energy into my right cheek muscle. His expression didn't change.

"How's your daughter doing, Mr. Collier?" Mark asked. "Has she explained what happened yet?"

Rote gestured dismally. "Confusion created by the fog, I guess. They made a wrong turn and stopped on the tracks. You know the rest."

"Funny neither one of them heard the warning bell."

I heard it, Mark, I protested wordlessly. Why can't you hear me? Didn't Fawn say she thought we were being followed?

The doctor bent nearer. "Did you see that?"

"What?"

"Her right cheek. I think it moved."

Mark pressed his hand on my face. "I—I don't feel anything."

His fingers were freezing cold and wet. The shock ran the length of my body and, before I knew what was happening, my teeth sank into his flesh.

"Ow!" Mark yelped. "Honey, you're all right!"

My mouth relaxed, releasing his finger. "I—I think so," I announced, glad to hear the sound of my own voice again. "Help me up."

"You had a close call, Honey, you'd better…"

I stumbled to my feet. "How long have I been here in this gully?"

"Almost two hours. They're pulling the wreckage loose from the engine now. How come you didn't hear the warning signal?"

"Car engine was idling too loud," I said. "Windows were rolled up. Where's Fawn?"

Mark gestured toward the top of the bank. "She's all right. Been bawling ever since we arrived. She thinks you're dead."

Rote and Mark assisted me up a soft, muddy slope to the railroad crossing. Police and sheriffs' cars were parked in all directions. An ambulance waited near the highway.

"You take Fawn in your car, Mr. Collier," Mark said. "I'm going to run Honey by the hospital for a check-up and then…"

"I'm all right, Mark," I insisted.

"Okay, if you say so. We'll follow you, Mr. Collier."

Rote nodded. He walked toward the front of the train where a massive crane worked in the spectral light of arc lamps, clearing the remains of Fawn's expensive convertible. Mark helped me into his car.

While we waited for Rote and Fawn, Mark said, "I'd appreciate the complete story, Honey. Fawn hasn't been able to put two words together."

"We were being followed," I explained. "At least, that's what Fawn imagined. She got excited and swerved off the highway."

Mark scratched his forehead. "That's funny."

"What do you mean?"

"Rote Collier was actually the first person on the scene."

"Well, that explains everything," I said. "Rote became worried when the fog rolled in. He went out searching for Fawn, spotted her car and followed us to the railroad crossing."

"Yeah," Mark said. "You're probably right." He took my revolver from his coat pocket and tossed it into my lap. "Your purse was found in the wreckage, but this wasn't inside."

"I know. Fawn got excited and started babbling about Reed Walker trying to kill her. I had the gun in my hand when I got out of the car. Where'd you find it?"

"In the gully. That isn't where you dropped it, though."

I shrugged. "I suppose the gun crawled down from the road."

"Nope. According to one of the conductors aboard the train, Rote Collier picked up your revolver near the crossing only a few minutes after the collision and then tossed it into the gully."

"That is *funny*," I mused.

"Yeah, but the funniest part of this bit comes in between the picking up and the tossing. The conductor claims that Fawn was thrown into a ditch on the other side of the road. She must have landed on her head and was unconscious for a few minutes. Anyway, long enough for Rote to aim your gun directly at her."

"You're not serious, Mark?"

"The conductor swears by his statement. He claims Rote probably would have pulled the trigger if it hadn't been for a car turning off from the highway."

"That's ridiculous! Rote idolizes that girl!"

Mark nodded. "That's what I thought, too, Honey. I'll tell you something else maybe you don't know."

"What's that?"

"Fawn Collier isn't really Rote's daughter!"

Mark explained his startling allegation as we followed Collier's black Cadillac through the thinning fog. "Erik Ford tipped me off. He said Fawn sort of sprang out of nowhere about four years ago."

"Of course. She'd been living with her mother."

"Rote's first wife has been dead for over ten years. That, I personally verified. Also, we haven't been able to locate a birth registration for a Fawn Collier either in New York State or California."

"She could have been born in any one of forty-six other states, or Canada."

"On the form we had her fill out she listed place-of-birth as New York City. On the missing persons report Rote Collier wrote Glendale, California. Now, one of them is lying. Why?"

"That's idiotic," I murmured. "Especially that business with the gun."

"All right, how idiotic does this theory sound?" Mark demanded. "Fawn arrives in Shark Beach, a frivolous young nineteen-year-old seeking a rich millionaire. She meets Rote Collier who's over fifty and loaded. He moves her in with him and to prevent any embarrassment they assume the daughter-come-home-to-father situation. This continues until Rote meets Helena. Then, tired of an older man, Fawn urges him into marriage, still clinging to her daughter role for obvious financial reasons."

"Sounds too fantastic, Mark."

"Sure, until you fit this into the theory. Helena discovers the truth about Fawn and threatens to expose Rote, so he kills her. He's forced to shoot Hel Gandy because of an incriminating photograph. Then he realizes Fawn may catch on, so…"

"And what about the two other kissing murders? How do you fit those into your theory?"

Mark frowned. "I don't know. Rote might have decided to capitalize on them for his crime. That old geezer, Butler—even dead-still isn't in the clear for the first two murders."

"Not a very clear deduction, Mr. Watson, especially in the light of Rote hiring me to prevent anything from happening to either Fawn or Helena."

"Don't you see, Honey, you were Collier's ace-in-the-hole to throw off any possible element of suspicion. And, too, he didn't know, any more than we did, who the kissing killer really was."

"Maybe," I said. "Still too many loose ends. One very important one which I'm sure you haven't considered."

"What's that?"

"Fawn Collier looks enough like her old man to be his twin."

Dawn was folding purple streaks into the hills above Shark Beach when we arrived at the Collier mansion. Rote made some coffee while Fawn and I showered, changed our clothes and freshened our makeup.

She met me on the stairs on the way down to join Rote and Mark. "Honey," Fawn said, "I can't tell you how sorry I am about what happened at the railroad crossing. It was a terrible blunder on my part." She was wearing a white satin tunic over tight red velvet trousers.

236

"Nothing serious resulted," I said, "except the loss of an expensive automobile. Hope you'll still help me find that movie film."

"I will. I promise."

We found Rote and Mark in the kitchen bent over half empty cups and looking at baby pictures. They were obviously of Fawn. There was no doubt of that fact.

"This one was taken when Fawn was three," Rote said, holding up a faded, hand-colored print of a raven-haired, green-eyed child in a pale green dress. "Fawn was always very photogenic. Her mother was constantly having pictures taken."

"Oh, Father, will you please stop. I'm sure lieutenant has more important things to do than look at old pictures of me."

Rote took another photo from his album. His face sagged slightly and he started to replace the picture when Mark grabbed the glossy print from him.

"That's my son, Frank," the ex-director said sadly. "I guess you know he was—killed in Korea."

Mark nodded. The photo revealed a handsome, pink-cheeked boy in his early teens astride a white palomino. He wore a dark polo uniform and a jaunty helmet was pushed back triumphantly on his young head.

"He always loved polo before he went into the service," Rote said, grimacing. "The day that picture was taken he and his team had won an important match with.." Tears sprang into Rote's eyes. He pulled the picture from Mark's hands, clumsily pushed it into the album and stood up. "Well, anyway, you asked about my family in their younger days, Lieutenant. Now you've seen them and, if you don't mind, I'd like to be excused. I'm very tired. It's been a long night."

"Of course, Mr. Collier." Mark glanced at me, a chagrined expression on his face. "I guess we could all use some sleep."

Rote nodded, wiped his eyes and strode from the room, his chin raised as high as possible, the album clutched tightly under his arm.

Fawn went to the stove and picked up the coffee pot. "Father's such a sentimentalist," she said, refilling Mark's cup. "He's never quite got over losing Frank."

Mark stirred in some sugar, then asked, "Has he demonstrated as much remorse over the loss of Helena?"

I shook my head angrily. "Mark, that isn't nice!"

Fawn took two more cups from the cabinet and smiled thinly. "That's all right, Honey. The lieutenant has a job to perform. It isn't easy—for anybody."

"I'll tell you the truth, Miss Collier," Mark continued, "an hour ago I didn't believe you were his daughter."

Fawn nearly dropped the cups. "You—you're joking!"

"No, I'm not. A couple of things happened before and after your accident which created a reasonable doubt—at least in my mind. That's why I asked your father to show me those photographs."

"What—what happened, Lieutenant?"

"Well, for one thing you and your father gave different states as the location of your birth. And for another…"

"Mark," I interrupted, "you're not going to place any real importance on a conductor's opinion based on a view from the inside of a train following a collision. That's insane!"

Fawn drew up a chair and sat down. "Just what are you trying to get at anyway?"

Mark scowled. "All right, Miss Collier, where were you born? Neither New York State nor California has any record of your birth."

"Is that it?" Fawn laughed. "Father's missing person's report. In his anxiety he must have given you Frank's place of birth, Glendale. And as far as my report is concerned, I was born on a train enroute to New York. I've never known for sure how they listed it on my birth certificate, but I've always assumed, since my first stop was in a New York hospital, that Gotham was it. Does that satisfy you?"

Mark's chagrined expression deepened. "Yes, I guess so."

"Now what was this other business about after the accident?" Fawn asked.

"Well," Mark stammered, "one of the conductors on the train saw something which he thought was rather odd. But I guess maybe he was a little cock-eyed at the time."

"What did he see?"

"Nothing important."

238

"It sounded important the way Miss West came back at you," Fawn said. "I'd like to know, even if it was an error."

"Well," Mark stammered again, "as Honey says, it's rather inconclusive and quite improbable, so let's just forget it, okay?"

Fawn nodded half-heartedly. Then she said, "If you're talking about father picking up Miss West's gun, that's nothing important because I saw him."

"You..." Mark faltered. "Why didn't you tell me?"

"I haven't had a chance. Anyway, as I said, it wasn't important. He didn't actually aim the gun at me if that's what you think."

"That's what he thought all right," I said. "The conductor claims he saw Rote through a train window."

Fawn poured coffee, her hand trembling enough to spill some of the hot liquid. "He should have had the view I had. For a minute I wondered myself. But then he tossed the gun away."

"Why, Miss Collier?" Mark demanded. "Why should your father pick up a gun and then throw the weapon down again? It just doesn't make sense."

"Doesn't it, Lieutenant?" Fawn said. "Have you ever been in a position to pick up a strange gun and then suddenly realize the implications and suspicions that go along with such and act? No. Of course, you haven't because you're the law. On the other side of the fence it's a shaky proposition."

"I guess so," Mark said. "Let's just say I was barking up the wrong tree. I apologize for my suspicions."

Fawn smiled. "Lieutenant, let me say one more thing. My father is not a murderer. He may be guilty of many wrongs, but not murder. I'm afraid Miss West heard a very bitter conversation New Year's morning. At that time, I angrily accused my father of wanting to kill me and of doing away with Helena. Believe me, this was merely a spoiled child's way of demonstrating wrath. I'm sorry for what I said."

Mark got up from the table and squashed his hat on his head. "I hate to admit this, but you make sense, Miss Collier. And in a case of this type, believe me, it's genuinely refreshing. Good night."

After Mark was gone, we sipped our coffee in silence. The sea battered distantly against the rocks and the sky lightened to a tawny gray streaked with crimson.

Finally Fawn looked at me. "You know something, Honey," she said, "Lieutenant Storm was right."

"Right about what?"

"Father really did aim your gun at me. If that car hadn't come up the road when it did I'd be dead now. Deader than a doornail."

Chapter Eleven

I took a long swallow of coffee and felt fire all the way down. "Fawn, you couldn't mean that?"

"Couldn't I? Do you think I enjoy accusing my own father? He hates me, Honey. He hates me with a vengeance because I wrecked his marriage."

"That doesn't make sense."

"Doesn't it? You don't know how I resented Helena. How I tried to upset her in every way possible. How do you think you'd feel having a step-mother younger than yourself?"

"I don't know. That's still no reason for your father to aim at you..."

"That's where you are wrong. He worshipped the ground she walked on. I wouldn't even be surprised if he suspected I killed her."

"You? Fawn, that's impossible."

"Is it? I hated her enough, believe me. Father knows I would have liked to have killed her if I'd had the chance. He's convicted me for my thoughts if nothing more."

"I still don't see..."

"Then maybe this will clarify. I was the one who took those movies of Helena in Hel's bedroom."

"You—?" I stammered. "Then you lied before."

"Yes. You wanted to know who the man was with her? Wolf Larson."

"Are you sure, Fawn?"

"I held the camera, I ought to be sure. Hel loaned Wolf his house. He knew about Wolf's plans with Helena and tipped me off. I hid in the closet. The details of the get-together, as you might imagine, are rather gruesome."

"Wolf Larson, of course. I wondered where I'd seen that broad sun-tanned back before."

"What?"

"Nothing. Fawn, do you know much about Wolf Larson? What he does in his spare time? Where he goes?"

"Sure. I already told you. He's exactly the way he looks and acts. A crude, rough, egotistical beachcomber. He operates a diving bell down on the pier and spends most of his time there. In fast, I believe he lives on the damned thing."

"You said before you thought Reed made Helena pregnant. Do you still agree with that theory?"

"I don't know," Fawn said thoughtfully. "I took pictures of her and Wolf together. And I imagine there were dozens of similar situations with other men I might have filmed—given the opportunity."

"Why did you shoot that particular sequence?"

"To teach my father a lesson. And to ruin Helena. But the whole deal boomeranged on me."

"How?"

"Father added the film to his collection of pornography featuring Helena. I think he almost thought of it as a triumph."

"Then why should he want to harm you?"

"Don't you see, Honey? Having that film was a shot in the arm to father's dwindling virility. Realizing I was the one who filmed the sequence sort of spoiled his fun. He highly resented the idea. Almost to the point of—of insanity."

"Do you think he's insane, Fawn?"

"He's my father. Of course, I can't allow myself to think that." She paused, then added, "He's always been a very peculiar man. I hate to say this, Honey, but more than a little effeminate, if you know what I mean."

"Yes, I noticed. Still that doesn't seem to change his feeling toward women."

"Nor toward men," Fawn said. "I've always been somewhat suspicious of his association with Hel Gandy."

"In what respect?"

"I can't tell you exactly. It's only something a—a daughter might feel—or sense. A feeling of great—comradeship."

242

I sipped at my coffee again. "That is odd when you consider Hel Gandy was the man who led Helena astray to begin with. Hel did tell me he couldn't stand being called a 'queer'."

"Naturally," Fawn said. "Because they can't live with that word. But he was one of them. A very twisted sort. Do you know why he photographed nude women? Why he got them into horrible pornographic situations? To ruin them! He hated women. His only pleasure in life was to smash them, to show up their weaknesses. He liked me. That's why he let Wolf Larson use his house that weekend. That's why he told me of the meeting and even loaned me the camera. He hoped to crush Helena, especially since she'd married my father. I think he hoped to show him what she was like once and for all. Father likes Hel Gandy. I think even more than he cares for me. That's why I'm sure he didn't murder Hel Gandy."

"But, Fawn, you said…"

"That he nearly pulled the trigger on me? Yes, I know. But he didn't. And, I don't believe he ever will now. He had that brief opportunity we probably all have once in a lifetime—to murder someone we love in a blinding fit of rage. He had his one chance and he failed. I don't believe the same opportunity will ever present itself again in his lifetime. Nor, do I think he'll ever have the same desire. Once you reach that ultimate goal—gun in hand—sight aimed—you realize—afterwards—what a horrible moment it was. I don't believe Father will ever feel that way again."

I got up and peered out the window at the new day that was carving its image on the gray horizon. "You don't believe he killed Helena?"

"No. Absolutely not."

"You said you knew the two other women who were murdered. What were they like?"

"Social climbers. Snobs. Lorraine Reynolds was constantly inviting me to her home for afternoon cocktails. She was a beautiful woman with more body than brains. Joan Lacey was a bleached-out little blonde who couldn't resist booze and beach bums—the strong boys with muscles and volley ball fever."

"Do you know if they ever posed for Hel Gandy—in their birthday suits?"

"No. I wouldn't be surprised though. He tried to get them all, especially those with a little prestige, too much vanity and money. They were a real conquest."

"Did you ever pose for him, Fawn?"

The way she answered gave me the feeling she was lying. Her "No!" was too positive, too resentful, too filled with anger.

We finished our coffee and went to bed. I didn't sleep too well, though. I dreamt about Wolf Larson and his Bathysphere. The fish that swam by the tiny portholes kept puckering up. Wolf Larson called them kissing fish. Then a mermaid swam by. She looked like Helena will full red lips curled back passionately. The tip of her tongue protruded slightly between her teeth. Suddenly her mouth exploded into a billion pieces. And Wolf Larson stood at the top of a watery staircase laughing his fool head off.

I didn't wake up until after three in the afternoon. Every muscle in my body ached from my tumble into the gully and my head was still sore from Hel's punch.

The castle was deathly quiet. I listened. Only a consistent crash of breakers cut the ugly silence. I grabbed a blue cardigan and matching skirt and stiffly dressed.

Then I checked Fawn's room. She was snuggled peacefully under a silken quilt. Her breathing was as regular as the quaint French clock on her dresser. Rote's room was a mess. His album of pictures was scattered wrathfully across the floor and he lay slumped in a chair, a pile of old newspaper clippings at his feet. His breathing was harsh, distorted and uneven. Most important it was loud. The newspaper clippings told a heroic story of a handful of American men in Korea who fought in a war nobody cared about. An article from a local newspaper mentioned one of these heroes— Private Frank J. Collier.

I didn't arrive at the Pleasure Pier until almost five o'clock. Wolf Larson was already in the front booth tallying his day's take. It seemed extremely lean.

I nudged against the window and grinned like a little girl embarrassed by the size of the world. "Gee," I said sadly, "I guess it's too late to see all those beautiful fish."

244

He didn't waste two seconds vaulting out of his glass chamber. "Honey! Honey, am I glad to see you!" He wrapped two big arms around me and his grip was at its usual rib-cracking best. "I've been thinking about you all day."

"Why?" I asked, trying to untangle my diaphragm.

"I read about you in the newspaper. You were almost creamed by a train. You and Fawn Collier. How do you like that?"

"I don't. And I'm talking about your strength, Wolf. You should farm yourself out as a machine. You'd work wonders in a nut cracking factory."

He stepped back and grinned. "Oh, Honey, you'd make me mad if I didn't know you were kidding. Listen, you've got a body that just screams to be hugged."

"Yeah," I said. "Polar bears go crazy over me. How's business in your part of the world?"

Wolf glanced at his diving bell, still glistening from a recent dip in the blue Pacific. "Not bad, not good. You know how the winters are in this neck of the woods. People starve with more humility than in Christmas goose in the middle of July. Come aboard."

He led me out onto a steel shelf which supported the Bathysphere on three curved I-beams. A heavy watertight door was swung open revealing the inner chamber of the ball-shaped undersea elevator.

"Works on a newly-developed principle for undersea operations," Wolf said proudly, "called static compression. She travels up and down on that steel rod in the middle."

I stepped inside. "it's much larger than I imagined."

"Biggest in the world. Weighs seventy-eight tons. Carries thirty passengers. I even live aboard her. Some people call her Larson's Lair." He laughed, showing his white fangs. "Other beach bums on the pier have their own name for it. Wolf's Wombat. Only they pronounce it like zoom. Get it?"

"Vaguely," I said, with a sarcastic note in my voice. "The bell-bottom trousered bachelor's boudoir. Is that what you're trying to say?"

"Yeah," Wolf said. "I knew you'd come up with something better."

He drew the watertight door closed and whirled the wheel lock. "Well, now, let's have a look-see," he said, turning around and planting his eyes on the roundness inside my sweater.

"Down, Rover!"

"Down, that's what I'm talking about. Don't you want to take a dip? It's on the house."

"Didn't I see you in the *Hound of Baskervilles?*"

"Quit kidding, Honey."

He strode to a panel of wheels and switches and turned on an overhead light. A motor began to hum under the floor. The Bathysphere trembled. I looked out one of the portholes. Greenish bubbles swirled up over the glass thrashing quickly into a thick inky blue. Air hissed down through a narrow vent in the ceiling as the chamber continued to descend.

Wolf finally turned another wheel and said, "This is it. Main floor. Starfish, sharks, seashells and shucks."

"Shucks?"

"Yeah," he said, moving toward me. "Shucks, you're beautiful, Honey. You've got more cleavage than the Suez Canal."

I shook my head, unable to force back a grin.

"Thanks, pal, and here I always imagined myself in the Panama class."

"You're in a class all by yourself."

"Oh, I bet you say that to all your canals."

"Stop joking. I'm serious."

"As serious as you were with Helena?"

He flinched noticeably. "Why do you always have to bring her into the conversation?"

"She's dead, Wolf."

"I know she's dead. So's Hel Gandy. So what?"

"New Year's Eve you said you'd just left her in a pool of kisses, remember?"

"That was a bad joke."

"It sure was," I said, "on Helena."

"Okay. Tell it to Erik Ford. He's the one who killed her."

"What makes you think so?"

"The police arrested him, didn't they?"

"That doesn't mean he's guilty."

Wolf bared his fangs angrily. "What does it mean? I suppose he's been

246

chosen treasurer of the Policeman's Ball."

I crossed to the bed Fawn had described. "Ever bring Helena in here?"

"Will you stop that kind of talk!"

"Or were these quarters too cramped for your scale of operations?"

"I never had a thing to do with Helena—not that way—and that's the truth."

"I saw a film yesterday morning which makes you about as truthful as George Washington before he cut down the cherry tree."

Wolf snarled, "George Washington was always truthful. Now you're making me mad. I don't like smart dames making with smart talk that adds up to zero."

"This adds up to Hel Gandy's bedroom. Ever been there?"

"I wouldn't be caught dead in the stinking place. Mesh curtains, bare black mattress. That stuff's for the fairies."

"You looked perfectly normal in this picture."

"What picture?" Wolf demanded, clenching his fists.

"Fawn Collier shot the reel from Hel's bedroom closet. You and Helena were on the bed together and you weren't playing charades."

"What were we playing, parchese?"

"You tell me."

"I'll tell you nothing," Wolf snarled. "I know you're a private eye. It's all over town."

"News travels fast."

"In Shark Beach news doesn't travel. It's shot out of guns like puffed wheat and filled with just about as much air. Like the stuff you're firing at me."

"I saw the film, Wolf. This don't come via Battle Creek, Michigan."

"You saw my face?"

"Not exactly."

"How do you know it was me?"

"A few other things were showing."

"Yeah, I'll bet," Wolf said. "Helena was a very curious doll."

"Then you admit it was you?"

"Hell, no, it wasn't me. Did Fawn say so?"

"Yes."

247

"Well, she's a liar. I always thought so. Now I'm convinced."

"Take off your shirt, Wolf."

His forehead ridged deeply and his eyes brightened. "Now you're beginning to make sense, Honey. Your type always goes for me. I knew that was just a lot of talk New Year's Eve."

"Take off your shirt and turn around."

"What?"

"I want to see your back."

"My back? Say, what kind of a nut are you?"

"That's one of the parts of you I saw in the film."

"I can show you others," he said.

"No doubt!"

"The odds are with you."

"The odds are never with me. Take off your shirt!"

"I'll be damned if I will. You take off your sweater."

"That wouldn't be fair," I said, reclining on the bed. "I'm not wearing a bra."

"Me neither. So we're even. You take off your sweater and I'll take off my shirt."

"You drive a pretty hard bargain, Mr. Larson."

"I'm known for that. Is it a deal?"

"I don't trust you," I said.

"And I don't trust you. So we're still even. But, I'll tell you what I'll do with you. I'll take off my shirt if you just unbutton your sweater."

"Still no bargain, Wolf."

"We're twenty feet below the surface, Honey. You haven't got much bargaining power when you analyze it. Now, have you?"

"I guess not.:

"All right. Start unbuttoning."

"Are you threatening me?"

"Nope, I'm just appealing to your better judgment."

"What if I asked you to take this thing to the surface and let me out right now?"

Wolf grinned wolfishly. "I'd say I can't. The mechanism is busted and we're stranded here. It happens you know. The police would have to believe me

248

because I could foul things up pretty easily. Anyway, you still want to see my back."

"Not that badly."

"All right, so you unbutton. I still couldn't see anything, right?"

"I'm not Little Lord Fauntleroy."

"You can say that again. I guess something's got to give. That's what I'm gambling on."

"You flatter me, Wolf," I said, still grinning inside at his naïve, school-boy tactics. "You could be disappointed."

"That deep groove is at least a promise. I'll still stand pat."

"Do you think my seeing your back is that important?"

"It seems like it. This is fun. Now don't spoil it."

"What do you mean?"

"Well, every doll I bring down here can't seem to get her clothes off fast enough. This is a refreshing change."

"I'll bet."

Wolf laughed. "The pari-mutual windows are still open. Put your money where your mouth is."

"All right," I said, throwing up my hands. "But, don't expect anything. This doesn't work like a jack-in-the-box, you know."

"I can dream, can't I?"

He said it in such a way that I couldn't help laughing. Suddenly I wasn't afraid of this big burly guy anymore. He seemed real now. Real and terribly human. He was a man, a rather attractive man, with the same compulsions and boyish cravings that were born in the male animal. Somehow it was impossible to get angry at his earthly remarks. They were too logical and, in a way, somewhat flattering. I pulled open the first button. Maybe he was the man in the movie wrapped in pornographic wrath with Helena Collier. Before long I'd know for certain. Until then I was still a female. And, truthfully, the gambling spirit behind our little game created a funny warmth down the middle of my spine. He sensed he wasn't going to see everything, but he still wanted me to unbutton those buttons. That sort of challenge was about as human as human could get. And I knew for sure, it was ten times more exhilarating than Hel Gandy's savage exposure of my upper anatomy.

"I'll go you one better," Wolf said. "I'll dim the lights."

"That's not necessary, Mr. Larson. I'm the one who needs clear vision, not you."

"Are you kidding?"

I opened the second button and things began to give a little. In fact, more than a little. His eyes widened a notch. My hand tried to stem the tide.

"I—I'm waiting," he said expectantly.

"So am I. Maybe this isn't such a good bargain. Let's look at the fish instead."

"I'm sick to death of fish. Honey, you're really a nice gal. It's obvious. Real obvious. And it's nice. I—I mean,: his tongue got all tied up, "I don't mean what you think I mean, but I mean every word. How mixed up can you get?"

"I think I know what you mean, Wolf." I grinned, then sobered. "You were a prize fighter once, weren't you?"

"Yeah. I took one too many punches and then decided to quit and go into this business. I don't make much money, but who cares?"

"You were a heavyweight, naturally!"

"Yeah. I might have gone all the way if I'd stuck with the dirty rotten business. There were just too many shysters telling me what to do."

"You don't like taking orders, do you, Wolf?"

"Who does? Maybe a nincompoop. There are plenty of those in the fight racket. They look like they're tough, but they're just a bunch of pantywaists. I began to feel like Hannibal."

"Who?"

"Hannibal. You know the old story. Hannibal was the strong guy with the elephants. People said he could never conquer Rome. He knew that was bunk. He could have done it with one finger, but the challenge was too easy. So, he decided to forget about Rome and go someplace else. That was the way I felt. I was the white man scheduled to lower the boom on the dark supremacy of the heavyweight crown."

"Hannibal was a Nubian," I said, "from a dark race. He was supposed to conquer the white."

"Yeah, I know. The story's a little twisted, but it still adds up to the same thing. I was supposed to be a conqueror and then all the guys behind me were supposed to be my army. But, they weren't. And I was no conqueror. I didn't want to take Rome. Not the way they wanted me to take it. So, I took a different route. I'm not the heavyweight champion of the world, but who cares?"

"They say Amytis was the one who stalled Hannibal."

"Who's he?"

"She," I said. "The Roman emperor's wife. She stole into Hannibal's camp and made love to him. Is that what happened to you, Wolf?"

"Maybe. Hey, what's happened to our bargain?"

"I got bogged down with the Nubian army."

"That was over two thousand years ago, Honey. There were no pari-mutuals in those days."

"You're not so dumb, are you, Wolf?"

"I read a little. Thomas Wolfe—because of the name. Theodore Dreiser because he makes a lot of sense. Ernest Hemingway, Faulkner."

I glanced around the bare steel walls of the Bathysphere. "I'd never guess! Where do you hide your books?"

"Naturally, under the mattress. Where else?"

I tucked my hand under Wolf's mattress, but didn't come up with any thick volumes of fiction. Instead, my fingers closed over a piece of fabric. When I brought it out in the open, Wolf's eyes opened wide.

"Is this your deep-sea outfit?" I demanded.

"No, of course not," he returned quickly. "It belongs to a friend of mine. Maybe to Amytis."

"Hannibal," I said flatly, "you've got your Alps crossed. This bathing suit belonged to Helena. She wore it New Year's Eve."

"You're wrong, Honey. The last time I saw her she wasn't wearing a thing."

"That's right, Wolf. Helena wasn't wearing a stitch when the murderer tucked her into that mummy case."

Chapter Twelve

Wolf Larson snatched the bathing suit from my grasp and hurled it savagely to the floor. Gold sequins flew loose in all directions.

"All right," he admitted, "so it's Helena's swim suit, so what? Is there any crime in the fact that she left the thing there?"

"When?"

"New Year's Eve."

I picked up the suit again. It was practically in shreds. "You say she left it here?"

"If you must know," Wolf growled, "I—I tore it off her, We had an argument."

"What about?"

"Nothing important."

"The police might not think it was nothing important if they saw the condition of this bathing suit."

"They're not going to see it. Our argument had nothing to do with her murder."

I closed one of the buttons on the front of my sweater. "They might imagine you ripped off the suit in some secluded spot at the party while you were smothering her."

Wolf banged his fist against the watertight door "I didn't kill her. She was trying to blackmail me. Sure, I wanted to kill her, but didn't have the nerve."

"What was she blackmailing you for?"

"She said she was pregnant. She threatened to tell Rote I was the father if I didn't pay off. New Year's Eve was H-hour for my payment."

"Were you the father, Wolf?"

"Hell, no! I told you before, I never had a thing to do with Helena Collier."

"Well, then, what did you have to worry about?"

Wolf ran his big hands across his face and they were trembling when he drew them away. "Rote and I are partners in this business. He owns the largest share. She figured he'd force me out if she told him."

"So that's it. How much was she asking?"

"Three thousand dollars! Ever hear of anything so ridiculous? She knew I didn't have that kind of money."

"Where did she expect you to get it, Wolf?"

"From Rote. Now doesn't that take the cake? Borrow money from my partner to pay his wife to keep her from telling him about an incident that I had nothing to do with. How screwed-up can life get?"

I stared at him skeptically. The scattered gold sequins on Reed Walker's carpet kept flickering across my mind. "Where'd this little argument of yours take place?"

"Right here. She was waiting for me when I got back from the party"

"What time was that?"

"I don't know. I didn't look at my watch. I'd say about fifteen minutes after I left you on the staircase."

"Go on."

"She had a sickening smile on her face. She put out her hand and I slapped it down. She knew I hadn't asked Rote for the money, and she just wanted to goad me, but I wasn't about to let her. I grabbed the front of her bathing suit. The damned thing was cut so low in front of her bathing suit. The damned thing was cut so low in front that it practically fell apart in my hands."

"I'll bet."

"You're still on," Wolf countered. "Sure, I was drunk and mad as hell and I could have killed her right then and there, but that isn't the way it went."

"You just tore off her bathing suit."

"That's right. Helena was a spoiled, ruthless little brat, so I turned her over my knee and spanked her bare bottom until it was raw. When I finally let her up, she dashed out the door stark naked and dove into the water."

253

"Then what?"

"I started after her, but it was too dark because of the storm. She'd left her car keys and a cigarette case behind, so I ran down to the pier parking lot, found her red Thunderbird and tore out along the shore road. Helena was like a fish in water. I knew she could easily swim the distance back to her place under normal circumstances. New Year's Eve the sea was at its worst. Breakers were topping eleven feet and busting hell out of every-thing. I never saw Helena again. When I reached the Collier place. I parked her car in the garage, left the keys in the ignition, the cigarette case on the seat and walked on back to the pier."

"Exciting story," I said.

"It's the truth, Honey, every word."

"Is there anyone who can corroborate that business about Helena div-ing into the water?"

"I don't know There were a lot of people on the pier that night. Maybe one of them saw her."

"Maybe," I said, re-examining the torn suit. "Maybe not."

"What are you going to do, Honey?"

"I don't know. The medical examiner did say Helena had a red fanny, as if she'd been spanked. I still want to see your back."

"And I still want to see your front," he said.

"The game's off, Wolf. Called on account of a misplaced sequin. Take off your shirt and turn around!"

"No."

"You were the man in the film, weren't you, Wolf?"

"No!"

"Then why do you refuse to take off your shirt?"

"Because I'm a stubborn Swede."

"Fawn's testimony in court would almost hang you, Wolf. And if we found the film…"

"I don't care what you find," he said, eyes narrowing. "You'll never be able to prove a thing."

I got to my feet, buttoned the last button and shrugged my shoulders. "Okay, Captain, let's surface and find out"

He gripped me savagely around the middle. "Honey, don't let this damned bathing suit spoil everything, please."

"I'm warning you, Wolf, let go of me!"

"You're the only woman I ever really wanted. Dames are always hanging around here, but I'm not interested. Helena was one of those. She had beautiful white hips and big breasts that turned up, but…"

"Like Lorraine Reynolds?"

"Yeah, but neither one of them could have competed with you…" He fell back awkwardly, his face contorted. "You—you tricked me."

"Lorraine Reynolds was one of the murdered women, wasn't she, Wolf?"

He slumped against the side of the Bathysphere. "I didn't. I knew them, that's all. A lot of guys were living off Lorraine and Joannie. I was no different."

"Except for the fact that you were apparently the last person to have seen Helena alive. That makes you different, Wolf. Very different." I moved to the control panel.

"Don't touch anything!" he roared, coming after me. I flipped two switches, but nothing happened. Then I whirled one of the small wheels. Water shot through a vent in the ceiling.

"You crazy fool!" he shouted, hurling me back. "You'll sink us to the bottom!"

The Bathysphere shook violently and began to descend. Wolf fell, tried to get up, but was knocked galley west as the diving bell jolted viciously. Sea boiled on the floor of the steel chamber. I picked myself up and waded to the panel. The switches clicked back into their original position easily. The wheel wouldn't budge.

"Don't release the brake!" Wolf wailed, trying to rise. "We'll blow higher than a kite!"

He stumbled to his knees, then lunged up and grabbed an axe fastened to the wall as the Bathysphere ground to a stop. He glanced at me with wild eyes that were blown open worse than a pop-eyed fish fleeing from a shark. The axe gleaned in his hands. "You know what I ought to do with this, don't you?"

I darted back as he slashed the blade into the raised wooden floor. After a dozen hard strikes through the rapidly rising seas, he tossed the axe aside and plunged his head and shoulders under the water. In a moment, the Bathysphere began to rise, a howling roar searing the steel plates angrily. White bubbles boiled around the portholes and the overhead light flickered.

When Wolf's face broke through the water, we had stopped again. "This—is—as—far—as—we—go," he said, gasping for air. "We're—we're still down about fifteen feet. We'll have to wait until she fills up and then I'll open the main door. Why'd you do this, Honey?"

"I'm sorry, I didn't realize…"

"You—you'll probably never believe this now, but I'm not a murderer. You ask Reed Walker, he knows."

The water swirled around my shoulders. "What does he know, Wolf?"

"That film you were talking about. He knows all about it—more than he'll ever admit. Get up on the bed!"

I took his advice as the overhead opening spilled new water almost to the ceiling. "Wolf, what do we do now?"

"Take a deep breath and pray I can get this door open. Then follow me. You jammed the escape hatch when you fooled with that emergency switch. The pressure is…"

His voice was swallowed up in the bubbling sound that overtook the Bathysphere as the water rose up over our heads. The light went out and we were plunged into an inky blackness. Then, faintly, the movement of Wolf's hands on the steel door glinted through the dark green bubbles. I swam toward the glimmer, bumped against something solid and reached out. My fingers closed over a rounded edge. I swung myself underneath and felt the cold icy touch of the open sea. The surface never looked or felt so good. Stars winked in a soft darkness overhead like tiny beads of fire in black tissue paper. My hands grasped one of the mossy pier pilings and my mouth sucked in fresh air hungrily. Then I looked around for Wolf Larson. The sea was calm, unusually calm, its surface traced faintly by the pier lights. He was nowhere in sight.

Mark didn't say much after two handsome deputies brought me wet and bedraggled into his office. He asked only one sterling question. "Honey, what keeps you alive?"

256

"My built-in waterwings, Lieutenant. Where were you when the lights went out five fathoms deep?"

"I was watching a Sputnik. At least, they say those babies send out signals."

"My Indian blanket wasn't handy," I said. "Helena's bathing suit was. Only trouble, it didn't send up big enough bubbles."

"Okay," he groaned. "Spell it out for me, Miss detective."

I told him the story of Wolf's Bathysphere and the events which led to the flooded chamber. He flinched when I mentioned my discovery of the gold sequined outfit.

"Will you, please, stop digging up suspects," Mark pleaded. "This joint's getting to be like Grand Central Station. We had to release Erik Ford this afternoon—under special guard—to perform an emergency operation."

I took a cigarette from the detective's pocket and lighted it "You'd better get a man after Wolf Larson."

"We're way ahead of you. Those two deputies weren't down on the pier just to watch your swimming exploits. We dusted Helena's car this afternoon. His prints were all over the steering wheel, her cigarette case and keys. Incidentally, he's been on trial."

"What for?" I asked, drying my hair with a towel. "Speeding in his diving bell?"

"Murder. He was acquitted in Seattle in 1947 on lack of sufficient evidence. A girl friend of his was found dead in her waterfront apartment."

"Cause of death?"

"What do you think?" Mark said grimly. "Suffocation. Could be compared with Helena's murder in every respect except this dame didn't have bruises on her mouth"

"Well, what do you know," I said, stubbing out my cigarette. "I guess Mr. Larson didn't take me down to see fish after all. What are your plans now for Erik Ford?"

"Continue to hold him. I'm still not convinced he didn't take care of Hel Gandy. He's a very peculiar man, Honey."

"There are a lot of peculiar men in this town, Lieutenant, not excepting present company. Is it all right if I use your phone?"

Mark grinned. "Go ahead, but if you're calling Buck Rogers, I'll save you the time. He's out."

"Out where?"

"The Marine Corps calls the assignment a night instrument flight. Perhaps to the moon, who knows."

"Very funny. You ought to write dialogue for Buster Keaton!"

"He's dead."

"That's what I mean."

The telephone jangled on Mark's desk. He lifted the receiver, still smiling. When he put it down again, his mouth was twisted into any angry scowl. "That was one of my men at the hospital. Erik Ford's escaped."

"How, Mark?"

The big detective lunged to his feet. "Ford added a new gimmick to the old shell game. He had two other doctors assisting in the operating room. They all wore masks, naturally. My men had Ford spotted as number two in the lineup, but he must have switched positions while they were wheeling the patient out of the room. He calmly waltzed out a side door while the deputies were handcuffing the wrong man."

I patted Mark consolingly on the shoulder. "That's all right, Lieutenant, I know where he's gone."

"Where?"

"After some instruments. Get it? He's on a night instrument flight—to the moon"

Mark didn't look back as he banged out of the office door. I waited five minutes and then started up the hill to Reed Walker's house.

Fog was beginning to drift in over Shark Beach when I reached the cantilevered structure at the end of Hilledge Drive. There weren't any cars in the driveway and the lights were out. Somewhere in the distance a dog howled.

I crept down the stairway to the front door and found it locked. A sliding glass panel facing onto the patio was a different story. A curtain fluttered through the opening, wafted gently by a slight breeze that continued to lift new fog up off the sea.

Reed's living room was unchanged from the previous evening, except that the thick wall-to-wall carpeting seemed freshly vacuumed. No more gold sequins glittered near the coffee table. Dirty dishes were piled in the kitchen sink. A glass on the drain board still bore the imprints of orange-painted lips.

I went into Reed's bedroom. A book lay on the nightstand. The title was, MURDER IS EASY, an autobiography smuggled from the San Quentin death house. One of the pages had been badly dog-eared and a paragraph circled in blue read:

"My seventh murder was the easiest. Perhaps, the symbolism behind the number had something to do with the ease, but I doubt this highly. She was a wealthy woman as in the first and fifth instances. Specifically, I had nothing to gain monetarily from this crime; however there was a financial element involved. She had been blackmailing me for suspicions she held on my sixth misdeed. It is unfortunate that such underhanded individuals exist. Their felonious endeavors often far surpass the crime of murder. For theirs is a crime of no-equal upon society. Blood thirsty and beyond reason are their demands. Why did she seek more money when she was already wealthy beyond any means? The answer was in the warped desire to possess more than she could possibly attain. This is seen in life and more viciously in business. Every day big men work brutally to squash the small in their efforts to attain more power. It is unending and horribly treacherous. For this reason I decided to put her out of her misery. I sealed our bargain with a kiss. A kiss which never ended for her. By a shutting off of both the mouth and nasal passage, she died of suffocation. To conceal the mode of murder from the police I placed her body in a bathtub and filled water to the brim. With her head submerged, I applied artificial respiration. Thus, later, the police autopsy report showed water in the stomach and lungs with foamy mucous in the trachea. The blood chlorides on the left side of the heart were thirty per cent lower than those on the right. This revealed positive drowning in fresh water. Afterwards, I was sorry I had concealed the method because the police stupidly called her death—suicide."

I closed the book and glanced around Reed's neatly-arranged bachelor bedroom. Other books were racked on a small shelf near the window.

Their titles ran the gamut from science-fiction to aeronautical engineering. I couldn't find a murder-mystery or crime detection book in the group. A pair of Reed's shoes were tossed carelessly in a corner, completely out of place in the extreme orderliness of the room. Their soles were covered with thick mud which had dried into a hard red crust.

In the night outside, the dog howled again, the sound dulled even more by the swiftly gathering fog. This time it seemed faintly mournful as if the animal were cold and alone. I shivered and opened Reed's closet. Two crisp Marine officer's uniforms hung neatly on hangers. Next to these were his civilian clothes: a brown suit with a white carnation wilted in its lapel, a gray wool sports coat with a slight red check woven into the material.

My attention strayed to a dresser built into the closet. One of the drawers was partially open and a white military glove protruded, the fingertips soiled with reddish clay.

This didn't startle me as much as the black, slightly bent negatives stuffed under the gloves.

I held one of them up to the light. A nude woman poised on a diving board, sprang unmistakably into view.

Chapter Thirteen

The negatives still smelled of developing fluid and were lacerated along one edge where they'd been ripped from Hel Gandy's metal hangers.

A car door slammed rudely outside the house. Footsteps thudded on wet asphalt and then vanished, creating a happy clamor from the once-mournful canine. Reed's next door neighbors must have arrived home.

I held a second negative up to the light showing costumed figures chaining a white manikin to Rote's sacrificial altar. The third was badly over-exposed. Faint images could be seen enveloped in a panorama of ribbons. The last was a poolside tableau. Dr. Ford clasped a woman in a cat costume. One of his hands was stuffed inside her blouse and the raw edge that I'd seen on New Year's Eve projected starkly. They were surrounded by bottles, bodies and a black sea that foamed over the edge of the rocky sea cliff in ominous white folds.

That was the extent of the negatives. It wasn't the extent of Reed Walker. He stood inside the bedroom door with a pistol barrel cocked straight at my forehead.

"I didn't expect you—yet," I said, lowering the negatives.

"That goes double," he said, examining my wet outfit. "I saw the lights and went down the neighbors' stairway under the house."

"That explains the dog," I continued. "He knows you."

"You're so right" Reed said flatly. "He used to be mine until I couldn't keep him any longer. What are you doing here, Honey?"

I couldn't think of a better answer. "Looking at old photographs. Very boring."

"Is that right? Where'd you find them?"

"In this drawer. You ought to keep such things in your photo album.

They wouldn't be so obvious."

"I don't have a photo album," he said. "They look like negatives. Big negatives."

"They are," I said. "A little too big for you, I'm afraid, Reed."

"Where they from?"

"Hel Gandy's darkroom. Ever been there?"

"Not in a long time. What'd you bring them here for, Honey?"

"I didn't. Let's not play games, Reed. You're the one with the gun. Mine's still down in Wolf's Bathysphere."

"You still talk in riddles, don't you? This is my house. You're the one who's broken in. Now let's get to the point."

"The point is, Captain, somebody shot Hel Gandy to get these negatives. Now, let's skip the formalities. They were in your bureau."

"I never saw them before in my life."

"And I suppose you never clapped your big brown eyes on this before either." I tossed him the book on murder.

He nodded. "That's exactly right. Say, what's been going on here anyway?"

Reed Walker seemed genuinely puzzled. He lowered the pistol and opened his bureau drawer where I'd found the negatives. His soiled gloves fell to the floor.

He picked them up and said, "Now how did these get there? I put them in the dirty clothes hamper this morning. And those shoes! They were out on the patio."

And Helena's bathing suit, Reed, where'd you leave that?"

"I—I don't know," he stammered. "I guess I burned it."

"Where?"

"In—in the fireplace."

"Now you know that's a lie."

"I don't know what you mean, Honey."

"Sure, you do. I found Helena's swimsuit in Wolf's Bathysphere where he admits he ripped it off her New Year's Eve."

Reed dropped his pistol into a bureau drawer and jammed it closed. "I'm a damned fool," he whispered. "I should have known I couldn't get away with that story. I should have realized her suit would turn up sometime."

"I have a weird feeling you're going to say Helena was blackmailing you, Reed."

His eyes narrowed. "How'd you know?"

"It's par for the course. How much was she after, three thousand?"

"No, five."

I whistled. "She had your number, but good. When were you supposed to pay off, New Year's Eve?"

Reed's head swung up sharply as if he'd been clipped with a hard uppercut. "That's right. She came up here just before the party. She was drunk and mean as hell." He gestured toward the living room. "She fell over the coffee table and almost knocked herself unconscious."

"You're sure that's what happened?"

"Of course, I'm sure. That's how those gold sequins got littered all over the floor. I told you that other story about finding the suit down in the vault because I couldn't tell you the truth."

"Why, Reed?"

He unloosened his tie and groaned. "Honey, I just can't tell you. It would ruin me. I'd lose my commission. Go to jail."

"If you don't tell me you may go to the gas chamber. This is serious business, Reed. At the moment you're like a man walking a tight rope over Niagara Falls. The evidence in this room alone might be enough to convict you of murder."

"I can't understand how all this got here, I swear."

"You lied before, Reed. How can I be certain you're telling the truth now?"

He took out a cigarette and pushed it between his dry lips and lit it. He moved mechanically to a bottom drawer in his bureau, lifting a pile of freshly laundered military shirts and took out a folded white paper.

"Read this," he said, handing it to me. "No one's ever known. You'll be the first. I suppose this means the end of my Marine career."

I opened the paper and read the printed script at the top: MARRIAGE CERTIFICATE. Below were the words: State of Nevada, County of Clark.

"Reed," I stammered, "you—you're not married?"

"I was," he mumbled, sitting on the edge of the bed.

The remaining words on the license were half-printed, half-written:

This is to certify that the undersigned Robert L. Williams did on the 21ˢᵗ day of May A.D. 1957 join in lawful wedlock Reed Samuel Walker of Shark Beach, State of California, and Helena Warren of Shark Beach, State of California, with their mutual consent in the presence of…..

I threw down the marriage license and glowered at Reed. "So, you married Helena six months ago in Las Vegas."

"Yes," he mumbled faintly. "I don't even remember the ceremony. In fact, I don't even remember the trip across the desert. She drove all the way. I was drunk. Drunker than a skunk. I guess this adds up to bigamy or something, doesn't it?"

"Are you crazy, this document isn't worth the paper it's printed on. It never has been."

Reed lunged to his feet. "What are you talking about?"

"You were both residents of the State of California. Helena was already married to Rote Collier. She gave her maiden name which was false. Thus, the marriage, in this state where you're a legal resident, was automatically null and void and not worth the money you paid for it."

Reed bent down slowly and picked up the paper. "She—she cheated me," he said, almost to himself.

"She lied. She—she said I'd be ruined if this ever came to the attention of the Marine Corps."

"You are naïve, Captain," I said, shaking my head. "Even if the marriage had been valid, Helena was the one guilty of a crime, not you. She was the one who committed bigamy."

He seemed to freeze like the horrible shapes at Rote's party the night I arrived. "I admit I'm not very smart. In fact, I must be a one hundred percent dope. I paid Helena that five thousand dollars New Year's Eve."

"Reed, you didn't!"

"I did. I had to. She had a copy of this marriage license. She said she'd send it to Headquarters in Washington if I didn't pay up. She said no matter what happened there'd be a scandal."

"You crazy fool."

"Yeah," he said. "Yeah, you can say that again. Whoever killed her probably got that money. It was every cent I'd saved for the last ten years."

"How'd you pay her, Reed?"

"Five twenty dollar bundles. She wouldn't accept a check. You can look at my bank book if you want to. It's all there in black and white. A one hundred and twenty dollar balance. What a crummy lousy break."

I studied the Marine Captain in his freshly pressed uniform and shook my head. "You could have drawn the money out and still not paid her, Reed."

He peered at me and his face was ashen white. "Yeah, that's right. I thought about that when she was here. I thought about blackmail and how it never really stops." He paused and his eyes lowered to his hands. "I even thought about killing her, but I didn't have the guts. When the police found my Buck Rogers wings in that mummy case, I nearly flipped. It seemed almost as if Helena were still trying to ruin me even after she was dead. Then you told your little white lie. That's why I checked on you The whole business didn't total. I even suspected you were the murderer until I found out your profession."

"Listen, Reed, you're not as dumb as you make out. I admit the wings in the mummy case were probably a plant, but this stuff—I just don't know!"

"Honey, I didn't kill Helena and I wasn't anywhere near Hel Gandy's place last night. You probably think the mud on my shoes…"

"How'd you know there was mud tracked into Hel's studio?"

"I—I read about the footprints in the newspaper."

"You've got an answer for everything, don't you? And your answer to the big question is: I'm being framed!"

"Of course," he said angrily. "What else could this mean?"

I mixed a couple of wet curls around on my forehead and said, "As far as I know there's been only one person to cast suspicion in your direction."

"Who's that?"

"Fawn Collier."

"That bitch!" Reed said "She'd say anything to get me in trouble."

"She claims she saw you in bed with Helena once."

He exhaled sharply. "Maybe she did. I don't know. Since that trip to Las Vegas I've been drunk so many times you couldn't count them on the legs of a centipede."

"Then that one-time business with Helena wasn't the truth," I said.

"I don't know, Honey. I really don't know. The time I told you about was when I woke up in Las Vegas. If there were any others I was too far gone to remember."

"Fawn says she thinks you were following her on the beach early last evening. Were you?"

"No! He got up and slapped his hands together. "I've got a lot more important things to do besides follow that dame. She's crazy. In fact, I think she's a dike."

"A what?"

"A dike. A female who goes for women. A lesbian. She's all twisted around. Sure, I'll admit she's attractive. Guys make passes at her all the time. I never go near her. She was pretty friendly with those two other gals who were murdered. Almost too friendly, if you know what I mean?"

"No, I don't know."

"Oh, what difference does it make? He paced across the room. "Maybe she isn't what I think she is at all. Who am I to call the kettle black?"

"What is that supposed to mean?"

He shook his head dismally "I don't know. I lied about having a sister, too. Maybe you guessed. That sweater you're wearing belonged to Helena."

"This isn't the same sweater you loaned me, Reed."

He froze again. "But—it looks like the same. Buttons down the front..."

"The other sweater was gray, Reed. This one is blue."

He slumped down on the bed again. "I guess I didn't notice. I just assumed..."

"Okay," I said, "we'll skip it for the moment. Did you know Erik Ford had been arrested by the police?"

"Yes, I read that in the paper, too. So what?"

"He's escaped. I'd like to find him, Reed. I'd also like to dig up Wolf

Larson. Do you have any ideas on the subject?"

I filled Reed in on the details of Erik's escape from the hospital and Wolf's disappearance in the night sea. Ten minutes later we were in the Booby Hatch. The fancy restaurant-bar looked the same as it had the night before except for the sea nymph. Somebody had forgotten to remove her bra. Fawn was seated at a corner table hunched over two tall drinks. She was alone. Reed and I pulled up two chairs and sat down.

"Hello, hello," she said, coldly drunk, a flat impersonal tone to her voice. "I'm celebrating, goodbye."

"What's the occasion?" I asked.

"Helena's two days dead," Fawn said. "Two days, two drinks each round, get it?"

"Get this, Fawn," Reed said. "You told Honey something I want straightened out right now. What gives you the bright idea I was following you on the beach last night?"

"Oh, that, Fawn said, sipping at her straws. "Well, weren't you?"

"You know better than that!" Reed nearly knocked her drinks off the table. "I don't even know what beach you were walking on or why and I couldn't care less if you were stone cold dead and hung by your heels in the middle of Times Square. Now, does that answer your question?"

"Perfectly, darling." Tears suddenly sprang into Fawn's wide green eyes. "I don't think you killed Helena if that's what you think I think. Go away will you, please? Please!"

I placed my hand on her shoulder. "Fawn, we're not here to upset you. Reed didn't mean what he said. We're looking for Erik and Wolf Larson. Have you seen either one of them?"

She wiped at her eyes with a silk handkerchief. "No. No, I haven't. Please, leave me alone."

"Fawn, did you know your father is a part owner in Wolf Larson's business?" I asked.

She looked at me. "No. Is he?"

"That's what Wolf Larson claims."

"I don't understand. Father couldn't be in business with Larson. You know what I told you about Wolf and Helena."

"Yes," I said, glancing at Reed. "That's not important now. Finding

267

Wolf Larson is."

"Fawn," Reed said, "you told Honey you saw me in bed with Helena once. When was that?"

"I—I don't remember," she answered faintly. "Whatever you've done, Reed Walker, doesn't concern me, understand?"

"Certainly it concerns you if you tell people about it!" Reed's eyes lit up. "Now when did you see us?"

"About two months ago. Now leave me alone!"

"No, I won't!" Reed said. "You've set me up for the kill—and I don't like it! Not one bit!"

Fawn tried to rise, but fell back in her chair. She was too drunk to make her legs work. "Don't you say that to me, Reed Walker! You never looked at me once, did you? No! You were too crazy about Helena. You were too fascinated by her big breasts and big hips to see me! All right, so I don't have big curves! I couldn't give you as big a time, could I? No!" She crumpled over the table. "You—you dirty louse!"

Reed didn't move. He seemed completely baffled by Fawn's outburst. So were a few other people within earshot. I put my arm around her shoulders again. This time I wasn't as tender.

"You're coming with us, Fawn," I said. "You've had enough. More than enough."

"Where—where we going?"

"I want to see that film in its entirety." I studied Reed Walker. "I want to compare backs, or faces, or what have you."

Fawn staggered to her feet. "Father's probably burned the reel by now. We'll never find it."

"Why do you say that?"

"Because," she said, 'he opened his wall safe this afternoon. He took out everything, including a gun."

It was nearly midnight when we arrived at the Collier castle. Thick fog shrouded the old mansion and waves beat below the cliff.

"Good night for a murder," I said. "Glad you two are still on your feet."

Fawn got out of the car and fell headlong on the road.

Reed snickered. "One down and two to go."

We picked her up and half carried her down the steps to the front door. It was slightly ajar. The living room was dark and smelled faintly of orange blossoms.

"Rote!" I called. "Are you home?"

"Sure, he's home," Fawn said, her words slurred. "He's always home. The sandman bites him about eleven-thirty. After he's watched Fu Manchu or some other idiotic mystery melodrama on TV. Why don't you two leave me alone?"

"Not until we see that film," I said. "And what's this business about your father taking a gun out of his safe?"

"I don't know," she said, staring up at me. "He owns one. Don't we all?"

"Do you, Fawn?" I asked.

"No, but you do, Honey. And he does. I've seen it. A pistol. A .38. We live in a world of artillery. God save the bullets and the bastards," she screamed and collapsed on the staircase.

Reed carried Fawn into her bedroom. "She's out like a light," he said, putting her down on the bed.

"Maybe she's right. Maybe we ought to go home and call it a night."

"Not until I find that film, Reed. If you want to leave, go head."

He shook his head and squeezed my hand. "I want to see those pictures as much as you do. Lead the way."

We walked down the hall to the staircase. Something brought me to a quick stop. A bottle of cologne had been spilled on the top step. I picked up the ornate bottle. It smelled of orange blossoms.

"Something's haywire, Reed," I said. "Something's really haywire."

"What give you that idea?"

I didn't answer his question. Two doors down from the staircase was Rote Collier's bedroom. He was seated at his desk, staring straight at us, his pink cheeks rosier than ever. In fact, they were too rosy. They were covered with blood.

Chapter Fourteen

Rote Collier had been shot through the right temple at extremely close range.

"My God!" Reed whispered.

"Don't touch anything," I managed to say trying to catch my breath. "Give me your handkerchief."

Reed didn't move. The sea rumbled in the distance and an old clock ticked in the corner of the room. After a momment, he fumbled in his pocket and handed me a neatly-folded handkerchief.

I bent down beside Rote's chair and found a .38 weapon that smelled like firecrackers after they had been exploded.

"He—he must have shot himself," Reed said.

I flipped open the cartridge cylinder. One empty case fell to the rug. An envelope addressed to Honey West lay on the desk. I opened it and found a check for one thousand dollars made out in my name and signed by Rote, and a terse, disquieting letter. It read:

> Dear Honey:
> We never discussed your fee, so I hope the enclosed will cover everything. You're probably wondering why a man who loved life as much as I did would ever commit suicide. To tell you the truth I couldn't stand the shame any longer.
> By now you know what I mean. I should have confessed the truth long ago, at least to you, but how does one put this sort of things into words. I never could before and I still find it impossible. Helena was as much in the dark as anyone. I shall never forgive myself for her death. It was all my fault. If I'd had any real courage I would have exposed the whole ter-

270

rible business long ago, but I never realized how treacherous it was—or how far it would go. You can add the two other women and Helmet Gandy to my erroneous blunderings, too.

For all of this, please forgive me.
Rote.

"So, he was the murderer," Reed said, over my shoulder. "I can't believe it."

"That makes two of us," I said.

Fawn appeared in the doorway. She didn't say a deeply in her eyes that they seemed like two monstrous green holes drilled in her ashen-white face. She staggered into the room screaming at the top of her lungs and pitched over on her face.

Lieutenant Mark Storm came out of Fawn's bedroom well after midnight. Rote's body had already been examined by the coroner and moved to the morgue. Mark looked like a corpse and removed to the haggard and unshaven. He sagged against the staircase banister and offered me a cigarette.

"The doctor had to give Fawn a shot," he said, as he fumbled for a match. "Damn near out of her mind. Who wouldn't be? Poor kid!"

I drew on the flame until smoke filled my mouth, then I exhaled slowly. "Mark, do you really believe he committed suicide?"

"Is there any doubt, Honey?" he asked sadly. "I know it's a shock to you. Even to me."

"Nothing adds up," I said. "The note for instance. He doesn't actually confess to any of the murders."

"He said, and I quote," Mark said," "I should have confessed the truth long ago, but how does one put this sort of thing into words'."

"I know that's what he said…"

"We checked the handwriting."

" I know that, too…"

"The bullet penetrated the lower right temple at close range. He obviously held the gun. A paraffin test will be just a formality."

"You don't understand," I argued. "I believe he shot himself. I even

271

agree that he wrote the letter—without any intimidation on anyone's part, but…"

"It still doesn't add up," Mark finished for me. "Look, we've talked about this before, Honey. Murder never adds up. That's why we have detectives instead of accountants handling homicide."

"But, Mark…"

"The case is over, Honey, you might as well face it. You were wrong—I was right, partially. My suspicions about Rote after the train accident bore fruit—a little too late."

"I know what he said, Honey. I've got every word memorized. The case is closed. You've got your money. Now, take my advice. Go home and forget Rote Collier, Shark Beach, Buck Rogers, the whole shooting match. I'll call you tomorrow."

I shrugged. "The fog's too thick. I'll wait until morning. Maybe a good night's sleep will snap me out of the doldrums."

"Okay," he said. "Good idea if somebody does stay with Fawn. She's pretty broken up."

"So am I."

He kissed my cheek and started down the stairway, then stopped and forced a grin on his whole mouth. "Why don't you quit this damned foolishness and get married? I can be had—very easily."

I smiled. "Thanks, Lieutenant. I'll keep your name on file. Okay?"

"Okay," he said. "I'll be around when you're ready. Do me a favor, though, will you?"

"What's that, Lieutenant?"

"Don't wait until I'm in a wheelchair. You can't make much love in the darned contraptions."

I grasped his outstretched hand. "You can make love anywhere, Lieutenant—with me."   He groaned. "Honey, you're fabulous. I wish I were anything but a detective."

"Why, Mark?"

"Because maybe, then, I could figure you out. He walked down the stairs with his head hunched forward and his battered hat pulled tightly to his eyes.

I went into Rote's bedroom, not even realizing why. His chair was drawn away from the desk and red stains still gleamed on the polished dark wood. On the wall near his bed was a photograph of Helena. Her shoulders were naked and the stark cleft of her breasts gouged down into the frame. She was smiling and black hair curled around her face like dark strands of velvet. I wondered who took the photograph and how long ago. She was obviously in her teens and the fresh sparkle of her eyes was as bright as diamonds. Under the portrait, on a narrow shelf, was a bronze cup with the inscription: MISS BLOCKBUSTER, 1952, *Helena Warren.*

Footsteps sounded on the staircase. The doctor was almost to the front door before I stopped him.

"How is she?"

He frowned. "She's tough. I'll tell you that, Miss West. That injection still hasn't knocked her out—completely. She's fighting it like a Trojan. I'd suggest you look in on her as often as possible."

I nodded, let him out the door and then crossed into the kitchen. Ten seconds later, Fawn was in the doorway, her dress wrinkled, face stained from tears.

"You ought to be in bed," I suggested.

"I know," she mumbled. "I just wanted to count heads. I suspected yours would be present and accounted for."

"I'm sorry about your father, Fawn. Believe me, I feel more deeply than you could imagine."

"You've got your money," she said, clutching the door frame. "What more do you want?"

"Nothing," I said, putting the coffee pot on the stove. "I haven't earned my salary yet."

"You mean your nurse maid's fee?"

"You might call it that—until tomorrow morning."

"Get out of here!"

"You don't mean that," I said.

"Oh, don't I?" She shook her head dazedly and nearly toppled over. "He's dead. It's all over, Miss West. The film business, the New Year's Eve parties, the little presents with his name scrawled on the packages, everything. It's all over now. SO you can go home. And I can go home."

"You're mixed up, Miss Collier." I started toward her. "Your home is

273

upstairs—in bed. Now let's move in that direction, shall we?"

She swung at me viciously and missed. Her fist struck the wall and a dish clattered off a shelf and crashed into a million pieces on the linoleum floor. She didn't utter a sound. Her eyes stared at me as if they were caught in a steel vise.

"You killed him," she whispered. "You killed him. If you'd never come here…"

I caught her arm as she went limp. The trip up the staircase was arduous. Fawn sprawled several time before I could get her into the second-story bedroom. A noise downstairs jolted me to a stop as I was unbuckling her belt. I tossed a blanket over her and headed for the kitchen. Erik Ford met me halfway. He still wore his green operating costume and his red hair was wet and matted.

"Where is he?" Erik demanded.

"The morgue," I said. "He had something no doctor could ever plug up. Where have you been?"

"Walking," Erik said, "on the beach. I finally went back to the police station and turned myself in. They told me what happened."

"Want a cup of coffee?"

"I guess so," he said. "I don't know what I want anymore. I feel as though I'm shell-shocked."

"That's exactly the way Rote Collier felt," I said, going into the kitchen. "Except the bullet didn't give him much of a chance to feel anything, did it?"

"You're horrible," he said, following me. "I came here to tell you that. Now you know."

I wet my lips. "See, it's true. Even your best friends won't tell you. I'm glad you had the courage."

"You're despicable," he continued. "You open people up and you feed on their insides like some damned vulture."

"That's right," I said, pouring two cups of coffee. "You might say I'm like a doctor. Only I don't sew my patients up after the operation. Most of the time they're too dead to sew up."

His eyes blazed fiercely. "You tried to ruin me just as Helena did. Except you did a better job. You got me arrested. My name in the headlines."

274

"That happens, Doctor. When murder raises its bloody head no one's considered innocent. You won't believe this, but I argued for your release."

Erik's fists tightened. "You stole my keys. You broke into my office. You accused me of Hel Gandy's murder!"

"Right on two counts, wrong on the third." I said, pushing a chair in his direction. "You're upset. Sit down and cool off."

"You're damned right I'm upset. Do you have any idea how many years I've worked to establish myself in the medical profession..."

"Sit down, Doctor! I don't care how many years you've worked to do anything! You're no saint!" I swallowed hard, touched by his anguished expression.

"All right, sure I care! I care about a lot of things but they don't seem very big right now. And what you're telling me is even smaller! Now, sit down and drink your coffee or get out of here!"

Tears ran down my cheeks and dropped into the folds of my shirt. He sighed heavily and slumped into a chair.

"Lousy damned women!" he whispered harshly. "Always got an answer for everything. And it's always a moist answer. Heavily saturated with mascara and nonsense."

My eyes sprang to his face. "What'd you say?"

"It doesn't matter."

"What'd you say, Erik? 'Heavily saturated with mascara,' is that what you said?"

"That's what I said. So what?"

I rose and wiped at my face clumsily. "You said 'heavily saturated with mascara.'"

"Are you crazy?" he said. "I'm beginning to believe you are."

"I think you've hit something, Erik!"

"Hit what?"

I dashed for the staircase. The stain from the spilled cologne still clung wetly to the carpeting. I sniffed closely to be sure. Orange blossoms. Erik followed me up the staircase.

"Honey," he said. "You'd better see a good psychiatrist."

I glanced at him and the smile that dented my cheeks was the warmest expression to touch my face in hours."

"You can say that again, Doc. I should have seen one two days ago, but I couldn't see the forest for the trees."

"And what does that mean?"

"I don't know exactly," I said. "But one thing's certain."

"And what's that?"

"Rote Collier wasn't a murderer!

Chapter Fifteen

Dawn touched my bedroom curtains, slanted through and blew its breath on my stomach bringing me fully awake from a bad dream about nude men and orange blossoms. My bedcovers were strewn all over and I was shivering where the cold had crept under my hip-length nightie. I rose slowly in the dim light, rubbing my hands over my chilled legs to stir some life back into them. Below my window the sea lay ominously quiet in a white foggy shroud. I slipped a one-piece bathing suit over my goose-pimpled body and went downstairs to the kitchen.

After a hurried cup of coffee and a slice of toast, I put on one of Rote's old jacket and walked out onto the cliff top. A sea gull squalled bitterly in the mist and a cool wind tangled my hair.

An old-fashioned stone incinerator squatted in a smoke-smeared hollow near the opening into the ashes. My fingers came up with a few scorched fragments of movie film. Under a bright light inside the house, the salvaged frames revealed a naked Helena prancing passionately in the forest. I went outside again and dug further. Nothing could be found of the scene in Hel Gandy's bedroom.

Mark sounded as if he were chewing on old wet rags when I got him on the phone.

"Take the receiver out of your mouth, Lieutenant," I said. "Then maybe you'll make sense."

"Who makes sense at six o'clock in the morning," he groaned sleepily. "For heaven's sake go to bed."

"I've been to bed. I dreamt about naked men and orange blossoms."

"Great. Go back to bed and dream about naked women and me. I'll

277

try and tune in on your wave length. Good-bye!"

"Wait, Mark! What'd you do with the cologne bottle we found on the staircase?"

"Sent it to the lab. Why?"

"Did you notice the fragrance?"

"Sure. Orange Blossoms. It was Helena's favorite. We found two or three more bottles on her vanity."

"What do you think it was doing on the staircase?"

Mark laughed. "Having a conversation with the banister, what else?"

"Listen, smart guy, Rote Collier didn't murder anybody but himself. That spilled bottle of cologne proves it."

"Proves what? All you managed to established last night was the fact that the cologne bottle was dropped after Fawn left the house for the Booby Hatch. What difference does it make? Rote probably penned his letter to you, then, feeling heartsick he went into Helena's room, picked up a bottle of her cologne and broke into tears. He staggered out onto the landing and, in a moment of bereavement, the bottle slipped from his fingers."

"That bottle didn't slip, Mark. It was thrown."

"What gives you that bright idea."

"Some of the cologne splattered as far as the landing and on the floor below the steps. A few drops even sprayed all the way to the wall leading into the kitchen."

"All right," Mark said. "So, he threw the bottle. He probably felt a moment of panic as he stood outside her bedroom door. She was dead. He had killed her and his brain pounded with morbid anger."

I shook my head. "Music up. Curtain. For my money your production stinks. It'll never make Broadway."

"That's what you think. For the last time, the case is closed. Go home!"

I told him to mind his own business and hung up.

The old house creaked from new winds off the sea as I went upstairs to Fawn's room. Her bed was empty. The dress she'd worn the night before was thrown over a chair. It smelled faintly of orange blossoms.

Fawn wasn't in her bathroom either. I glanced out the window. The fog had lifted slightly over a calm sea and a solitary swimmer cleaved the blue surface, kicking up a soft white spray that concealed his identity.

I raced downstairs to the spiral steps. My heels clanged on the metal treads as I hurried to reach the bottom before the swimmer disappeared. The door leading out to the rock shelf was jammed. I heaved my shoulder against it several times before the panel gave. Wind ruffled my hair and stung my eyes as I stepped out near the pool. The figure in the water was gone.

Now a small fishing boat drifted about fifty feet offshore. Its foamy trail lay in the water like a strip of heated popcorn and a broad hairy-chested man stood in the bow. He waved at me.

"Hi, Honey! Come on out!"

"Wolf! What are you doing here?"

"Guess you didn't know I owned a fishing boat. I been out all night. I want to talk to you about something very important."

"The police have been looking for you."

"Yeah, I know," he returned. "They caught up with me this morning down in Newport Harbor. I heard about Rote. Come on out. I want to talk to you."

"I've learned my lesson, Wolf. This is about the right distance for a conversation with you. Go ahead."

"Can't shout it over the clifftops," he said, shaking his shoulders. Beads of water ran down his chest. He obviously was just out of the flat sea. "I'll come ashore."

"I've a better idea. Meet me tonight at Hel's studio. Seven o'clock. All right?"

"I don't get it," he shouted.

"You will," I said huskily, winking. "You will—tonight."

He grinned. "Okay, I'll be there."

Wolf swung his boat around and vanished in the fog. I looked up at the house. A figure moved back from one of the windows, rustling in the curtain. I counted the number of windows from the balcony. My room!

I rushed back upstairs and scoured the house thoroughly, but found nothing out of the ordinary except a few drops of dried blood on the kitchen floor.

I called Mark again.

"Fawn's missing."

"Are we going to go through all of this again, Honey."

"I found blood on the kitchen floor."

"Sure it isn't orange blossoms cologne?"

"You better find her, Mark."

"Thanks, but no thanks."

"Okay."

"Okay, what?"

"I'll find her," I said. "You may not like my methods, but I'll find her, Mark."

I spent the greater part of the morning going through Rote's important files which were hidden in one of the vaults. One document spelled out the legal percentage arrangement of a business called Bathyspheres, Inc., which was operated under the joint partnership of Wolf Larson and Rote Collier. The ex-movie director held two-thirds of the stock. One clause specified that upon the death of either partner the entire profits, stock and holding of the business would revert to the survivor.

Something else caught my eye. It was a Shark Beach newspaper clipping, dated January 22, 1954. The two-column headline read: RETIRED MOVIE DIRECTOR'S LIFE SAVED BY EMERGENCY OPERATION. In the second paragraph of the story the doctor who performed the brilliant piece of surgery on Rote Collier was named. Erik Ford.

Two marriage licenses were filed in a folder marked *personal*. The first was a soiled document dated June 15, 1928 which revealed the wedlock of Rote to his deceased wife, Mary, in the First Methodist Church of Los Angeles.

The other license was a Photostat of an original filed in Clark County, Nevada. Helena Warren's name was typed neatly on the transcript. Rote Collier's wasn't. My eyes widened. This was a copy of the marriage document Reed Walker had taken from the bottom drawer of his bureau. This last transcript could mean only one thing. Rote had known all the time about Helena's elopement to Las Vegas with the handsome Marine Captain. It also meant, in all probability, that Rote Collier and Helena had never exchanged vows.

After lunch I made three phone calls. Doctor Erik Ford's receptionist put him on the wire immediately. When I asked him to meet me at Hel Gandy's studio at seven his voice changed.

"No, thanks," he said. "Enough is enough, Miss West. My bones have been picked clean already."

"I told you last night, Erik, something new has developed. You still owe me a favor for that wrestling match you put me through New Year's Eve. Now I'm asking you nicely, please."

He hesitated for a long instant, then said, "All right. But, I'm warning you, don't pull any fast ones."

"I won't keep any promises," I said. "Tell me, Erik, you weren't by any chance out swimming in the ocean early this morning, were you?"

"No, of course not! The water's freezing this time of year. Why?"

"Nothing. One more question. What's the fishing like close to shore around Shark Beach?"

"I don't know!" he snarled. "Call the Chamber of Commerce! I'm busy!" He hung up in my ear.

My second call took twice as long, but was worth every moment of waiting. A cracker-voiced operator at the Marine Base had to track Reed Walker down at the "ready room" where he was preparing for a flight. His abrupt tone warmed instantly when he realized who was at the other end of the line."

"Honey, I've been meaning to call you all morning. I've been worried about you."

"Why, Reed?"

"Well, you took Rote's death pretty hard last night. I'd never seen you cry before. It made me feel awful bad. I couldn't sleep."

"Reed, did you go for a swim around daylight?"

He pause was electric. "How'd you know? Yeah, I went for a dip this morning. Funny, you should ask. My nerves were all tied in knots. The swim sort of loosened me up."

"Were you anywhere near the Collier place?"

"No. I climbed over the fence at the high school. Went swimming in the pool. It was wonderful."

"How's fishing in these parts, Reed?"

"Not bad. Lot of yellowtail right now in deep water."

"How about the shallow areas, close to shore?"

"I never cast off the rocks. The surf's usually too high to fool with."

His voice seemed to tighten with each word of the conversation. When I asked him to meet me at Hel Gandy's studio at seven, he choked audibly.

"What for, Honey?"

"I want to give you something, Reed," I whispered. "Something, you want more than anything else in this world."

"Well," he stammered, "why not my place?"

"At seven, Reed," I said. "I'll be waiting, so don't be late."

This time I hung up first. I waited for a few moments to see if he might call back, but he didn't. I dialed the Chamber of Commerce in Shark Beach. A crisp male voice answered my question about fishing in shallow waters. He practically repeated Reed's statements verbatim except for one minor addition.

"Lobster fishing is very good this time of year." The man said. "Some people have pots, you know."

"Have what?" I asked.

"Lobster pots."

"What are these lobster pots? How do they work?"

The man's voice warmed with my interest. "They're wire cages anchored in the water. They trap the lobsters and keep them alive until the pot owners show up for the kill. Personally, the lack of sport involved is what makes me against them and besides…"

"How deep in the water are they usually anchored?" I interrupted.

"Oh, just a foot or so beneath the surface. Sometimes during an extremely low tide you can see them from shore."

"Thanks," I said. "Thanks very much."

"Happy lobster hunting," he said.

He had no idea how happy my hunt was going to be. I walked down to the rock shelf again and plunged into the cool water. It was still calm, but now, fog lay on the surface like cotton candy pressed to the face of a little child. The sound of my arms cleaving the water seemed unusually loud.

After a few minutes, I lost sight of shore and the gentle swells grew colder and wider apart. The odds of my finding a lobster pot in this kind of weather were terribly slim, but I persisted in my course out into the bay. I tried to recall the path traced by the swimmer earlier. The fog mixed me up as it thickened into a filmy cloak that was dense as pea soup.

I finally turned around, heard something slapping gently in the swell and tried to locate the sound. The square, wooden-frame box with chicken wire tacked over its sides was half out of the water and filled with huge lobsters that flashed beady, frightened eyes in my direction.

The prospect was not to my liking, but I lifted the lid of the cage and reached in after one of the hard-shelled creatures, trying to keep my fingers well back on its body. The claws snapped, sending a shudder through my whole arm. I managed to escape the pincers and tossed the lobster into the sea. The others scuttled against each other as I reached for a second, their backs snapping and fluttering like a rattler's tail.

In all there were six. Only three had to be removed before I saw a tin box wedged in the corner of the cage. An ugly, partially-broken pincer snipped at my hand as I lifted out the box and opened its spring lock. Under the battered corroded cover were five wet bundles of twenty dollar bills.

Here, at last, was Reed Walker's missing five thousand dollars.

Chapter Sixteen

Erik Ford was the first to arrive at Hel Gandy's studio. He was fifteen minutes early and sweat beaded his forehead as we stood in the dark entryway.

He removed his topcoat and asked, "What's the new development?"

I led him into the studio where the furniture and lamps were still in disarray. We straightened up two chairs and sat down. He offered me a cigarette.

"I drove over to your house late this afternoon," I said. "You weren't home."

His body snapped rigidly. "Of course, I wasn't. You know I was at my office. Don't tell me you broke in?"

"No, that wasn't necessary. Your clothesline was as far as I had to go."

"My clothesline?"

"I found a pair of bathing trunks hanging there with your initials stitched on the pocket. They were still wet from that swim you took this morning."

"You're crazy!" he slammed, getting to his feet. "They were still wet from the fog. They've been out there for the last three days."

"Your neighbors say you left the house early this morning, Erik Ford. Even before daybreak. The lady next door woke up when you started your car."

"It was an emergency call, I..."

"I checked, Erik. You had no emergency calls today at any time. Want to tell me about it?"

He slumped into the chair and winced. "I—I went driving down to San Clemente."

284

"Why?"

"I was disturbed by what you said last night. About Rote Collier not being a murderer."

"Why should that disturb you?"

"Because I feel the same way. I knew the murderer was still at large and might kill again."

"Who do you think is the killer, Erik?"

"Wolf Larson."

A huge shadow filled the door. Wolf Larson entered the studio, his fangs glistening in the bare light. "And I figured you picked up the tab, Doc, so what do you think of that?"

"What are you doing here?" Erik asked, shooting a side glance at me.

"I was just going to ask you the same question," Wolf asked. "This party is supposed to be exclusively in my honor."

I smiled. "That may be truer than you think, Mr. Larson. Pull up a chair and sit down."

After Wolf was settled comfortably I handed him the business contracts on Bathyspheres, Inc., with the death clause circled in red. He straightened.

"So help me, you're barking up the wrong tree," Wolf said. "He committed suicide. The police proved that."

"Sure they did. But you know, Wolf, I just found out something very interesting about you. You're a rich man."

"What are you talking about?"

"Rote's will," I said. "His lawyer allowed me to read that illustrious document only an hour ago. You not only get Bathyspheres, Incorporated, but Rote Collier divided his entire estate between you and Fawn."

"You—you're joking!"

"He speaks of you very warmly. Refers to you as having been like a son to him. The son he lost during the Korean war."

Wolf Larson bit his lips, then said, "How do you like this? I didn't know he felt that way about me. I always wondered why he backed me so quickly in that business. He was friendly, but…"

"Do you think he ever had any reason to feel ashamed of you, Wolf?"

"Ashamed?"

"Don't you think he knew about you and Helena?" I demanded sharply.

His face reddened. "I told you before there was never anything between Helena and me! Rote was too nice a guy!"

"Rote had a movie of Helena and ..."

"I know! You told me! But, whoever it was—it wasn't Wolf Larson."

The doorbell jangled. I went into the hall and returned to the studio with Reed Walker. He was carrying a bottle of champagne and his expression changed when he saw the two other men.

"Honey," Reed groaned, "I thought you told me.."

"This is what you call the triple-cross, my friend," Wolf said, setting up another chair for him. "We've been had—but good. Take your place of execution."

"So that's it!" Reed said to me. "A quiet little wake! Or is it a purge?"

"Sit down, Reed."

"Sure," he said. "Sit down, Reed. Cool off, Reed. Boy, did I have you figured wrong, sister. You're nothing but a damned machine stamping out the crest of justice on every hunk of humanity you get your hands on. Here!" He handed me the bottle of champagne. "Why don't you launch us all into San Francisco Bay and float us to San Quentin."

Erik Ford got to his feet. "I've had enough of this. I'm leaving."

I pulled a revolver from my purse and leveled it at the doctor. "Sit down, Erik. You, too, Reed. You're all staying here until I'm finished saying what I have to say, understand?"

The three men stiffened.

"Honey, you'll go to jail for this," Erik said.

"Maybe I will and maybe I won't," I said. "I'll have to take that chance. Now, sit down."

The doctor slid back into his chair. Reed Walker shrugged his shoulders and followed suit.

I sat on the edge of a table a few feet away, gun lying close by my side. "Now," I began, "for one reason or another each one of you fine gentlemen had a warm niche in the heart of Rote Collier. You, Doctor, because you saved his life four years ago when you operated on him. I'm sure Rote respected you more than anyone else in this world."

Erik frowned. "Well, if he did he was a damned fool. A doctor just tries to do his job the best way he knows how. With Rote Collier I was successful. With one or two others," his voice faltered and his hands brushed together, "I wasn't so lucky."

"Yes, I know," I said quietly. "But, with Rote Collier you were successful. He must have been proud of you, Erik. Do you know of any reason why he might, also, have been ashamed of you?"

The surgeon's face turned ashen white and his hands began to tremble. "No, why should I? I never did anything…"

"You had relations with his wife."

"He didn't know anything about that!"

"How do you know—for sure?"

"I—I don't. I just…"

"Would he have been ashamed of you if he thought you'd murdered Helena—and two other women?"

Erik bolted for the door, but my gun stopped him.

"Let me out of here!"

"Sit down, Doctor," I said, waving the .32 toward his chair.

Hesitantly, he resumed his seat. I glanced at Wolf Larson.

"And you, friend. What did Rote Collier think of you? He thought of you as a son. He was so proud of you he could burst. In fact, when everything popped you were left with nearly a million dollars. Do you think he would have been ashamed if he thought you were the murderer?"

Wolf picked up the bottle of champagne and tore off the wrapper. "Sure, I guess he would have been ashamed. But, if he thought that, he was wrong—dead wrong. Now, let's all have a glass of champagne and go home."

I took the copy of the Las Vegas marriage license from my purse and tossed it to Reed Walker.

"What's this?" he demanded.

"It's a Photostat," I said, "of a little certificate awarded six months ago for valor above and beyond the call of duty."

Reed scanned the document and his eyes widened. "Where'd you get this?"

287

"In Rote's private personal file. It indicates to me that he knew you were married to Helena."

Wolf and Erik reacted as if they'd been struck in the back with pitch-forks."

"Reed!" Wolf looked astonished. "You were married to Helena?"

"Yeah," Reed said, after a moment. "I was drunk. She poured me into a car one night, six months ago, and drove me to Las Vegas. Fortunately, the ceremony wasn't legal. Helena gave the wrong last name."

"That's where you're wrong, pal," I said. "Did any of you gentlemen attend Rote and Helena's wedding?"

One by one they shook their heads.

"I'll tell you why none of you were ever invited," I said. "Because it's my guess there never was a wedding, or a ceremony, or anything. Rote Collier was just living with Helena. That's why she doesn't even get an honorable mention in a will which was drawn up more than a year ago."

Reed's face fell thirty thousand feet in a straight, headlong dive. "You—you mean Helena was actually my wife after all?"

"That's right, Captain. She gave her right name and for good reason. The handwriting was already on the wall. She was on the verge of being ousted from the Collier castle. In fact, in desperation she stooped to black-mail, intimidation and subterfuge. She pitted herself against the world—people against each other. She even went so far as to smash you in Rote's eyes."

"What do you mean?" Reed asked.

"You were in Rote's will, very prominently, one year ago. He thought of you as a heroic officer of the United States Marine Air Corps. He knew you'd fought in Korea. He considered you a son up until six months ago when you eloped with Helena. That's when he crossed you out of his will in heavy black ink. But, I have a feeling he never crossed you out of his heart."

"That—that's absurd," Reed stammered. "Rote didn't like me—he couldn't have liked me if he knew."

"He knew all right," I said. "He was still proud of you—for your war record, at least. I wonder how much shame there was in his heart, Reed, the night he committed suicide?"

Reed said, "You—you make this out like it was a war, don't you? With two or three sides not knowing which way to go. Not knowing what's right and what's wrong. You can't do this, you know, Honey. You can't take three men or three armies and bend them to the point of busting wide open. Because they'll revolt on you, do you understand? They'll tear you to pieces. Some thing in life are sacred—and a man's insides are on the them. You can't just cleave him open and leave him dripping, because he'll tear you to bits before he dies. I—I'm warning you! You'd better stop this right now!"

"He's right, Honey," Erik said, hands clenched on the arms of his chair. "You may kill one of us possibly two at the most, but there's bound to be one left to take you. Put down that gun because we're leaving—now—and there's not a thing you can do about stopping us."

"I'm afraid there is, Erik" I said, pointing the gun at his head. "Murder is a pretty rough business. Maybe all three of you have wondered why I'm in it—clear up to the armpits."

"Breasts would be a better word," Wolf interjected. "Lord, have you been endowed, Honey."

"All right," I said, "however you want to put it! I don't like murder or murderers, understand? You sort of get that fixation when you find your own father lying in a gutter with his head torn open by a bullet. And you get that way when you discover three people as self-centered as you three, gentlemen. None of you really knew how Rote Collier felt about you. You never took the time to find out what he was, how he lived, or what Helena really meant to him. Sure, he was no angel—who is? And Helena was one of the worst. She was blackmailing all three of you. And you want to know why? Because New Year's Eve was a deadline for her, too. The party was her swan song. Rote was turning her out the next day. That's why he cried so bitterly when we found her dead. He felt guilty. More than that, he knew who the killer really was and he felt so ashamed that he finally took his own life because he couldn't face the prospect of life any longer—with that shame hanging on his shoulders."

The three men stiffened, almost in unison, as if they'd been welded together in some fantastic triple birth.

"The murdered went to the Collier place last night." I continued, "and

Rote told him what he knew. The killer was obviously a sensitive man. He wanted to kill Rote, but couldn't. Instead, he promised to turn himself in to the police and left the house. Accepting the killer at his word, Rote penned a note admitting his shame and then took his own life."

A champagne cork exploded against the ceiling and pale amber wine followed after it like the gust of a roman candle ignited on the Fourth of July. Wolf put his finger over the opening and stopped the foamy liquid. The plastic cork had missed me by inches.

I aimed the gun at Wolf's ponderous head. "You're not a very good shot, Mr. Larson." I said, wiping away some of the wine that had gushed over my skirt. "Another inch one way or the other and you might have been ahead in this game."

"You know," he said, a sardonic smile creasing his thick mouth, "I believe you're right, Miss West. When you suddenly come into a million dollars, one inch can make a lot of difference. Especially if that measurement belongs to the nose of a horse and your million is riding on his proboscis."

"Stand up," I said to the three men, gesturing with the gun.

They rose slowly, their knees bent slightly, their backs as stiff as boards.

"One thing the killer didn't know," I said, after a moment, "is that Hel Gandy did take a picture New Year's Eve which showed the murderer in all his glory. Hel didn't realize this fact until the next morning when he developed the negatives. Once he knew, he wasn't beyond a little blackmail himself. He called the murderer and revealed what he had—or at least, what he thought he had. Perhaps, to Hel Gandy it wasn't incriminating evidence at all. That's why he didn't call the police. The murderer knew different. He came up here and gave Hel a bullet instead of money. Unfortunately for him, though, he couldn't find a negative anywhere which proved him anything more than just another gay figure at a wild New Year's Eve party. So the murderer wrote off Hel's phone call as a novice attempt at blackmail. He'd faced more convincing attempts on the part of Helena. That was where he was wrong!"

"What do you mean?" Wolf demanded.

"Hel really did have a negative which would have convicted the killer. He knew a lot about blackmail, too. Helena had been giving him the same kind of business. Isn't that funny? Everyone was being blackmailed by Helena, and nobody else knew about the other."

"What did Gandy do with that negative?" Erik asked, his breath tight in his throat.

"He hid it in a place he figured no one would ever think of looking."

"Where?" Reed Walker demanded.

I smiled. "I hoped one of you might be able to answer that question."

Wolf Larson rose, flexing his big biceps. "I'm getting out of here!"

"That's Erik's line," I said, leveling the revolver at him. "Surely you can come up with something better."

"I came here for a party," Reed said. "This is a poor excuse."

This was the moment I'd been waiting for. The three men stood staring at me. I snapped my fingers. "I've got it! His waste basket—in the darkroom! No one would ever think to look in there!"

I went after a cardboard box under the sink, dumping its contents on the darkroom's slate floor. Spoiled negatives, cigarette butts, trash, and discarded prints spilled out. I placed my revolver on the edge of the sink and poured through the debris. The three men stood outside the darkroom door, staring at me intently. Then, for a brief second, my attention strayed as I picked up a discarded negative and held it up to the green light.

"I've found it!" I shouted.

There was no reason for my yelling so loud. The lights went out in the studio and my shout only dulled my own eardrums to the sound of bodies jostling in the darkness. One thing that wasn't dulled was the thud of a heavy instrument slamming on my skull. In fact, that sound just seemed to take off for the moon. Then, it hung there for the briefest of seconds until it exploded.

And when it did, my head couldn't have cared less.

Chapter Seventeen

When my eyes opened, Wolf Larson was wiping my face with a damp cloth and Fawn Collier stood in the faint greenish pallor of the sink light freshening her makeup.

She peered down at me and smiled, "How you feeling?"

"Terrible," I said. "Where'd you come from?"

"Sheriff's office. Lieutenant Storm and I just arrived."

Wolf spread the cloth over my forehead. "You've been out for about twenty minutes. That was some wallop you took. It raised a lump the size of an ostrich egg."

Mark bent over me. "You're right, I don't like your methods. Was this a personal or private inquest you were staging here tonight? I feel very disappointed I wasn't invited."

I tried to sit up. "Where are Reed and Erik?"

"They got away," Wolf said.

"I guess they didn't appreciate your séance," Mark said. "They've been picked up, though, and are being brought back for the finale. I assume you do have a closing number in this show."

I looked at Fawn. She wore white gloves and a gray suite with a faint red stripe running through the weave.

"Where have you been all day, Fawn?" I asked.

Mark helped me to my feet. "She dropped by my office about fifteen minutes ago to tell me you might be in trouble."

I studied the green-eyed woman for an instant. My head still throbbed from the blow. "What gave you that idea, Fawn? And how did you know where to find me?"

"I was upstairs in my room this morning," she announced, "when I heard

292

you ask Wolf to meet you at Hel's studio. I knew there might be trouble, so as soon as I got back from Dago I went to Lieutenant Storm's office."

"That was nice of you," I said, going unsteadily into the studio. "Too bad you weren't more prompt. You might have saved me from getting my brains knocked out. Where's that bottle of champagne?"

"I'm sorry, Honey," Wolf said. "It got broken in the scuffle."

"Too bad," I said, studying his face. "I wanted to drink a toast to the murderer's one last mistake."

"What was that?" Wolf asked, hesitantly.

"He didn't hit me hard enough to kill me."

Two sheriff's deputies brought Reed and Erik into the studio a few minutes after I finished explaining to Mark what had happened earlier. Both men were white-faced and trembling. Reed had a slight cut under his right eye.

"All right," Mark demanded, " which one of you jokers pulled this stunt?"

Neither man answered. Mark bent over Erik's chair.

"So they found you at your office, Doc? What were you doing, filing that negative you took from Honey in your bottom drawer with all the rest of your mementos?"

He flinched, but didn't say a word. Mark whirled on Reed. "And what about you, Walker? What were you doing down on the beach near the Collier place? Did you dig a nice deep hole?"

I put my hand on Mark's shoulder. "It doesn't matter about the negative, Lieutenant. That was just a hoax to bring the killer out from under his shell. The only thing visible on the piece of film was a side view of plump buttocks belonging to a model named Lois."

"You mean that was just a trick?" the doctor said, wiping his forehead with a handkerchief.

"That's right, Erik," I said. "It's a shame you didn't stick around. The negative was much clearer under good light."

I took five packages of twenty dollar bills from my purse and tossed them onto the Marine officer's lap.

"There's your money, Reed," I said.

Mark cut in before the captain had a chance to examine the bills. "What money?"

I answered, "Helena put the blackmail bite on our war hero for five thousand smackers. He paid off on New Year's Eve, but the murderer wound up with the dough."

"Where'd you find it?"

"In a lobster pot," I said. "The killer hid it there when he realized he might get caught with a big bundle of marked money if we ever made an extensive search."

"What do you mean marked money?" Mark demanded.

"You'll notice a tiny R has been scratched in India ink in the lower left hand corner of each bill," I said.

"Did you mark this money, Walker?" Mark asked.

Reed pinched his lips together. "Yes. I know it sounds crazy, but I thought she'd demand more money later, so I marked the bills as a possible jail threat."

"Sounds flimsy, Captain," I said. "She could have spent it all before she asked for more. Tell me, what color is Fawn's suit?"

The Marine officer said, "Gray with a red stripe."

"Then you're not color blind?"

"Of course not," Reed growled. "I'm a jet pilot. We take tests all the time. Now what are you driving at?"

"Nothing," I said, turning again to Mark. "Around daybreak this morning the murderer swam to a lobster pot stationed out in Collier Bay and deposited Reed's money in a metal case inside the wire cage. I saw him from an upper story window. Not his face exactly—but his back. I believe it might be the same one I saw in a movie film not too long ago. Mark, I'm positive I'd recognize that man's back if I saw it again."

"Okay," Lieutenant Storm said, "rise and shine, gentlemen. Off with your shirts and turn around."

Wolf Larson sat rigid. The other two men, after some protest, got to their feet.

"What's the matter with you, Larson?" Mark demanded. "Rigor mortis set in?"

"You don't mean me, too, do you?" he said, tapping his chest with his fingers. "I didn't run away. I stayed here with Honey."

"Yeah," Mark said. "Maybe you stayed behind so you could finish her off. Stand up!"

Erik Ford removed his shirt first. His shoulders were much bonier than I imagined and a wide scar ran jaggedly across his white skin.

Reed Walker followed suit. The freckles on his broad shoulders were so prominent that even from a hundred yards in a hazy sea they would have been noticeable.

Wolf Larson, moving at a deliberately slow pace, glowered at me as he opened his buttons. "You cheated," he said. "I don't like cheaters. You were supposed to take yours off first."

His back was broad and deeply sun-tanned. Now there was no doubt in my mind that Wolf had been the man in the movie with Helena. He wasn't the man I'd seen in the water.

I turned to Fawn. "Okay, let's see yours?"

"What?" she choked.

"Take off your blouse and let's see your back," I said.

"Honey!" Mark started toward me. "Are you out of your mind?"

I ignored the Lieutenant. "Take off your blouse, Fawn, or I'll take it off for you."

Her green eyes widened with horror and she backed against the wall, arms raised in defense.

My fist plowed into her stomach viciously, turning her cheeks the color of her eyes. Fawn doubled over and I tore at her blouse, ripping the buttons loose, then reached inside to the white silk fabric underneath. One hard yank was all it took to send two rounded rubber pads flying.

Fawn opened her mouth to scream, but what came out was more like the huskily contorted howl of an animal driven mad by the scissoring grip of a heavy trap.

She got by me, thrashing her arms wildly, and ran toward a glass door leading out onto Hel's front balcony. She seemed caught in a blind panic. We started after her, but the sound of her body striking the hard surface caught us all completely off-stride. For a terrifying instant, we froze in grotesque positions if movement as Fawn Collier kept on going, vanishing in a cloud of jagged glitter that seemed to tear her image to shreds.

When we reached her she was still breathing, very faintly. She had plunged sixty feet down the side of a hill and her face and throat were slashed almost beyond recognition. One part of her body that was recognizable through the tears in her clothing brought instantaneous gasps from the men. Even under the harsh glare of Mark's flashlight it was impossible for them to comprehend.

Fawn *wasn't* a she.

Fawn Collier was a man!

Chapter Eighteen

Mark met me outside the morgue after the medical examination. We walked silently for a long while through faintly-lighted corridors, our heels creating the only sound, except for a rhythmic buzzing of doctor's numbers flashing on numerous overhead call boards. Finally, we turned onto a small balcony near the edge of the dark sea.

"Honey," Mark said suddenly, "when did you first suspect Fawn was really *Frank* Collier?"

"I don't know," I said, shivering from the chilly air. "Maybe the night of the train accident when you said you didn't believe Rote had a real daughter. And, then again, maybe not until two seconds before I ripped out those rubber pads. It was such an intangible theory, Mark. The thought gnawed at the back of my mind and yet, as a woman. I couldn't accept it. I guess Rote's suicide note convinced me I should at least try to investigate the situation—no matter how absurd it seemed."

"That's why you held the private inquest at Hel Gandy's place."

"Yes. I was pretty sure Fawn had heard me make a date to meet Wolf Larson and I guessed, if she were guilty, she'd be there someplace near enough to see what I was up to. When I pulled that ruse with the negative she—I mean he—was able to flick a light switch, hit me over the head and escape with the film. I'm certain he never even examined the negative and just destroyed it, driving straight to your office hoping to create an iron-clad alibi in case I'd become suspicious."

Mark shook his head. "It's fantastic. Fifteen minutes ago a couple of our men found an old diary stuffed in the back of a bookcase in his bedroom. The memos inside were for the year 1953 and traced his movements and emotions from his last days in the Marine Corps and as Frank, through his return to the United States and finally to his arrival in Shark Beach as

297

the beautiful Fawn."

Mark glared at his hands. "He says somewhere in this diary that one reason he took the role of a woman was because he couldn't stand the possibility of ever being drawn into any more war and violence. If I'd only had the sense to check with Washington for confirmation of Frank Collier's death."

"Don't get mad at yourself, Mark. Fawn's lived in this town for four years and apparently no one's been suspicious on that count."

"But, Rote knew."

"Sure, Rote knew from the very beginning. Of course! But he was a man with deep, strange emotions himself. He had no way of knowing how Frank's masquerade would turn out. At first it must have shocked him horribly, but what could the poor man do? He'd expected a son to come home a war hero, a conqueror and got a daughter instead. Another man might have rebelled immediately, but not Rote. That boy meant everything to him. He never let the secret out. Between the two of them they even managed to keep the truth from Helena. Having a gorgeous big-bosomed woman living in the house was probably the straw that broke Frank's female back."

"What do you mean, Honey?"

"I don't think Frank Collier had any sexual irregularities; they were all psychological. A real woman prancing around in her birthday suit must have aroused some strongly imbedded male instincts in him."

"I can imagine," Mark said. "Helena was an exotic woman even lying on a slab."

"You can imagine what she was like in the living flesh. Suddenly Frank needed an outlet. Enter Lorraine Reynolds and Joan Lacey. They became friendly with Fawn. Lorraine began inviting Fawn over for cocktails in the afternoon. She was a buxom redhead with a passion for men and money. They probably spent a lot of time lolling around Lorraine's expensive Three Arch Bay home, sipping martinis and swapping stories. Lorraine wasn't shy in the least. She probably told Fawn all the gory details of her affairs and sex life. No doubt, she dressed and even occasionally bathed in Fawn's presence. Then, one fine day, Frank Collier couldn't stand the pressure any longer and exploded from under all his makeup and mascara. He pinned two strong arms around her naked waist and grappled her to the floor. Lorraine was strong, too, and Frank had to use both arms to hold her down while he tried to get his own dress up. Lorraine must have gone mad at this point. She screamed and Frank crushed his lips over her mouth to shut out the sound. You know the rest."

"Yeah," Mark said. "Same business with Joan Lacey, only she was small and blonde and not so strong."

"He got Joan down on the beach one moonlit night when her husband was on duty and suggested they go for a nude swim together. Frank went wild when he saw Joan's body, but Joan went even wilder when she saw Frank's."

"Exit Joan," Mark said.

"And enter Helena. Frank discovered his father was about to dump the dark-haired goddess. He also knew about Helena's marriage to Reed Walker. He hated them both with a vengeance, so with two murders already on his conscience it didn't seem too terrible to get Reed drunk and into Helena's car and wind up at the Pleasure Pier before Frank could make his move. Helena got out, probably said she'd walk home and pinned Reed's wings on Frank—or Fawn's—costume in a gracious gesture of turning Reed over to her stepdaughter. Frank waited, saw Helena leap off the pier and followed her on foot along the beach. She must have come out of the water somewhere near the Collier house where Frank was waiting with a blanket. He took her up the lower side staircase to the study, removed the blanket and..."

"—Helena ended up in the mummy case. But, why, Honey? This time there doesn't seem to be any motive—any real motive."

I rubbed back the goose pimples on my arms. "Frank Collier really loved his father. That was obvious. He would have killed him otherwise. I'm sure Frank knew Helena had hurt Rote deeply with her elopement with Reed. He wanted to get back at them both for what they'd done. That's why he left Reed's wings in the mummy case."

"Honey, when do you think Rote first suspected Fawn was the murderer?"

"The night of the so-called accident at the train crossing. He picked up our trail when we left the Booby Hatch. Frank knew he was being followed. He thought also that we were getting a lot warmer than we actually were, that perhaps it was the police and not his father or anyone else who was hot on our heels. He sensed I was going to unmask him sooner or later. After asking the time and figuring a train was about due, he drove recklessly onto the tracks."

"Wasn't that taking a helluva chance?"

"Sure. He'd taken plenty before. He took a chance swimming out to that pot this morning. He got nipped by one of the lobsters and bled enough to leave those drops I told you about on the kitchen floor. That's probably why he was wearing gloves tonight. He took even a greater chance in Hel Gandy's studio. The truth of the matter is that Hel had taken a picture of Helena and Fawn together, but the negative was so badly fogged that all it showed were two very faint figures. The night he went to see Hel, Frank probably made the mistake of trying to buy the negatives and when Hel became suspicious, Frank got him after Hel, panic stricken, climbed up to the overhead platform."

"So Rote suspected Frank of Hel's murder, too?"

I nodded. "When Rote found my revolver near the tracks, he aimed it at his son and probably would have shot him right then and there if that car hadn't turned onto the road. Last night he faced Frank with the truth. Rote was obviously mad and very ashamed. He ordered Frank to turn himself in and Frank, torn to pieces by his father's accusations, agreed to do so. As he walked down the staircase, Rote angrily grabbed a bottle of Helena's cologne and threw it at this son of his dressed in female clothes. When Frank was gone, Rote wrote the note confessing his shame and then quietly shot himself."

"But Frank didn't turn himself in."

"Nope. He didn't have the courage. Instead, he stopped at the Booby Hatch and got drunk. He probably sat there and thought about his clever plan and how it had all blown to pieces. He'd even carried his attempts to incriminate Reed Walker to the point of marking a book on murder and planting this, along with the stolen negatives, in Reed's bedroom. It had all been very carefully thought out—everything except his own father's reaction. Frank was so drunk by the time Reed and I arrived at the Booby Hatch that he'd even drowned the fear of his father exposing him to the police. He had to be practically carried home. Unfortunately, he fell on the staircase as we tried to get him up to his room. If that incident hadn't happened I would have known this morning that he was the murderer because his dress smelled faintly from the cologne where he'd been struck by the bottle."

Mark took a pack of cigarette from his pocket, lighted two of them and handed me one.

"You know, you are pretty clever, Honey," he said. "Frank Collier spelled it out exactly the same way just before he died."

I glowered up at him. "Well, why didn't you tell me before? Why'd you let me ramble on like this?"

He smiled. "Because I like to hear you talk and anyway, I wanted to know if you really had figured the case out to the last letter."

"Figure this one out, Lieutenant, I'm cold."

He put his big arms around me and drew me tight against him. "How's this feel?" he asked.

I shrugged. "Not bad. Tell me something, Lieutenant. How can I be sure you're a male?"

His grip intensified. "Well, for that matter, I don't know that you're really a female."

"Lieutenant Storm! You make the silliest statements."

"And Miss West," he said softly, "you ask the craziest questions."

"Lieutenant, I don't have the slightest idea what you mean by that."

"Oh, don't you? He said, squeezing me until I could hardly breathe. "Give me forty years and I'll prove it."

I looked at him and his mouth reached down for mine. "Lieutenant, I'll give you forty seconds and then…"

He kissed me and my toes felt so warm they tingled.

"Then what, Miss West?"

I didn't answer. He was a man all right. And I was a woman. And I was glad someone had thought up this wonderful idea. It beat anything else. Hands down.

The End

Girl on the Loose

G.G. Fickling

The Honey West Files
ISBN: 9781936814176
Cover Design:
Erik Enervold/Simian Brothers Creative
Prepress: Lewis Chapman
Editorial assist: Yolanda Cockrell

www.moonstonebooks.com

Chapter One

Through the partially opened, frosted-glass door I saw a shadow emerge from the semi-darkness of the third floor corridor. A revolver was clutched in its hand.

"Honey West?" a deep voice asked, as the office door closed.

"Yes."

"Stand up. Take two steps toward me."

"What is this?" I said, getting to my feet.

"Don't ask questions. Just take off your clothes."

"What?"

"You heard me. You have exactly one minute. Get started!"

"Look," I said angrily, "it's three o'clock in the morning. Too late to play games. My office hours begin at nine. Come around tomorrow and we'll begin all over again."

"I said strip down," the man in the shadows growled. "You've got fifty seconds."

A chill raced up my spine. "Put down the gun. I'm not going anywhere."

He laughed. "That's what you think. Forty seconds, Miss West. I'm not kidding!"

The tone of his voice told me he wasn't, I reached for the top button of my sweater. "What's the angle? What happens when I'm finished with my strip tease?"

He took a package from under his arm and tossed it at my feet. "Get into this outfit! You've got exactly half a minute."

I opened two buttons, keeping my eyes riveted on his dark bulk. I could see that he wore a trench coat and a hat and I noticed that his gun hand trembled.

"Are you sure you've got the right party?" I asked, slipping a third button loose.

"I have it memorized," he said. "Female. Private detective. Third floor of the Wilks Building. Blonde. Blue eyes. Twenty-eight years old. Five feet five. About one hundred and twenty pounds. You figure it out!"

"I'm trying, but nothing makes sense. What's this outfit in the package?"

"A Marine uniform," the man said. "You've been drafted."

"Is the world situation that bad?" I asked. "Come on now, this doesn't add up."

The revolver raised threateningly at my head. "It adds up to me, Miss West. That's all that matters. Now are you going to wear that uniform while you're alive—or after you're dead?"

I slipped off the sweater and reached for the zipper on my skirt. In the distance, a ship moving through the night fog of Long Beach harbor moaned its awesome warning.

"I hope I brought the right size bra," he said.

My skirt and slip dropped to the floor. "Thirty-eight," I said, trying to focus my eyes in the semi-darkness. "Like the revolver of the same caliber. Is that what you're carrying?"

"In the package, yes," the man said. He waved the gun. "This is a little out of your class. Forty-five. Finish the job, please."

I grinned. "I'm glad you said 'please'. That makes every difference. You know this could add up to all sorts of charges, including kidnapping, if you walk out of here with me."

"That's right. And it could add up to murder if I don't. The bra and panties, Miss West!"

"But I don't even know your name," I said stalling.

"Just call me G.I. Joe. Time's up."

His finger tightened on the trigger. I picked up the package and removed the uniform. Second Lieutenant's bar glistened on the shirt collar. "I thought people were drafted into the rank of *private*," I asked.

"We're giving you a head start," the man answered. "We thought you'd like that."

"We?"

"The General and me. You're so clever, Miss West, with your questions. How many cases have you solved anyway?"

"Not enough," I said quickly. "I'd give a lot to solve this one right now. How about it?"

His fingers tightened again. "The bra and panties, Lieutenant. You don't want to be out of uniform at reveille."

I examined the shirt in the dim light. The name Sylvia Verse and a serial number 089099 were stamped inside the collar. "Old issue," I said. "What's the matter with the Marine Corps? Don't you know officers are supposed to buy their own uniforms?"

"We've changed our policy," the man said. "This one is on the house. No more stalling, Lieutenant. We've got an important roll call to make."

He moved toward me menacingly. The hat couldn't hide the narrow eyes harshly glinting in the desk lamp's dim light. I turned around. "Undo my bra, please! I'll be glad to take it off if you'll unhook it for me."

He took another step and then stopped. "You're smart, Lieutenant. Real smart. You know it takes two hands to undo one of those things."

"I haven't got a gun," I said, my back to him. "I'm sure you'll agree to that. What could I do against a big man like you?"

He laughed cynically. "Miss West, you're a riot. I know all about you, so you can quit fooling. You know more judo than half the Japanese army. Now, no more tricks, understand?"

I whirled. He was only a foot away and his revolver nearly touched my bare stomach. His face, coated with thick black grease, grimaced.

"What beachhead are you aiming for?" I demanded. "Or is it a party for ghouls?"

"Wouldn't you like to know! I'm enjoying this, Miss West. Really enjoying it. Reminds me of my soldiering days in the infantry. I remember one time we came into this little town in Italy, and there was this little Italian girl. Imagine that? A real blonde I-talian. She was built like you. Built for action. Twice as big across the top as she was in the middle and could she make love! Brother!

"I'll bet," I said, edging nearer.

"Then I got back and all I knew was how to handle a gun. Funny isn't it? I went to college once. Played around too much. Never really learned anything."

I touched his coat and the gun barrel sank into my stomach. He trembled again as he looked down at me. "You're awful smart, Miss West. And awful pretty. I'd hate to spoil all that. Now, please? For the last time!"

"Who's paying you to do this?" I asked, moving back into the shadows and undoing my bra."

"Last time, Lieutenant," was the curt reply. "One more question and they'll bury you without military honors."

I removed the bra and threw it in his face. He flinched and grinned.

"You got a lot of guts, lady. And that's not all you got a lot of. I could go for you in a big way. A real big way. But that isn't what I'm here for. Now finish it and be quick. I'm taking you out of here one way or the other. So you'd just better make up your mind which way right now."

My fingers gripped the top of my panties. "Who's Lieutenant Sylvia Verse?"

"No more questions!"

"Is she dead?"

"Damn you!" the man cursed angrily. "Why did they have to send me after a woman? Now get into that uniform! He roared.

"You won't kill me!" I said, reaching for the package. "You need me! Why?"

The man flattened against the wall, his gun hand trembling with emotion. "Lady, I can understand now why you're a private detective. You just don't give up, do you?" His massive shadow slanted crookedly across the ceiling. "You finish getting undressed and put those clothes on fast, understand? I won't answer for what I might do if you don't." His voice stopped as he inhaled a deep breath. "You're right! I won't kill you. But you'll wish you were dead, because I'm strong and I'm lonesome. And I need somebody like you. Just the way you are. Mad enough to hit me and soft enough to—for Lord's sake get those clothes on!"

Again I knew he meant what he said. The bra and underpants in the package were both stamped with the name Sylvia Verse. I slipped them on quickly.

"That's better, Lieutenant." He breathed a little more easily. "Now you're acting like a real lady officer."

"Where are we going?"

He grinned faintly. "El Toro Marine Air Station."

"Why?"

"I'm supposed to deliver you there by five o'clock this morning. And we're going to be there on time."

I put on the uniform. It fit as if it had been made for me, everything including the shoes. I saluted when I finished dressing. "I'm ready. Remember, though, this is still against the law. You can quit now and be ahead."

He gestured toward the door. "March, Lieutenant. My car is parked down in front. One false move and..."

"I know."

In the hallway, he slipped the gun under his trench coat. We went down the stairs and onto the street. Neon lights winked eerily in the wet fog. There was no one on the sidewalk. He opened his door on the driver's side.

"Crawl through," he said. "And don't bother to try the other door. It's jammed."

I got in and pushed the passenger side handle. It wouldn't budge. "You've figured it all out," I said.

He nodded, climbed in behind the wheel and started the engine. "With you, lady, it's a necessity. Now lean back and relax. We should be there in about an hour."

Fog pressed in tightly as we reached the outer fringes of Long Beach. He flicked on the windshield wipers, cursed and brought the car to a slow crawl. As we moved cautiously through the swirling mist, I tried to fill in the complicated holes of this jigsaw puzzle. One of the biggest gaps belonged to Sylvia Verse. She was obviously a woman exactly my size. Probably attached to the El Toro Marine Air Station. But what had happened to her? And why was I chosen to take her place?

My mind fled back to the minutes before the grease faced hunk had emerged from the shadows of my office building corridor. I had received two phone calls. One from Lieutenant Mark Storm of the Sheriff's office, homicide, asking about a date for Saturday night and the other from a muffled-voiced man who drunkenly begged my pardon for dialing a wrong number. The last had undoubtedly been the final check on my whereabouts before the actual kidnapping. Now I recalled a similar wrong number several days ago. A woman had asked for—for Sylvia! I knew that name had rung some sort of bell.

The man rolled down his window and peered out at the elusive white line snarled grimly in fog. "We've got to be there by five," he said, almost to himself. "They won't wait."

"Who won't wait?"

"Nobody," he snapped.

"Why am I supposed to pose as Sylvia Verse?"

"Be quiet!"

I leaned toward him. "Look, if you need money…"

"Stay back!" he said. "I'm warning you." He took the revolver from inside his coat and pointed it at me again. "This is a big thing. I don't know why it's so big, but it is, you understand? You add up to about a hundred dollars a pound. And when somebody pays that kind of money for live-stock, sister, I'm willing to supply and deliver. Can you match that officer?"

"Not exactly."

"I thought not." He reached over the seat. "Here, take this! But don't open it!"

He tossed a shoulder-bag in my lap. It was Marine style with the initials SLV stamped into the leather.

I shook my head. "You've got her uniform, her shoes, her purse—even her underwear. Where'd you bury the body?"

"I don't know what you're talking about."

"Up until now," I said, "it might have been an accident that all the pieces to this uniform were marked with the name Sylvia Verse." I held up the bag. "But, this was no accident. It smells more like murder."

"You got me," he said, peering through the open window at the fog-bound highway. "I don't know the lady. You're my sole claim to fame in this lashup and I don't plan to pull any triggers to get my money."

"Who hired you?"

"Kilroy," he said grinning.

"Did you call me a couple of hours ago?"

310

"Sure. I've had your building covered since this afternoon. I would pick a night when you were working late. Don't you ever go home?"

"Who's the payoff man?"

"Never met him. This is a C.O.D. order. Cash on the line when I hand you over."

"How do you know there won't be a double-cross?"

He grinned again. "I don't. That's where you come in, beautiful. They want you; I want the money. An even exchange or no deal. For your sake you'd better hope they forget their wallets."

"What do they want me for?"

"I don't know and I don't care. Any more questions?"

"You don't strike me as the kind of guy people hire for this kind of work."

"It takes all kinds of people to make a world," he said. "Now you, for instance. If I didn't know for sure, I'd never take you for a private eye."

"They used to say the same thing about my dad. He was in this racket until he caught a bullet one night in a dark alley. Funny though how a private eye always looks like a private eye when he's found dead."

"What do you mean?"

"They have such nice broad backs for characters like you to take a few pot shots."

He stiffened. "I never ambushed anybody in my life, understand?"

I didn't answer. He pulled off to the side of the road and cut his engine. Through the mist I could make out a high wire fence on one side of the road and a grove of eucalyptus trees on the other.

"El Toro?" I asked, gesturing toward the fence.

"Yep."

"Where's my honor guard?"

He glanced at his wrist watch. "They should be here shortly. Don't be nervous, they won't let us down."

Headlights suddenly flashed about a hundred yards down the road and then blinked out.

"Last chance to reconsider," I said. "Kidnapping is a federal offense. You could get the gas chamber."

The headlights went on again. He trained his gun at my head.

"That's them," he said. "Come on, let's go."

He got out onto the road and I followed slowly. The fog was damp and dripped from eucalyptus branches as we walked up the road toward the two glaring yellow cones. He kept the gun at my back.

Ten yards from the car he ordered me to stop, then shouted, "Lieutenant Verse, reporting for duty as ordered!"

We heard a door open and slam shut.

"Advance and be recognized!" a harsh voice commanded.

The man pushed me forward. Our shoes cracked audibly on the wet asphalt. Suddenly I had an uneasy feeling that I was about to die. Etched in the brilliance of headlights I saw two shadowy figures. One held a snub-nosed submachine gun. I dove for the pavement. My massive, trench-coated escort swore, took one step toward the trees and then literally fell apart from a furious blast of bullets."

"Get the girl!" one of the men shouted.

I rolled toward a ditch along the edge of the wire fence as another hail of lead from the machine gun zinged off the pavement, barely missing my head. Darkness and fog swirled over me as I fell into the ditch and started crawling on hands and knees. Sharp stones tore at my legs. The clatter of metal-tipped heels rang in the night.

"Come back, Sylvia!" a man called. "We mean you no harm. It was all a mistake!"

I visualized my grease-faced friend sprawled headlong on the road and I knew their only mistake was that they hadn't nailed two with the same blast. Gears clashed behind me as an engine exploded into action. Then tires squealed on wet pavement and one of the cars droned away.

The silence that followed was disturbed by the distant howl of Marine jets winding up for their morning fights.

Cold fear touched my insides as I listened. One of he men might still be around and waiting for me to come out of hiding. I couldn't believe they were both gone. The character with the machine gun had been too anxious to drill a few new openings in my hide.

Footsteps came again, running close by. I slumped down, holding my breath.

"This way!" a voice yelled.

A light pierced the darkness.

"Over here!"

A yellow wedge sliced through the fog about five yards away. I got to my feet and ran in the other direction. Another beam stabbed into my eyes.

"Halt or I'll shoot!"

Three Marines clutching pistols converged on me and one of them, with three stripes on his sleeve, shoved a flashlight in my face.

"Here, Major!" the sergeant called.

"A tall, thin officer with sloping shoulders and a graying handlebar mustache strode out of the fog. He peered at me hard.

I breathed a sigh of relief. "You don't know how glad I am to see you, gentlemen."

"I'll bet you are," the major growled. "Welcome back aboard, Lieutenant. We've missed you." His eyes darted to the dark pool swiftly spreading under the twisted body on the road. "Looks like you didn't miss him."

Chapter Two

It was daylight before Lieutenant Mark Storm of the Sheriff's homicide division burst into the Marine military police barracks. His gray eyes were glazed from rudely interrupted sleep and deep lines etched his ruggedly handsome face. His voice was almost as fierce as the banshee wail of jets climbing off the runway into a pale morning sky.

"Where's this dance you called me about?" he said, flicking his deputy sheriff's badge at the Marine Major.

"Over there." The officer indicated my location with a nod of his head. "Who'd she say she was?"

"A private eye named Honey West." The major snickered, "Craziest damned thing I ever heard of. Every piece of clothing she's go on, including her BVD's, is stamped with Sylvia Verse's name. She has a Bam purse with Lieutenant Verse's ID card. Even her boyfriend had an official Marine Corps photograph of her in his coat pocket."

Mark glanced in my direction. "Have you fingerprinted her yet?"

"Nope, we were waiting for you."

"Let me see that picture you took off the dead man." Mark pushed his hat back and regarded my face. "What's your name, baby?"

"Salome," I said. "Want to dance?"

"Don't be funny!"

"Don't be so loud," I returned. "I'm not deaf."

"No, you're just dumb," Mark said. "What sort of weapon did you use on the murdered man?"

"A bulldozer."

The thin-faced major with the handlebar mustache handed Mark a five by seven photograph. "That's the kind of smart talk we've had to put up with for the past two hours."

Mark nodded.

"You can see it's the same girl. No need for fingerprints. Same full mouth, same eyes, same big…" the major stopped, coloring slightly.

"Yeah," Mark said, comparing me with the photo.

"What are you looking at? I demanded in a loud voice. "You know darn well who I am!"

The deputy sheriff laughed awkwardly. "You're not Monroe, Mansfield or Ekberg and Brigitte Bardot speaks French."

"This has gone just about far enough. Now cut out the kidding, Mark, and tell these people who I am!"

Mark shook his head. Who is she, Major?"

"Sylvia Verse. Lieutenant, Woman's Reserve Corp. Joined twenty-two months ago. Attended officer's training school and graduated last summer with high honors. Returned to El Toro six months ago. Went absent without leave two weeks later after assuming exec position at base hospital. Officially charged as a deserter." The major flicked at his mustache. "Does she really resemble this—this Honey West she's talking about?"

"Vaguely," Mark said, glancing at the photo again.

I leaped to my feet, but a husky MP sergeant stopped me before I could reach the deputy. "You know that's not true," I said. "I saw the photograph. We could almost pass for twins."

"Yeah," Mark said, "and so could the Smith Brothers, except they didn't have hair on the same end of their heads. Come on, sister, let's go."

"Where?"

"The Sheriff's office. Desertion's a pretty serious crime, but murder's worse. What'd you do with the tommy gun after you pumped your friend full of air?"

"Gave it back to the Easter Bunny," I said. "Okay, fingerprint me if you don't believe who I am."

"That won't be necessary, Lieutenant Verse," Mark said, snapping handcuffs on my wrists. "I got a telephone call from Honey West just forty minutes ago. She's in San Francisco!"

Mark swung his sheriff's car to the side of the road, outside the Marine base, glanced back at the distant sentry box and then grinned at me.

"Had you worried, huh?

"You sure did," I said, holding up my manacled wrists. "For a few minutes I began to wonder who needed a strait jacket-you or me."

Mark unlocked the handcuffs and shook his head. "We can't tip our hat to the military-not yet. It's quite possible someone at the base is involved. How in hell did you get into this, Honey?"

"Easy. I was minding my own sweet business, for a change."

I gave him a quick rundown on the odd circumstances that forced me into a change of clothing, the trip to El Toro with my abductor and, finally, the murder. "It was grisly, Mark. I've never seen that end of a tommy gun before. Then that major calling me Lieutenant Verse. I nearly flipped when I saw her picture. Do you have any idea who my friend was?"

"Sure. A local small-time hood named Kemp Gimbel. A three-time loser. He'd served time at Quentin for assault with a deadly weapon. One of those handy guys with a gun who always winds up looking like a hunk of Swiss cheese.

"Tough."

"You don't know how tough," Mark groaned. "You're involved in a real mess, Honey."

"What do you mean?"

"We checked out your office after the Marine base called. It was pretty obvious what had happened. Your clothes were strewn all over the place Then your phone rang."

"Who was it?"

"Margo Stevens."

"Who?"

"Margo Stevens. She was calling from a hospital in San Francisco."

I pursed my lips. "You got me pal. Who's Margo Stevens? The only Margo I ever knew was a sex-hungry doll named Margo Henry. I went to school with her at Long Beech jaysee."

"Same girl," Mark said. "The call was person to person for H. West so I accepted. She thought I was your father—wanted to hire me for a private investigation. I tried to tell her your dad was dead and you'd take over the business, but she didn't stop talking long enough to listen. She said she was married to a guy named Web Stevens and had just had a baby. She was incoherent as hell. Said she was in trouble. Big trouble. Thought she was being watched and was frightened for her life."

Images began flooding back from my junior college days. Images of a pretty, dark-eyed girl in loose-fitting sweaters and saddle shoes, a girl who had been one of my friends and sorority sisters. One image was etched sharply on my memory. The night she ran to the Long Beach police screaming rape. She had accused the tall, handsome student-body president of luring her to the beach at Belmont Shores and ripping off her clothes. Several newspapers hit page one with the story before it was discovered the boy was innocent. Margo had hoped to force the wealthy student into marriage through her cleverly planned fraud.

"Margo was always crying wolf," I said. "Who was her adversary this time?" Her husband?"

"No. She's been separated from her husband for over six months." Mark stopped abruptly.

"Well, then what?"

"She started to cry. Said some woman was trying to trick her. She didn't know the woman's real name because she'd been given a phony."

"Sounds like Margo all right."

Mark wiped his mouth with the back of his hand. "I thought it sounded sort of crazy, too. I tried to get her to put somebody else on the line, but she kept right on talking and said this woman had insisted she have the baby yesterday by induced labor."

I ignored the faded images of Margo Henry and tried to picture her lying in a hospital maternity ward somewhere in San Francisco. I wondered what sort of trouble a woman with a new baby could be involved in. How dire could circumstances be to provoke a phone call four hundred miles away?"

"Was the baby all right?" I asked hesitantly.

"Yeah, the baby was, but Margo wasn't. She kept crying and when I asked to speak to her doctor she said he was gone. She was all alone in a private room and plenty frightened." Mark stopped again and winced.

"Well?" I demanded.

"That was the last I got out of her. She suddenly started to choke and

317

I heard the receiver drop. I tried to reach the operator who originated the connection, but you know these long distance calls. Ten minutes must have passed before I got the hospital switchboard."

" You can cut the long story short," I said. "How did she die?"

"Smothered. With a pillow. She was murdered while I was talking to her."

"Great," I said. "So two people interested in the West family of fine detectives meet untimely deaths four hundred miles apart. One with a submachine gun. The other with a pillow. What does that make me?"

Mark started the engine and pulled out onto the road. "Honey, gal, that puts you smack dab in the middle of one of the biggest mysteries I've run up against in my ten years with the Sheriff's office."

I could tell he wasn't kidding. "All right," I said, "let's go back to the beginning, to three o'clock this morning when I was free, white and Honey West. What suddenly compelled this character Kemp Gimbel to transform me into Sylvia Verse?"

"Money."

"Sure. Money he never got. But why pick on me in the first place?"

"Because you look a lot like this Sylvia Verse dame. At least, close enough to pass in the dark wearing her Marine uniform. Same blonde hair, similar features, build…"

"Okay. So this female Marine and I are look-alikes. Who are the two bright boys with the tommy guns who obviously don't go for our type?"

"I don't know," Mark said, turning toward Long Beach. "That's one part of the mystery. There's still Margo Stevens. Why does she call you less than an hour after you're taken from your office at gunpoint? Why was she murdered? And who is the woman who supposedly tricked her?"

"Not Sylvia Verse?"

"Hardly."

"Then what the devil are you driving at, Mark? I was abducted and my kidnapper murdered. That's a mystery, yes. And it's a mystery why an old friend calls my office an hour later and is also put out of commission. But I don't see any connection between the two cases if that's what you're trying to draw."

Mark's face hardened again and his eyes blazed as he glanced to me.

318

"Of course, you wouldn't see the connection. And, of course, you are mixed into it right up to the armpits. But you wouldn't be if you weren't in this business. If you weren't always trying to prove you're something more than just a woman!"

"Get off it Mark!" I said. "Why do you always have to act the hard-nosed, knuckle-fingered deputy sheriff with more brawn than brains? Sometimes you've got less understanding than a one-celled molecule with a grain of sand caught in his one-celled craw!"

"Damn you, Honey!" he roared, in the same hurt way a man with a bullet in his belly yells when he knows this time it's for keeps. "Damn you for being in this crummy racket, for letting yourself in for capers like this where somebody is either stripping you down or taking wacks at you with a tommy gun. You haven't got enough sense to pound into a rate hole!"

"Who says?"

"I do! Any sensible woman your age would be married by now with a couple kids. And instead of dodging lead you'd be dodging burps from the newest baby."

"Yeah," I returned. "That's what Margo was planning to do, so what happens? She winds up dodging a pillow with her number written all over the hem. How do you figure that, Lieutenant?"

"I don't. I just figure you and murder are going to end up in the same hole. In a big fat coffin with your name stamped all over the lid."

I knew one thing for certain about Lieutenant Mark Storm. When he began preaching about my life expectancy as a private eye either he was about to propose for the ten thousandth time or else was holding back some mighty important information.

"Look, Mark, I was minding my own business when suddenly this grease-faced hulk came along and put the snatch on me. So what?"

The big deputy glanced back at the road. He said it so quietly that I almost didn't realize what he meant until it was all out.

"You're not the only one who was minding his own business," he said. "At about the same time Margo Stevens was murdered, a baby belonging to a San Francisco millionaire was kidnapped out of the nursery of the same hospital. And by a woman fitting your description!"

319

Chapter Three

The jangle of a truck's tailgate, bouncing over a torn-up section of Coast Highway, drew my attention away from Mark for an instant, just long enough for me to fully grasp what he was trying to say. A definite connection did exist between my abduction and Margo's murder. Apparently the woman bearing my description was that link.

"Okay," I said, after a moment. "You think the gal who grabbed the millionaire's kid was Sylvia Verse?"

"I don't know what to think, neither do the San Francisco police. They can't understand the motivation behind Margo Stevens' murder, or why she was so worried about her life. There must be a connection somewhere between your abduction, her death and the infant's snatch—but what?" A small note of disgust crept into his voice. "The dame, sure, but it's just possible the guy who spotted her in the dark outside the hospital has a penchant for blondes built like brick roadhouses."

"I resemble that accusation."

"Look, Honey, let's face it. Busty blondes are a dime a dozen. If you put a hundred of them up against a wall in a dark alley you couldn't tell Marilyn from Mamie or Jayne—much less Honey West—unless they were all stripped naked and one has a fluorescent birthmark inside her right thigh."

"Who said my birthmark's fluorescent?"

"You get what I mean. You may not look exactly like Sylvia Verse, not if the two of you were matched together under a bright light. But in a Marine uniform on a dark road you probably look more like Sylvia Verse than her official Marine Corp's photograph does. The same goes for the doll who waltzed out of that hospital with a newborn infant under her arm. The man who identified her thinks she was a blonde. He knows she was stacked. He thinks she was about five feet five and weighed around one hundred and twenty pounds. He knows she had blue eyes and a lean tanned face. He thinks she was about twenty-eight years old. But when the San Francisco police asked him what kind of car she got into, he couldn't remember. He didn't know if there was anyone else in the car or why he thought she was carrying a baby, except that she was carrying some kind of blanket-covered bundle and wore a green cap. You know, the kind nurses wear in surgery."

"Oh brother, I wouldn't give you a plugged nickel for that identification. How mixed up can you get?"

"I don't know," Mark said. "But you're mixed up in this in more ways that one. The police found one of your father's old cards on the table next to Margo's telephone. Apparently she used it to make that call to your office. But why would she have had one of your father's cards after all these years?"

I took off the Marine officer's cap and ran my fingers through my hair. "Margo was not the usual junior college type, Mark. She got into several jams, all involving men. My dad tried to help her on one occasion."

Mark turned off on Anaheim Street, angling toward my apartment near Alamitos Bay. He grunted. "The San Francisco police doubt there is a connection between Sylvia Verse and the kidnap-murder despite the odd similarity in descriptions—and Margo's phone call."

"What do you think?"

"I told you, I don't know. I'm just convinced you'd better quit right now while you're ahead. Lock up your office, take a vacation and dye your hair black."

I laughed. "What for? Are blondes suddenly out of season just because two guys with tommy guns go hunting for one?"

Mark braked his car in front of my apartment house, reached across me and opened the door on my side, then said, "Get out!"

"Is that a nice way to talk to a lady?" I asked.

"You're no lady, you're a private eye. Get out!"

"I'll report you to the Sheriff's office."

"You do that," he said gruffly, "and when you call, please ask for the coroner."

321

"Why?"

He tossed my Marine cap to me and scowled. "Because I've got a hunch if you hang around these parts for very long, baby, you're going to need one—bad."

I hardly had time to shed the military duds before my kitchen phone rang. The stove's clock indicated five minutes after nine on this sunny April morning. Hardly six hours had passed since I climbed at gunpoint onto this crazy merry-go-round. Now it seemed I was more than a passenger. Especially after I picked up the receiver.

A crisp female voice said, "I have a person to person call for Miss Honey West from Mr. Phillip Sharkey."

"Speaking, operator. Where's the call from?"

"San Francisco. Hold on please."

In a moment, a deep, intensely nervous male voice broke onto the line. "Hello Miss West, this is Phil Sharkey."

"Who?"

"Phillip Sharkey. It was my son who was kidnapped early this morning. I've been trying to reach you for the past two hours."

I suddenly remembered a recent issue of a national news magazine with a cover drawing of a lean hard face with piercing eyes and a thick mouth. The caption under the grim portrait had read, MILLIONAIRE PHILLIP SHARKEY—NO FISH TOO BIG!

"Hello, Miss West, you are there?"

"What? Oh, yes, Mr. Sharkey."

I felt sorry for that face on the magazine. It had looked miserably unhappy, one jump ahead of a psychiatrist's couch and two jumps behind an ulcer tablet. He looked about thirty-five. In a hundred, miserably unhappy words he now spat out his version of the San Francisco kidnapping. How his wife had been taken to the hospital yesterday noon. How she had suffered numerous complications and was rushed into surgery following the birth. She was still unconscious but was expected to pull through, although an additional shock might change things.

"I've got to find that baby, Miss West, before she wakes up and starts asking for him. She's blind."

322

"I'm sorry."

"Are you? I want that boy back alive Miss West."

"Of course."

"I'm willing to pay anything." His voice broke. "What has Margo Stevens got to do with this?"

"I haven't any idea."

"She was talking to someone in your office when she was murdered, wasn't she?"

"Yes, but it's possible there's no connection…"

"There has to be! The police say a woman took my son. That it was love, the need for a child that provoked her, not ransom. I can't believe that! I'm one of the richest men in the world!" He paused, as if for a terrible instant even he was stunned by this realization. "I don't know you, Miss West, but somebody told me you look a lot like the woman who kidnapped my son. What does that mean?"

"You've got me Mr. Sharkey, but I'd like to find out."

"All right," he said, "I'm going to gamble with you, Miss West. I don't like private detectives in any shape or form, including female. They're all scum, you understand? Willing to work for a fast buck just as long as it exposes some private citizen—especially a rich one—to ridicule and humiliation. But I want my boy back—alive! Get him before my wife comes out of her coma and you can name your own price."

"Wait a minute, Mr. Sharkey," I said. "You sound as if you think I'm involved in this kidnapping."

"I didn't say that."

"No, but you inferred it."

"Hang it, woman, I don't care what I infer. At this moment, I'd be willing to suspect my own father if he was still alive. Now do you want the job or don't you?"

"I don't seem to have any choice."

"No. I don't believe you do."

"Mr. Sharkey, just for the record, I want you to know I don't like you. Not one bit."

"The feeling's mutual. I just want my son."

Anger surged into my throat. Hot anger. "Mr. Sharkey, I don't know whether you deserve to have your son back."

"What does that mean?"

"If I were the kidnapper I don't think I'd feel any pity for you."

Silence came, silence punctured by loud breathing. Then, "One thing I'll say for you, Miss West, you've got guts. I still want my son. And it's got to be within the next thirty-six hours, understand? My wife was in a bad auto accident once. Almost died. She can't take another shock. The next thirty-six hours—or else!"

"Or else, what?"

"Or else I'll break you. I'll break you and every important member of the San Francisco police force. And I'll have every official of this hospital staff in so much trouble they won't know what hit them."

"You don't impress me, Mr. Sharkey."

"Miss West, one of the men here described you to me. He said he met you once during a murder case. He said you were one of the most beautiful women he's ever seen in his life. I'd sure hate to spoil all that.'

My mind raced back to the grease-faced hulk with his .45 braced against my stomach. "You know, Mr. Sharkey, somebody else said those very same words to me not more than five hours ago. Isn't that funny?"

His voice flattened. "Hilarious. Thirty-six hours, Miss West. Not a minute longer." The rude click in my ear told me he'd hung up.

I replaced the receiver and found the magazine with Phillip Sharkey's harsh countenance reproduced on the cover. He had a deep scar on his right cheek.

I leafed to the article titled, Heir Apparent to the Throne. It spelled out a fabulous story of a young man who had grown up along the wharfs of San Francisco's waterfront. His father had been a known thief, his mother a prostitute. Phillip Sharkey had fought his way out of the bowery when he was fifteen, lied about his age and joined the Navy a year later on December 7, 1941. After four months he landed in submarine training at New London, Connecticut, emerging at the top of his class. From there he had gone into the Pacific, assumed command of his wounded sub and personally torpedoed three Japanese battleships. In the space of thirty-three months, Sharkey catapulted from Ensign to Rear Admiral through his sometimes heroic, but more often bull-headed attempts to win the war sin-

324

gle-handed. Once, on the flight deck of an aircraft carrier, in the midst of a savage attack by kamikazes, Sharkey had taken over one of the gun emplacements and knocked out eight suicide ships before they could sink several American vessels. At the war's end, he was awarded the Congressional Medal of Honor before a throng of newsmen and radio commentators on the White House steps. True to form, Sharkey performed one of his inimitable deeds by abruptly removing the medal from his chest and pinning it on the bosom of a woman who'd lost three sons in the Battle of the Coral Seas.

Sharkey's unselfish heroism, plus his unequaled bravado, caught the attention of Llewlyn James, the wealthiest U.S. industrial magnate. He was hired to an executive position, married James' daughter, Pat, and five years later took command of her father's vast business enterprises when Llewlyn died of a heart attack. This was the story behind Phillip Starkey's rise to fame. The article went a step farther and told the struggle he'd had to maintain his hold on this lofty peak. It was a grisly tale of a cocky little Ensign taking control of the nation's biggest submarine and sinking every piece of private enterprise he could find within range of his periscope. The final paragraph read, "There is no fish too big for Admiral Sharkey, for his torpedoes are bigger, more destructive, more war-like than any other. 'Crash-dive' Sharkey knows, in any battle, he cannot lose."

I tossed down the magazine. What was it with "Crash-dive" Sharkey? Was he still the heroic Admiral who helped keep his country's freedom? For the James' empire? Beneath his cloak of power I could sense the stirrings of a cocky little Ensign who had never forgotten how easy it was to take a pot shot at somebody when they couldn't see him coming. Now, suddenly, the tables were reversed. An unseen enemy had found Sharkey in his periscope and split him wide open.

I shucked off my undies (Marine style without frills) and jumped under the shower. The thirty-six hour deadline kept jolting through my mind. Did he really believe I was involved in his son's kidnapping, or was that just another torpedo lobbed out in hopes it might strike a target of opportunity? It was true, the similarity in features between me, the girl who supposedly kidnapped the Sharkey baby and Sylvia Verse was odd. Almost too odd to be coincidental. But the oddest thing was what I suddenly saw in the shower

325

door as it slowly opened.

Through the soapy, eye-smarting suds that streamed down my face, I saw the faint outline of a revolver.

Chapter Four

The shower stall was about three feet wide by six feet deep. It would have done justice as a fancy glass casket if I had fancied it as such. Which I didn't. That's why the slippery bar of soap in my hand suddenly made like a soap commercial. It shot up toward the windowless bathroom's only light. At the same instant my other arm chopped down on the revolver. That was when all hell broke loose. Glass shattered, the light blinked out and I hurtled through the door after the hand and body which still clutched the gun.

I could barely see from the raw, blinding smear in my eyes that made everything look red and stringy like infinitesimal blood vessels under a microscope. I didn't intend to die easily. Not after the tommy gun on the lonely dark road. Not after Mark Storm's snide remarks about my life span. Not after Phillip Sharkey's accusations of my possible connection with his son's kidnapping.

The glass door caught my intruder full in the face and sent him reeling against the wall. Through the soapy haze I saw him crumple to the floor and I dove, naked as a jaybird, after the target. I missed. He squirmed to his feet, still grasping the gun, and whirled for the bathroom door.

I shot after him, soapy water streaming down my body. He made a wrong turn in the dark, shade-drawn bedroom and tripped over my bed. This time I didn't miss. My leap caught him full-length, knees digging for his stomach, one fist aimed for his throat. His free hand fought to push me away and came up under my shoulder, clawing for a hold, finding one for an instant and then slipping away. I fell forward on his face, rolled over and caught his hand in a stinging vise between my legs. That was when he lifted his gun hand and brought it down on the back of my head. An H-bomb went off in my brain and practically spun me upside down. The last I remembered was going limp.

"Now what have you got yourself into?"

Mark Storm's battered felt hat crystallized into view. So did the ceiling of my bedroom. His hat was suspended eerily on a thin piece of hickory clutched by an equally thin hand. I blinked, raised my head slightly and studied the gray eyes of the man seated next to my bed.

"Fred? What are you doing here? Where's Mark?"

"Down the hall talking to your landlady. She's the one who heard the ruckus and called the Sheriff's office."

My hands felt around. They touched dried soap suds flesh, and more flesh. They reached my right side, still sore from the intruder's grasp, before they came in contact with the blanket that was thrown over me.

I smiled. "For a minute there, I thought..."

Fred's lean face, furrowed from too many years on the news beat and too many months on a battlefront, crinkled into a small grin. "She found you unconscious on the bed in—in rather awkward circumstances. She took the liberty to cover those circumstances before calling Mark."

"I'm glad of that."

"She said it looked like you had been..."

"Taking a shower," I interrupted quickly. "That's all I'd been doing—I think."

Fred lowered his cane and flipped Mark's hat onto the floor.

Fred Sims carried a cane for two reasons. Several times he'd used it to great advantage against thugs he'd cornered in his search for a headline. The other reason was even more important. He didn't have a left leg. Not one that was worth the powder to blow it to kingdom come. Which is exactly what had happened to Fred outside Cologne, Germany during an infantry assault in 1945. Despite his handicap he still managed to cover more mayhem for the *Long Beach Press-Telegram* than a fifteen-legged mayhem-follower.

Mark Storm barged through my bedroom door, picked up his hat and glowered at me in his own inimitable way.

"Who did it?" he demanded.

328

"Who did what?"

Mark hung his hat on a doorknob and grunted. "Mrs. Libby, your landlady, says…"

"I've heard what she says. I was in the shower. He came after me with a revolver. We struggled on the bed. He hit me on the back of the head. That's it."

"What were you wearing?" Mark's mouth tightened.

"What does anybody wear in a shower?" I asked.

"A bar of soap. If you're thinking what I think you're thinking, then the answer is, I don't know."

"Why not?"

"Because I haven't had time to find out—what with press conferences and deputy sheriffs trooping in and out of my bedroom. Is that answer enough?"

Mark glanced at Fred, then his eyes darted back to my blanket-covered body. "Did you recognize him?"

"No. I had soap in my eyes. I think he was big. At least, he felt like it."

"I don't care how he felt!" Mark boomed. "Was he one of the men you saw on the road?"

"I told you…"

"I don't care what you told me!" Mark returned. "You must have seen something between the shower and your bed. Was he fat big, slim big? Was he wearing a coat? What?"

I glanced at the crippled newspaperman. "Fred, you'll have to forgive the lieutenant for his juvenile outbursts. His mother still bathes him, so he can't understand how anyone can get soap in his own eyes."

"Why didn't he just kill you instead of…"

"I told you, Lieutenant, I don't know why he did or didn't do anything. My female intuition tells me he didn't. Possibly because he wasn't planning to or possibly because Mrs. Libby's ponderous movements down the hallway stopped him before he had a chance."

"Good for Mrs. Libby," Mark said, grabbing his hat. "She says the position she found you in definitely indicated he was planning to do more than commit murder."

"I'll be glad to mail you a full report in the morning."

329

The deputy went to the door. "You do that. Meanwhile I'd be more careful who you talk with on the telephone."

I raised on my elbows nearly forgetting my state of undress beneath the blanket. "Have you got my wire tapped, Lieutenant?"

"What if I have?"

"Don't kid me. If you had a man in this building, he'd have been up here five seconds after you heard from Mrs. Libby. Quit sniping in the dark."

Mark crushed his hat down on his head and laughed. "I don't have to have a man in this building to know what you're doing, baby. How much did Sharkey offer you?"

"Who's Sharkey?" I demanded innocently.

Mark groaned. "Same old Honey. Indestructible, infallible and in-trouble. Come on, Fred, were cramping the lady's style."

I sat up, holding the blanket around me. "What do you mean by that crack?"

"Just look at this place," Mark said. "Look at you. It's pretty obvious what sort of business she's running, wouldn't you say, Fred?"

Fred chuckled. "Leave her be, Lieutenant."

"Oh, so you're on her side!"

"I think she's telling the truth," the newspaperman said. "Now pull in your green horns and let's scram."

"You think I'm jealous?" Mark said.

"If you're not," Fred said, "You ought to have your butt kicked. Now move."

Mark hesitated, then shrugged his shoulders. "Okay, so I apologize. But, I would like to say one more thing."

"What's that?" I asked, pulling my blanket up another notch.

"If you're planning to stick on this case," Mark continued, "I'd suggest you stay away from Web Stevens."

"Margo's husband?"

"That's right. He was in our office this morning and he's mad. He says he's going to butcher the woman who killed his wife if he gets to her first."

"What makes him think a woman murdered Margo?"

"He saw that Marine Corps photograph of Sylvia Verse and he's looking for a blonde about your size and weight. You take it from there."

Mark whirled out of the room. Fred winked at me and followed him out of my apartment.

When they were gone, I went into the bathroom. I had to find out one thing for sure.

Mrs. Libby's best ear had been to the wall. She weighed over two hundred pounds and when she moved fast the rafters fairly shook from her jolting steps. My intruder must have heard her coming. The only real damage from his attack was where the purple bruises where his fingers had clung tenaciously.

I washed off the dried soap suds, applied some lipstick and brushed my hair. After slipping into a yellow cotton dress, I looked up Web Stevens' number in the phonebook. He answered immediately, a warm, deep voice with a touch of Joseph Cotton mixed with Clark Gable. We traded introductions, followed by a few terse comments about his wife, and he asked me to meet him for lunch at a café just off the Hollywood Freeway on Sunset Boulevard. I hesitated until he said he had a hunch where we might find Phillip Sharkey's son.

"Okay," I said, "but you're in for a surprise."

"What do you mean, Miss West?"

"Do you carry a gun?"

"Well no, not on me. What's this all about?"

"Just leave all your hardware, cutlery and bolo guns at home. I'll be wearing a yellow dress, yellow hair and blue eyes. Don't be surprised by the package Mr. Stevens."

It turned out I was in for a surprise myself. And what a handsome wrapping it had. A tall, broad-chested man stood outside the Dolphin Café, his head and shoulders caught in the sunlight's brilliant glow. He had bold features, pale blue eyes, a mass of blond curly hair, and his smile revealed straight white teeth against deeply tanned skin. I guessed he was about thirty.

He approached me without hesitation. "So that's why you warned me," he said, taking my arm. "You look like the girl in the picture."

"And you look like…"

331

"Who?" he asked, still smiling.

"The new fullback for the Los Angeles Rams. I saw his picture in the paper only yesterday."

He escorted me into the café. "I guess there must be some truth in that old bit about everyone having a double somewhere in the world. Except you're a lot prettier than that Marine gal."

"Thanks. How do you rate with a football?"

"Terrible. In college my forward passes were always being blocked."

We sat at a table near the bar and ordered sandwiches. Web Stevens' smile faded after a moment and his eyelids narrowed as he glanced at the distant rush of traffic on the freeway. "Do you mind if I call you Honey?"

"Of course not."

"You went to school with Margo?"

"Yes."

He spread his large hands out on the table and scissored them together around a glass of water. "What was she like in those days?"

"Strange. A little wild."

"Neurotic? Oversexed?" he asked.

"You might have called her that," I said.

He nodded. "That was Margo all over. She had it bad. While I was on road trips she used to pull some pretty weird parties."

"How long have you two been separated?"

"Little over five months."

"Did you know she was living in Frisco?"

"Sure." Web stopped and shrugged his huge shoulders. "I'd see her every chance I could when my business took me into town."

"Was she living with anybody?"

"Not that I know of."

"I mean, another woman."

"No." Web lifted his eyebrows. "Well, it's possible, I guess. She never mentioned a roommate."

"Weren't you ever in the bedroom?"

He blushed slightly. "Sure."

"You never noticed anything, another woman's clothes, shoes?"

"No."

332

"The bathroom? An extra toothbrush, shower cap, dressing gown?"

"Not that I remember. What are you driving at?"

"It can wait," I said. "Let's hear more about what you were saying on the phone."

Web straightened up, offered me a cigarette, then flicked a table match with his fingernail. "I've got a theory. Maybe it makes sense, then again maybe it doesn't. But, I intend to find out, if it kills me."

"I'm listening."

"I picked up a special news bulletin on my car radio a few minutes ago. Maybe you heard it. A San Jose supermarket box boy found a baby blanket this morning which matches those at the hospital. This definitely convinces me."

"Of what?"

"That the kidnappers are heading for Mexico by way of Nevada."

"What gives you that idea?"

"As I said over the phone, it's just a hunch."

"And why do you say kidnappers when only a woman has been identified with the crime so far?"

"Another hunch," Web said quickly. "But you know yourself it would take more than one person to execute the kidnapping of a child less than one day old."

"Maybe," I said, "unless, as the police say, it really was a snatch for love. The woman could have done it alone. Parked her car on a side street, walked into the hospital wearing a nurse's uniform, lifted the baby, waltzed out and drove to San Jose."

"You forgot one thing."

"What's that?"

"When did she have time to kill my wife and why?"

I crushed out my cigarette. "I don't know. But, then, there're a lot of things I don't know. For instance, what are you doing here in L.A.? Why aren't you in San Francisco investigating the situation up there? Arranging for the funeral? Looking after your own baby?"

Web's face hardened. "It might interest you to know," he said, after a long moment, "I wasn't really in love with Margo. I—I guess I was at first before I found out about.." he paused. "It wasn't my idea—the separation.

She just walked out one day after telling me she was pregnant. It really shook me up. Like somebody hit me with a car and just left me there. She was at least honest enough to tell me the baby was mine. I didn't know whether to believe her or not until she rubbed in the fact that she had been careful with—with the others."

His eyes darted to mine. "I—I've always wanted to be a father. I guess more than most men. I was injured once and didn't think I'd ever be able to..." he grimaced from embarrassment. "Anyway, I tried to get her to stay, but she wouldn't. And suddenly it was all gone. I—I felt empty inside..."

"You don't have to finish," I said.

"I want to finish!" His hands tensed into hard knots. "Yesterday, Margo called me before she went to the hospital. She said she wanted to come home with the baby, I was really happy..." He shook his head. "Sure, I've got a son. I've never even seen him. But, I don't want to see him now. I don't want to see him until I find the people who did this to Margo, the same people, I'm sure, who kidnapped Sharkey's baby. I just want to get my hands on them for five seconds. Now, do you understand?"

"I thinks so."

"Okay, do you want to come with me?"

"Where?"

"The Mojave desert."

I blinked. "Are you kidding?"

"Look, Honey, I'm a salesman for a company here in Los Angeles. My territory extends north to Frisco and all the way east to the Nevada border. I've handled this area for eight years. I know every inch, every curve of those roads. Just for fun I used to work in my mind various routes of escape from that rock in San Francisco Bay—Alcatraz."

"Why?"

"For no particular reason except to keep my mind occupied while I was driving. I worked out two routes."

Web spread a large map of California on the table. It was a detailed road map showing San Jose and two routes running southeast from that city marked in heavy red pencil.

I shook my head. "So, what does this mean?"

"They've got to be stopped," Web said. "Before that baby dies on the

334

way to Mexico."

I studied the man sitting across from me. "Who says he's taking a ride that far?"

"I do."

"All right," I said, examining the map again. "Let's hear your theory."

Web's index finger touched San Jose. "Here's the last known point of contact, according to that news bulletin. The police figure it's a woman and she's headed farther south or planning to hole up in San Jose."

"That makes sense."

"They figure if she's going anywhere it's down one-oh-one toward Los Angeles. But she *isn't* going in that direction.

"Why not?"

Web's forehead ridged. "In the first place, three men have got that baby, besides the woman."

"Wait a minute," I said suspiciously. "A witness has already testified to the fact that a woman, and only a woman, a busty blonde, was seen leaving the hospital in a nurse's cap with a blanket-covered bundle. The theory is that she had a hankering for a baby so she walked in and took one. Now where do the three men come in?"

"Maybe it isn't three men. That's a wild guess. Maybe it's two, maybe four. Only I'll bet my bottom dollar this is a Lindbergh snatch. That it's not for love, but for dough. Big dough. That's why my wife was murdered."

"Just where does Margo fit in?"

His eyes drifted back to the freeway. "They showed me a rough drawing of the hospital floor plan at the Sheriff's office. Margo's private room was down the hall from the nursery. My hunch says this woman took the Sharkey baby, ran for a back stairway where she met one of her male accomplices. They heard someone coming and dodged into Margo's room. She was on the telephone and started to scream. So, they smothered her." His teeth clamped tight. "Lousy son-of-a..."

"Okay," I said quietly. "Going on your theory, the man and woman escape down this back stairway. The woman is noticed by a witness and described as blonde and blue-eyed. They head for San Jose. Then what?"

Web's gaze riveted on my face. "So, this morning—let's say around

335

nine-fifteen-they pull into this supermarket parking lot. They need some things for the baby. They're desperate. The baby's too young to take this kind of treatment and they know they're in trouble. During the hassle in the parking lot one of the baby's blankets drops from the car."

"So, then, according to your theory, they lam out of San Jose. Taking which one of your well-studied routes?"

Web's finger touched the map again. "They might have decided to avoid one-oh-one entirely and gone over this old road through Mt. Hamilton to Turlock. Or, they might have figured to make better time and taken one-oh-one to Gilroy, then veering off on one-fifty-two which leads to Fairmead. These are the only two practical routes east out of San Jose for Nevada."

I shrugged. "Which way do you think they went?"

His fingernail traced the southern-most red line. "Straight down through Fresno, Tulare, Delano, Bakersfield to this bridge over the Los Angeles aqueduct."

"What do you plan to do out in the Mojave Desert?" I asked.

He grinned wryly, touching the map again. "I'm going to barricade this bridge over the aqueduct with my car. Now, do you want to come along or don't you?"

Chapter Five

"It'll be dark before we reach the aqueduct," Web said when we reached the turnoff one mile from the bridge. I had slept most of the way from Los Angeles. He glanced at his wrist watch under the faint glimmer of dash lights. "By my calculations they can't possibly reach the bridge for at last another hour. We should have plenty of time to set up the barricade."

I brushed some dust off my wrinkled dress and tried to smile, but my mouth was as stiff as the rest of me from the long, hot ride across the desert. We'd been on this wild goose chase for almost five grueling hours, ever since I'd had the crazy impulse to say "yes" back in the Dolphin Café. Exactly why I'd decided to come along was still a mystery to me. All I knew was that Web Stevens' theory paralleled Phillip Sharkey's contention that ransom was involved. Since I had only thirty-six hours to find that baby, Web's fantastic plan was a shade better that just sitting around my office waiting for another customer with a spare Marine uniform and a gun. Besides, Web Stevens interested me. He was a man with a purpose. And he was more than a little attractive.

"Web, will you answer me one thing-honestly?"

"What's that?"

"How long do you really think we'll have to wait?"

"Three hours. Maybe three days. Depends on how many stops they make."

"What do we do in the meantime? Brush up on your forward passing?"

Web's forehead ridged. "Don't joke, Honey. I've got blankets in the trunk. We'll take turns sleeping after I set up the flares."

I grinned. "Sounds very practical. I just wonder how long this dress will hold up under the punishment. I object to looking like a worn-out dishrag."

"I—I meant to tell you, Honey," Web said, glancing at me. "You're the first gal I've ever seen in a chemise dress who doesn't look like a dishrag."

"Thank you, kind sir." I said. "Now, let's talk about what the well-dressed kidnapper is wearing this season?"

"Aren't you ever serious?"

"Not if I can help it. In my kind of business things get too serious too often."

"Yeah, I guess so."

"Web, I thought the aqueduct was all underground."

"Most of it is. This is one of the few open stretches. Lasts for about a half mile and then dips back down into a tube. Have you got a gun?"

"Now aren't you curious? Of course. I want you to know, just for the record, Mr. Stevens, that I think your whole theory is as wacky as a banjo. But, just in case you're some sort of mathematical genius, don't expect yours truly to be throwing her passes barehanded."

"Where is it? In your purse?"

"Nope."

He glanced quickly at the front of my dress. "Don't tell me…"

"You're more curious that I thought," I said. "Where do you keep yours? If I may be so bold…"

"Open the glove compartment."

In the tiny gleam of light, a .38 revolver's muzzle glinted. I removed the weapon and opened the cylinder, revealing six fully loaded chambers.

I shook my head. "You know, I'm beginning to think you're really serious about this barricade bit. And here I thought you drove me all this distance just because you liked my chemise."

"Why didn't I meet you in Long Beach four years ago?"

"Because I was living in Lakewood. Now tell me again about these flares."

"We'll set three on the western side, two on the east, five hundred feet apart in the center of the road. That should stop any traffic from either side."

"How can you be sure?"

"Because our car will be turned broadside on the eastern end of the bridge. At that point the road narrows making it virtually impossible for another car to get past unless it stops and carefully eases by."

"What if this other car doesn't stop?"

Web shrugged. "Then we pick up the pieces and go home."

"Very funny."

"Believe me," Web added, "if that happens I'll be picking up the pieces. Yours."

I grinned. "You're awfully familiar, Mr. Stevens."

"Honey," he said quietly, "with a figure like yours even in a chemise dress, I don't have to be familiar, just aware."

"Okay. I'm glad I wore it. Now, please, change the subject."

The narrow bridge over the aqueduct rose in the glare of headlights. Web braked his new Thunderbird, pulled to the side of the road and got out. Warm wind ruffled his hair as he stared across the inky desert. Beneath the bridge, water gurgled against the steep walls and, in the thick brush beside the highway, crickets scratched out their repetitious sound.

"I can just about see the lights of Monlith," Web said, keeping his eyes toward the western horizon. "Nothing coming from that direction. I'm going to set up the flares."

He took two flares from the trunk and walked over the bridge. On the other side he spaced the dark, pot-shaped objects about five hundred feet apart in the middle of the road and ignited them.

When he returned, illuminated in the yellowish smear of headlights, his mouth was set in a grim smile.

I climbed from the car and scanned the eastern skyline. It was etched faintly with the lights of Mojave. Web moved in that direction placing two more lighted flares. Then he swung his car around broadside, blocking all but a very narrow space at the end of the bridge.

"All right," Web said, after setting the fifth flare near the rear bumper. "We're ready for them."

As we climbed back into the car, I had to lift the hem of my dress because it was binding my knees. My garter holster and its tiny, pearl-handled Hi-standard .22 revolver peeked out from under. Web's gaze moved above

339

my knee to my thigh where the blue garter held its weapon.

"What do you know?" he said. "Will wonders never cease!"

"I told you I had a gun."

He shook his head. "A prize in every package. Now I can see the advantage of a private eye being a woman. You've got firepower from just about any angle."

"Believe me, I need it." I thought about the grease faced hulk, the two desperate men with tommy guns and my shower assailant. All had caught me with my garter down. That wasn't going to happen again if I could help it. "Who takes the first watch?" I asked, covering my thigh.

"Me. Climb into the back seat and get some rest."

I lifted myself over, trying to keep my dress from doing nip ups. "Mother told me there'd be nights like this."

"Yeah."

"Why'd you ask me along?"

Web took his .38 out of the glove compartment and flicked off the dash and headlights.

"You called me, remember?"

"Did you tell anyone at the Sheriff's office about your theory?"

"Nope."

"Why not?"

"They'd have thought I was crazy."

"You mean you're not?"

He lighted a cigarette and handed it to me. "Maybe. You stay well hidden if we get any customers, understand? I'll get out and do all the talking."

"What if they don't speak your language?"

"Then I may have to call on you and that blue garter. Just be sure you don't snap it at the wrong guy."

I rolled down one of the rear windows and laughed. But I didn't laugh for long. Peering straight at me were a pair of beady, red-rimmed eyes.

"What's bugging you silly creeps? You're not going to get any space action with this kind of stuffy ritual."

Web lunged around, the .38 concealed in his big right hand. I went for my garter, but the little man beat me to the draw. He reached through the window and grabbed my wrist.

"That's all right, sister. You don't have to hide anything from the old Perfessor. What have you got under there, a Vernusian Grounding Device?"

He didn't have a chance for further investigation. Web leaped from the car and pinned our sudden intruder against the rear door. The little man's grizzled face glinted in the light of the flares. He must have been seventy if he was a day and the bald flesh on his wrinkled head was burnt darkly from too much sun.

"What are you after, gramps?" Web asked sharply, his gun still hidden from view.

"You know what I'm after," the man said, "and I think I've found 'em."

"Get to the point. Where's your car?"

"I walked."

"From where?"

The old man's mouth pursed cynically. "You know! From the convention campsite. I was out looking for 'em when I saw you light those flares."

I climbed from the back seat and joined them beside the car. The Perfessor stood about five feet tall and was as skinny as a rail. He grinned when he saw me.

"You're the ones all right," he said triumphantly. "The man who witnessed the landing said they were big and blonde. You're the ones. What a discovery!"

"Are you crazy?" Web said. "What are you talking about?"

"I wasn't even going to the flying saucer convention this year," the Perfessor continued, "until I read about this new grounding device in that fact science fiction magazine. Who'd ever guess I'd catch two honest-to-gosh Venusians. I'll bet they'll have my picture in the newspapers tomorrow." He was quivering with excitement.

Web glanced at me and shook his head. Another case of mistaken identity. Only this time I was apparently something from another planet.

"Look, gramps," Web said, "you haven't caught anybody except two people in distress. Our car broke down and we're waiting for a tow truck to haul us into Mojave."

341

"Likely story. Likely story," the Perfessor repeated, licking his crusty dry lips. "I been warned you'd know our language and tell a pretty fancy story if you were intercepted. What's she got under that dress?"

"Nothing!" Web said. "I—I mean, nothing of an interplanetary nature. Now take my advice, turn around and walk back to your convention. At this very moment flying saucers are landing there and you're missing the whole show."

The Perfessor's eyes widened. "Then you are landing more ships. I knew it. I knew that grounding device would work once you made contact."

"We won't confess to a thing," Web said, trying to keep a straight face. "But what you'll find back at convention headquarters may change the whole course of the world. Now go!"

The little old man slithered past me, ran to the side of the road and disappeared in the thick brush.

Web almost doubled over with laughter when the Perfessor was gone. "Oh, brother, has he got a story to tell when he gets back to the camp grounds. Ten foot tall Venusians are barricading the bridge on Highway Four-sixty-six. One of them has a grounding device strapped to her leg."

"Thanks, pal. The next landing's on me. I've never had anyone so gallantly protect one of my devices in my life."

"I only hope all the other flying saucerites think he's as looney as we did. We wouldn't want the whole convention on our necks."

"You can say that again. I have visions of being forceably stripped and examined for foreign objects."

Web opened the car door and regarded me in the flare's reddish reflection. "If that ever happened," he said, "I'll bet they wouldn't find anything foreign. Unusual is the word."

He suddenly looked beyond me to the bridge and the dark road leading to Monolith. "Get in."

"What's your hurry? This is the first chance I've had to stretch my legs."

His eyes were riveted on the highway. "Maybe you'll have a chance later. Here comes our first customer."

I whirled. Two pinpoints of light were threading their way hurriedly across the desert.

"Moving fast," Web murmured. "Moving damned fast. And you can bet they're not from Venus either."

Chapter Six

We got into Web's car. The roar of the approaching vehicle dented the still desert night.

I groaned. "If that's a sheriff's car, we're going to be in real trouble. Blocking a state highway is good for about ninety days in these parts."

"Our engine's on the blink," Web reminded.

"Yeah, it is until they press the starter. Then we may wish we did own a flying saucer."

"Now listen carefully, Honey," Web said. "If that car passes the first flare and slows to a stop, let me handle it alone. You stay completely out of sight. If it doesn't, dive for cover in the brush and for heaven's sake, stay down."

"Aye, aye, sir, but I still think you're banking too heavily on this theory of yours."

He nodded. Across the bridge the flares sizzled, eerily illuminating a horny creature as it crawled onto the road, clicking its tail. The car drew nearer, its lights bathing the dark, jerking angrily in their wild course. Peering through the rear window, the scene was enough to make my flesh crawl. This was no place for a woman, with or without a gun.

"About a half mile now," Web murmured. "They must be traveling eighty or more."

"What's that other thing on the road?"

"Looks like a Gila monster. On second thought you'd better stay out of the brush."

The approaching car raised a cloud of dust as it careened around a curve leading to the bridge.

"Holy jumping Venusians," I said, "he's going to plow into us!"

Caught in the angry glare of the onrushing car's headlights, the Gila monster's mouth slid open, his stubby legs turned him head-on toward the howling attack of the mechanized creature. Churning wheels skidded past the first flare, struck the giant lizard and split him open. His horned remains thudded against the bridge, spewing reddish-purple, tail still flicking wildly.

Web lunged awkwardly for his door and missed the handle. I found mine. That was all I found, though. My heel caught under the rear seat spilling me headlong on the road. The hurtling steel mass thundered onto the bridge straight at me. I thought about a lot of things in that frantic instant. Most of all I wondered how the Gila monster had felt when those three thousand-odd pounds popped him like a pretzel.

Suddenly the car swerved in the center of the bridge, grazed a wooden buttress, glanced off another and slid to an ear-shattering stop about ten yards from where I lay.

Web's voice split the quiet that came after the paralyzing screech. "Get inside, quick!"

I didn't waste time with words. I got to my feet and realized I was plainly visible in the car's headlights. I felt like an actress caught in the lonely glow of the stage. Or a thief cornered in a blind alley.

Web hauled me through his door and pushed my head down in his lap. "Be still!"

"I didn't say anything," I whispered. "What's happening?"

"Nothing, yet. It's a black sedan. Fifty-four Chrysler, I think. Did that man at the hospital give any description of the car?"

"You talked with them at the Sheriff's office," I said. "You know as much as I do. Can you see anybody?"

"No. Headlights are full on us. Wait a minute! His voice rose. "A man's getting out on the driver's side."

"Has he got a gun?"

"Can't tell. I can only see his head and shoulders. He's wearing a hat. Looks about my age."

"How old is that?"

Web groaned. "Will you please be serious!"

"I'm trying. But now that I'm in your arms I'm wondering if you didn't plan this whole scheme, including the little old man with the popped eyeballs."

"Quit kidding, he's looking us over carefully. You would have to take a high dive right in front of him."

I felt my ribs. They were sore. So was the spot on my scalp where the gun had knocked me into dreamland early this morning. "High dives are my specialty. The only difference between me and Esther Williams is the molecular fortitude of water in contrast to asphalt. What's he doing now?"

Web's arm stiffened around my waist. "Nothing."

"You don't feel like he's doing nothing," I said, trying to get up.

"Stay down!"

"All right, but five'll get you ten the guy's alone and just didn't see the flares in time."

Web moved his .38 toward the window. "He's coming in our direction. Slowly. Looks about five-ten. I don't see any gun. Hey!"

I lunged from underneath Web's arm and peered through the window. The man lay face down about three feet from his car. His hat was titled sideways over a thick head of black hair.

"What happened?" I demanded.

"He—he took two or three steps," Web stammered, "and—and then just fell. I—I don't get it."

"Ten'll get you twenty he's drunk. Probably been over to Monolith at some bar. That's why he didn't see the flares in time to slow down."

"I'll bet he's faking," Web said. "I wish the devil we could see if there's anyone else in that car. Must be a trick. Somebody's got him covered from inside."

"There you go again," I said. "Making mountains out of molehills. It's a hot night. The guy is thirsty so he drives over to Monolith, gets loaded and drives back. Boom! He's so plastered he nearly runs us down and then, half stupefied and half lit, he drops over in the road. He might have had a heart attack for all we know. I'm going to check."

Web jabbed his revolver in my sore ribs. "You stay put! He's not going to lie out there all night."

"He is if he's dead."

I pushed the gun aside and climbed from the car.

"Honey, come back here!"

"No," I said, advancing toward the prone figure. "I've had enough fantasy for one night."

As I drew nearer I realized the car's engine was still idling. Desert wind suddenly blew the man's hat across the road into the brush. I jabbed his shoulder with my toe. He didn't move. I rolled him over on his back. He was dressed in a blue suit and his tie was pulled loose at his throat. He smelled of alcohol.

I bent down and yelled, "He seems to be breathing. Probably knocked himself out when he hit the pavement. You'd better give me a hand."

"Come back here, Honey, while you still got a chance!" Web's voice was contorted with anger.

The man wasn't as young as Web had guessed. I figured him to be in his early forties. He had a bulbous nose and blood trickled from the corner of his mouth where he'd hit the pavement. I lifted his head and his eyes gaped open."

"How dry I am," he began to warble. "How dry I am. Nobody knows how dry—I am."

I glanced toward the Thunderbird. "Did you hear that? This guy's hung clear to the eyeballs." I slapped the man's face lightly. "Hey! Wake up!"

He shook his head and leaned on one elbow. "What—what seems to be the trouble, offishur?"

I helped him to sit up. "Our car broke down and you didn't see the flares."

He rubbed his eyes, fixing a new glance on my face, then his gaze drifted down. "Wow! I'm in heaven!"

"Not quite," I said. "You're on Highway Four-sixty-six at the aqueduct. I'm a Venusian who just landed in a flying saucer."

He blinked. "You're—kidding—they don't come like you in flying saw-shurs. Let's have a drink."

He staggered to his feet and nearly pitched over again before I caught him. "Come on, pal," I said, "we'd better get you home before you drill a big fat hole in the desert."

He laughed. "Very funny. I like your sense of humor. That shurtinly calls for a drink. And ask you friend. There's a full bottle under the seat."

"Hey!" I yelled to Web. "I told you you were crazy…" I stopped dead. A new sound reached my ears. The cry of a baby.

"What's that?" I demanded.

"What?" The man straightened all too quickly. "Must be the wind…"

I went for my blue garter, but his gun was easier to reach than mine. His hand darted inside his coat and produced a .45. I dropped the hem of my dress, reared back and hit him in the Adam's apple. He didn't say another word. The hideous choked sound that gurgled up into his throat couldn't begin to compete with the scream that split his pained lips when he hit the ground. I added one well-placed kick, picked up his automatic and started for the black sedan. Then I saw it. It was practically sticking in my face so I didn't have to strain my eyes in the flickering light to recognize what it meant. A sawed off shotgun has a way of making you know this even before it speaks. This one, with a snubbed double-barreled snout, was just about to talk its head off. And mine, too.

Chapter Seven

"Make one move and you're dead," a male voice growled behind the shotgun.

I froze. It didn't seem possible Web's theory was correct, but here was living proof poking in my face. New wails of an infant drifted from the sedan.

"Drop that gun!"

Again I complied without argument. The man with the big nose tried to rise and then crumpled on his face as if he were praying his guts wouldn't fall out from my kick.

The voice from the sedan continued, "Tell your boyfriend to come out with his hands up and be quick about it."

"I'm alone," I said, trying to make out the shadowed face behind the shotgun. "My car broke down and…"

"Tell him to come out or I'll cut you in two!"

The other man stood up, gagging, clutching his stomach. He pressed the snout of his revolver under my chin and groaned. Blood streamed from his mouth and nose. This really looked like it was it. I'd never had so much firepower aimed at me at one time in my life.

"My insurance agent," I said trembling. "Would you excuse me please while I go sign my new policy. I promise to come back." The automatic jabbed my words to a stop.

"I ought to scatter you all over the highway."

He whirled, pumping two quick shots at Web's car. One rocketed off the metal top. The other smashed through the front side window.

"Are you coming out, Buster?" the man behind the shotgun shouted. "Or are we going to have to blow you out?"

349

For a long instant there were no sounds, except for the hiss of flares and the sedan's engine. Then the man beside me swore. He leveled his gun in Web's direction, but never got a chance to pull the trigger again. A bullet tore through the patch of black hair, skidded across his skull, and smashed sickeningly into a bridge buttress. Big Nose's grim expression didn't change. He didn't seem to realize he'd been hit. He swore again, moved a few steps, took better aim. Web's second bullet was about two inches lower. Big Nose's head snapped back, spurted new blood and went limp. His body spun against me and we thudded to the pavement together before I had a chance to move.

The man with the shotgun found himself caught in the same embarrassing position. He didn't know what to do first. His twin barrels swung toward the Thunderbird, then sensing his mistake swerved back to me. I couldn't afford to make the same error. The sticky weight of the bling under the sedan's rear wheels. Death was only a fraction of a second behind me as the shotgun seared the pavement, sending up a howl that ricocheted across the desert's brush.

Web roared, "The aqueduct, Honey!"

I started in that direction when another sound froze me in my tracks. The sedan's engine thundered and suddenly spit power into the wheel near my head. The tire spun on the pavement and leaped forward a few feet, then reversed its course. I didn't know which way to go. I screamed, fell face down and clawed toward the bridge. Big Nose's shattered hulk wasn't so lucky. The sedan bumped over him, missed my left arm by inches and ground to a stop. I had just enough time to pull myself out from underneath, run wildly to the bridge and throw myself over the side before another burst of the shotgun hammered after my torn and blood-spattered dress. In the next instant I struck the dark water and its cool impact was so wonderful I almost screamed again. This time with joy.

I should have realized I couldn't get away that lucky. The swift current of the aqueduct and its steep walls threw me into even greater panic than the shotgun. I swallowed enough water to sink a battleship and tore half a dozen fingernails on the sheer cement sides before getting a break. The channel suddenly narrowed and I remembered Web's remark about it going

350

underground. I managed to grab a metal stud that protruded about a foot above the waterline.

Then began a battle to hang on against a stiff suction that lead down into the tube. Its hungry mouth lay only a few yards away! I was about to give up when I heard Web's voice shouting my name.

"Here!" I cried. "Here, Web! Quick! I can't hold on much longer!"

His legs thrashed through the brush and his big frame rose above the wall. He reached for me, but only our fingertips touched.

"I thought you'd gone into the tube! I'll have to get a rope!"

Tears sprang into my eyes. "No use," I whispered. My hands loosened on the stud.

"Honey!" Web shouted. "You can't give up now!"

"It's no use, Web. My fingers are too numb."

He swore, straightened up, tore off his coat and vanished. Seconds later I heard a loud splash upstream. He appeared beside me in the water and his arm encircled my waist just as my fingers slipped loose. He seized the stud with his other hand.

"Catch your breath," he said gravely. "I'm going to help you up to my shoulders. You'll be able to reach the top from there. Are you hurt?"

"Just bruised," I managed. "Are you okay?"

He nodded. "The sedan got around me after you jumped. I thought sure you'd gone into the tube. Come on now, up!"

"Web, I can't leave you here."

He lifted me onto his shoulders. "There's a rope in the trunk of the car."

"But, I won't be able to pull you up," I protested.

"I know that. The brush isn't too thick. Drive the car here. Tie the rope to the frame. I'll be waiting, I hope."

He pushed me against the wall and I clawed my way over the concrete wall into the brush. My legs were too weak to hold me up as I ran toward the car and I fell, crawled a few feet, got up and pitched over again. Web's Thunderbird was still parked at the end of the bridge. I dragged myself onto the road. The upturned body of the kidnapper lay tipped to the dark sky, his face twisted and stained from the impact of death. I climbed inside the car and started its engine. Headlights flickered through the brush as I plunged off into the desert, bouncing over ridges until the underground tube swelled out of the night. I backed the Thunderbird as near as possible to the channel side and tied a rope under its rear axle.

Web still clung to the wall. His hands finally grabbed the rope and he pulled himself to safety. He dropped to one knee, dazedly shaking his head.

"Honey," he whispered, "you're okay." He gasped for air. "How—how you kept from getting killed…"

"You saved my life," I said softly. Beads of water ran off my cheeks onto his face as I leaned over and kissed him. His mouth was wet and hard. It wasn't easy to draw away. I ran to the car.

"Honey!"

I wrapped a car blanket over my wet and tattered dress and started the engine again. Web crawled in beside me and stared silently as I brushed a few strands of blonde hair off his forehead.

"Web, how could you be so right?"

"About what?"

"About the bridge, the barricade, those men?"

"I was as surprised as you were, Honey." He kissed me under my chin and I drew back.

"But you weren't surprised. You warned me when I got out of the car as if you knew…"

A look of anger crossed his face. He caught my shoulders. "It was a hunch. I told you we might wait three hours and maybe three days. They might never have come. They could have taken a dozen other routes."

"But they didn't."

I studied his face. It was unshaven and still wet from the channel.

"All right, so they didn't," he said. "I figured it out mathematically and it worked."

"The baby's still alive, Web. I heard him crying."

"I know," he said. "I heard him, too."

Suddenly I realized the garter on my right thigh was empty. "I lost my gun."

He tossed me the kidnapper's .45 automatic and grimaced. "I didn't want to kill him, but he gave me no choice. Here's his wallet. Name is Rice. Wilt Rice. Lived in San Francisco. Who else was in the car?"

"I saw only one other man," I said, " and him I'll never forget."

"What'd he look like?" The intensity in Web's voice was unmistakable.

"Fat. With a mustache. A thick mustache."

We drove to the highway where Web picked up all but one flare. I wiped any fingerprints off the dead man's wallet and returned it to his coat pocket. Then I did the same thing to the .45, first removing its bullets.

"What's that for?" Web asked.

"Are you kidding? Never steal from a dead man unless you're planning to wind up on death row."

"But I was the one who shot him, Honey. Shouldn't we turn these things over to the police?"

I tossed the bullets off into the brush. "Let them find things for themselves. They like it much better that way."

Web took the wheel this time and swung his Thunderbird toward Mojave. After a few moments he glanced at me out of the corner of his eye. "You're sure there was nobody else in that car besides the baby?"

"No. It was too dark inside."

"You didn't see her?"

"Who?"

"Sylvia."

I whirled in the seat. "What do you know about Sylvia, Web?"

"She's the one, isn't she, Honey?"

"She's the one, what?" I demanded.

"She's the one who killed Margo, isn't she?"

"Maybe."

"No maybes about it." A smiled twisted the corners of Web's mouth. "I've got another hunch."

"What's that?"

"We're going to find her. You and I together, Honey. We're going to find Sylvia and that baby. I'll stake my life on it."

I thought about Web's sudden mention of Sylvia Verse. I thought about it all the way into Mojave. He had said her name as if it belonged to the Devil's mistress, as if he knew it as well as he knew his very own. And yet, we'd never discussed her by name.

At the Kern County Sheriff's office in Mojave they loaned me a woman's loose-fitting jail outfit to replace the blanket and torn dress. The lanky deputy on duty seemed much more interested in my shape than the story of the dead man at the bridge."

"You mean to tell me," he grumbled, "there's a body laying out by the aqueduct that we don't know nothing about?"

"Two of them," I said. "A kidnapper from San Francisco and a Gila monster from the Mojave desert."

"What's your name?"

"Honey West. I'm a private detective hired to find the abducted child."

"That's what I thought." The deputy removed a note from his clipboard. "You're supposed to call Lieutenant Storm at this L.A. number."

"What?"

"He phoned about two hours ago. Said he had a report you were heading in this direction and that you might wind up here."

A Mojave operator put me through to Mark's office.

"Lieutenant Storm speaking."

"Is that so," I said, "and here I thought sure it was Mandrake the Magician."

"Honey, where are you?"

"What's the matter, Lieutenant? Has your crystal ball gone dead? Or did your bird dog lose my trail?"

"Both," he grunted. "Are you in Mojave?"

"Yes. You didn't by any chance have a man follow me to the Dolphin Café?"

"Of course, but the damned idiot lost you later on the freeway. What's going on? My man sat too far away to hear your conversation at the Dolphin. He said he saw the two of you pore over a map and did manage to catch the words Mojave desert."

"Good catch," I said. "Too bad he fumbled the ball. We could have used him about a half hour ago. Even as a spectator."

Mark swore when I told him what had happened out at the aqueduct.

"How do you know it was the kidnappers, Honey?"

"A sawed-off shotgun told me."

354

"Did you actually see the baby?"

"No, but I heard him loud and clear."

"This is too fantastic."

"I know. It was Web's brainstorm. I was just crazy enough to go along after he told me about the baby blanket."

"What baby blanket?"

"The one found in San Jose. It seemed reasonable that if..."

"Wait a minute. As far as I know no baby blanket's turned up in San Jose—or anywhere else for that matter."

"You—you're sure?"

"Of course. Where'd he get this information, Honey?"

"I don't know," I lied, remembering Web's comment about a bulletin he'd picked up on his car radio.

"I just talked with San Francisco. They haven't had a whiff of anything new. In fact, they're still working on the woman angle—canvassing houses in the immediate area of the hospital."

Web was too far away to hear any of our conversation. He and the Mojave deputy were talking to three other men in an outer office.

"Well, they can stop canvassing," I said. "Look, Mark, do me a favor. Call Phillip Sharkey and tell him his son's still alive. I guess he'd like to hear."

"Okay, but what's with Web Stevens?"

"I don't know. Was he in L.A. last night?"

"Yes. That's already been checked out thoroughly. He was in a four-man poker game from about midnight until five this morning. He never left the room for more than a few minutes at a time."

"Did he win or lose?"

"That we didn't bother to find out. You don't suspect he had anything ot do with his wife's murder, do you?"

"No."

"Well?"

"Did you or anyone else mention the name Sylvia Verse to Stevens this morning when he was in your office?"

Mark paused. "I—I think so. Dammit, how can I remember everything when I've got you in the middle of this whole mess!"

"You don't have to yell, Lieutenant. Bell went to a lot of trouble to perfect this instrument."

"You don't have to tell me about Alexander Graham Bell," Mark roared. "I want to know about Web Stevens."

"He saved my life. Twice in the space of twenty-eight minutes. That's a lot more than I can say for some other people in the space of twenty-eight years."

"Are you kidding? I've saved your neck so many times in the space of twenty-eight hours that a cat would drop dead just trying to count 'em all."

"All right, so I'm living on borrowed time."

"Yeah, mine and Web Stevens'. Where'd he get that stuff about a baby blanket?"

"I told you I don't know."

"And what's this brainstorm he came up with?"

"We're wasting time, Mark. I've got to find that kid inside twenty-four or else."

"Or else what?"

"Nothing. Do me another favor, Lieutenant. Ask San Francisco police to check out our friend Phillip Sharkey. He smells sort of bad to me."

"He smells bad to a lot of people. Especially to a guy in Las Vegas named Manfred Beech. Beech owns a gambling casino. Sharkey ran out on a big investment deal one time which cost Beech nearly a million bucks. Then there's the Bureau of Internal Revenue. He really stank up that joint. They claim he's managed to beat the government out of ten million dollars in back taxes. They're on the verge of working him over in court. Listen, Honey..."

I hung up, moved quickly into the outer office and grabbed Web's arm. "Come on, let's go!"

"Wait a minute, Miss West," the deputy said. "We still have a few matters to straighten out." He glanced at the three other men. "Okay, boys, get out to the aqueduct. Bring back anything you can find, understand?"

When they were gone, the deputy eyed me suspiciously. "You know, Miss West, we don't believe stories around these parts until they're actually proven. What with nudist colonies and space conventions sprouting up all over the desert we get some pretty crazy tales, I'll tell you. For instance, about twenty minutes ago I got a call about a flying saucer landing near the aqueduct. It supposedly contained two nine foot characters from another planet." His eyelids narrowed. "Now you couldn't possibly have had anything to do with that story, could you?"

"No." I said innocently, glancing at Web. "But, I understood they were ten feet if they were an inch."

The deputy sneered. "I thought so. What the hell have you two been drinking anyway?"

"Water," I said.

"Yeah, I'll bet." He surveyed my frame again. "What'd Lieutenant Storm want?"

I winked. "My name, rank and Venusian serial number. Now can we go? I promise to return the dress only right now I've got a big date with a grounding device."

"A what?"

"You wouldn't understand," I said. "It has to do with an interplanetary invasion."

The deputy's lean shoulders tensed angrily. "Get out of here! I should have known better. I've never met a female private detective before, but I read about one in a paperback book one time. She was nuttier than all hell. I ought to arrest you both for wasting my valuable time with your phony stories. If I ever hear about you fooling around these parts again you'll wish you were anyplace but on Earth, believe me. Get out!"

I ran for the door, pulling Web after me. I didn't even say thanks. We didn't have time. The phone in the deputy's office began to ring insistently and I guessed it was
either another space invasion or Lieutenant Storm. If it was the impetuous lieutenant from Los Angeles, I knew we were grounded for sure.

Chapter Eight

We drove about a mile before I asked Web about the baby blanket.

"Okay, so I lied," he said. "There was no special news bulletin. I made the whole story up."

"Why?"

"Well, my hunch was pretty wild to begin with. When you called me, Honey, I figured you'd never believe my story unless I doctored it a little. So, I added the San Jose bit."

"Why lie to me?"

He shook his head. "I don't think you would have come with me otherwise."

"Probably not. But why am I so important?"

"I—I don't know."

"That isn't much of an answer."

"Of course, it isn't," he said. "What do you want me to say? That I'm crazy about you?"

"No."

"Well I am." He wiped his hand over his mouth. "Back there by the aqueduct I almost—I never felt anything as strong as that before in my life."

I ignored his comments and asked, "Web, are you sure barricading the bridge was just a hunch or did Margo tell you something that you haven't told anyone else?"

He swallowed nervously. "She only said she was coming home, that's all."

"Withholding evidence is a serious business."

"I know that. Telling you that lie, having the hunch come out almost on the nose-this all seems very suspicious. I don't blame you for thinking

I'm involved."

"I didn't say I thought you were involved. Just unusually psychic especially for a salesman."

"Don't kid yourself, Honey. If I hadn't been a salesman in this area I'd never figured that out in the first place."

I lighted a cigarette and watched the smoke drift up slowly. "This afternoon I mentioned the possibility of Margo having a roommate."

"Yeah, I remember."

"There was someone who influenced her to have her labor induced."

"So I heard at the Sheriff's office."

"Do you think that someone was Sylvia?"

Web exhaled loudly. "If she had a roommate, yeah."

"Is this another of your profound hunches?"

"Maybe. Look, Honey, why don't we just do an about face, go back to Mojave and turn me in."

"What for?"

"Because I murdered Margo," he said. "Sure, maybe I didn't push the pillow in her face, but I might as well have."

"You're talking nonsense, Web."

"If I'd been more of a man she'd have never walked out on me."

"That's ridiculous. You said yourself Margo was a strange woman."

"I know." He nodded dismally. "I know."

"If Sylvia Verse was that influence, Web, why did she insist Margo have her labor induced on the same day Mrs. Sharkey had her baby?"

"I—I wish I knew."

"Could there have been a connection? Could Margo have been involved and then changed her mind at the last minute and called me?"

"She didn't act strange when I talked to her last, Honey. On the contrary, she seemed normal for the first time in months. How could Margo have been involved?"

"Did she know Phillip Sharkey?"

"Maybe. I don't know."

"Did she like money, lots of it?"

"Don't all women?"

"Web, Margo was in trouble when I knew her because she tried to pull a fraud on a wealthy Long Beach jaysee senior. That's why she had one of my father's business cards."

"I—I heard about that incident indirectly before I married Margo. It didn't bother me."

"Well, maybe this will. Have you ever considered the possibility that Phillip Sharkey used Margo in a plot to kidnap his own son?"

"That—that's crazy, Honey. No man would kidnap his own son. Especially Phillip Sharkey. He's a war hero."

"What's a war hero, Web?"

"Well, he's a man who does something great. Saves lives. Gets a medal for it."

"You saved my life, but I don't see any medals hanging on your chest."

"Honey, let's be sensible. Phillip Sharkey has all the money in the world. What would he gain by kidnapping his own child?"

"Money. He'd pay himself ransom, what else?"

"But, why?"

"Sharkey's in trouble with the Bureau of Internal Revenue. About ten million dollars worth of trouble. Why couldn't he write off the ransom and plead for leniency in the tax court. A man with a kidnapped child can get a lot of sympathy—even from the government."

"I doubt it," Web said. "Besides, ten million dollars is just chicken feed to a man like Sharkey."

"Maybe."

"And beyond that I still say no man in his right mind would have his own child kidnapped. There's too much danger, Honey."

I thought about that for a minute. It did make sense. A man values his own child usually beyond all other things. Even money. I glanced at Web.

"Ever hear of a guy named Manfred Beech?"

"No."

"He's a big gambler in Vegas. Owns a casino. Sharkey once cost him nearly a million bucks. Do you think a man in his position would like revenge?"

"Why not? Money is his business."

I glanced out the window at the vast stretch of desert. "Where are we?"

"A few miles out of Mojave."

"What's the next big town?"

"Barstow. The road forks there. The northern route leads to Vegas. The southern to Needles and Arizona."

"Want to play a hunch of mine for a change?"

"Why not?"

"Take the northern route to Vegas."

Web grinned. "My hunch is with you."

A light flashed on the highway ahead.

"Now what's that?" I said.

"Don't tell me it's a barricade," Web said.

He slowed the Thunderbird to a stop. A man stood in front of the car waving frantically. We poked his face out the window and groaned. A thin, grizzled face poked back. It was our old friend the Perfessor.

"So, it's only you stuffy fools," he said, glowering at us.

"Afraid so," Web said. "We're on our way to a rendezvous with some twelve foot Martians."

"It's going to be a cooperative plan," I added, hoping the same absurd psychology would work on the old man. "We're going to split the Earth up into two equal parts."

"You don't have to pull my leg anymore," the Perfessor said. "You pulled it once and that's enough. I know you're not from Venus. The man who told that story about the landings was found out to be a liar."

"Glad to hear it," Web said. "Now we'll be on our way if you don't mind."

"I thought you were from the Sheriff's office," the Perfessor said. "A terrible thing's happened. Worse than an invasion. Worse than anything."

"What's that?" I asked.

"My nephew's car was stolen. But the worst part is, whoever stole it left another behind." His eyes opened wide. "And the one they left behind's got blood all over it!"

It was nearly midnight when we reached the flying saucer camp grounds. Wind-buffeted sand had begun to swirl around us. But threatening weather didn't seem to faze the carnival atmosphere of the saucer convention. Telescopes protruded in every direction. Soft drink and hot dog vendors hawked their wares, while other barkers milled through the crowds selling saucer-shaped ashtrays, authentic Martian grass (cut during the vendors' last interplanetary journey), photographs of a buxom nude Venusian stepping from her space ship, Pluto Water (for those unfortunate space bugs who drank too much Jupiter Juice the night before), even long playing records with the Martians singing "I'll be down to get you in a space ship, honey, better be ready about half past doom," and "Look up, look up, you lonesome humans before we blast you away."

"Holy smokes," Web said, pushing me through the crowds, "if it isn't the circus of tomorrow."

We bumped past miniature rockets, campfires, tents, kids and barking dogs. In the midst of all this chaos my prison garb didn't make the slightest impression.

Cars were squeezed together in the parking area like a bunch of sausages in a German meat market. The Perfessor showed us where his nephew's car had been parked at the outer edge of the confusion. A sleek black Chrysler sedan glistened in the moonlight, its left rear window still partially rolled down where the shotgun had taken aim at my head.

"There's where my nephew left it," the old man said, "keys and all. He was always leaving his keys behind. Crazy fool."

Blood was splattered on the sedan's left front fender. I climbed in the back seat. The Perfessor poked his head in behind me.

"May I have your flashlight, please?" I asked.

"There's nothing in there," he said. "We already looked." He handed me the flashlight with a sigh.

Web watched as I began to carefully examine the interior for possible clues. A small white stain was dried on the seat. I glanced at Web, then scratched at the crusty remains.

"Milk," I said. "Probably some formula the baby spit up. What kind of car was your nephew driving, mister?"

"A Mercury, of course. Most important planet in our solar system. Nearest to the sun. Nearest to..."

"What year?" I said, examining the ashtray.

"Fifty-six convertible. Beautiful car. Power steering, power brakes. White with a black top."

I held up a lipstick-stained cigarette butt. Web swore.

"Say, what is this anyway?" the Perfessor asked. "You two are a couple of bugs. Positive bugs."

"How long ago did your nephew discover his car missing?" I asked.

"He actually saw 'em steal it. About twenty minutes ago. There were two of 'em. A man and a woman."

"Were they carrying anything? A bundle maybe, with a blanket wrapped around it?"

"He didn't say. The man was fat."

"What about the woman? What'd she look like?"

The old man hunched his shoulders. "Who knows. She was a bug. Only a bug would steal a car."

I got out and returned the flashlight to the Perfessor. Wind blew sand in my eyes and I groped for Web's arm. "Come on," I said. "Let's get out of this flea circus. They've probably got a half hour on us at least. We still might be able to catch up."

"Just who are you?" the old man asking, flashing his light in our faces.

"Don't you know," I said. "We're not humans. We're Mercurians. It makes us mad when anybody fools with a Mercury."

A car's engine roared. We whirled around. A few hundred yards away, partially hidden by a clump of desert cactus, sat a white convertible hazily etched in the swirling sand.

"That's it!" the Perfessor yelled.

Web ran past me. I tried to follow, but the rising wind pushed me to the ground. He was a dozen yards away before I could get to my feet.

"Wait!" I called.

Sand filled my mouth. I staggered back to the kidnapper's abandoned sedan and got behind the wheel. The key was in the ignition. I started the car and rammed the indicator into drive. The white convertible was swiftly vanishing in the gritty wind. I clamped my foot to the floorboard, swerved around two parked cars, skidded past the Perfessor and onto the bumpy desert road. I saw Web dive for cover to avoid being run down. Suddenly everything was obliterated and the car shot over a ravine. My head hit the ceiling, bounced off the steering wheel and kept on bouncing until my foot found the brake pedal. I ground to a halt, pushed some hair out of my eyes

363

and leaped out.

The white convertible was faintly visible farther down the ravine. My hands dug in the desert soil in search of a weapon and came up with a gnarled piece of wood about two feet long. I staggered down the slope, trying to shield my eyes against the blistering sand that burned as it struck the exposed parts of my body. The convertible's windows were rolled up. I could see a white face through the glass. I pushed down on the door handle and swung viciously.

A hand caught my swing and it pulled me against a sweaty bare chest. Dark, angry eyes glared down at me.

Then something else reared into view. It was the head and shoulders of a young girl. She couldn't have been more than sixteen. She was stark naked.

Chapter Nine

It was too late to rectify my mistake. The arm around my middle loosened, and I was pushed back into the ravine. I scrambled clear as the car spun around. Its wheels tore into the sandy surface, caught hold and pushed the convertible back up to the top of the slope. In another instant it was gone.

Web came down the steep side and lifted me to my feet. "What happened?"

"Another case of mistaken identity," I said, feeling my ribs.

"What do you mean, Honey?"

"If I tried to explain, Web, we'd be here for hours. Come on, the kidnappers have got a big enough jump on us now as it is."

He assisted me to the top of the ravine. The little old man was waiting, a sneer on his weather face.

"That wasn't my nephew's car," he said. "That one was all white."

"Yes, so I noticed," I said. "Outside and in. What are you people running here anyway? A space convention or a nudist camp?"

The Perfessor stared at me as Web and I walked toward the highway and our car. Enroute I told Web what I'd found inside the convertible.

"How old were they?" he demanded.

"Not old enough, I'll tell you that. They probably saw our flashlight, got scared and ran. They plunged off into the ravine and so did I."

Web helped me into his Thunderbird. Sand piled up on the windshield and its impact shook us as Web drove out onto the highway again.

"You've got a cut on your forehead," he said, handing me his handkerchief. "You can't keep up this pace, Honey. I'm dropping you at the train station in Barstow."

"Thanks," I said. "But I'm going on to Vegas. How long do you think I'd last at a ticket window wearing a jail outfit?"

"I forgot about that."

"Well don't forget they're probably an hour ahead of us thanks to my blunder. You dealt me in, Web, and I'm staying to the last hand. Win or loose."

"Okay, only just remember one thing, Honey."

"What's that?"

"I'm the guy who was willing to pick up your cards while you were still ahead."

The dashboard clock indicated five minutes to two when a furious gale of wind pushed us off the highway into a ditch. We hadn't seen the lights of another car in almost an hour. Web's face was deeply lined from the strain of trying to stay on the road. He smashed his fist against the door.

"We're in trouble, Honey. Real trouble. This is the worst storm I've ever seen out in this desert. And believe me, I've encountered some bad ones."

"Where are we Web?"

"As near as I can figure we're about fifteen miles from Baker. Seems to me I remember seeing an old cabin just about here. Maybe we can get some help." He opened his door. "I'm going to check."

"Web, wait a minute! Wouldn't we be better off to stay in the car? It can't last forever."

He pulled his coat over his mouth and mumbled, "That's what you think."

It seemed an eternity after he left, before I had sense enough to open the glove compartment. In its light I saw Web's map, a paper cup and some bullets. The .38 was gone. I removed the map and spread it across my knees. This time I examined it more carefully that I had in the Dolphin Café, but I found nothing to indicate Web knew any more than what he'd told me. Under the paper cup was a piece of paper, a memorandum from Web's office in L.A. Scrawled across the paper were the words, "Stevens— a woman called—wouldn't leave her name—long distance from Frisco— said she'd try to reach you tomorrow." The date at the top showed the message had been written about a week ago. I refolded the memorandum and tucked it inside my bra.

A fist banged against my window and I saw Web's coat-covered head.

"Come on, Honey! Throw that blanket that's in the back seat over you!"

I hesitated, then followed his orders and climbed into the ditch. Wind hurled me against him. He caught me in his arms and lead me up over a sandy embankment.

"Web! Are you sure you know what you're doing?"

We staggered on, my question left unanswered, the storm screaming back its own deadly retort. I thought about his gun. It seemed to me he'd replaced the weapon in the glove compartment after we left the aqueduct.

A building loomed up in front of us. He pushed me through a door and I blinked with amazement as he shut out the howling wind.

"Like it?" he asked, brushing sand from his face.

A large, cozy room stretched around us. At one end was a pot belly stove, reddish tongues of flame licking in its mouth. There was a wooden table in the center and a smaller one in a corner, both with flickering candles on them. A double bed with bare springs and mattress was pushed against one wall.

I blinked again. "Now look, Conway, Shangri-La is supposed to be in Tibet. When did you move it to the California desert?"

Web stuffed some more wood in the stove. "The aces must be stacked in our deck," he said grinning. "I found the house I was talking about."

"Whose house?"

He shrugged. "Probably belongs to some desert rat out looking for uranium. I had to break the lock to get in."

I studied the room suspiciously. It was clean, well insulated, and had a faintly perfumed fragrance. "No rat lives in this house. Smells more like mink if you ask me."

Web laughed. "All the comforts of home. It smelled pretty awful when I broke in, but look what I found."

He removed a spray bottle of deodorizer from a cupboard. "Now that's what I call a rat with a conscience. Maybe he even drinks the stuff, but who cares."

Wind tore against the house, wrenched furiously, drawing our eyes toward the roof for a long instant. Web removed his coat and pulled me toward him.

"Y know what else I found?" he said.

"No."

"How would you like a little midnight—I mean post-midnight snack?"

"What's on the menu? Baked sand?"

"Are you kidding? We go first class."

Web took some cans from the shelf and examined their labels. "Pork and beans. Vegetable soup. And—hey, look at this!"

"What is it, canned steak?"

"Lasagne. Man oh man, when in Rome let's eat like the Romans do."

I began searching for a can opener. "I always thought sand dunes were in Egypt."

"You see, you've got your geography all mixed up." His arm encircled me warmly. "How about this, Honey?"

I thought about the memorandum I had tucked in my bra, started to show it to him, then tossed the pink paper into the fire. "I like it fine," I said, smiling. "Even if I still don't believe it."

Web took a handkerchief from his pocket, folded it over his wrist and bowed. "What would you care to drink, madam?"

"Champagne, of course, James."

He lifted a green bottle with a fancy label from the same cupboard. "Champagne, it is, madam. Vintage 1936, bottled in Brest, France. It's not chilled, but…"

"You must be kidding!" I roared, examining the bottle. Sparkling champagne shimmered inside. My eyes toured the room again. "What is this, the Desert Hilton?"

We removed the wire shield from the bottle's neck and pried its cork loose. He poured the bubbly liquid into two old jelly glasses and we clinked to each other's health.

"Mmmm, good," I whispered, feeling a warm tingle in my throat.

"Yeah, even at room temperature. Hey! What about our dinner?"

I heated the lasgane and we ate by candlelight, sipping more champagne and listening to the howl of sand and wind and the crackling fire in the pot belly stove. And we talked, too. Low, intimate talk about things we liked and places we'd been and the bruised elbows, snake bites and swimming holes of our childhood. Web grinned when I told him the police picked me up when I was six for swimming in the nude.

"First offense?" Web asked, pouring the remainder of the champagne.

"Not exactly. I was picked up when I was four on the same charge." I smiled. "Only this time they caught me strolling through Westlake Park wearing only a hat with a big feather."

"Pretty sexy. No wonder they tossed you in the clink."

"They even had my picture in the paper."

"I don't blame them. Although, if they'd waited twenty years I'm sure they would have sold more copies."

"Mr. Stevens," I said, rubbing my eyes and stretching, "you're getting out of line again."

"That's the specialty of the house, madam."

"So I noticed at the aqueduct." I shook my head. "This champagne has really knocked me for a loop."

"You must be tired, Honey."

"I am, and I hurt, too. I've taken some banging around lately, I'll tell you."

"Why do you do it, Honey?"

"What?"

"Stay in this business." Web paused, "I mean, you're pretty. You could do almost anything."

I smiled. "So I've been told. Come on, let's go to bed."

"What?"

"I said let's go to bed."

Web stood up slowly. "Okay, I'll curl up on the floor and you take the.."

"You'll do no such thing," I said, stretching again. "You'd probably catch cold. The bed's plenty big enough for both of us."

"You—you're kidding."

I ran my fingers through my hair and laughed. "Don't get excited, Conway. This isn't Shangri-La and I'm not going to turn into an old lady overnight. I didn't mean what you're thinking."

Web's cheeks flushed slightly. "Well, what am I supposed to think when you…"

I crossed to the double bed. Two thick wool blankets were drawn over the mattress. I tossed him one. "We'll each roll up in our separate little bundle. What could be more proper?"

"It stinks that's all. I'd rather have been in Westlake Park when you were four."

Sand drilled against the cabin walls in a new frenzy. I stood by the bed, still feeling a warm glow from the wine and stared into his angry eyes. His shadow ran crazily across the ceiling, flickering eerily in the candle's glare.

"That's a funny thing to say, Web."

"Is it, Honey? I would have been about five or six. I think I would have liked you better than. At least, you were doing what came naturally."

"What's wrong with what I'm doing now?"

"You know the answer to that." He glanced at the blanket in his hands. "You've got a birthmark on your leg."

I stared down at the baggy jail outfit. "What makes you think so?"

"I saw it when you pulled me out of the aqueduct."

I wet my lips with my tongue. "Flattery is liable to get you somewhere, so you'd better stop."

"Where will it get me?"

"Curled up on the floor."

"You wouldn't do that," Web said. "I might catch cold, remember?"

"I'm trying to forget. Why don't you put out the cat and come to bed?"

"Stop testing me, Honey, or you'll be sorry."

"Will I? You know, we have exactly the same color hair and eyes."

He started for the door. "That's where the similarities end. I'm going outside."

"What for?"

"You're inquisitive as hell. I think I'd better sleep on the floor."

"Maybe you had."

He shrugged his shoulders, opened the door and vanished in the swirling sand and darkness. While he was gone, I removed my dress and wrapped one of the blankets around me. I felt funny inside and hot. I tried to blame the champagne, but it didn't work. Web Stevens was too big an influence to overlook.

When he returned I was lying on the bare mattress smoking a cigarette.

He rubbed sand from his eyes and then glared down at me. "Didn't anybody ever warn you about smoking in bed?"

"Nope. Nobody ever did."

"Well, I am," he said, bending over me. "Put it out. We'd be in a pretty fix if this cabin caught fire."

"Make me," I taunted.

He snatched the cigarette from my mouth and jammed it into his own. The red tip gleamed angrily as he stared at my bare legs sticking out of the blanket.

"You ought to be spanked, you know that, don't you?" he said.

"Says who?"

"Says me. This isn't a kid's game."

"I didn't infer that it was, did I?"

"No, you're just the little girl who takes walks through parks, all very innocently. I wouldn't be surprised if you weren't born that way."

"What way?"

He ran his hands down the front of his shirt. "Open up that blanket and take a look."

"Oh, come on, Web. You're the one who's acting childish. We're both over twenty-one."

"So, I've noticed. You'd better get out of that bed!"

"What?"

"I said get out of that bed. We're leaving here."

"But, the storm…"

"I think we can make it now. I got the car out of the ditch. It'll be rough, but it will be better than this."

I rose on my elbows, forgetting all about the blanket. "Why do you say that, Web?"

He groaned. "I told you I'm crazy about you. I'm not to be trusted. I hate blind man's bluff and when I was a kid I always cheated when we played spin the bottle."

"So?"

He paced across the room. "So, get yourself another boy. I play for keeps."

371

"So do I," I said quietly. "You've overlooked one thing about me, Web. I'm pure, unadulterated female."

He peered at me through the flickering candlelight. "I haven't overlooked a thing about you, Honey. That's the trouble. Now let's get out of here."

I slid off the side of the bed, tripped on my blanket and sprawled on the floor. He bent to pick me up.

"Honey, you drive me crazy."

I got to my feet. "Let's just write it off as a bad bottle of champagne and leave."

He caught me in his arms and his hands moved down my back. The fire in my stomach exploded. His mouth brushed against my cheek and then closed over my lips. His fingers fumbled under the blanket at the hooks of my brassiere.

"Wait—a—minute," I whispered, drawing back.

His mouth found mine again and it hurt this time as his unshaved face rubbed my flesh. He pushed me toward the bed.

"Web..."

He crushed out my protest with his mouth again, one hand pulling off the blanket, searching my body, the other holding me against him.

"Web—Web—WEB!" I cried.

His fist shot up and blotted out my cry. I fell on the bed. He lunged for me, but my foot snapped up instinctively and struck him hard. He dropped to the floor as if he'd been shot, rolled over and staggered to his feet again. I tensed myself for his next assault, but it wasn't aimed at me.

He grabbed the empty champagne bottle and hurled it toward the door. And for a very good reason. A sawed off shotgun was poked through the opening. Web's toss put it out of action long enough for me to dive for cover. In the next instant glass and death sprayed in every direction and Web Stevens was right in the middle of the blast. He dropped, only this time he didn't get up. He didn't even move. Nothing moved except those ugly twin barrels pouring their venom into the room.

Chapter Ten

Being a woman has its advantages. When the shooting was over and I lay on the floor in the inky darkness, I thought about my half-naked appearance rather than death and I didn't shake so much.

For a long moment, there was no sound except the howling wind. I thought I heard an infant's cry, but I wasn't sure. I wasn't sure of anything until I heard Web's hushed voice in the furious dark.

"Don't move!"

"Are you kidding?"

"If I am, I'm dead. My gun's in my coat pocket near the bed. Get it!"

"Yes sir."

"And don't be smart."

I got the .38 and whispered, "I was only trying to be apologetic."

"For what?"

"For kicking you. It must have hurt."

He groaned. "It still hurts. Be quiet!"

"You're the one who's making all the noise."

"I've got a right to."

"So do I. Your fist didn't exactly feel like a piece of Kleenex."

"I'm sorry, but you shouldn't have yelled."

"What was I supposed to do?"

"I—I didn't mean to hit you," he whispered.

"Your aim was pretty good. I doubt if you ever threw a forward pass so accurately."

"Be quiet. They're right outside. Have you got my gun?"

"Of course."

"Slide it across the floor."

"I've got a better shot from here. Just yell and I'll be ready."

"I've been yelling all evening, but you haven't been ready."

"This isn't Westlake Park, Mr. Stevens."

"So I've noticed. Either smog has moved in or the air's getting awfully thick. Did I hear a baby a minute ago?"

"I think so."

Web's voice tightened. "They must have got behind us in the storm. Probably saw our car on the road."

I searched for matches in Web's coat pockets. "What are we waiting for? They must be gone by now."

Web jammed the door closed as I relit one of the candles. He stared at me for a long moment.

"I'm sorry," he said.

I glanced down at my bra and panties. "What for?"

"Your face," he said. "I hit you pretty hard. I saw him out of the corner of my eye."

I pulled the jail outfit over my head and smoothed back my hair. His shirt was almost torn off his shoulders. "I'm sorry, too," I said.

"What for, Honey?"

I kissed Web's mouth softly and handed over his coat. "If you don't know, you're a bigger fool than I am. And that's pretty big, believe me."

Web caught my hand, then blew out the candle. We plowed out into the violent, sandy night.

We pulled into Las Vegas around dawn, having failed to overtake the white convertible. The wind storm had subsided after we passed the Nevada border and orange streaks traced lightly across a gray cloudless sky. Nightclubs and million-dollar hotel-casinos, still neon-lit and belching tired patrons, lined the fabulous Vegas stip.

Mark Storm was waiting outside the Clark County Sheriff's office when we pulled to a stop. So was newspaperman, Fred Sims. He pointed his cane at my dress and laughed.

"Who bailed you out, Honey? And when?"

Mark didn't have a laugh in him. "All right, let's have it," he said. "Where have you been?"

"On the Atcheson, Topeka and Sandy Fe," I said. "What are you doing here in the land of loaded women and loaded dice?"

"I got a special leave," Mark growled, "to pick you up in one piece." He examined the bruise on my cheek.

"I come in more than one piece, Lieutenant. So, just crawl back into your woodwork and take your friend with you."

Fred hooked me with the crook of his cane. "If you're referring to me, champ, I'm the guy who's got enough woodwork to last us until hell freezes over. Now smile."

I smiled. "Tell your friend to smile, or I'll crack him one right across his big flat arches."

Mark did his best to smile, but worry and lack of sleep still ridged his forehead. "Look, Honey, we've had half the Sheriff's offices in Californa looking for you two. Where's the baby?"

"I don't know."

"That's what I thought," he said, glancing at Web. "What's been happening?"

"Not a word until I've had some breakfast," I insisted. "And some civilized clothes."

Mark crossed to Fred's car and hauled out a suitcase. "Here," he said. "I grabbed just about everything in your closet. They may not be folded to your satisfaction, but Fred said it didn't matter."

I tossed a kiss at the crippled newspaperman. "Thanks, pal. Remind me to pack a suitcase for you sometime—with a bomb in it!"

Fred winked. "Honey, I been worried about you, even if Mark wasn't."

"Yeah, I'll bet. And just how worried was your city editor?"

"Oh, him?" Fred laughed. "He's a bug. An absolute bug."

I reacted at the coincidental mention of the word. I glanced at Web and threw up my hands. "Here we go again!"

After Web and I told our stories at breakfast, Fred Sims cornered me alone outside the ladies room. He pushed me against a wall with his cane and grinned.

I said, "What's on your mind?"

"I've got something important to tell you and it's not for publication. At least, not in the Sheriff's office."

"Well fancy that," I said. "Withholding evidence from old hound dog Marcus is a federal offense. I'd be careful if I were you, Fredrick."

He pushed even harder at the mention of his Christian name. "I've killed me for less," he said grinning.

"What have you done to women?"

He shook his head. "I'm not convinced you fit into that category."

"Well, then, watch where you poke that stick."

"Is that so?" Fred murmured. "The way Web Stevens looks at you I'd be willing to guess you'd add a lot to a party."

I stiffened. "Fred, I resent that."

He removed his cane and sobered. "All right. Then resent this, if you will. I think I know who engineered the Sharkey kidnap."

"Who, Fred?"

"A gambler here in Vegas named Beech. Manfred Beech."

"Where'd you get this information? And why haven't you printed it?"

"Who says I haven't?"

"Come on," I said, "that isn't the kind of barrage you put up outside Cologne when the Jerries had you pinned against a tank."

"Okay, so I haven't released a word," he said. "I don't know whether it's true or not. I'm gambling on you and me to find out."

I loved this guy, but we was strictly a newspaperman and not to be trusted when it came to you's and me's.

"What do you want out of this?" I asked.

"What do you think?"

"And here I thought it was just for me alone…"

"You can cut female private eye approach number six-five-six. I love you, too. But, I know your angle in this case. You've got about twelve hours left to produce that baby or your name is Sylvia Verse."

I patted his cheek. "How information does leak into your pointed little ears. I'm surprised you didn't wind up at a listening station during the war."

He tapped his cane briskly. "So am I. The only reason I didn't was because the German frauleins were almost as pretty as you. And almost as shrewd. You know, Honey, we have one thing in common."

"What's that?"

"We've both dodged bullets. Only difference is, I wasn't so lucky."

I played an invisible violin and hummed some appropriate dirge. "Private Sims, if I wasn't so familiar with your sob stories I'd kick you right square in the middle of your Medal of Honor. Admit it. You need me. I need you. Enough said."

"Okay," he said, "we're going to a party. A big party. It's very exclusive and supposed to last twenty-four hours in honor of a new Beech casino-nightclub just opened on the strip."

"Thanks for the invitation," I said. "Who invited you?"

"Nobody," Fred answered. "That's why I'm taking you, baby. In your newest slashed to the waist-slashed in the back gown. In other words, we're crashing. Get me?"

"Yeah," I said, "but you don't get me. I haven't got a gown like that."

"You do now. I just bought one next door at that fancy dress shop. Go try it on and then duck out the back door. I'll meet you in the parking lot."

"But, Fred, you can't afford a dress like that."

"Who says I'm paying for it, baby? The city editor said, 'Go get Honey West even if you have to put her in a strait jacket.' This dress is the next best thing I could find. Now, get going!"

Fred's backless-frontless gown was anything but a strait jacket. Two narrow strips of fabric folded over the top of my bosom and that was all. The back went all the way down to hell and gone. The whole gown was held together by three straps, two of them criss-crossing over my shoulders.

Fred was waiting for me in his car. Even he did a double take when he saw me.

"My Lord, I didn't realize it was that low."

"Neither did I until I got inside. Then it was too late. Where are Web and Mark?"

"Finishing their breakfast. They still think you're in the ladies room. Oh, brother, are they in for a surprise."

I tossed my bra and other dress in the back seat and groaned. "They're not the only ones in for a surprise. If this thing doesn't hold together, mister, everything's going to hit the fan, including you."

377

Manfred Beech's party was jammed with a weird variety of people; shrewd-eyed gamblers with silver dollars bulging in their pockets, suckers who hadn't slept for three days and who were trying to salve their wounds with another thousand martinis, flimsily-clad women with too much makeup and too many ridges below their uplifts, chorus girls with phony eyelashes, handsome men with the stamp of "queer" or "male shill" so indelibly impressed on their spindly legs that they could hardly walk without their knees rubbing together.

Fred did the "crashing" honors. He was an expert at that game. With a limp, a cane and a low-cost gown beside him, he could do anything. The grease ball at the front door didn't get a chance to argue. Fred pushed his walking stick between the guy's eyeballs, put me through a deep knee bend and the doorman didn't know what hit him. Not until we were lost in the crowd. By that time it didn't matter.

"What a layout," I said, escorting Fred to the bar.

"Yeah. The only thing missing is dancing girls on the ceiling."

I glanced up. Above the glistening chandeliers were five unobtrusive slits where five delicately-shaped barrels protruded.

"That ceiling's got something dancing girls will never have." I gestured.

Fred got the message. "They look like they're all aimed at me," he whispered.

"Don't be such an egotist. They don't know you from Adam."

"I hope not," Fred said. "I wouldn't want to be mistaken for Eve."

We split up and began circulating after Fred described Manfred Beech's sturdy, middle-aged physique. I didn't have to look far to find him. He was gray haired, green eyed and clutching a tall drink and two red-haired beauties. They were jostling around near his massive, A-shaped pool. He took a long look at me and the action stopped. Dead.

I thought it might have been because Beech had never seen three or four G-strings sewed together into a gown. Or that one of my straps had snapped, dropping the front as low as the back. Neither was the case.

His thick mouth curved into an awesome smile. Then he said, "Hello, Sylvia, welcome home."

I was stunned to hear the name. but even a little more uncomfortable at the same time. Two of Beech's vultures had come down out of their nests, and they had two fat eggs planted hard against my back.

I was certain, staring at the gambler's face, when those eggs hatched, I'd be dead.

Chapter Eleven

My head jerked sideways. There was no mistaking what I saw. A bloated white face, small, bloodshot eyes and a thick purplish mouth. For a second I thought it was a joke. Then I saw the other vulture. His face was gaunt, pock-marked and toothless. I knew the joke was on me. These were a couple of ghouls, not vultures. They gestured with their coat-pocket-covered roscoes for me to accompany them to their chamber of horrors. And quietly.

That's when I made up my mind. I took a quick step toward the swimming pool. The slobsy twins followed, but not fast enough.

"Last one in is a Beech-nut!" I shouted at the top of my lungs.

People around the pool stopped in their tracks. So did Beech's gruesome twosome, but I kept right on going, splitting the water and kicking up a tremendous spray to cover my path. I figured they'd expect me to head for the other side, so I planned to circle back to the metal steps near where I'd jumped. I was in for another surprise. Bloodshot Eyes had not been left behind Dr. Frankenstein's door when the brains were passed out. He leaped in the pool and whirled me around. Almost everyone had accepted my challenge and people were diving in from all sides, splashing and yelling at the top of their inebriated lungs. This was something else I hadn't counted on. Noise and confusion was exactly what Bloodshot Eyes wanted.

"Nice try, Sylvia," he said, grabbing me in a bear hug. "But, it was your last."

I recognized his voice instantly. He was one of the killers from the El Toro Marine Air Station road. Pock Face must have been the one with the tommy gun.

He pinioned my arms and I figured the next stop would be the bottom. Luckily I guessed wrong again. A slender hard object snapped against his thick skull and his arms flew up like a jack-in-the-box. I glanced around for my benefactor, but the local talent was creating such a frenzy in the water I couldn't see anything except the metal ladder I climbed up and surveyed the clamoring crowd. Then I saw Pock Face. He was moving fast in my direction, one hand still stuck in his pocket. I saw Fred Sims, too, sitting at a table between Pock Face and me, swinging his cane idly between his legs. Beech's ugly killer was quick, but not too quick for Fred. He passed Fred's table just as the newspaperman's cane flicked into position. Pock Face tripped, tried to catch his balance and crashed headfirst through a glass table. Fred's cane withdrew so fast that no one even noticed what had caused the startling noise.

I headed for a building at the end of the swimming area and dodged inside, while a crowd gathered around Pock Face. I found myself in a gym filled with exercise equipment. Hearing the sound of running water, I tiptoed down a corridor, past a steam-filled shower room and into another narrow passageway where six foot lockers lined the walls. This was as far as I could go because the door at the far end was padlocked.

The sound of water stopped abruptly and voices drifted from the shower room, gradually growing nearer. I opened the nearest locker and closeted myself inside as two men swung around the corner into the dressing corridor.

"Some party," one said. "Loaded with beautiful dolls."

"You can say that again! When Man Beech throws a big one, he booby traps the whole joint."

The first man laughed. "Yeah, he's got a little black book a mile long. I ought to know. I used to work for him."

The locker next to mine snapped open. "No fooling, Joe, I didn't know that."

"Sure," Joe said. "Hell, I was lucky to get out when I did. That was about two years ago. Believe me, Jerry, I know things about Manfred Beech that would make your head spin."

"You wouldn't be talking about the Macelli rubout, would you?"

Joe's voice lowered. "That's right."

"You think he did it?"

"I know he did. I was with Macelli that night at the party. I knew Beech was setting him for a scare, but I didn't know he was serious. After it happened I blew town. Hit for Reno until it was all over."

Jerry rattled something in his locker. "You're damned lucky you did. He might have fingered you for the trigger man like he did Paul Bates. You really think Beech did the squeezing?"

"Hell, yes! But, as I see it, there's only one person who could have put Beech in the gas chamber. And I'm damned sure they got her by now."

"Who's that?"

"You remember that stacked blonde, used to hang around Beech's joint?"

"He's had dozens of them."

"Sylvia—Sylvia Loring."

"Don't think I ever knew her."

"Doesn't matter," Joe said, leaning against the locker that contained my dripping, breath-held shape. "The name was probably a phony like most of 'em around Vegas. But I'll tell you one thing, Jerry, there wasn't a phony curve in her body. She was built in Texas by Texans. If you ever got home on the range with that, brother, you wouldn't forget."

"I gather you did all right."

"Once," Joe groaned. "Never again. She was like dope. Once you were hooked-really hooked, you could offer your soul to the devil for five cents and he wouldn't buy it. She was the kind who really gives. But when she started to take, look out."

"How'd Beech get mixed up with her?"

"Easy. She was a nurse here in town. Beech needed an aspirin one night and called her."

"So?"

"So, Beech liked what she gave him. He kept liking it all the way to the night he squeezed Macelli into the obituary column."

Jerry rattled his locker again and I nearly jumped out of my skin. "This Sylvia dame, she was there?"

"Was she? It just so happens our fair buxom Sylvia practically engineered the squeeze. She knew Macelli held the wedge against Beech's expansion plans. And Man was hooked, but good. You take it from there."

"So, Sylvia saw the shooting, right?"

"That's what I think. They tell me she disappeared right after. Whether she ran or whether they got her then and there, I don't know. In fact, I really don't know anything. I'm just talking, understand, and you never heard a word!"

"Sure, I understand, Joe. Hell, we're old pals. Now come on, get dressed and let's get back to the party."

I stiffened. Clothes hung outside my locker. Joe moved, banged his fist loudly.

"You're okay, Jer, I don't know why I said that. We both work for respectable joints. I never squeezed a trigger in my life."

"Me neither."

"I'll tell you one thing I'd like to squeeze, though."

"Sylvia Loring?"

"You're damn right. Just one more time. She had everything but the kitchen sink."

He snapped open my locker and his square jaw slid open as if it had been hit with a sledge hammer. He was a husky, broad-shouldered man with a niche in his chin. He had a lot of hair on his chest and his hips tapered down like the "after" photos in a physical culture ad. All this was obvious, and much more, because at the moment he didn't have a stitch on his back. For a long instant, we both stood silently, staring. Jerry had his back turned and was bent over tying his shoes. Joe finally made his move. He picked up his towel, wrapped it around his middle and slammed the locker closed in my face.

"Jerry?"

"Yeah. What's the matter, Joe, you look like you've seen a ghost?"

"No!" Joe laughed faintly. "I just decided to skip the party for a while and work out in the gym. I need the exercise. You don't mind, do you, Jer?"

"No, of course not. Hey, you're not mad are you? You look mad, Joe."

"No, just forgot what I said about Manfred Beech that's all. Just forget it."

Jerry laughed now in the same forced way. "You know me, Joe. Old

383

pals, remember? I'll see you outside."

"Okay."

When Jerry was gone, I emerged from my hiding place. Joe's mouth was till somewhat askew and he wiped his hand across to straighten it.

"How'd you get in there, Sylvia?"

"I've been inside for almost two years, Joe," I said, pitching my voice in the sexy way I thought Sylvia might talk. "Don't you feel sorry for me?"

"Cut the ad libs. Does Beech know you're here?"

"Of course. We've already kissed and made up."

"I'll bet. And did you kiss and make up with Pigeyes and The Worm, too?" I winced.

"I thought so," Joe continued. "You see, I happen to know more than what I told Jerry. Those two cozy characters have been looking for you, I understand. They've been hoping to blow you up like a balloon. Only they wouldn't have to work very hard on your upper story, would they, Syl?"

I caught what his eyes were feasting on and pulled my soggy gown back into place. That's when he saw my identification card pinned inside. He ripped it loose.

"What's this?"

"If you must know, I'm not Sylvia Loring. The last time I saw Pigeyes he was making like a submarine hit by a depth charge and The Worm was picking glass out of his toothless mouth."

Joe read the words on the card aloud and then reread them, shaking his head. "What kind of a gag are you pulling now, Sylvia? You're no private eye."

"Name's Honey West," I said, lifting my skirt. "You said you knew Sylvia pretty well. Did she ever have this fixture?"

He stared at the birthmark on my thigh. "I—I don't remember. What difference does it make?"

"Plenty. You seem like a fairly honest guy. Sylvia Loring's back in town. Only this time she's mixed up in a kidnapping. It's possible Manfred Beech engineered the theft. Use your head. If I really were Sylvia would I be hanging around this place?"

He grimaced. "No. I guess you wouldn't. But, dammit, you sure look like her."

384

"Yes, I know."

He handed me back my ID card and I tucked it inside my gown."

"A private dick, huh?" he said suspiciously. "I never met one with a birthmark before."

"I only showed you for identification purposes."

"Yeah. Well, if you are a private eye I don't know nothing, understand? Nothing!"

"You don't sound that way."

He advanced a step. "You couldn't be carrying mini tape inside that damned gown, could you?"

"You know better than that."

His hands tightened on the towel around his waist. "The Macelli squeeze is just hearsay. It wouldn't stand up in any court. That's why Beech doesn't bother me. But that doesn't mean he wouldn't if I opened my trap at a hearing."

"I didn't ask you to, did I?"

"And as far as any kidnapping is concerned, I don't know a thing. So, next time pick on someone else's locker, will you?"

"Look, Mister..."

"Williams. Joe Williams. I work for a clean joint on the strip. Nothing funny at the tables and no trigger squeezing. Get me?"

"I got you," I said. "But unless you help me, Mister Williams, I'm not going to help you."

"What do you mean?"

"I mean if I get out of here in one piece—without your help—I'll see to it you're subpoenaed for a hearing on the Macelli job."

His fists clenched. "You're asking for trouble."

"I've got trouble." I said. "I don't have to ask for it. Beech's ghouls are outside. They think I'm Sylvia. And they're not going to change their way of thinking until I'm six feet under."

"What do you want me to do?"

I glanced down the corridor. "There must be some clothes in one of these lockers that'll fit me."

"You mean you want to masquerade as a man?"

"Alone I probably wouldn't stand a chance. With you I might..."

385

Footsteps clattered on the floor inside the gym.

"The locker, quick!" Joe said.

I wasn't back inside two seconds before the footsteps reached the corridor. Then they slowed to a halt.

"Oh, it's you, Jerry," Joe said. "I'll be out in a sec. Had a helluva workout with the bar bells, I'll tell you."

Jerry didn't say a word in return. He didn't have to. Other footsteps moved in the corridor. Joe let out a harsh gasp and then pitched over hard on the floor. The bullet that killed him apparently came from a silencer because all I heard of its deadly passage was the sound of its ricochet off the door of my locker.

Chapter Twelve

Manfred Beech's deep voice said, "Here's the key. Take him out the back way—fast."

"What about his clothes, boss?" I couldn't mistake the gravel tone of Pigeyes.

"He won't need them where he's going. A car's waiting outside. Jerry, you and Pigeyes take him out to Boulder Dam. I want The Worm to stay here with me. We've still got to find that dame."

"Okay, boss."

They moved in the corridor. Somebody unlocked the back door and Joe Williams was carried outside. I waited, wondering if they'd all gone out to the car. They wanted me bad. So bad they were probably going to turn Beech's desert mansion upside down after Williams' body was out of the way. They might even begin with the lockers. Now was really my only chance.

I opened the door a crack and peered out. The Worm stood a few feet away, near the door, apparently watching the others outside. Distant sounds told me they were placing the body in a car. Other noises drifted from the pool area where drunken voices still rose gaily. I squeezed through the locker opening, taking great pains not to release my pressure too suddenly on the metal floor.

Once on the cement, I crept stealthily toward the gym, never looking around, fearing at any moment The Worm would turn. He didn't. At least, not until I was past the shower room and out of sight. Then my steps quickened. Fred was waiting outside.

"I thought sure you were dead by now," he said, grabbing my arm.

387

"Beech and his playmate went barreling in there a few minutes ago with blood in their eyes. How'd they miss you?"

"I was wrapped up in a Turkish locker," I said. "Let's get out of here before Beech comes back. He just had an old employee fired."

Fred got the innuendo and grimaced. "Who was it?"

"Guy named Joe Williams. He took an old friend into his confidence. What he didn't know was that the old friend was on Beech's payroll. Come on."

"Which way? That goon at the front door surely must have been tipped off by now."

The desert mansion enclosed its Z-shaped swimming pool like the claw of a giant lobster. Glass windows and doors created the inner walls. Somewhere behind those sun-splashed mirrors there had to be an unguarded exit.

I jerked Fred through the first available opening just as The Worm come out of the gym, closely followed by Beech. His bandaged face told me all I wanted to know. They had discovered the open locker and put two and two together.

We ducked behind a curtain and waited. They surveyed the people around the pool, then Beech's eyes strayed to the partially open glass door near where we were hiding.

"Have you got a gun?" I whispered.

"Are you kidding?" Fred groaned. "Where's yours?"

"Probably in L.A. by now. It went into the aqueduct tube. Haven't had a chance to buy a new one."

"Some private eye you are."

Beech's gaze froze on our door. He tapped The Worm on his skinny shoulder.

"They're hot," I said, glancing around the room. "Do they know yet you're with me?"

"I don't think so."

"You want to gamble?"

"I've gambled all my life, baby. You name it."

I crossed to a bar built against the far wall, poured a tall shot of bourbon in a fancy glass and handed it to Fred.

"Take a swig," I insisted.

"I'm a teetotaler," he said, gulping half the contents of the glass.

"So I notice."

I spilled some of the whiskey down the front of his suit.

"Hey!" he protested. "That stuff stains."

"Not as bad as blood," I said.

"Beech and his Buddy were already heading in our direction. I tore Fred's tie loose, ripped open his shirt and jerked him toward a bed in the corner.

"Judas Priest, Honey, what the hell are you doing?"

I threw back the covers, dove underneath face down. I managed to peel my gown off the threw it on the floor. I pulled a pillow over my head. At the same time I hurled the remainder of the bourbon over the bed and went limp, still clutching the glass.

Fred had about a second to figure out my plan before Beech and The Worm barged through the door.

"What's going on here?" Beech demanded.

Fred wasn't much of an actor, but he had guts. I watched him from under the pillow and he wasn't about to let them investigate my prone, half-naked body. His cane flew up angrily, pointed directly at The Worm's chest.

"What do you think is going on?" Fred demanded, feigning a drunken stupor. "I'm having a little party of my own, do you mind?"

"Do you know who you're talking to?" The Worm said, advancing a few steps.

"Sure, I know," Fred said, staggering slightly. "The great and magnificent Manfred Beech. I'm having a wonderful time as you can plainly see. Thanks for inviting me. Now scram."

Beech said, "I don't think I did invite you. Who let you in, gimpy?"

Fred stiffened. "I let myself in. Your boy at the door didn't have a chance to argue. Now blow before my breakfast gets cold."

"Who do you work for, gimp?" Beech asked.

"Myself. Who do you work for? Money?"

I tensed myself for the attack, but I didn't come. Manfred Beech just stood there, openly awed by this frail, crippled man who baited him so viciously.

After a long moment, he said, "I like you, gimp. I ought to break you in half, but I like you. You got real guts. I could use a man like you."

"Yeah," Fred returned, slumping down on the bed. "Well, I couldn't use a man like you. Not right now. Don't you see I'm busy?" He began to stoke my bare back.

Beech said, "Sure. Who's the doll? Anybody I know?"

Fred's hand stopped, almost too quickly. "Just a broad I picked up around the pool. Works downtown. No class, but plenty of you know what."

"Hey, boss," The Worm said, "let me work this creep over. I don't like his looks."

I could hear Beech's first slam off The Worm's bandaged face, driving the toothless man against the glass door. Then Beech flattened him with another hard right that made the skinny gunman scream with pain.

The gambler stood over the fallen man. "I don't like your looks either! If you ever try that again, so help me, you'll never live to tell about it!"

"I'm sorry, boss," The Worm said, "I wasn't going to…"

"Get out of here and find her, you'll find yourself in trouble. Only this time you won't be chewing glass, understand?"

Beech turned back to Fred. "Well, do you want to work for me?" the gambler asked. "I think I may need a good man one of these days. As sort of a replacement."

"Maybe," Fred murmured.

I sensed the ease with which Manfred Beech could hurl his vehemence. Fred's fingers, digging at my back nervously, told me he sensed the same thing, but his mouth didn't seem to get the message.

"Call me sometime," he said to the gambler.

Beech was not a person to fool with too long. I suddenly knew Fred wasn't the man for the job. Any job, except the newspaper writing. He didn't have the finesse. And, besides that, he was a lousy drunk. I put my arm up from underneath the blanket and savagely pulled him down next to me.

"Love me, baby," I mumbled.

Beech laughed. He went for the door. "Have a good time, gimpy. It's on the house." Then, he stopped, "What'd you say her name was?"

"I didn't," Fred managed to say, despite my tight grip.

Beech whistled. He must have picked up the dress. "You really must have something there. Sure you can handle it alone?"

Fred couldn't stand remarks leveled at his physical handicap. He tried to rise, but my arm around him stiffened. "If I can't," he said, after an instant, "I'll call, okay?"

"Okay," Beech said. "And don't forget to call me on that other matter as well. You'll come out ahead in the long run, believe me."

Fred nodded. Beech must have started to toss down my gown, when he noticed my ID card lying on the floor. My heart stopped as he said, "This looks interesting." I realized he was examining it.

"I thought you said she worked downtown," he said suspiciously. "It says here she's a private eyeball from Long Beach."

"I didn't say what downtown she works," Fred said. "In fact, she didn't even tell me. I just took one look at her and guessed."

"Well, you guessed wrong, gimpy." He moved toward the bed. "And I'm beginning to think I guessed wrong about you. Let's see what she looks like."

Fred didn't waste any motion. He took the pillow from my head and threw it in Beech's face. The gambler fell back, reached inside his coat, but Fred was too fast for him. His cane rose twice and fell both time on Beech's skull. He didn't make a whimper. Fred's cane came off second best. It broke in half and flew across the room. I swung around in bed and grasped my dress.

"Is he dead?" I demanded.

Fred stared at Beech's swiftly reddening face. "I don't know. He's still breathing. Do people usually do that when they're dead?"

I pulled my gown on and helped him to his feet. "Now you've really fixed us, haven't you? We might have got away free, if you hadn't been so smart."

"He called me a gimp. I can't live with that kind of talk."

"No," I said. "But you seem perfectly willing to die with it. Come on."

I pulled him toward the door, but he faltered without his cane.

He sank to his good knee and grinned. "Leave me, baby. I've had my fun. Now scram. I'll make it alone."

He was almost dead weight, but I jerked him to his feet. "Listen to me, buster. I may not be as big as the guy who hauled you in off the front lines at Cologne, but I'll bet I'm just as mad. Anybody who takes a Brodie as easily as you do!"

Fred's teeth gritted together and he stood alone before I caught him again.

"Damn you, Honey! I knew I loved you for some reason, but I never thought of you as a crutch."

Well you'd better readjust your thinking," I said, moving toward the door again. "Because once we're out of here I'm not going to be stuck with any gimp, understand?"

His eyes widened as I had hoped they would. He was really mad now. And he was going to stay mad. That was the way he had to be if we were both going to get out this place alive. And, in a way, Fred knew it. He jerked me through the opening onto the cement rim of the swimming pool.

"Which way?" he demanded.

"If I know Beech, there's only two ways out and one of those is padlocked."

We veered toward the front of the house.

"I told you I was a good gate-crasher," Fred murmured, as we entered the palatial living room. He picked up an expensive vase. "You haven't seen nothing yet."

The man at the front door managed to dodge Fred's vase, but I had something he hadn't counted on. Beech's fancy-handled .45 revolver. I pushed it into his ribs and smiled.

"Don't make a sound," I said. "Just be a perfect gentlemen and help my friend and me out to our car."

He grinned back, almost too broadly, and placed his arm under Fred's shoulder. We moved out quietly to Fred's car. Beech's doorman helped Fred inside and then I encouraged him to crawl into the back seat. He didn't argue. Especially after I relieved him of a neat little .38 he had tucked in an underarm holster. Then I got behind the driver's seat and handed Fred the artillery.

That was before I realized we had another passenger in the back seat. Somebody I'd never expected to see in a million years. Sitting there so ca-

sually, you'd almost think he'd been installed in Detroit, was Phillip
Sharkey. And he had a gun, too.

Chapter Thirteen

"Don't move, Miss West," Sharkey said. "You either, Sims. Just deposit those weapons on the floor, if you please."

Fred didn't please, but he complied. "Now what?"

I studied the millionaire's red-rimmed eyes. "Thought you gave me thirty-six hours?"

"That's right," Sharkey said. "I did. But that was before I knew you were playing around with Man Beech."

"Playing around?" I laughed. "If you call that play then hire a mortician to referee the next game, not a private eye."

"I'll do that," Sharkey growled. "Drive straight to the Sheriff's office and no funny business."

"Exactly what I had in mind," I said. "The sooner the better before Mr. Beech wakes up and starts counting his teeth."

"What's that supposed to mean?"

"Nothing," I said, "only our friend here from the Fourth Estate may be pushing up daisies instead of pencils if he's not careful."

Fred swallowed deeply. So did I. We both knew Beech and his gruesome twosome would make us really suffer if we were caught.

After I changed into something more suitable, I told my story to Mark Storm and a half dozen deputies in the Clark County Sheriff's office.

"You actually heard this guy Williams state as a fact that Beech squeezed the Macelli trigger?" one of the deputies questioned.

"He didn't witness the shooting, but he said it was pre-arranged by Beech. I think Williams got all of this from Sylvia Loring Verse before she blew town two years ago."

394

"She was the murderer?"

"That's Williams' version," I answered.

"And Beech has been gunning for her ever since."

"I would assume so."

"Why did Beech mistake you for Sylvia Loring?"

Mark rose. "I can answer that one. They're look-alikes. Same height, weight, build. Same color hair and eyes."

A tall Vegas deputy handed me a cigarette. "What happened to Williams after you overheard his conversation with this Jerry?"

"He was carried out feet first. I think you'll find him floating around in Lake Mead."

"Who did it? Jerry?"

"I'm not sure. I was inside the locker when he came back with Beech and his two stooges. I have a hunch it was either Pigeyes or The Worm."

The interview broke up abruptly. They issued warrants for the four men on suspicion of murder. Half of the deputies headed for Beech's party. The others were dispatched to Lake Mead. Temporarily the man we'd brought in was jailed on the same charge.

Mark and I walked to a nearby hash house squeezed between two garish, neon-lit gambling joints, and ordered two coffees, black. Tinny western music clanged off-key and the repeated *Zunk-Zunk-Zunk* of the cylinders grinding to a stop inside slot machines created a background reminiscent of an aircraft factory during the war. Mark told me Fred had borrowed a cane and gone somewhere to file his story.

"You should have stopped him," I said. "Beech is not going to be satisfied until he pays Fred back for that beating. And don't think he's still at his party just waiting for a caravan of sheriff's cars to drive up, either."

"I know," Mark said. "Fred conned me into believing he'd wait until we were through questioning you."

"What happened to Sharkey?"

"Slipped out a side door, I suppose. He flew in from Frisco about two hours ago. I met him at the airport. He's convinced you're mixed up in the kidnapping somehow. I've tried to explain what went on out at the aqueduct, but he's a very stubborn guy. He's certain you were hired to engineer the crime. And since he found you out at Beech's place, he's more convinced than ever."

"How did he happen to be in Fred's car?"

Mark shrugged. "He says he took a taxi out to Beech's joint because he wanted to talk to him. He knew you were with a newspaperman, saw the Long Beach press card in the window of Fred's car, so he climbed in and waited. I guess he didn't have long to wait."

I stirred my coffee and thought about Sharkey and his income tax problem. "What do you think about Sharkey? Could kidnapping his own son save him ten million dollars?"

"I don't see how, Honey. The Bureau of Internal Revenue takes a dim view of tax delinquents. Especially those in Sharkey's bracket."

"Guess so," I said.

"Beech seems more logical. He knew Sylvia and he had a grudge against Sharkey."

"Yeah, but, Mark, assuming Sylvia Verse was the blonde woman who snatched Sharkey's baby, why would Beech be after her if they were in this together?"

"He might have changed his mind at the last minute."

"Why?"

"Maybe because he realized if she were caught she'd spill the beans about the Macelli killing. Or maybe they had a run-in, who knows?"

I shook my head. "I can't buy that, Mark, especially in view of the fact that Beech's gunmen were searching for Sylvia in the L.A. area instead of Frisco. Wouldn't it have been obvious to Beech—if he were involved—that Sylvia was operating in the Bay area, since that's where the kidnap took place?"

Mark pushed back his hat and squinted at the mammoth replica of a cowboy across the street which symbolized Las Vegas. "Okay," he said, after a moment, "it should have been obvious to Beech's men where to locate her. But maybe they went to Frisco first, found out she had changed her address and apparently gone to L.A. Once they reached the Los Angeles area, they were stymied. So they hired Gimbel, a local squeeze man, to produce the goods."

"Only he had the same kind of luck trying to locate Sylvia because she was in San Francisco."

"That's right," Mark continued. "Then one fine day he saw you waltzing along the streets of Long Beach, figured you were Sylvia until you wound up in your office."

"Sounds good, keep going."

"He decided the only way to make any money was to pull a switch. He got your measurements, bought a complete woman Marine's outfit and had each piece stamped with her name and serial number."

I raised my hand. "That's where I get confused. How'd he know her serial number? Where'd he get her ID card?"

"He had one made using the picture Beech supplied him. The serial number and other pertinent information were supplied by a girl friend of Gimbel's who worked in the El Torro disbursement office."

I gazed at Mark suspiciously.

"Oh, it's a fact," he added. "She's already been arrested. We think we've also found the man in Long Beach who printed up the ID card."

"Got it all figured out, huh?"

"We think so. Now why don't you go home while the going's good."

I took out a mirror and applied some lipstick. "Tell me one thing," I said. "Why did Gimbel put me in a Marine uniform if Beech knew that Sylvia had deserted months before?"

"That was Gimbel's mistake," Mark said, "and he paid for it with his life."

"Maybe. But, I have a crazy sort of hunch he was going to pay for it anyway whether he produced the real McCoy or me, Marine uniform or not." I moved out of my chair. "You take it from there, Lieutenant."

He caught my arm. "Honey, I'm warning you…"

"And I'm warning you, Lieutenant. I'm going to find that baby. Phillip Sharkey hired me with the understanding that I could name my own price if I found him alive before midnight tonight. Well, my price may be Sharkey's neck."

Mark followed me to the door. "Honey, there's one other thing I didn't tell you."

"What's that?"

"Web Stevens has been arrested."

I whirled around. "What for?"

"Murder. Kern County deputies came after him about an hour ago. They found that stiff out by the aqueduct. He's being taken back for a formal inquest."

"What do you mean, being?"

"He checked in at the Cortez. The Kern County men went to pick him up just before you came in with Sharkey and Fred."

"Did they get him?" I demanded.

"I imagine so. He was in his room when they telephoned the desk."

I exhaled angrily. "Nice going, Lieutenant. A man saves my life and what does he get for it? A phony charge slapped against him. You know that was justifiable homicide."

Mark scowled. "Sure, I know it and you know it, but we both know the law doesn't work that way. He has to be formally exonerated at an inquest. Your testimony's about the only evidence that'll clear him."

"Thanks," I said. "It couldn't be possible that I smell a rat sticking his nose in this, could I? A rat named Mark Storm?"

"Now, Honey…"

"Now, Honey, my foot!" I said. "You know darn well Web's arrest could have been averted until after Sharkey's baby was found. And you also know that as the only material witness to that shooting at the bridge I could be taken in on a trumped-up warrant and shipped back to Mojave—now—this very moment."

Mark grinned. "I hate to hear you put it that way, Honey, but it's for your own good."

He pulled a paper from inside his coat pocket, but I was two jumps in front and stayed that way until I reached the street. A cab came bolting around a corner and I ran for it. Mark was fast, even for his size. He caught me again, momentarily, and only lost his hold when I dashed between two parked cars. His coat snagged on a partially raised trunk lid and flipped him over. The last I saw of Lieutenant Storm, as I climbed into the cab, was one of his hands struggling to pull himself up, still clutching the warrant for my arrest.

An empty sheriff's car was parked in front of the Cortez Hotel when my cab drew up.

398

"Pull around the corner," I directed.

The driver eyed my tight-fitting white dress and smiled. "Okay, lady, you're the doctor."

I ignored the remark, stepped from the cab and paid him from money Mark had given me back at the Sheriff's office.

When he was gone, I scrutinized the outside of the four-story hotel. A fire escape zigzagged down from the roof. Web Stevens wasn't on it, but somebody else was. A man wearing a Sheriff's office uniform. And even from where I stood, the tall, lanky frame of the deputy from Mojave was too big to miss. He got the same impression about me and yelled.

"Hey! Miss West! We want to talk to you!"

I didn't want to talk to him. He was three flights up and I knew I had a bigger jump on him then I'd had on Mark Storm. I ran down the side street, turned into an alley and kept on going until I reached a gambling establishment loaded with one-armed bandits and people. I pushed inside, brushed past a few loose hands clutching loose change, and wound up beside the craps table.

"Come on, baby," the man rattling the dice moaned, "make it eighter from Decater."

His fist lashed out, releasing the two cubes. They spun against the bright green felt, bounced off a sideboard and ground to a sickening stop. Snake eyes. I didn't wait to hear the loser groan again. A man wearing a uniform stepped through the front door and surveyed the crowd. I headed for the back way, but there didn't seem to be one. A long, jam-packed bar circled the rear wall of the gambling joint. I squeezed in between two stools and discovered too late that I had squeezed my way right into trouble. Two highly intoxicated young men, obviously in their early twenties, grabbed me fast.

"Hello, sweetheart," the one with a crew cut and dimples said, gripping me tightly. "Where you been all my life?"

I glanced toward the door and saw the deputy moving toward us, so I smiled instead of prying loose the familiar fingers.

"I've been looking for you two handsome dogs."

The last word carried way too much emphasis, but they were long gone and didn't notice.

"What are you drinking, baby?" The one with a tilted nose and freckles was a hand's length below my spine and heading for trouble.

"Any sort of poison that's available," I said, trying to stem the tide. There were just too many hands to cope with. "A martini?"

"Coming up!"

That's not all that was coming up. One hand was working down my ribs and angling for the promised land. So was the deputy. He was past the craps table and angling for the bar like a homing pigeon. That's when I decided it was do or die. I grabbed Freckles and drove my lips against his wide mouth. He nearly went off his stool before the impact hit his dulled brain. His hands slid up to my face allowing me to cradle his head with my right arm, blocking off any possible view from the deputy's side. Then I poured my heart and soul into the ruse.

I must have poured too much because when it was all over, the crowd around the bar applauded riotously. So did the deputy. Only his applause was directed on my shoulder as he prodded me to come along. Fortunately, my display of affection made Freckles and his friend hesitant to see me leave. Crew Cut started to argue with the deputy and was pushed out of the way by my lipstick-smeared lover who had more hands than brains. I could testify to that, and for a moment, I thought I was going to have to. Freckles lashed out with one of his endless hands rolled into a fist. Luckily the blow missed the deputy, but landed on another patron and all hell broke loose. Bodies began to fly. A pair of knuckles found his range and he went out of the picture completely. SO did I. The street outside the gambling den was filled with curious, wide-eyed onlookers and even more deputies, but I managed to slip through unnoticed.

Blistering mid-day Nevada sun had me in a sweat before I stopped running two blocks away and caught my breath. This sort of exertion, especially the variety I'd experienced squeezed between the two Rover boys, had to go. I walked back to the Cortez Hotel. The sheriff's car was gone. At the front desk I learned that Web Stevens had escaped arrest.

"Did he leave any messages?" I asked.

The desk clerk's eyebrows knitted suspiciously and he made a pretense of checking Web's box. When he returned, shaking his head dismally, I flashed my ID card.

"I work with the Sheriff's office," I lied. "Now shall we try again."

He drew a piece of paper from a drawer near the switchboard. "I was afraid you were on his side. We don't appreciate this sort of investigation, but if it's in the interests of law and…"

"What's the message?"

"It just came in a few minutes ago," the clerk said. "After your——your deputies left."

"Well?"

"It was from Mister Stevens himself. Doesn't make much sense. He said, 'Tell Honey, I'm funny.'"

"What?" I grabbed the message.

"Tell Honey, I'm funny," the clerk repeated. "He's funny all right. In fact, for my dough, he's nuts."

I walked outside, still clutching the note. It really didn't make sense, that was the trouble. I crossed to a newsboy on the corner.

"What's funny mean to you?" I asked, buying a paper. "What's that lady?"

"You heard me. What's funny mean to you in Vegas?"

He shrugged his narrow shoulders and stared at me as if he thought I was ready for a white coat with wrap around sleeves. "It means have a good time, lady. Everybody does in Vegas. Don't you?"

"Sure," I said. "But doesn't it mean something in particular. Some place, for instance?"

He shook his head. "The Dunes, that's a funny place. Everybody says it has a very funny show. That TV comedian is playing there. You know who I mean."

I walked off down the street and opened the paper to its theatre and entertainment pages. That's when I saw the full page advertisement announcing the opening of a new nightclub out on the strip. What really caught my eye was the name of the girlie extravaganza debuting tonight. It was called, "What's funny, honey?" I didn't laugh. At the top of the ad were giant block letters, MANFRED BEECH PRESENTS….

I hailed a cab, but didn't go directly to Beech's new casino. I stopped at a swank hairdresser's shop and bought a long black wig. It took almost every cent I had, but it was worth the money. For the first time in my life I was tired of being a blonde. And for a very good reason.

Then I phoned person-to-person to San Francisco and talked with another newshound friend of mine, Sid Lowman of the Chronicle. I asked him to check on Phillip Sharkey's marital status. He returned my call twenty minutes later with some very surprising answers, including a few tempting morsels he had extracted from a lawyer who formally worked for Llewlyn James, Sharkey's deceased father-in-law. My next step was Beech's new multi-million-dollar casino-hotel.

Web Stevens sat in a far corner of the Four Leaf Clover Room, wedged between the wall and a table crawling with visiting salesmen noisily celebrating the rebirth of the human race.

He didn't recognize me through the black wig until I put my arm around him and whispered, "The next bundling party's yours, mister."

"Honey!" he exclaimed. "What in the world?"

"Haven't you ever met a dark-haired Venusian before? They're very common where I come from."

"You did get my message!"

"Of course. How'd you manage to dodge those long armfuls of law?"

Web grinned. "Luckily, I happened to see them arrive outside the hotel before they saw me."

I scanned the elegant confines of the Clover Room. It was about as ultra-modern as Manfred Beech could get for several million bucks. The room, bar and tables were all shaped like four-leaf clovers. The curved ceiling, flood-lighted in cool green, had at least fifty thousand silver dollars embedded into the plaster. Web followed my gaze.

"Genuine, naturally," he said. "Just knock on the walls. I'd love to have been the plasterer."

"Beech may wind up digging them out with his fingers, believe me."

"What do you mean?"

"Apparently he killed a man two years ago. The local gendarmes are searching for him now. They have an idea he engineered the kidnapping as well."

Web's eyes narrowed. "Where'd they dig that up?"

"I loaned 'em my shovel after Beech nearly buried me with his."

Web listened intently while I told him the story. His face showing more anger with each new word. When I stopped, he said, "So that's the reason for the wig."

"That and the fact that Mark Storm wants me out of the way as well. There are so many warrants for arrest floating around Vegas right now, nobody's safe—with or without a wig. Come on, let's get out of here."

"Where are we going?"

"After a submarine."

"A what?"

"Ever hear of the U.S.S. Sharkey?"

"You mean Phillip Sharkey?"

"That's right."

"But, Honey, he's in Frisco."

"Not any more. He arrived this morning. He's got a hunch I'm mixed up in the kidnapping. Only I've got the same hunch about him."

Web gripped my arm, glanced at the loud, boisterous men at the next table and said, "Honey, I told you. No man would have his own child kidnapped, not for all the money in the world."

I shook my head. "I don't think you have any idea how much money there is in the world, Web. Or how much is available at Phillip Sharkey's fingertips."

"Then if money's the motive that lets Sharkey out, doesn't it?"

"I'm afraid that lets him in, but good. You know, Web, aside from his income tax problems, there's something I just learned about Phillip Sharkey's financial status that's quite amazing."

"What's that?"

"He's the richest poor man who was ever born."

"All right," Web said, "he came up the hard way. I've read articles. He fought his way out of the slums, so what?"

"So, you must not have read what I read between the lines."

"I read only what's on the paper." Web said, losing patience.

"What I'm referring to is on paper. A San Francisco lawyer has it in his possession. The paper is Llewelyn James' will. He's the late great father of Sharkey's wife. A very shrewd man. One of those corporation magnates who earned every penny the hard way and expected to take it with him, but couldn't find a hole deep enough. So, he did the next best thing and left everything in his daughter's name. Her maiden name. And then, just to be sure no one ever changed his last will and testament, he named a trustee to handle the estate in her name. Phillip Sharkey was left running the business, sharing in its profits, but never to share in James' legacy if divorce ever occurred."

"What makes you think a divorce is.."

"Philip Sharkey's a gambler, both in business and out. He got in trouble years ago with Manfred Beech, two years ago to be exact. Despite big losses at the gambling tables, Sharkey was able to recoop part of it by pulling out of an investment deal with Manfred Beech, thus costing Beech around a million dollars."

"I read about that," Web said. "It was on paper. Now get to the point."

"The point is, wives often get fed up with gambling husbands, especially when they lose. How did Margo feel about your losing streaks?"

Web glanced away. "I don't know. I suppose that was one of her reasons for walking out."

"Well, it may interest you to know that Pat Sharkey, formerly Pat James, did file for divorce before she went to the hospital. And, it may also be of interest that she was in a serious automobile accident years ago which caused her blindness and other complications. Another blow might…"

Web slumped back into his seat. "You don't think Sharkey would…"

"I don't think anything," I said. "All I know is that Phillip Sharkey will inherit a fantastic fortune if his wife doesn't come out of this. A fortune big enough to pay off any gambling debts, any back income tax and still leave him rich enough to live out the rest of his life in ease. Beside that," I added, "he was associated with Manfred Beech two years ago in a business deal—at about the same time that Beech was going with a buxom blonde named Sylvia Loring Verse."

Web lighted a cigarette and finished his drink. "Amazing," he said, after a moment, "how fantastically interwoven lives can get. Margo and me. Sharkey and his wife. We've never even met. Never spoken two words." He shook his head sadly. "And yet here we are. Margo's dead and Sharkey's wife is on the brink of dying if her child isn't returned." He looked into my eyes. "Maybe you're right, Honey. Maybe he's the one."

"I'm sorry, Web, I know this only stirs up bad memories, but…"

He tried to smile. "And then there's you, Honey. Twenty-four hours ago we hadn't even met." His jaw hardened angrily. "Where do we find Sharkey?"

"He's got a place here in Vegas. Not far. Are you game?"

"Are you kidding?"

Web tossed down some change and we threaded our way out of the crowded Clover Room. A clock in the lavish foyer told me it was noon.

I veered off for the powder room to redo my makeup for the battle ahead. On the way back, my face was reflected in a pane of glass between the horseshoe-shaped dining room and the corridor. I stopped to be sure I hadn't made any mistakes, when I noticed a very extraordinary thing. My hand flicked at a dark spot of my cheek, but it wouldn't come off. In fact, my reflection didn't even move. That's when I saw something else that nearly knocked me for a loop. My reflection wasn't wearing a black wig.

My hands flew to my head. This time the reflection did move, but not in the same direction. It pulled away from the glass and ran. It ran just the way I'd imagined it would—when Sylvia Verse and I finally came face to face.

Chapter Fourteen

I whirled, searching for an entrance into the dining room from this end
of the corridor, but there wasn't any. Web was still waiting in the lobby
when I raced through toward the huge gold doors which lead into the palatial theatre-dining room.

"Hey!" he yelled, ignoring startled onlookers. "What's going on?"

"Sylvia!" I managed to say, bursting into the dimly lighted, lavishly-dec-
orated room. Tables were arranged on four levels surrounding the sunken
stage like a gigantic horseshoe. I scanned quickly for the blonde woman.
Then, a light flickered and went out far up on the top tier and I bolted
around tables and chairs until I reached the door she'd vanished behind. A
fat man in a cook's hat faced me on the other side.

"Where'd she go?" I demanded.

"Who?" he said, started by my sudden appearance.

"The blonde. Where'd she go?"

"What blonde?"

I tore off my wig and the cook staggered back as if he'd been hit with
an H-bomb.

"Momma mia," he whispered. He crossed himself and stared dumbfounded at a rear door to the kitchen.

On the steps leading down to the parking lot, the harsh Nevada sunlight
blinded me for an instant. But not long enough to hide Sylvia's flight to a
white convertible with a black top, parked near the bottom of the steps.
She leaped inside as I sped down the cement ridges three at a time. She was
too far out in front. By the time I'd reached the asphalt, her car was crossing the lot toward the distant highway. And then it vanished in a cloud of

dust and traffic.

"Are you sure it was Sylvia?" Web said, as he drove his Thunderbird past the strip's fabulous clubs toward Sharkey's house.

"If she wasn't," I said, "I'm turning myself in for a new model. There are too many of us running around as it is."

"What would she be doing in Beech's club if he's gunning for her?"

"You could ask me the same question, except you know the answer. I read an advertisement in the paper. I don't know what she was applying for, but you can bet it wasn't for a cook's job."

We jolted around a corner, at my insistence, and whirled past expensive sprawling mansions on the west side of town.

"What do you expect to find at Sharkey's place?" Web asked. "We're wasting time. Sylvia wouldn't go there."

"Why not?"

"Well, it just stands to reason. She'd go where the kid is, wouldn't she? Sharkey wouldn't be fool enough to..."

"I don't know what kind of a fool he is," I said. "But he was foolish enough to hire me with threats. I don't work too well under those conditions."

Sweat streamed down Web's face. "I hope you know what you're doing."

"So do I. Where would a woman hide a kidnapped child in Las Vegas?"

"A million places. Maybe even down town in one of those crummy hotels."

"Where's your gun?" I asked.

"Open the glove compartment." I found his .38 back in its old resting place.

"How much further?" Web asked.

"About a mile." My dark wig lay between us on the seat. "Guess I won't need this thing any longer."

"What sort of clothes was Sylvia wearing?"

"A blue suit. Rather tailored as I recall. You know, there's one thing I can't figure."

407

"What's that?"

"She had a spot on her right cheek. Like a mole. High up underneath her eye. Sylvia Verse's photograph didn't show any such indentifying mark."

"Maybe the photographer removed it," Web suggested. "They can do a lot with retouching."

"That was an official Marine Corps photograph. I think you'll agree the service usually prints pictures as if they were shot under a microscope. Nothing is left to the imagination."

"How about an eyebrow pencil?" Web said. "A simulated mole. That is if she was Sylvia Verse."

We passed through a long stretch of yucca trees and desert before reaching Phillip Sharkey's weirdly elevated residence. The house jutted out atop a six-foot concrete foundation on three exposed I beams. Glass and aluminum rose into a formidable pyramid shape, capped by a round black chimney. Part of the house was suspended over Sharkey's S-shaped swimming pool and a high diving board protruded at the base of one slanted window. A gray Cadillac was parked in the driveway. We climbed a flight of over-sized butcher boards fastened to two black metal rods and knocked. Sharkey's thin face was bleached stone white when he opened the door.

"Oh, it's you, Miss West," he said dazedly. "Come in."

The steel magnate's desert home had an even more fabulous interior. It was a maze of thin steel wires which supported blocks of color, massive unframed aerial photographs and expensive oil paintings. Even the furniture was suspended on these rods, rich fabrics stretched taut over foam rubber in shades of orange, gray and white. Nothing touched the thick wool carpeting except the cables which slashed through its charcoal surface like rain on a stormy lake.

I introduced Web Stevens. "Sorry about your wife," Sharkey said, pouring us a drink with one hand. "I just talked to the doctors at the hospital. My wife's having a rough time. They're pretty worried and so am I. She's been asking about the baby."

Web nodded, crossed to one of the triangular windows that swept from floor to ceiling and stared silently at the snow-capped mountains in the distance.

Sharkey was wearing a lounge jacket and he kept his left hand in the pocket.

"May I look around?" I asked, moving toward a sheet of orange-colored peg board that lead into another room.

His voice stopped me cold. "You may not, Miss West! What do you think this is, open house?"

"No," I said, glancing at his angry face. "I thought you wouldn't mind if I took the ten-cent tour. This is a fantastic place. I take it the design was tailored to your wife's…"

"It's not for sale, Miss West, and neither is your story. At least, I'm not buying it. What do you want?"

I smiled. "The ladies room. Do you mind?"

He gestured at a conglomeration of wires and pictures and I snaked my way through, ending in an antique gold bathroom equipped with everything from wall-to-wall women etched vividly in the rubber tile, diamond shaped mirrors, an elevated bathtub with a dictaphone and books built into the side, a slot machine that dispensed paper towels after jerking on the handle and heat lamps and electric lights automatically controlled by the path you followed inside the room. One other feature really made my eyes bug. Blankets were stacked neatly on one of the marble top cabinets. They were small and blue and bore the imprint of a San Francisco hospital.

I snatched up one of them and showed it to Sharkey. He didn't flinch.

"Where'd you get this?" I asked. "And the others in the bathroom?"

"It's perfectly obvious," he answered. "You can read, can't you?"

"Sure," I said, tossing the blanket to Web and producing his gun. "Can you read this?"

He stared at the muzzle, frowning wryly. "So, it comes to this, does it, Miss West? Where's my baby?"

"You take a crack at that question, Mr. Sharkey. He can't be far with all those blankets on hand. Where's the nursery?"

"There isn't any. I brought these from San Francisco myself."

"Sure you did," I said.

"For identification purposes!" Sharkey blurted.

"Six blankets?" I demanded.

"Yes! Now get out of here!"

I didn't move. "How much were you planning to pay me, Mr. Sharkey, if I produced your child—alive—inside thirty-six hours?"

"I figured you'd ask for about ten thousand."

My shoulders heaved. "I'm sorry, but my price is one hundred thousand dollars."

"Get out!"

"Why not a hundred thousand?" I said. "In fact, why not a million? Be big about it! I'll never have a chance to collect. Not as long as you've got your own child in hiding."

"What?" He stepped back like he'd been struck with a whip. "You've got a lot of nerve to accuse me of such a thing! You must be out of your mind!"

Web stepped between us. "Honey, I tell you this is all wrong."

"Is it?" I said, pushing past Web and shoving the revolver into Sharkey's stomach. "Raise your left hand!"

"I will not!" he roared. "I'm calling the Sheriff's office. I know they have warrants out for both of you and…"

"Lift it, Admiral," I insisted, "or I'm going to torpedo you so hard your periscope will pop."

We pleaded, "Honey, don't…"

Sharkey knew I meant business. He raised his hand slowly. There were bloodstains on both palm and fingers.

"You'll never believe me," he said.

"I can believe that," I said, handing Web the revolver. "Here, cover him while I check the other rooms."

Sharkey protested, but I went into the kitchen. There was bright splatter linoleum on the floor. Something else, too. A big fat body with a dark mustache and a red hole in his chest. He was splattered around a bit himself. Enough to reveal he was quite dead.

Phillip Sharkey stared down at the dead man and shook his head dismally. "I didn't do it, believe me."

"Then who did?" I asked, examining several empty glasses on the sink. "There's nobody here but us chickens."

410

"I came home a short time ago," Sharkey stammered, "to get those blankets and take them to the Sheriff's office."

"Lieutenant Storm met you at the airport, why didn't you give them to him then—or later at the office?"

"I—I forgot."

"You seem to have a terrible memory, Mr. Sharkey, and besides that you couldn't have been in a very big hurry to give them those blankets."

"Why?"

"Well, do you usually change into a lounge coat when you rush home to get something important?"

"No, I—I changed when I saw your car coming into the driveway. You see, I didn't want you to…"

"Find the body?" I finished. "Naturally, who likes to have fat, old, bullet-riddled bodies found on their kitchen floor. Very embarrassing." The glasses were clean. No lipstick stains. "Finish your story."

"Look here, Miss West," Sharkey said suddenly, "you can't treat me like a criminal."

"I'm not," I said, checking the back door. It was unlocked. "I'm treating you like a client. Go ahead."

Sharkey wiped nervous fingers across his face and winced. "Well, it was hot after I got inside. This house gets that way with all this glass. I came in here to get a bottle of beer out of the refrigerator and—Well, he was lying there face down. I didn't know he was dead. I rolled him over and—That's how I got this blood on my hand!"

"Have you ever seen this man before?" I said.

"No!"

"Have you, Web?"

"No."

"Well, I have. He's great with a sawed-off shotgun. Examined my tonsils once."

Web snapped his fingers. "The bridge. You said he had a mustache. How do you like that?"

"I don't," I said. "According to the information the Perfessor gave us, that would leave only Sylvia."

"Sylvia who?" Sharkey demanded.

"Sylvia Verse, know her?"

The thin-faced millionaire shook his head.

"How about Sylvia Loring?"

"No."

I crossed the room and examined the stove. "You know few people for such a big man, it's pitiful. Do you own a gun?"

"Yes," Sharkey said. "Several. I go hunting frequently."

"How about pistols or revolvers?"

"A few of those, yes."

"Where?"

"Back home," Sharkey said angrily, "in Frisco! I have a gun case in my library. Now, look here, Miss West…"

"I'm going to look," I said, "but not in your library in Frisco."

He stopped me near the door. "All right, I do keep a revolver here. For protective measures. It's in a drawer in the master bedroom. But, I'm warning you…"

I dodged around steel cables until I reached a triangular bedroom with a fourteen foot photographic reproduction of Phillip Sharkey plastered from floor to ceiling on one wall. He stood firm-legged, eyes piercing down like two molten pools of metal being poured at one of his steel plants. Several bureau drawers were open and a white shirt, still wrapped in a Las Vegas cleaner's band, lay upside down on the carpet. A .38 revolver was tucked inside one of the drawers. I picked it up with a handkerchief and smelled the barrel. Web and Sharkey came into the room.

"This gun's been fired recently," I said.

"It—it couldn't have been," Sharkey stammered. "I've never used it. You're trying to frame me, Miss West."

I took another article from the drawer and held it up. A face peered at me from inside a white frame. A very familiar face. One I'd seen only an hour ago reflected in a window at Beech's casino. A face circled with taffy-colored hair. A face like mine, except for one big difference. It had a small dark spot high under the right eye.

"It's a frame, all right," I said, flashing the photograph at Sharkey. "Read the inscription."

His mouth sagged and for a very good reason. The inscription, in a

412

neat feminine hand, read, "To Phillip—The most powerful man in the world—I surrender! Sylvia."

"Where are you, Honey?" Mark Storm said, when I got him on the phone.

"Well, I'm not stuck in Mojave, no thanks to you," I said. "Hope you enjoyed that warrant with your lunch."

He groaned. "Are you with Web Stevens?"

"How could I be, Mark? Didn't they arrest him?"

"No, they didn't arrest him! And all because of some dumb blonde who sent half a dozen deputies on a wild goose chase through the downtown gambling joints!"

"Oh, I wouldn't say that blonde was so dumb," I said. "She got away, didn't she?"

"Yeah, she got away all right," Mark said. "But, if I have anything to do with it she's not going to keep getting away—and neither is he!"

"Fred's right," I said. "You are jealous."

"Jealous of what? It may interest you to know, sweetheart, that Beech and his killers are still on the loose. If I'm jealous it's only because they're probably nearer to ringing your neck than I am!"

"Did you find the stiff in Lake Mead?"

"No! I'm beginning to think you're off your rocker. Where are you? I hope it's a rest home, you need one!"

I glanced at Sharkey's bent figure, still held at bay by Web's revolver. "The only person taking a rest around here is lying in the kitchen, Lieutenant."

"Is he drunk? Are you at another damn party?"

"No, he's dead. I'm at a funeral."

"What?"

After hearing the condition of Sharkey's kitchen linoleum, Mark swore. "Are you sure it's the same man you saw out at the aqueduct, Honey?"

"If it isn't," I said, "he's got the same double trouble I've got, only his problems are over."

I described the eventful meeting with my reflection in Beech's new casino. This time the deputy didn't swear, but muffled sounds told me he

413

was swearing out a new warrant.

"Hey, Mark," I said, "while you're at it make one out for Phillip Sharkey, too."

"What for?" the deputy said.

"I've got a smoking revolver belonging to him and a photograph of Sylvia Verse that I lifted from his bedroom drawer. Now you take it from there, Lieutenant. I've got to run before your hound dogs start nipping at my heels again."

"Honey, wait…"

"Yes, Lieutenant?"

"Look, I'm sorry about trying to haul you in. I should have known better in the first place. If you've got evidence against Sharkey I promise you won't have to go back to Mojave."

"How about Web Stevens?"

Mark growled. "That's slicing it pretty thin, Honey."

"Yeah, I know," I said. "And when it comes to slicing me, Lieutenant, you've got a big badge with a pretty sharp edge and the slices come out looking like swiss cheese. Thank you, but no thank you. I'm not testifying at any inquest. Bye."

"Wait!"

"Yes?"

"All right, no formal inquest for either you or Stevens until after the child's found. That's all I can promise."

"Do I have your word?"

"Yes, but only if Sharkey, his gun and the stiff are still part of the surroundings when we arrive."

"Okay," I said, glancing at the two men. "They'll be here, including Stevens, but I've got your word Web won't be taken into custody."

"Yes."

"Thanks. Good-bye, Lieutenant."

"But, Honey, where are you? Where you going?"

"We're at Sharkey's place. I've got some unfinished business. See you."

"But…"

I hung up and said, "You stay here, Web, until the Sheriff's deputies arrive. I've got Lieutenant Storm's word that you won't be held for an inquest until after the baby's found."

Web's mouth tightened. "But, Honey, you…"

"Just keep that gun trained on Mr. Sharkey. I'll meet you in the same old place at seven-thirty. I'll explain more then." I tossed them both a kiss and sprinted down the steps to Web's car.

On the way back to the strip, I thought about Phillip Sharkey. He was in a tough spot. A real tough spot. But, so were a lot of people, myself included. There seemed to be only one solution. I started with some of the big hotels first, then migrated down to motels when it became obvious that my ruse would never work with desk clerks who served large clientele. I was about ready to give up when I finally hit pay dirt at a fairly big, new motel at the very end of the strip. I used the same pattern as I had with all the others, waltzing into the lobby as if I owned it, crossing to the desk and dangling my hand in the clerk's face.

"My key, please," I said, with an air of flip assurance.

"What room?" the young man asked, staring straight at my chest.

"Don't be silly," I said, leaning over the counter to give him a better view. "You know very well you don't have any other tenants who look like me." My mouth drew close to his. "Do you?"

"I—ah—What happened to your key?"

My index finger traced a heart on the back of his trembling hand. "I'm so forgetful. I must have misplaced it. Now isn't that silly?"

His mouth began to quiver and he glanced around the lobby. "You— you lonesome?" he asked.

"What do you think?" I moistened my lips with my tongue. "My husband's gone out of town for a few days. I think I'm going to be terribly lonesome in that dismal, old room."

His eyelids narrowed. "I'll bet. What about your baby?"

I nearly spoiled the whole thing with my reaction, but managed to convert it into condemnation. "What's the matter? You afraid of a little baby? I thought you were a great big strong man." I winked. "He won't say anything. He sleeps most of the time."

The clerk leaned back suspiciously, then he grinned. He didn't say another word. He didn't have to. He handed me the key to Room 91.

I patted his cheek and walked outside into the blistering sunlight. The motel was two stories high and plunged back into the desert, taking advantage of less boulevard frontage and more inexpensive sand. Room 91 was on the ground floor at the very end of the motel, beyond the swimming pool, the children's play area, everything. I noticed a few dusty cars and drawn shades. Two empty fifths sat outside 90. Inside the room, behind its dark open window, was the drunken laughter of a woman and loud music. As I passed by, she screamed delightedly and a man swore.

"Not so loud, baby!" His next words were drowned out by the increased roar of the radio.

I move to 91 and knocked. Nothing happened, so I tried the key. It was the last thing I tried for a long long while. As I started to open the door, a fist tried my jaw for size and found it adequate. So adequate, in fact, that my eyeballs spun like wheels on a slot machine. I don't know how they looked when they stopped spinning. All I knew was that somebody had it the jackpot. Me.

Chapter Fifteen

Manfred Beech was looking down at me when my vision cleared.

"Where's the baby, Sylvia?"

I groaned and felt my aching jaw. The motel room swam around a few more times and slowed to a stop. That's when I saw The Worm. He was standing next to Beech, rubbing his boney knuckles.

"Where's the baby, Sylvia?" Beech repeated.

"Alaska," I managed. "He prefers a cooler climate."

One of The Worm's metal-tipped shoes sank into my ribs and I spun across the room, nearly coming apart at the seams from the pain. I tried to rise, but a hollow eyed hulk clutching a .45 automatic pushed me down again.

"Let me work her over, boss," Pigeyes pleaded. "She'll talk."

"Yeah, I'll bet," Beech said, shoving his fat trigger man out of the way. The gambler's gray hair was streaked with dried blood and an ugly welt ran across his forehead. He studied my bruised face. "You're going to die, Sylvia, so you might as well come clean."

Clutching my sore ribs, I raised myself on one elbow and grinned. "There's too much dirt in here for that."

Beech straightened, then he smiled. "Same old Sylvia. So smart and yet so dumb."

"I'm smart enough to keep that kid away from you," I said, "until you pay off."

He laughed, deep in his throat. "Are you kidding? I wouldn't pay you a dime. You were crazy to have crossed the California border. Now the feds-s'll be in on it. Lift her up," he said to Pigeyes.

The radio in the next room roared, intermittently split with delirious squeals and laughter. Pigeyes pulled me to my feet, a fiery pain searing my left side. He smashed a stinging slap across my cheek that nearly dropped me again. In the reddish haze that followed, I noticed baby equipment stationed about the room. An electric sterilizer, bottles, a bassinet, blankets.

"One more chance, Sylvia, that's all I'm giving you."

"Don't—don't bother," I gagged.

Pigeyes reached up to slap me again, but Beech pulled him away.

"Leave her alone!" he roared.

"Still go for her, huh, boss?" The Worm said.

"No! You numbskulls just don't know how to treat a lady. You don't gouge and brass knuckle them to death." Beech rolled up his sleeves and his lips pulled back savagely over crooked yellow teeth. "Come here, baby!"

He jerked me into his arms and his ugly mouth welded itself over my bruised lips. I gave him something back. My knee. He fell screaming. The Worm and Pigeyes converged on me and this time everything went terrifyingly black.

Burning low afternoon sunlight pierced under my pained eyelids. Purple desert shrubs tilted into view. So did an upside down horizon with dark hills spilling down into a vast blue pool. I realized I was on my back and that my head partially hung down a sandy embankment.

"Well?" a voice said from a great distance.

I tried to lift my head, but it was a painfully impossible task. Somebody helped by grabbing a handful of my hair. It was The Worm. Behind him stood Beech, etched against the huge desert sky. He seemed as big as all outdoors and his green eyes were filled with hatred.

"I'm waiting, Sylvia," he said.

My mouth hurt when it moved. "What for? For me to die?"

"No," he said. "I got the message you left at my new club. I know you're trying to frame me for this kidnapping, but I'm not holding still for it, any more than I am for Macelli. Now where's that baby?"

"What'll you do if I tell you?" I asked.

"What do you think? Get rid of it. And get rid of anything you might have planted to throw the feds on my trail."

I wiped at the corner of my mouth and my hand came up red. "I thought you wanted to bleed Sharkey and get your million bucks back."

"Are you crazy? I had nothing to do with this and you know it. Sure, Sharkey took me, but I'd be a fool to try and get it back by pulling a snatch."

"You had nothing to lose," I said. "The authorities know your murdered Macelli."

"You dirty, stupid, little wench. I should have realized what kind of a woman you were when I first met you. Even Macelli warned me, but I didn't have enough sense to listen."

"What'd he say?"

"He said you were insane. And you proved it when you squeezed my gun and killed him."

I sat up, jerking my hair loose from The Worm's fingers. "So, that's what happened!"

"You know damn well that's the way it was," Beech returned. "You were going to pin it on me, weren't you, Sylvia, only I didn't give you a chance. You got away with the gun, but I knew you'd turn up sooner or later. Your picture in the newspaper was all I needed."

"What picture?"

"In the L.A. Times. You looked gorgeous in a uniform. Lieutenant Sylvia Verse, deserter, Marine Woman's Reserve. The rank and last name threw me, but your face didn't."

"So, you sent your butcher boys after me?"

"Yeah. They needed a little help because they're stupid. But they almost got you." Beech grinned wryly. "Believe me, you're not going to break loose this time. Now, where's the baby?"

"Why did you have Williams shot, since you knew I got Macelli?"

"That was strictly a case of self-defense. Of course, the police wouldn't buy it. I only wanted to set Williams straight on the facts. He got all shook up when he saw us walk into the locker room and he pulled a gun."

"I'll bet," I said. "Where'd he get it from, his belly button?"

"It was wrapped in his towel."

"I don't believe that!"

The gambler's shoulders lifted. "I don't care whether you believe it or not. Where you're going it won't make any difference." He snapped his fingers at The Worm and he grabbed my hair again. "I'll make it easy for you, if you tell me where that baby's stashed."

"All right," I said, gritting my teeth against the pain. "What if I did believe you? About Macelli, about Williams, about the kidnapping? Would you let me go if I proved I wasn't Sylvia?"

Pigeyes moved into view behind Beech and even he laughed, his fat belly jiggling furiously.

"That's funny," Beech said. "Real funny." His face sobered. "But I don't have time for jokes."

I touched my cheek. "Sylvia has a mole under her right eye, doesn't she?"

Beech moved nearer. The Worm jerked my head around so he could examine me, too. The gambler shrugged. "You could have had it removed in the service."

I laughed half-heartedly. "Have you been able to remove those lumps you got on your skull this morning form the gimpy guy's cane?"

Beech's eyes widened. "I thought you were the dame in bed. Chalk another one up to you, Sylvia. You always did know how to work every angle in the book. We'll take care of your boy friend later."

My rib cage felt like it had been stomped on by an elephant. I stared at Beech. "Brother, if you do, I'll guarantee you'll be on page one in ninety-six point type. The gimp's a newspaperman and he's already filed a story on the Williams shooting. Knowing Fred, I doubt if he carelessly omitted your name. His obituary would really put you in the gas chamber, but quick."

"You're lying!" Beech spat. "You wouldn't get mixed up with a reporter, the hole you're in."

"Wouldn't I, Mr. Beech? Well, what about that ID card you found inside my dress?"

"That was a phony!"

"Was it?" I jerked loose from the toothless wonder and surveyed Beech's puzzled face. "How do you account for your goons taking pot shots at Sylvia Lorning on a deserted road outside L.A. when she was pulling a snatch on the Sharkey baby at the same time four hundred miles away?"

"I don't know any of the facts about the kidnapping!" Beech roared angrily. "All I know is what I read in your note. You said you had the

Sharkey kid and you were going to pin it on me, if I didn't pay off!"

"Look," I said. "You've been taken in by the oldest con game in the world. And so have I. It almost had to be either you or Sharkey who engineered the kidnapping. You both had enough motive and you both knew Sylvia."

"Stop conning me, Sylvia," Beech said, advancing another step. "There's not another woman like you in the world."

"There may not be another woman like Sylvia," I said, "but it just so happens there is one who looks like her. And that, unfortunately, is me. Check with the Sheriff's office if you don't believe me."

Beech laughed again. "Sure, so they can lock me up for murder—and kidnapping."

I sank back in the sand. "If what you've told me is the truth, then you're in the clear. Would I ask you to get in touch with the Sheriff's office if I really was Sylvia?"

"Are you kidding?" Beech said. "You've got my gun. The one that killed Macelli. You also know I'd have a tough time proving Williams was a case of self-defense. Add those two charges together, plus kidnapping, and I'd have the front row seat in the gas chamber. Oh, sure, you might get a few years as an accessory. But, knowing you, baby, you'd come out into court with a dress cut clear down to your kneecaps and you'd even beat that rap. Now start talking straight, where's that kid?"

I began to shake inside. Beech wasn't kidding. Innocent or not, he was going to kill me. The fear of losing his empire, and perhaps his own life, had thrown him into a panic. There didn't seem to be any way of stopping him now.

"I'm a private detective," I said. "Even if my body's never found it won't keep you out of the gas chamber. You'll still have to contend with the real Sylvia Verse. She knows I exist because she's seen me. And beyond that she's still got the Macelli gun."

Beech flicked his green eyes toward The Worm. "I guess she's just going to keep on stalling until we have to…"

That toothless face leaned over me with a gun, but I still had enough energy to spin out from under him and stagger to my feet. The Worm swore, scrambled up and took aim at my stumbling figure. I dodged past

Beech, heard the gun's sharp report and fell headlong in the sand. That was the surprising part. Somebody else fell at the same moment, only he had the bullet and I didn't. When he hit the ground, Manfred Beech looked like a man who'd just seen the heavens open. His arms flew up, but before he could reach what he was after he was dead.

Pigeyes bent over the fallen gambler, then lifted his gaze to the toothless cavity that hung open in The Worm's pock-marked face.

"You killed him," Pigeyes said incredulously.

The Worm stammered, "No—no, I couldn't—I…"

"You meant to kill him, didn't you?"

"No—no—I—I…"

The fat man snatched a gun from inside his coat, trained it on the other killer and squeezed. The Worm's head snapped. So did his right wrist as his gun spat again. A red stream geysered out of Pigeyes' monstrous frame. He tried to stop it with his hand, but it spilled down the front of his suit as his legs sagged from the impact of the bullet. He pitched over on his knees, took another desperate sight on The Worm's face, but before he could get enough pressure into the trigger a second slug spun him upside down in the sand. That was when I noticed The Worm's mouth. It hung open and he looked as if he were trying to swallow something. His hands slid to his throat. Blood suddenly gushed over his shapeless lips. Then I knew. Pigeyes' bullet hadn't missed. The Worm dropped at the top of the embankment, and died, screaming his lungs out.

Chapter Sixteen

The three corpses, sprawled in the day's dusk, seemed nothing more than twisted desert shadows.

I crawled to Pigeyes' crumpled fat remains and tried to remove the automatic he still clutched in his dead fingers. The gun was frozen in its meaty vise. The Worm, his ugly face pushed deep into reddening sand, released his weapon at my touch. There was blood on the handle and its warm stickiness made my lips twist with revulsion.

After an unsuccessful search of Beech's pockets for Sylvia's note, I crawled to his car, parked near the ravine where they had expected to leave my body. Night swiftly climbed the distant mountains. My face glinted in the car's rear view mirror, outlined dully in the wan glow. I gasped. My cheek was livid purple where I'd been struck. Blood ran from a cut in the corner of my mouth. My scalp was in worse shape. There were too many lumps to count and some of them were still bleeding. My ribs really worried me. They were too sore to touch and my insides hurt when I took a deep breath.

I drove slowly toward the lights of Las Vegas, doubled against the steering wheel, gritting my teeth from the pain. All the way I kept thinking about Sylvia Verse. What kind of a woman was she? A deserter from the military service? A murderess? A blackmailer? A kidnapper? A user of human beings for whatever evil purpose she could construe? The answer was "yes" on each count. But what about the baby? Why had she taken such pains to keep him alive? Why had her motel room been outfitted with everything a newborn baby might need? Surely, not out of pity. The answer had to be Sharkey. There was only one drawback to that conclusion. Where was the baby?

On the outskirts of town, I pulled up to a small hospital and managed to make it through a side emergency door into the arms of a nurse. She assisted me into an examination room and helped peel down my dress. When she unhooked my brassiere, she winced. The skin over my ribs was broken and badly discolored.

A young intern came in. He felt for a fracture, his fingers painfully working their way down to my waist.

"I don't feel any separation so far. My guess would be an undisplaced simple fracture of the seventh and eight ribs."

"Is that bad?"

"It isn't good. Hurt much?"

"Plenty," I said, still clenching my teeth from his examination of the lower side. "Will you need to X-Ray?"

"I think we'd better. That's a pretty mean bruise. Who kicked you?"

"A horse."

He smiled faintly, peering at my discolored cheek and cut mouth. "That horse didn't like you a bit, did he?"

"You can say that again."

He continued his examination. Finally he lifted his hand and helped me to my feet.

"We'll X-Ray, just to be sure my diagnosis is correct."

The X-Ray proved him right. He gave me a couple of codeine pills and taped the injured area. Then I phoned Mark. The big deputy laughed when I asked for money to pay a doctor's bill.

"I've been expecting your call," he said, laughter edging into anger. "Except I thought it would come from a mortician's office. We got a report a while back to investigate a murder committed in a motel at the end of the strip. It seems some damned blonde pulled a stunt on the desk clerk and when he went to investigate he found blood on the carpet. I figured the plasma must have been donated by you."

"Now what gave you that idea?"

"Blood was splattered all over. People usually like you so much they want to spread you around a bit, if you know what I mean. How bad are you hurt?"

"Not as bad as Beech and his two ghouls."

424

"How bad is bad?"

I glanced at the young doctor. He pretended not to be listening.

"Lead poisoning," I said. "Real bad. Fatal for all three."

"What?"

"It was an epidemic, Lieutenant. Just blew up out of nowhere. They caught it from each other."

Mark said, "Where'd all this happen?"

"End of Dogwood Road, near a ravine. They were convinced I was Sylvia and nothing would change their minds."

"What did they do to you, Honey?"

"The Worm tried to kick me for a field goal."

"Anything busted?"

"Simple rib fracture. It did hurt, but right now I'm on cloud nine. I've just had a couple of codeines on an empty stomach."

"Well, you'd better climb down and fast. Phillip Sharkey got away. I guess your theory wasn't so wacky after all."

"What do you mean, he got away?"

"Just that," Mark groaned. "We went out to his house. The joint was in shambles. No Sharkey—and no Stevens, either."

"I don't believe it!"

"Not only that, but a white convertible with a black top was parked out front."

"Sylvia's car," I said.

"That's right, only Sylvia wasn't in it—and neither was the baby."

I knew he'd found something, but I was almost afraid to ask. "Mark, the baby…"

"No, we didn't find him. We did find Sylvia."

"Where?"

"In the kitchen. She was lying beside the stiff you mentioned. Only she was even stiffer."

"Mark, that isn't possible!"

"My sentiments exactly. Ballistics says they were both killed with the same gun."

"Sharkey's?"

"Guess so. We didn't find the weapon."

"You searched for Web inside and out?"

"Sure. We scoured the brush for a half mile around the house. We didn't find any more bodies."

"Glad to hear that."

"I thought you would be. We did find fresh footprints leading off into the desert."

"How many sets?"

"One. They were made by a man running. We lost the trail in an abandoned stone quarry."

"What's on the other side?"

"A small town about another mile and a half away. We sent a man there, but haven't received a report as yet."

I glanced at a clock on the doctor's desk. It was nine-fifteen.

"How's this stack up to you, Mark?"

"Well, going on what you told us, Web Stevens had Sharkey covered when you left."

"That's right."

"Somehow Sharkey turned the tables. Either when Sylvia drove up or by using some other ruse. They struggled. Tore furniture from those cock-eyed cables, knocked down pictures, even put a hole through a piece of fiberboard. Stevens got loose and ran off into the desert. Then Sharkey pumped a bullet into Sylvia and drove away with the baby."

"No," I said.

"What do you mean, no? There was enough evidence in her car to prove the baby's still alive. Dried mucus on several paper tissues in the front seat revealed particles of undigested formula very recently expelled from the baby's stomach."

I rubbed my forehead. "Something's crazy here, Mark."

"Sure, the whole thing's crazy! I've known that from the beginning. You don't figure Beech had anything to do with—?"

"No. He's out. Sylvia's out."

"We found Sharkey's Cadillac abandoned near the airport. His description's been circulated to all personnel in the field, but so far no luck. It's possible he got away, although a man carrying a baby…"

"Mark, we've missed the secret to this case."

426

He groaned. "What are you talking about now? Has that codeine rotted your brain?"

"The secret is the baby himself," I said.

"Of course," Mark answered. "The baby hired all these people to kidnap him so he could extort money from his old man. Juvenile delinquency obviously starts in the cradle."

"Mark, the answer's been sitting right in front of us and we've ignored it."

His angry voice almost tore my ear off. "What answer? You're bugged, Honey, really bugged!"

I began to tremble. "Listen, Mark, one of the biggest single questions has been Margo Stevens, right?"

"Right!" He said the word with as much exasperation as a chicken squawking out his last squawk on a chopping block.

"We've always wanted to know why she allowed her labor to be induced, why she tried to call me."

"Yes."

"All right, let's assume Sylvia Verse was the woman who inveigled her to do this. Let's assume it was Sylvia who smothered Margo."

"All right!" Mark blared. "It's assumed! So, what?"

"Then, have you ever asked yourself this question?"

"What question?"

"Didn't Margo realize that Sylvia looked like me?"

"She must have, unless—unless she was blind."

"She wasn't blind, Mark. But, somebody else is."

"Who?"

"Pat Sharkey. Phillip Sharkey's wife is blind, Mark, did you know that?"

"I heard it somewhere, yes. So what?"

"I want you to do something, Mark. Something very important."

"What's that, Honey?"

"I want you to phone the hospital in San Francisco. I want you to get in touch with the maternity ward. I want you to tell them to remove the Stevens baby from his crib and take him into Mrs. Sharkey."

"Honey, you must be nuts. She's a sick woman! You want to kill her?"

"No!" I returned. "Maybe this will bring her out of it. She's blind. Let her think the child is hers."

"That's criminal!" Mark roared. "What if we find her child—and he's dead? What would we say then? How would we explain? It's impossible, Honey!"

"It's not impossible!" I gripped the receiver with such force my fingers hurt. "You do this, Mark! I don't know how exactly, but you do it even if you have to fly to San Francisco and take that baby in yourself, understand?"

His voice suddenly softened so much it almost made me cry. "Honey, I love you. You know I love you. I think you're the greatest girl in the world. But, you're asking for the moon and I haven't got a rocket ship..."

"Get one, then! Mark, I'm begging you!" I slumped against the desk and my ribs felt like part of a head-on collision with a freight train. "Look, you said yourself she's a sick woman, that she might die. Isn't it better to try and save her—no matter the cost?"

"But, Honey, the cost is so high! I have no authority to do this. I could lose my badge. I could lose everything I've worked for..."

"Do it, Mark. You won't be sorry..."

A silence came. A terrible silence. One that did bring tears to my eyes. Then his voice came, so soft at first I hardly heard it.

"All right," he said. "But you've got to make me a promise. If I lose, you've got to support me for the rest of my life—and I've got pretty expensive tastes..." Then he broke, "Honey, what is this? What are you planning to do?"

"Mark, I promise," I said.

"But, what are you going to do?"

I hung up, dialed the operator and placed a call to the hospital in San Francisco, asking for time and charges. The head nurse on duty in the maternity ward answered my two questions efficiently and without hesitation.

After promising the wide-eyed doctor a check within a few days, I walked stiffly to Beech's car and eased behind the wheel. Now I knew. Now I knew everything and I hoped to God it wasn't too late.

Chapter Seventeen

The moon was high in the Nevada sky as I drove along the Las Vegas strip toward the airport. Neon lights flashed and people and cars darted through the big hotel's parking lots, creating more stirring, more frenzy, in the whirligig of darkness. That same impossible stirring was tight in my chest, caught in the pain and sudden understanding that constricted me like the tape across my ribs. How could I have been so blind? And yet, blindness was the key.

I drove into a small motel located a few hundred yards from the airport.

"You want a single for the night, lady?" the man inside the office asked, scanning my figure knowingly.

"No, thanks," I said. "I'm looking for my husband..."

"Oh." His grin faded.

"And my baby," I added softly. "I was supposed to meet them in Vegas, but I've forgotten the name of the motel. I think this is the place. He's a big tall blond fellow with..."

"Sorry, lady, no man with a baby's checked in here. That's pretty unusual. Don't see that sort of thing very often. Now, you might try the motel across the street. They sort of cater to children over there. Even have a baby-sitting arrangement and..."

"Thanks."

I got into the car and crossed the divided highway to the other motel. It was ancient by Las Vegas standards. The little old lady who came to the door was of the same vintage. She smiled sweetly when I gave her my story. Then she said, "Why you poor dear. He told me not to mention it to anyone, but he never said you were coming. I guess he thought..."

"Of course, he did," I interrupted. "He thought I knew where to find them. I have such a bad memory. Which room are they in?"

"Who, dearie?"

"My—my—husband—and my baby."

She was as smart as all get out and she knew it.

"What's his name, dearie?"

"His—his name?"

"Yes, dearie, you ought to know your husband's name, shouldn't you?"

"Of course, I—I…"

"Blow, dearie." Her smile faded into a wrinkled scowl. "It was a good try, but it didn't work. Divorcees are always pulling this trick. Now blow."

I knew Web wouldn't have registered under his own name, but I hadn't figured on this sort of resistance. A wild guess was in order. Only it had to be good.

"That's not very nice of you," I said. "My husband's name is West."

Her wrinkled face didn't change for a long moment, then it suddenly brimmed over with kindness. "I'm sorry, dearie, but you know how it is. In this sort of business you have to be careful. They're in sixteen. Registered only a few hours ago."

I walked to Room 16 and tried the doorknob. It turned. Inside was Web Stevens and in his arms he held a baby, wrapped snugly in a blue blanket.

"Okay, daddy," I said. "You can put him down now."

Web swung around and his eyes widened. "Honey, where'd you come from?"

"Out of the blue," I said. "The stork brought me."

A tiny, pink sleeping face was nestled inside the blanket and suddenly it sighed almost as deeply as I did as I slumped into a chair.

"Honey, you don't understand," Web said, holding the infant to his chest. "You just don't understand."

"Sure, I understand," I said, clutching my ribs. "You great dope. I thought you were smart, but no! You're the great big hero, aren't you?" I spread out my hands. "Father Divine. You and Sharkey should have been twins."

Web placed the baby on the bed and looked at me angrily. "What are you talking about? Are you drunk? Have you been in an accident? What's

430

the matter with you?"

"What's the matter with me," I sighed, "is what's the matter with the world. It's blind, it's sick and it hurts. What's your problem, Web?"

He straightened. "I have a hunch you know."

I laughed bitterly. "Are you kidding? I don't know anything. A couple of hours ago two guys tried to kick some sense into me. I guess it worked, a little." I rubbed the bruises on my face.

"Who did that?" Web demanded.

"Who cares?" I said. "All that matters is that it hurts. But what hurts worse is to see you standing there. And to see that baby. And to know…"

"Honey, I can explain."

"Sure you can," I said. "But I can explain better." The codeine was wearing off and I grimaced. "Have you got a drink in this place? I could really use one."

Web took a bottle out of his suitcase and poured me a tall straight shot of bourbon. I gulped it, choked and caught my breath. "Okay," I said, after a moment. "Tell me your story, only make it good."

"I've never lied to you, Honey," he said, glancing down at the sleeping infant. "No, I did tell you a few lies. About Margo's last phone call especially. She didn't tell me she was coming home."

"I guessed that," I said.

He paced across the room and ran his hands over his eyes. "She said she was never coming home and that I'd never see my baby. She threatened me—like she's always threatened-with all sorts of harm and misery. I didn't think much of it because she's always been that sort of person. Half-mad, half-woman, half-anything, but a human being. You knew her, Honey. You knew what she was like." He shook his head. "I never thought she'd stoop this low, be this insane." He stared down at the sleeping infant. "But there's the living proof, right there."

I shrugged my shoulders dismally. "You're a fool, Web. But, I guess you had to be to marry Margo."

"What are you talking about?" he demanded.

"You've been duped," I said, crossing the bed. I lifted the baby in my arms and smiled faintly. "This isn't your child."

"What?"

"This isn't your baby. It's Phillip Sharkey's. A switch was never made."

Web's face dropped like an elevator with its cables sheared. He stared open-mouthed for an instant, then jerked his head back with his hands. "But—but, Margo, said…"

"That your baby was going to be switched with another man's baby."

"Yes."

"Only you didn't believe her when she told you," I said. "To you it was just another case of Margo crying wolf."

"Yes."

"You continued to think that way until yesterday morning when the San Francisco police called and told you she was dead—and that Sharkey's baby had been kidnapped."

Web Stevens rocked unsteadily on his feet. His face blanched white and his hands trembled. "Honey," he said. "You don't know what I've been through the past thirty-six hours."

"You forget, I've spent most of those hours with you."

"I—I know," he stammered. "Inside me, I mean." He gripped his stomach. "I've been like a sponge without water—brittle, dry, falling apart, decaying inside. Not knowing, Honey. Not knowing," he repeated wildly, "not knowing…"

"You're a fool, Web." I stood up and groped for the bottle of bourbon. "You should have told me the first time we met. I know now you were the man who poked the gun at me in the shower." I poured another drink. "I suppose I have Margo to thank for that, too."

· Web turned away, biting his lips. "She mentioned your name over the phone." He sighed dismally. "She said you were going to be in real trouble when this baby switch took place. I laughed. I always laughed at her stories, they were so ridiculous."

I swallowed the whiskey and laughed myself, way down in my chest where the pain was the worst. "Margo never did like me. She pretended to be my friend, but…"

"Yeah, I can guess what it was like. That was the status of our married life. She was like some beautiful awesome snake—that you paid twenty-five cents to watch climb a rope. And suddenly you woke up to the fact that you were the rope—and she was strangling you in the bargain."

A neon sign clicked outside the window, flushing the room with its jaded phosphorescence, etching Web's hugeness against the wall, then exterminating itself with another faint click. I stared at his dilated eyes, still half blind from the flash.

"He's not yours, Web," I insisted.

"Honey, how can you be sure?"

"The wrist and ankle bands both say Sharkey."

"I—I know, but they probably switched those."

"That's not easy to do, Web." I lighted a cigarette, then crushed it out remembering the baby. "It could have been done, but not in this case."

"What do you mean?"

"This kid has a few things your baby doesn't."

Web shaded a new wedge of neon. "I don't understand."

"Margo had a girl," I said. "A cute little six-pound girl."

He staggered back. "A girl, but…"

"I just talked to the hospital a short time ago. Little Miss Stevens is doing nicely. Despite the fact her father's never taken the time to inquire."

"Honey, I thought…"

"—you had a boy," I finished. "I know. You even convinced me of that fact, but you didn't have a boy. That's the reason there was no switch. That's probably the reason Margo's dead."

Beyond the room's window the world was bitterly dark when the neon clicked off. Web stared into its coal smoke depths and shook his head. "Honey, I'm lost. I don't know what to do or say, I…"

"All right, I'll say it for you. You thought Margo was lying when she told you about the proposed baby switch. Then you saw the headlines yesterday morning on your way home from the poker party. They said, "Millionaire's son kidnapped; woman murdered!' Right away you assumed two things: Margo had told the truth and it was your son who had actually been snatched."

"I wasn't sure!"

"So you looked me up."

"I just wanted to ask you some questions!"

"Only you picked a very odd way of asking."

Web's face reddened in the blaze of light. "I—I was desperate. I didn't know whether you were involved or not. How did I know you'd be in the shower?"

I kept my eyes riveted on him. "My landlady claims she found me in an awkward position on the bed."

His mouth trembled and a hand brushed across his forehead. "I—I'm sorry. You were lying there on your face. I thought maybe I'd killed you. When I rolled you over…" His eyes lowered.

"You're just lucky I didn't recognize you."

"I know. When you called I thought maybe you had. Even at the Dolphin Café I still wasn't certain."

"So you went all the way on this thing never knowing whose child this really was."

Web nodded, peering down at the pink face in the blanket. "I couldn't go to the police, Honey, because I didn't have any proof. What could I have said? My wife was a neurotic? She was always calling me in a drunken stupor? She was always threatening suicide? Hell, Honey, she'd already been to the hospital once for throwing herself down a staircase and trying to cause an abortion. This threat was nothing new."

"Then why did you believe her this time, Web?"

"I didn't." He crossed to the window and pushed his forehead to the glass. "I told you I wasn't sure. All I knew was that a baby had been kidnapped and I had a hunch how to find him. Beyond that, I was in the dark all the way."

New light wreathed Web's shoulders. Another shaft of it streamed across me. I whirled, but not fast enough. In a half-open door stood Phillip Sharkey. A dusty, tired figure with a gun.

434

Chapter Eighteen

Sharkey kicked the door closed behind him.

"Both of you," he growled angrily, "up against that wall and be quick about it!" His words were thick and pressed through dried, cracked lips.

I moved back toward Web. "How'd you know where to find us, Mr. Sharkey?"

"He told me." The millionaire laughed hoarsely. "As I was running across the desert, he yelled it at me. Isn't that funny? I got a lot of laughs out of that while I was out there. A lot of laughs."

He glanced down at the baby and his grimy hand, gripping the gun, trembled.

"You're going to die for this, you filthy, rotten kidnappers!"

My chest ached horribly, but I managed to laugh. "You've got it all wrong, Mr. Sharkey."

"Have I? I suppose that bullet Stevens put into Sylvia was all wrong, too."

I turned and studied Web's rangy figure, suddenly illuminated by the neon. "You didn't tell me…"

"I didn't have a chance."

"You've got one now," I said.

Web grimaced. "She came in a few minutes after you left. Through the back door. Caught me by surprise. For a second I thought it was you." He shook his head futilely. "She had a gun. That one." He indicated Sharkey's revolver. "She took one shot at me and missed. I didn't."

"No, you sure didn't," Sharkey said. "And you didn't miss me either."

"Well you jumped me, what'd you expect?" Web demanded. "You knocked the gun out of my hand and I got mad, but I didn't hit you."

435

"No," Sharkey said, wiping a sweaty sleeve over his mouth. "You just knocked me around, that's all. Until I got Sylvia's gun. Then you started talking out of the other side of your face."

"You didn't scare me," Web insisted. "I could have taken that pea-shooter out of your hand, but you turned tail."

Now Sharkey held his ground without wavering, anger tightening into his dusty, raw features. "Of course I did. What'd you expect? I knew you were desperate. I knew you didn't care whether you lived or died. Do you think I would have been crazy enough to put a bullet in you like you did Sylvia?"

"I'm no hero," Web said. "I knew you'd never pull that trigger. That's why I went after you. That's why I told you where you could find me—if and when you decided you wanted to find me."

Sharkey said, "Well, don't try to test me this time because you won't come off so easy! I've just walked twenty miles through sand and dust and heat. I thought I'd die out there a couple of times, but I kept going just on the hope that I'd find you, Stevens."

"Well, you found him, Mr. Sharkey—and your baby," I said. "Now put down that gun!"

"No!"

Web shrugged. "The baby was in Sylvia's car. I didn't take him to the police because…"

"Because you're the one who engineered this kidnapping from start to finish," Sharkey said.

"You're wrong!" I said. "Do you want to know the truth? Do you want to know who really started this thing?"

"You might as well save your breath. I know the truth and I've already called the police. They're on their way."

New pain seared my left side and I groped for support. Web caught me. I groaned. "You're both a couple of fools. When are you going to grow up?"

"What are you talking about, Honey?" Web asked.

"It's obvious, it hurts," I moaned. "Really hurts. Sylvia Verse was the blonde who kidnapped the Sharkey baby, all right, but she had help, lots of it."

436

"Who?"

"Your wife for one, Sylvia found Margo in San Francisco. I don't know how, but she found her. Margo fit Sylvia's needs to a T. She was neurotic. She was pregnant. And she had gone to Long Beach jaysee."

"What is that supposed to mean?" Sharkey growled.

I slumped into a chair. "That's where I come into the picture. It was my misfortune that I looked like Sylvia. To Margo it must have been astounding. To Sylvia it was probably like a godsend."

"Honey," Web stammered, "I know I'm thick, but I just don't get it."

"All right, I'll start from the beginning. Somebody hired Sylvia Verse to steal the Sharkey baby, that we know. But, Sylvia was a smart girl. From what I've learned, almost too smart. Somehow, and only God knows how, she met your wife. Margo was hungry—money hungry. She was willing to do almost anything to get her hands on a few bucks, honest or not."

Web's head shook dismally in the neon glare.

I continued, "Sylvia devised a plan whereby Margo would go to the hospital the same day that Mrs. Sharkey was admitted. Margo's labor was to be induced, in an effort to make the two births occur as closely as possible. It was a fifty-fifty chance that everything would work out all right, including the sex of the babies."

"Stop me if I'm wrong," Web inserted, "but this sounds too fantastic."

"It was fantastic," I agreed, "but no more so than what Sylvia had arranged for me. She must have been thrilled when Margo showed her my picture in the school annual. She knew I was the answer to two very important problems. One, how to vanish into thin air after the kidnapping and, two, how to get Manfred Beech off her back before one of his guns squeezed her out of existence."

Phillip Sharkey took a menacing step toward me with his gun. "You're making this all up."

"Am I? I take it you never heard of a killer named Gimbel? I suppose you don't know that Sylvia hired him to set me up for Beech's hoods? That she hoped I'd be so filled with holes that nobody could identify me except the county coroner by means of Sylvia Marine clothing and her ID card."

Web bent over me, his forehead furrowed deeply. "Honey, what part did Margo play in this? Why was she murdered?"

"I can only guess," I said. "But it seems as though Sylvia convinced Margo that if they could switch babies and kidnap yours, Web, they'd be in the clear. Nobody could ever prosecute them for kidnapping because they were taking Margo's child with her consent."

"But, what about the switching of leg and arm bands?" Web asked.

"That could have been blamed on the hospital as negligence, if they'd been caught."

Sharkey's sunburnt face ridged in the sudden red glow. He stared at the blanket-wrapped baby. "You trying to tell me this isn't my child?"

"No," I said, clutching my sore ribs. "I suppose you're not aware that the big plan went haywire? That Margo Stevens had a girl?"

Before Sharkey could answer, I continued, "That twist of fate probably shook Margo like nothing in her lifetime. How she must have wept and trembled, lying in that quiet, lonely private room knowing she was about to die. Can you picture that, Mr. Sharkey?"

"No—I—I. . ." Sharkey stammered.

"I thought not," I broke angrily. "Nor can you probably imagine the following moments when she called my office, fear tearing at her throat like a mad dog, fighting for her life, and finally losing when Sylvia caught her with the phone in her hands."

Sharkey withered, gun hand trembling, sweat streaming down his face and caking in the dust. "I don't see how all this…"

"Of course you don't see! You don't see that any more than you see Sylvia smothering Margo. Or your own child being lifted out of his basket and carted down a twisting, dark stairway and into a car. You don't see any of that do you, Mr. Sharkey?"

"No, I…"

"Nor can you visualize Sylvia and her one surviving gunman arriving in Las Vegas already frightened by a blood barricade and a sandstorm and frightened even more by the complications and problems surrounding a two-day-old child. And these complications only becoming more complicated when the man decides to give himself up, but is persuaded by Sylvia to visit your house first in a daring ruse to gain some quick money."

Sharkey's narrow shoulders stiffened. "How could they have entered the house? All the doors were locked."

438

"You know better than that," I said. "Or have you forgotten that picture of Sylvia in your bureau drawer? Didn't she still have a key to your back door? Didn't she enter the house and shoot her compatriot as he stood defenseless in the kitchen? And then later, guessing you were in town, didn't she come back to get money?"

The door suddenly slammed open and Mark Storm with a half dozen Las Vegas deputies crowded into view, bathed weirdly by the glow of neon. Sharkey dropped his gun and whirled, his sunburnt mouth eddying open like frothy white tide drawing back from a craggy, red rocked beach.

"Lieutenant," Sharkey said, "you—you surprised me, I…"

"I'll bet," Mark said. A Vegas deputy slapped handcuffs over the millionaire's thin, dusty wrists. "We've been standing outside for the past five minutes listening to this conversation. I guess you can come along with us now, Mr. Sharkey."

"I guess not," I said, rising uncomfortably from my chair.

"What?" Mark said angrily.

"Did you boys bring an ambulance, Lieutenant?"

"Of course! You need medical aid, Honey?"

"I need plenty of things, you nitwit," I said. "I'm talking about the baby. He's sleeping peacefully, but it's my guess it's not because he's been overfed in the past twenty-four hours. Get those white-suited characters in here, on the double!"

After the baby was removed to the ambulance, Mark backed me into a corner. "All right, now! What's this all about?" he demanded.

The warmth of a new drink had eased some of the pain and I smiled. "Did you make that phone call to San Francisco?"

"Yes, I did,' Mark said.

"Did they do what you asked?"

"Yes, dammit!"

"I take it the reaction was bad."

Mark glanced at Sharkey, still manacled near the door, and grimaced. "Very bad. She went hysterical. They had to administer sedatives to quiet her."

"Good," I said.

"Honey," Mark groaned, "I could kill you for this."

"I don't think so," I said, "after you hear what I have to say."

"Well, say it, dammit say it! I have a hunch it'll be your last speech for a long time!"

Web stood near the window and his face seemed contorted in the repeated splashes of neon. I glanced at Sharkey.

"Your wife is blind, isn't that so, Mr. Sharkey?"

"Yes."

"Has she ever spent any time in Vegas?"

Sharkey's brow knitted. "Yes, but what has all this to do with…"

"Was she here two years ago?" I demanded.

"I don't know," he said, shaking his head. "I guess so, yes. She lived here for awhile. Six months, I think, why?"

I glanced at Mark's questioning expression. "Why has your wife filed for divorce, Mr. Sharkey?"

Sharkey backed against the wall, but met my gaze. "Who knows?"

"Was she afraid of you?"

"Maybe," he stammered, looking away. "She's always been obsessed with fear—ever since her father died."

"Was she afraid of you? I repeated.

"Yes!" Sharkey burst suddenly. Then his voice lowered. "Blind people have reason to be afraid. It's dark and fearful where they are. Pat's no different."

"But she is different, isn't she, Mr. Sharkey?" I drummed. "She's afraid of you because her father made her afraid."

"Yes," he whispered after a moment, his eyes staring down at the floor.

"He made her afraid of your power, didn't he?"

"Yes."

"In fact," I added, "he even made her afraid of you as a man, didn't he?"

Sharkey's face folded into a tight mask of sweat and grime. "Yes." It was hardly audible.

My eyes darted to Mark Storm and I sighed dismally. "There's your case, Lieutenant."

""What in hell are you talking about, Honey?"

"Fear," I said, shaking my head. "The fear of a blind woman for her un-

440

born child. Pat Sharkey was the one who hired Sylvia Verse to steal her baby."

The ensuing uproar was deafening. Deputies bolted through the door. Web lunged for me. Phillip Sharkey toppled over in a dead faint and the crude neon glared on his dirty, tear-stained cheeks.

Chapter Nineteen

Cool green light filtered down through the Four Leaf Clover Room's smoke and darkness, faintly outlining the blonde singer's face as she stood above the bar.

Web sat in the corner again, staring, not at the songstress, but at me.

Twenty-four hours had taken some of the fire out of my rib fracture and I was able to bend toward him without wincing. "Penny for your thoughts," I said.

Web glanced at the silver dollars in the ceiling and feigned disgust. "How cheap can you get? Sharkey gives her a bag full of those coins, practically makes her independently wealthy and she offers me a hunk of copper for my thoughts."

"Well?" I said.

"I was thinking about you, naturally. I was wondering how you did it."

"Did what?"

"Figured Pat Sharkey. She was the last person in the world I would have suspected."

"Me, too."

Applause rippled up, hung in the thick haze and then faded. Glasses began to clink again and sleek, mesh stockinged waitresses milled between tables.

Web sighed. "What's going to happen to her?"

"Nothing, probably." I smiled. "Funny, isn't it? She was afraid of Sharkey. Being blind, she had a fixation he might try and take the child away from her when their divorce came to trial. So she hired Sylvia to steal the baby and keep him until it was all over."

"But, Honey, where did she meet Sylvia? How could she have been sure Sylvia was competent enough to care for the child?"

"Sylvia was Mrs. Sharkey's nurse when she stayed in Vegas two and a half years ago. They became fast friends, but their friendship led to an affair between Sharkey and Sylvia. When it finally blew up and the Sharkeys moved back to Frisco, Sylvia dropped nursing and moved in on Manfred Beech."

Web lighted a cigarette and slipped it between my lips. "What a mess!"

"Yeah," I breathed lowly, "and who do you blame? Pat Sharkey? She only did what her instincts told her to do. A terrified mother hoping to protect her baby. Phillip Sharkey? He didn't have the courage to tell his wife the truth about Sylvia two years ago. If he had—if Pat Sharkey had known what Sylvia Verse was really like—none of this probably ever would have happened."

"And what about me?" Web asked. "The big hero who didn't have enough sense to take a warning, who had to kill two people to make up for his diffidence."

"Sharkey and I testified this afternoon, Web. You know the verdict. Both cases, justifiable homicide."

"Sure. Legally I'm as free as a bird. Morally, I'm all locked up-tight." He pressed his hands to his chest. "Here."

I lifted his hands away and put them on my taped ribs. "Me, too," I said with a half-smile. "So, what do we do about it?"

"I've got a wonderful idea," he said. "Remember the desert rat's cabin? Maybe he's got another bottle of champagne hidden somewhere. Let's go get drunk!"

I regarded his face for an instant, then said, "I've been meaning to ask you about that, Web. How come you don't have twin beds?"

"What?"

"I mean, not everyone likes to share a double bed."

"Honey, did you know I owned that cabin when we were there?"

"Of course. Nobody stumbles onto desert cabins with cupboards full of champagne, vintage 1936, in the middle of a blinding sandstorm unless their name happens to be Gable and MGM is footing the bill."

"I should have known. But I thought…"

"The trouble with you, Mr. Stevens, is you think too much."

He moved nearer. Holy smokes, I thought, what do you do with a man like this?"

The End

Printed by Publishers' Graphics LLC USA